# HORIZON
## OF WAR

# HORIZON
## OF WAR

### BOOK 1

## HANNE

Podium

Published in 2024 by Podium Publishing
www.podiumaudio.com

# HORIZON
## OF WAR

NOMA
Caladania
Tarraca
Kehldin
Centur
ELVEN SATRAPY
THIR
HUMA
Sarmatia
Elearis
Halicia
Ekionia
BEASTMEN CONF

Province of
Brigandia
PEOPLE
Province of
Arminia
Inglesia
Tiberia
Arvena
MERCANTILE
KINGDOM
Rhomelia
PERIUM
Midlandia
Elandia
Korimor
Umberland
Ornietia
Edessa
Three
Hills
White
Lake
opola
South
Hill
Korelia
Salceslia
Galdia
NAVALNIA
EMPIRE
Corinthia
Lowlandia
Plains
RATI
The
Great Marshes

# CHAPTER 1

# ORBIS ALIUS

Water sprinkled from the bottoms of the metal cans affixed to a wooden pole that Lansius carried, darkening the soil of the green vegetable patches as he passed. A strong, earthy scent arose from the moist ground.

Despite having done this dozens of times, he couldn't help but think that it would have been faster if he had sneakers or boots. Alas, all he had were sad-looking medieval leather shoes with hardened soles.

"Lans, are your legs getting wobbly already?" Marc teased from the well.

Lansius chuckled and returned to the well for a refill, but suddenly lunged at Marc with his wooden pole.

"Hah!" Marc parried with his pitchfork and launched a counter sweep.

Lansius blocked it, and the two engaged in a friendly spar, with Marc easily blocking and dodging Lansius's slow swings, taunting him all the while.

After a few more attempts, Lansius finally threw his arms up. "No more . . . hard to breathe."

Marc hadn't even broken a sweat, and Lansius's attacks only managed to mess up his disheveled, short brown hair. Having been trained to wield a polearm, a simple pitchfork posed no challenge for him. "Seems like the master soldier wannabe has poor stamina," he taunted with a smirk.

"Quiet, you." Lansius chuckled breathlessly.

Marc picked up the wooden pole, refilled the metal cans, and continued to water their family plot. Slowly but surely, he covered all their spring vegetables. Their livelihood depended on it.

Unlike last year, Lansius could now help with the work. Even though he could only do so much before becoming sluggish and exhausted, he found satisfaction in knowing that he wasn't a freeloader anymore.

"Marc, no other work?" he asked in broken language as they cleaned up.

Marc grinned. "Easier work for you, bro?"

Lansius could only nod. He had yet to master the language well enough to argue.

"Still won't do the wool shop?"

*Oof, anything but that . . .*

Lansius shook his head.

Marc snickered. "You can't cook, can't do carpentry, and can't write. So, either the wool shop or the tannery."

The thought of working in the tannery made Lansius's stomach churn. Tanneries used urine and manure to treat leather, and even used blood, brains, and other animal waste in their process.

"Well, at least you're a freeman," Marc said to cheer him up.

"Freeman?" Lansius said, testing the new word out and guessing at its meaning.

"Yeah, unlike us, you can go wherever you want and find work elsewhere."

Lansius furrowed his brow. "You . . . not free?"

"Well, we could be if we paid our debts. The land, the house, and the tools are provided by the lord. But we needed money for repairs, clothes, new fences," Marc explained.

Lansius grew worried. This was the first time he'd heard about this problem.

"No worries. It's only a small sum," Marc reassured him. "But at this rate . . ."

Lansius followed Marc's gaze and understood the situation. They were planting on not even a quarter of the allotted land. Moreover, the yield was small, and vegetables held little value.

"Oi, don't give me that look," Marc said. "It's true that we're in debt, but we're not planning to move, so it's fine."

"You like it here?" Lansius asked, looking at the vast green meadows.

"Yep, Father brought us here when we were little. It's far from the capital, but much safer from the war," Marc said.

A soothing wind blew softly, causing their loose, off-white tunics to flutter. The late spring breeze carried a distinctive fragrance and a touch of aridity.

"Marc! Lans!" a little girl called from beyond the field.

"Tanya, why are you here?" Marc, the girl's brother, asked.

Tanya grinned from ear to ear and announced, "Mother bought meat from the market."

"Whoops, gotta go." Marc quickly gathered his tools and sprinted home.

"Oh, man!" Lansius protested. He lacked the stamina to chase after Marc, so he took his time cleaning up. His stomach growled at the thought of the missed opportunity. Meat was a rare treat. When Mother Arryn bought some, it was usually just bones for broth, with very little actual meat.

By the time Lansius finished, the sun had turned completely orange, sitting low on the horizon. As he walked home, he spotted Tanya waiting behind the wooden fence. Her golden hair shone brightly in the sunlight. She was the only blonde in the village; everyone else, including her brother and mother, had brown hair.

"Tanya, why didn't you go with Marc?" he asked, trying to recall his vocabulary.

"I'd rather walk home with you," she replied with a grin, revealing her missing tooth.

Lansius couldn't help but chuckle. He genuinely enjoyed Tanya's company. Of the three people he knew in this world, she was the closest to him, the one who had kept him sane at the lowest point of his life.

"Hey, I was wondering, have you gotten your memory back?" she suddenly asked.

"Err . . . no, I remember some things, but not much."

"Aww, I really want to hear what your home and village look like." Like other kids, Tanya was curious about the world outside Bellandia.

"Maybe after I learn to speak more."

"You're doing well. Last year, you only talked with hand signals," she said, smiling sweetly.

Unable to resist her charm any longer, Lansius stopped, knelt down, and gestured for her to climb onto his back for a piggyback ride.

"Yay!" She hopped on and wrapped her arms around his shoulders.

"Oof, you heavier," he muttered.

Tanya laughed, pressing her knees against his sides as if riding a horse. In truth, she was underweight, like many other children in the village.

Lansius obeyed and started jogging. He adored the little girl.

Lansius had found himself here, in this unknown place, a year ago. He had been severely ill, and he nearly died. No one rushed him to a hospital or administered first aid. Not knowing the language or his location, he could only assume he had had an accident in a rural part of the world.

Yet, as he was recovering, he realized something: there were no light bulbs in Bellandia—no wall clocks or even tissues. This place didn't just resemble the medieval era. All evidence pointed to the impossibility that he was indeed in the Middle Ages.

Even worse, his entire past identity had become hazy. He could recall movie plots and books, and knew he had graduated and worked, but not a single name came to mind. No family faces, where his hometown was, or even his own name. The only name that remained was a nickname he had used: Lansius.

For someone raised in modern times, the prospect of living in a medieval era seemed bleak, filled with wars, plagues, and backbreaking labor. Lansius became depressed, barely eating, and he had suffered from a series of fevers. There would have been little hope for him if not for Tanya.

The little girl cared for him and kept him engaged with her curiosity. Gradually, her words became familiar, and he began to open up, trusting her to keep him moving forward.

The seasons changed, and summer arrived in Bellandia. Even in the heartland of the Arvena highland, the sun blazed hot, though tempered by the cool mountain breeze. Farmers who had cultivated their land sought shade within their homes during this time of the year, tending to tasks such as fixing tools and mending clothes.

The land surrounding the village ripened with yellowing crops, just a season away from harvest. Unlike staple crop farmers, vegetable farmers operated on shorter timetables, planting and replanting multiple times throughout the year. Consequently, Mother Arryn's family continued working during this unforgiving season.

Lansius also lent a hand on the farm today, but after two hours of hard work, he was soaked in sweat and had to stop. He leaned against the cool stone well, groaning in the shade of its roof as his body ached.

*So hot . . . damn it . . . just unbelievable.*

"Ha, told you," Marc exclaimed from beneath his large straw hat.

"Leave him alone, and help me with this," Mother Arryn called out.

With a resigned sigh, Marc returned to work under the relentless heat of the sun.

*This is so pathetic . . . at this rate, I'll be depending on them forever.*

Lansius observed Marc and Arryn. Despite the heat, they diligently tended to the cabbage and turnip plots, weeding and replanting as needed.

This was Lansius's second year, so he thought he was up to the task of helping them. However, the summer sun was nothing like the mildness of spring. The humidity, intensity, and heat easily overwhelmed him. He had tried several times, but always ended up with a nosebleed or a fever.

*I need a different job. Something other than manual labor if I want to stand on my own.*

"You're probably better off accompanying Tanya in the wool shop," Arryn suggested, cleaning the hem of her brown working gown from dirt as they finished for the day.

"Maybe . . ." Lansius answered indifferently while tidying up the tools. His palms ached, but he wanted to help.

He knew Arryn thought he was being too hard on himself, while Marc teased Lansius for being too proud to accept a woman's job.

The wool shop, true to its name, was a place where wool was dyed and spun into yarn. Although Lansius didn't mind this kind of work, the pay was meager, and the shop primarily served as a gathering place for village housewives to chat and gossip while working. As an introvert, it would be his worst nightmare.

Lansius was grateful that Arryn and Marc weren't pushing any particular decision on him. Despite their struggles, they didn't rely on his help. He knew he could be picky, especially about boiling water for drinking, but mostly he took care of himself.

As the sun began to set, the three fetched Tanya from the wool shop and headed home.

That night, Lansius felt a fever coming on and needed ointment for his blistered hand. Tanya applied a thin layer of salve on his injured palms and distracted him from his worries by sharing stories she'd heard at the shop.

While Lansius felt inadequate, the other family members seemed grateful for his efforts. He was learning the language and showing his willingness to help. Moreover, Marc was old enough to answer the Lord of Arvena's call, and instead of paying taxes, able-bodied farmers like them went into military service on a rotational schedule. When selected, men from the village would follow the lord into battle for up to four months each year. In those times, Arryn would work alone, and Lansius's presence provided Marc some peace of mind.

However, Lansius couldn't see it that way. His inability to work like the other men disheartened him. Even with only a fragmented memory, he knew his old life was paradise in comparison to this. He felt that medieval farming was nothing less than cruel. That night, like many other nights when beset by illness, he vowed to escape the farming life.

The wet season arrived, and drizzle fell almost every day. Winter was still a month away, but the chill in the air was enough to penetrate one's bones.

"Gah." Lansius panted as they endured the cold, light rain.

"A bit more, keep it up," Marc encouraged him.

The two were carrying firewood for the village chief. Marc carried a stack of wood on each shoulder, while Lansius managed only one with both arms.

"I—is there no other job?" Lansius asked. His shoulders ached, and his hips burned.

"Heh, you're still asking about that?" Marc teased.

Lansius exhaled deeply.

*Easy for him to say. I don't want musclehead jobs.*

Unfortunately, most jobs were manual labor. While there were some other trades, they were typically passed down from father to son and too small-scale to require additional help.

"Move it fast, lads. It's getting wet," urged the old man in dry, thick clothes as soon as he saw them approaching. In contrast, the two youngsters wore only two layers of coarse garments and were now drenched.

The two quickened their pace to a jog and hurriedly entered an old but sturdy-looking wooden shed. The place belonged to the village chief, who was wealthy enough to have a separate shed for storing firewood.

Both carefully dropped their stacks of wood on the floor and paused to catch their breath.

"Took you too long," the chief complained as he fretted about the firewood getting wet—unsurprising, as he was known to be rude, senile, and cheap. Marc had only taken the job because the chief's wife always shared some food.

But before they could claim their reward, the chief stopped them.

"Hey, where are you two going? Stack them first, neatly," he ordered.

Marc and Lansius groaned but turned around and stacked the firewood as requested. Unlike the small branches they used in their home, the chief's woodpile came from thick logs that were properly cut and dried. This wood was smokeless and burned longer.

When the two were done, the chief scratched his head, seemingly puzzled.

"What's the matter?" Lansius asked while rubbing his hands for warmth.

"Tsk—it's nothing. I just forgot to count them before stacking. Now it's hard to count."

"The wood? Why, it's thirty-six pieces," Lansius answered flatly.

The chief immediately looked at Lansius with doubt. Even Marc, who was busy cleaning his clothes from wood chips, watched with suspicion.

*What did I say?*

"I-it's only six and six . . ." Lansius explained while searching his vocabulary for the exact word for multiply. He couldn't find it and started to realize what went wrong.

"You can multiply without using a table?" Marc asked in disbelief.

"Y-yes," Lansius replied, realizing that in this era, people relied on multiplication tables for calculations. The use of numerals similar to Roman numerals made calculation even more challenging.

*They can't multiply? But of course! They have no formal education . . .*

Marc looked ecstatic, but the chief wasn't convinced. Even he, along with most merchants and several farmers, knew how to calculate without using a table. So he challenged him. "Try to calculate how many legs three horses have. You can use—"

"Twelve," Lansius blurted out without trying.

His answer startled the old man. "Eleven plus seven?"

"Eighteen."

The old man continued to furrow his brow. "How about, if five goats each give birth to three baby goats, how many total baby goats are there?"

"Fifteen baby goats," Lansius answered with a grin.

The chief was furiously engaged in finger-counting. In this method, each finger represented up to four units, corresponding to its three joints and the fingertip. He used his thumb as a pointer to keep track. With this technique, using all eight fingers, he could easily calculate up to 32 units—sufficient to count the days of a month.

When he arrived at the same result, he became slightly frustrated. He had always prided himself on being the cleverest one in the village, but this was his limit. Now, after witnessing Lansius calculate without needing a table or fingers, he was taken aback.

"Young man, have you regained your memory? Are you perhaps an apprentice to a merchant?" The old man's tone was less rude than usual.

Lansius shivered, not from the cold, but from the realization that this could be his ticket out. *To think, it's math—not something groundbreaking like making gunpowder or antibiotics.*

# CHAPTER 2

# BELLANDIA

After a brief but freezing winter, another spring arrived in the Arvena highlands. As the snow melted, the scenery changed dramatically. Meadows turned colorful with purple and yellow wildflowers, while hints of their floral scene were carried on the wind. The land was returning to life once again.

Like most villagers, Arryn's family spent the first week of spring cleaning their yard and making small repairs to their thatched roof. Afterward, the entire village welcomed the new spring with a week-long festival. Only after the soil was soft enough did they return to farming.

Last year, Lansius had unexpectedly assisted with the village's annual report, a job typically reserved for the village chief, scribe, or officials. However, his hopes for rapid advancement were quickly dashed. In a rural farming community, there were seldom jobs that required such skills.

Despite the setbacks, the townsfolk began to see Lansius in a different light. They collectively concluded that the only explanation for his skill with numbers, his odd-looking clothing, and his inability to speak the common language was that he must be a foreign merchant apprentice who was robbed and had gotten lost in the woods.

Since Lansius lost his memory, the rumor went unchallenged. Even the village chief wrote such in his reports. The officials learned about the appearance of a foreign straggler, but with the nobles locked in conflicts, they saw it as an insignificant tidbit.

Arryn's family followed their work routine as usual. During the warm spring season, Lansius was able to help out, and they planted more than usual. Things were looking promising.

After the planting season was over, Marc convinced Lansius to accompany him for daily strolls just before sundown. They would make their way around the village plaza, where the young people would socialize under the watchful eyes of their elders. Despite his social awkwardness, Lansius engaged in small talk and gradually improved his speaking skills.

In this world, the common tongue was rough-hewn and direct. Words were utilitarian tools, not elegant and well-articulated. Conversation was a matter of conveying necessity, not crafting poetry. The more polite and formal the conversation, the stiffer it became.

On one such evening, the two found themselves wandering aimlessly and ended up at the butcher shop. Though they were penniless as usual, they still went inside to catch up on the latest gossip and perhaps offer their help in exchange for some slices of meat.

The owner, a retired butcher from the city, required no help that day, but he halted them. "Lad, I heard you can do calculations?"

Lansius's eyes widened. "Yes, I can."

Connor, the owner, was tall, muscular, with a graying mustache. "Next week I'm going to deliver a new batch of meat jerky to the city. I'm thinking to buy some supplies. Problem is, I don't know whether my savings will suffice."

*Hmm . . . shouldn't be too difficult.*

"Can I have something to write with?" Lansius asked.

Connor gave him a waxed tablet and a wooden stylus. "Would this suffice?"

"Gratitude. This will do," he said, his words fluent and formal. "Now, name the items you wish to purchase, along with their prices and quantities."

Connor informed him about the goods.

Lansius tallied them and compared the sum against the savings. "You're still forty copper short."

"About three silvers short, eh?" Connor approximated while rubbing his chin.

Sensing an opportunity, Marc grinned and hyped it up. "Wow, you sure can count fast. Not even the chief can calculate that much."

Lansius could only smile sheepishly, but Connor nodding his head. "Indeed, lad, you're pretty good with this."

Marc found an opening. "Surely such assistance begets some—"

"But of course," Connor said happily.

They went home with three iron coins and a sausage. The treat was a pleasant surprise for Tanya and Arryn. Before eating, the boys smelled their cut multiple times to savor it. The meat was juicy, unlike the dry, salted meat they had for festivals.

One small favor led to another. In the following weeks, the number of people asking for help, while random and inconsistent, steadily grew. Lansius was happy, but knew that he couldn't count on them for a living.

When spring almost came to a close, Connor returned from his trip. He happily reported that Lansius's calculation had saved him from taking out loans. Now, he wanted Lansius to teach his oldest child calculation.

Lansius, ever in a hurry to escape from farming life, immediately agreed. With Mother Arryn's blessing, he took two students under his wing. At first, he thought that this was doomed to fail, but he soon realized that he was dealing with teenagers, not kids. They were well-behaved and curious, so the teaching went smoothly.

For his effort, he earned six iron coins or half a copper daily—half the price of a full meal with ale. It certainly wasn't enough to get by, but Lansius was content. This was progress, at least.

Soon, things took a positive turn. Over the summer, he gained two additional students: the village chief's son and the baker's child. With more students, his income increased, allowing him to earn a copper a day. Summer passed smoothly, but when autumn arrived, tutoring came to an abrupt halt as the entire village turned its attention to the harvest.

Harvest was the biggest celebration of the year, and other festivities like marriages and feasts were commonly arranged around it. Only after the festivity ended did things slow down as people prepared for winter.

One clear but windy day, without warning, hundreds of armed men marched toward Bellandia. It was then that the villagers learned that Arvena was at war. Young Lord Arte led a column of men, including wounded soldiers and refugee, toward Bellandia. They camped outside Bellandia and waited for reinforcements. Marc and the other villagers were called for training.

This unforeseen event worried Lansius. He had never had any experience with war or fighting before. Although he never said it, he felt sickened by not knowing what was going to happen.

Days passed in more or less the same routine. The only difference was that Lansius frequently spent his free time with other men from the village. During one such gathering, the topic of magic was raised. Some believed that the lord might employ a mage or a saint candidate as a healer.

Intrigued, Lansius found himself increasingly drawn to the subject. Magic was something he had always yearned to witness. Thus, he followed the crowds to the newly established camp nearby to listen and learn about the world beyond his village.

However, rather than learning about magic, Lansius found himself becoming an object of curiosity. The men at the camp were intrigued by his foreign features. No one had seen dark hair like his before. While they were familiar with various shades of blond and lighter brown, his near-black hair was a novelty. Even men who hailed from distant lands, such as the Mercantile Kingdom in the Far East or the Navalnia Empire, hadn't encountered someone with such distinct hair color.

Lansius came to realize his distinctiveness. Then, abruptly, a voice rang out. "You with the dark hair, the young lord wants to see you," someone declared in a commanding tone.

Everyone's gaze had turned toward Lansius as an imposing man in a fresh white tunic approached. The man motioned for Lansius to follow him.

The crowd's eyes dutifully followed as Lansius and the knight headed toward a particularly large tree.

Lansius saw young Lord Arte sitting regally on a small wooden chair, surrounded by burly men, presumably his knights.

Gulping, Lansius stammered, "My lord." The words felt foreign. He had never addressed a lord before.

"No need to be so tense," Arte responded. "I just heard a story of a foreigner who was robbed, lost his memory, and couldn't even speak the language."

"Indeed, that is my story," Lansius confirmed, relieved that he found the right words.

"Do you remember anything about your home?"

Lansius shook his head. "I can't remember."

"Ah," the young lord mumbled, then changed his tone. "Tell me, what do you do in this village?"

"I teach children to calculate," Lansius managed, feeling the constraints of his limited vocabulary.

The young lord laughed upon hearing this, appearing pleased about something.

"If you can count, why not calculate the number of our troops or something? Entertain us, will you?" said one of the burly men.

"That's a good idea. Can you do it?" the young lord agreed.

Lansius hesitated for a moment. However, his interaction with the young lord validated what others had said about him. The young lord seemed genuine. Thus, he answered, "I believe I can."

"Excellent," Arte replied, clearly excited.

The knight who had approached Lansius earlier now signaled to some men. "Assemble the men who can walk. No armor, no weapons. And make no unnecessary commotion."

Slowly, the camp came to life with calls and shouts as everyone who was able sprang into action, readying themselves for formation. The knights watched from the sidelines, clearly considering themselves above the call. For them, this was merely entertainment.

"My lord, the men are ready," the knight reported to Arte.

The young lord stood and inquired, "Well, can you calculate the number of men in their current formation?"

Nodding, Lansius realized that his actions had led a large number of men to assemble, many of whom were wounded. The pressure was immense, and the villagers watched intently.

Observing the formation, he noted that the men were arranged in five deep ranks. The first and subsequent ranks consisted of equal numbers, and only the last was missing a few men.

*The front consisted of 22 men and 5 ranks deep. So, 110. But they are missing three to complete the formation.*

"My lord, it's 107," Lansius answered. Clearly, Arte had fully expected him to count manually or to use a stylus and multiplication table.

"Oui, that was quick. Are you certain?" Arte asked, a fierce glint in his young eyes, perhaps a byproduct of this violent era.

"More or less, my lord," Lansius confirmed.

Fascinated, Arte ordered, "Send in the squires."

Three teenagers hurriedly began to count the men manually, each starting from a different point. They divided the formation into thirds and ran while counting. It was evident that they were accustomed to this method.

After a short wait, the squires returned and announced, "My lord, it's 107."

Lansius was inwardly pleased. The count matched his own calculation exactly.

The knights looked pleased, as did the young lord who dispersed the formation. The 107 men also appeared amused by the recent events. Many eyes turned toward Lansius, a level of attention he was unaccustomed to.

Arte returned to his seat and asked, "What is your name, man?"

"It's Lansius, my lord," he responded, surprised that Arte would even ask. The social chasm between them was so wide that it would normally be unthinkable for Arte to need to remember the name of a lowly subject like him.

"Lansius, you're an interesting man. How about joining my retinue?" Arte's offer drew chuckles from his knights.

At this, Lansius was dumbfounded, struggling to process the unexpected offer.


Two weeks had passed since the arrival of the armed column. The trees had shed their orange leaves, and the cold air from the western Targe Mountains had descended upon the Arvena highlands, signaling the approaching winter.

Despite the usual calm during this time, the towns and villages near Bellandia saw an influx of armed men arriving from distant towns and cities. The majority didn't stay long but continued their march eastward. Most traveled light, as supplies were plentiful and easy to come by so soon after the harvest.

The situation reached its peak when Lord Maurice of Arvena, Arte's father, arrived in Bellandia with his personal column.

Today was the second day after the lord's arrival. Despite all the military activities and the rising prices, Arryn's household continued their life as usual, except for the addition of a mother and daughter who were war refugees. Arryn gladly sheltered them in her house.

The guests helped with the chores and offered some coins for food. With the farm empty for winter, Arryn, Tanya, and the guests went to the wool shop. Meanwhile, the boys were busy fixing things like roofs, window covers, and fences.

Lansius found himself considering a rather memorable scene involving himself, the troops, and the young lord. While he didn't think much of this encounter, others insisted that he had impressed the young lord, who had asked him to join. However, Lansius felt that the young lord was only joking, as he was neither a fighter nor a competent scribe.

As the sun was rising and today was laundry day, Marc and Lansius busily scrubbed and beat their clothes with a wooden bat before rinsing them.

Suddenly, a woman's voice rang out from outside. "Lansius. I'm looking for Lansius."

Marc and Lansius stared at each other. Lansius cleaned his hands from the white ash they used as a detergent, but Marc headed straight to the front.

"Wow, a woman, not from Bellandia, either. I never thought this could happen to you," Marc commented sarcastically.

Lansius splashed water on Marc for his stupid comment.

"Bah!" Marc reacted by trying to smack Lansius's back as he went past him, but missed. He ended up grinning and shaking his head while returning to his laundry.

The woman leaned against the short wooden fence, her hands resting lightly on the rough wood. Unlike most of the women in the village, her hair was cut short.

"I'm Lansius," he said as he approached.

"I can tell from the hair," she quipped.

Lansius unconsciously frowned. He disliked the way his hair made him stand out.

The woman missed the subtle change. "Are you really a foreigner?"

"I think so. Even now, I'm struggling to talk." He wasn't being modest; despite two years and daily chats in the village plaza, he was only slightly better than basic.

"I understand you enough." She straightened her posture and revealed a weathered black gambeson. An exquisite-looking belt decorated her waist and a well-worn scabbard hung neatly on one side.

"I'm Stefi, a squire. They sent me to help you on the journey ahead." She gave a little bow at the end.

Lansius blinked several times to process what he just heard.

*Ehhh . . . a squire? Accompany me? A girl . . . !?*

Nervously, Lansius guessed why she was here. He concluded that the young lord's offer was real. However, nobody had informed him about this arrangement.

"May I call you Master Lansius?" she asked indifferently.

"Eh, no, I'm not someone important. Just Lans is enough," he clarified.

Stefi stared at him briefly. There was something about her gaze. It was so abnormally powerful and penetrating.

Not wanting to start on the wrong foot, Lansius decided to explain his stance. "Listen, before anything else, you should know that I haven't made my decision yet."

She looked surprised. An invitation from a noble was a formality. It was hardly refused, either due to its prestige and opportunity, or fear of punishment. "Are you by any chance afraid of the upcoming battle?"

"That is one concern, yes," he admitted. Life for him was already hard without sanitation and antibiotics. Adding war into the mix would be suicidal.

Stefi offered a stiff smile and explained, "Be at peace. At most, you're probably going to work as a scribe."

"But I never travel out, and I can't even write that well."

Lansius's confession broke the ice and made the squire chuckle. "That's why I'm here. And Lans, put more trust in your ability. I was there, you know, when you counted the troops."

"Ah . . ." he muttered.

"The troops had barely assumed formation. The squires just started their counts when you finished counting. How did you do that?" Stefi asked with great interest.

"It's just multiplication," he said, but he knew that mental math was uncommon in this era.

"But you didn't even use a multiplication table. That's amazing, you know?"

The way Stefi said it made Lansius rather proud. However, he still had doubts. "I'm just a farmer turned teacher. I only want to live in peace."

"Ahh, so you're that kind of man," she said, gazing out across the landscape.

"I'm not sure I follow," Lansius replied.

"Humble. Many people get a speck of skill and become pompous and haughty."

Lansius couldn't help but smile at her kind words.

"Is that your house?" She gestured at the small hovel.

"Yup," he remarked without any intention of hiding that he lived in poverty.

"Looks cozy and well taken care of, aside from the rotted thatched roof and wood panels," Stefi observed.

"Indeed, it needs a bit of repair," Lansius admitted.

Stefi nodded sympathetically. "Must be costly . . ."

"Yep." Lansius knew where the conversation was headed and braced himself for her sales pitch.

"So why don't you accept the offer? Being a lord's retainer brings wealth and status. What's not to like?"

Lansius was hesitant and asked sheepishly, "Do you know about the pay?"

"For non-combatants on a campaign, it's usually a half silver a day."

A half silver was six copper, six times his current income. Lansius started to see the benefit.

"I don't know about teachers' pay, but I think it's hard to pay for a better house," Stefi teased.

Lansius nodded in agreement.

"I heard you guys aren't related, but . . . don't you want to help them out? I imagine working the land is hard on the body."

Lansius exhaled deeply. Mother Arryn's back was getting worse while blue dyes wrecked Tanya's fingers. The family had taken care of him, a complete stranger. It was only natural for him to help them back.

"How about if I return tomorrow morning for your answer?" She knew not to push too hard.

"Yes, that's probably for the best."

"I hope you say yes; otherwise I'm stuck with half-pay," Stefi commented without sounding bitter.

"Eh, why?"

"Well, because I don't have a duty right now," she answered flatly.

"But you're a squire?"

"A masterless one. My knight master, unfortunately, died on a hunt. Maybe I'll tell you about her when we have the time."

"I'm sorry to hear that . . . but why won't other knights employ you?"

She giggled. "Because I'm a female and most all other knights are males. If I fuck around and become pregnant, then they'll be the one who gets the blame."

"Th-that's awful . . ." He felt embarrassed by the frank answer.

She laughed. "It's just a lame joke. But yeah, at any rate, you would be stuck with me. But don't worry. I'm more reliable than my looks."

Lansius smiled at Stefi's self-promotion. "Is it common for women to become squires or knights?"

Stefi furrowed her brow momentarily. "Oh, I guess you didn't know since you're not from here. It's rare. Probably my master and I were the only ones, so I usually work with the servants. Why, do you wish to change for another squire?"

"No, not at all," he said, shaking his head. "I'm just curious."

Sensing a change in his mood, she asked, "So, how about it? Are you coming?"

He mulled it over. "Are you sure about no fighting?"

"Of course! We're only defending against a small incursion. We'll be mostly at the rear, far from any battle."

Lansius was getting swayed. He looked around to settle his mind and spotted Marc hanging clothes.

"He, too, would get an exemption," she whispered.

Lansius's eyes widened. He looked her dead in the eye and asked, "Are you sure?"

"It's common knowledge that the lord can only levy one from a family."

He knew that most men in the village had already answered the call. While a lord couldn't legally force the same man to answer the call multiple times, they could impose a quota on the village or settlement. As a result, many volunteered multiple times on behalf of their sons or other male relatives. Youngsters and first-timers like Marc, who had no protection from their parents or uncles, were sure to get selected.

Lansius finally found his courage. "When will we depart?"

Stefi smiled brightly. "Tomorrow after sunrise."

"So soon?" he asked while trying to steel his resolve.

"Winter is coming in a month or two, so we're running out of time," she remarked. "Don't worry, I'll prep you up and show you the basics."

Lansius remained doubtful. He couldn't shake off the feeling that he was being treated as an exotic pet with a talent for numbers. If that were the case, assigning him a squire would make sense—not as an assistant, but more like a handler.

Despite his pessimism, he still wanted to repay the family's kindness. Lansius wasn't trying to play a hero. For him, it was about survival chances. Obviously, a scribe in the back lines was safer than the front lines. As he reached out to offer his right hand, he found himself already contemplating the words he would use to say goodbye to the family, preparing an excuse for Arryn, Marc, and especially Tanya.

Stefi took Lansius's hand, and the two clasped hands to seal the deal. "I swear to protect you from harm and injury until we reach our destination."

"I put my life in your care," Lansius said, taking a leap of faith.

Autumn of Elven Calendar 4422 was drawing to a close.

# CHAPTER 3

# CERESIA

On his last night in Bellandia, Lansius told his family about his decision to join young Lord Arte as his retinue. His family was mostly ecstatic. However, Mother Arryn felt the need to warn him, "Remember, we're just village folk, and you still have a lot to learn about interacting with nobles."

"It's not that scary, Mother. Besides, expectations are low for country folks like us," Marc reassured her. He then added, "Based on your abilities, you'll probably work in the supply camp. The worst that could happen is joining a scouting party to count enemy soldiers, but that's unlikely since you'd need to know how to ride a horse."

Lansius nodded, hoping Marc's assessment was accurate.

"You know what Connor told me?" Marc asked.

"The butcher? No, why?"

"Don't overthink it. Learn as you go if you have to. Opportunities are rare," Marc said, smirking proudly as he reiterated Connor's advice when Marc had been selected for training.

Mother Arryn crossed her arms and muttered, "Well, the worst that can happen is they'll send you home."

Marc laughed and patted Lansius's shoulder. "I'll lend you my rucksack and shoulder bag. Now, let's prepare things for the journey."

Lansius didn't tell them that accepting the offer would spare Marc from being levied.

Early in the morning after breakfast, men around the camp refilled their waterskins, packed their clothes and other gear, and saddled their horses. Everyone, including a number of camp followers, was ready to march. Mules and horse carts laden with supplies were also lined up.

Meanwhile, inside Arryn's household, Lansius was getting ready.

"Wear this for the winter," Arryn instructed as she unloaded items from a wooden chest.

"Gratitude." Lansius examined the woolen coat and found it to be in good condition despite its age.

"Lans, take this for good luck," said Marc.

Lansius looked at a small iron medallion resembling a coin with intricate patterns. "Where did you get this?"

"It belonged to Father."

Lansius furrowed his brow. "Are you sure you want to give me this?"

"Yep," Marc said, pulling out his own medallion. "I have a better one, see?"

Lansius grinned.

"Have you packed your mittens and thick gloves?" Arryn interjected.

"Yes, I've packed those already."

"Extra footwraps for the road?" she inquired.

"Already gave him two," Marc answered.

She nodded. "That should suffice."

Lansius's rucksack was now loaded up. Next was the shoulder bag, which he filled with packages of dried meat, hard biscuits, a small sack of flour, some raisins, and carrots.

"Here's the waterskin. It's old but still sturdy and not leaky," Marc said as he handed over what was essentially his own gear to Lansius.

"Gratitude, Marc. Let me pay you for this."

"No need, you've already shared enough. I can buy another one later when I need it," said Marc.

After they finished packing, Tanya came in and hugged him. "I was about to make you a hood, Lans, but it's not finished yet. I'm sorry I can't give you anything." Her voice was tinged with regret.

Lifting her, he reassured her, "Don't worry about it. Take care of Mother and Marc for me. I'll come home when I can."

"Hush, you're going to work in his retinue," Arryn corrected him. "Obey your master, and don't ask to come home too soon; wait until you've done something worthy. Don't worry about us."

Smiling at her wise advice, Lansius felt grateful. Given the hurried nature of his departure, he had little time to dwell on his emotions. His farewell might have been more emotional and potentially awkward if he had more time.

After saying his goodbyes and sharing warm hugs with everyone, Lansius stepped out the door with a heavy heart. His family waved as Lansius shouldered his rucksack and began to walk toward the camp.

Along the road, he encountered the mother and daughter who had been staying at Arryn's house. They had just come back from bidding their relatives farewell. Just like Lansius, many had joined the campaign to retake Riverstead.

"I wish I could give you something," the mother said while the little daughter grinned at him.

"That's alright, please look after Arryn and Tanya for me," Lansius replied and continued on way.

The sun was still low on the eastern horizon, and the wind was cool. Bellandia looked amazing at times like this. The farm and the distant meadows glinted in the light, while the grass, still wet with dew, took on an almost magical sheen that stretched on for miles.

As Lansius had expected, a woman in black gambeson waited not far from his house. Stefi approached Lansius and asked, "All set?"

Lansius tapped at his shoulder bag. "Hopefully it's enough."

"I'll share if you're missing something," Stefi reassured him. She then led him to a section of the camp where her horse was kept. It was already saddled and ready to go; a young servant stood by, waiting.

"Gratitude. Here's a coin."

Upon being paid, the servant darted into the crowd that was preparing to leave, apparently in search of his own master.

"What do you think of Horsie?" Stefi asked.

"She looks gentle, but I don't know anything about horses," he admitted.

Stefi chuckled. "Come on, take the reins, and let's go."

Lansius wasn't sure. "I've never held horse reins before."

"Don't worry, she's docile. Time to get acquainted," Stefi said, smiling.

He gazed at her questioningly. "You're going to train me to ride?"

"There's no reason not to. Just don't pull too hard. Guide her gently."

Lansius did as he was told, and they finally hit the road. It was bustling with a column of people, knights, horse carts, pack mules, and even donkeys, all marching eastward toward their final destination: Riverstead City.

*Elven Calendar 4422*

In an era marked by rising tensions and escalating raids, Viscount Karius, the formidable Lord of Inglesia, committed the ultimate act of aggression. He crossed the Great River and launched a large-scale attack on the jewel of the Arvena province—the city of Riverstead.

Despite Lord Maurice of Arvena's attempts to fortify the city, even sending his own son to bolster its defenses, the city of Riverstead fell prey to Karius's surprise assault.

The High Lords viewed this as an overt act of hostility and aimed to censure the Lord of Inglesia. However, the Imperium's archaic bureaucracy, slow and unresponsive, sought to label the incident as a minor border squabble among its vassal lords.

This attempt was a bid to preserve a semblance of peace within a realm already besieged by battles, particularly the western front's ongoing struggle against nomadic incursions.

Unwilling to wait for the slow response of the Imperium, Lord Maurice mustered his forces, marching them to Ceresia on the eve of winter.

*Two Months After Leaving Bellandia*

Lansius was suddenly awoken by a chilling gust of wind, causing his body to stiffen. Blinking, he found himself curled up around a faintly glowing campfire inside an old barn. Despite the fire's warmth, he could see his breath turning into vapor. His face and his whole body ached from the cold.

"It's still not dawn," Stefi whispered beside him.

Lansius nodded and pulled his rough woolen blanket tighter around himself. The wind outside howled and shook the barn, making it feel even colder. Despite the thick rags and hay mats on the ground, the cold still seeped through.

Only the crackling fire and the friendly faces of his comrades brought any relief. Gradually, Lansius began to drift back to sleep.

Lansius and the Arvena troops had been marching to retake Riverstead for almost a month when they encountered sudden, drastic changes in the weather. No one wanted to be caught in a blizzard, so they scrambled to find winter quarters.

Lansius's group had found refuge in an abandoned barn in the village of Ceresia. Here, they had made camp, in hopes of waiting out the weather, yet winter was still in full force, with frequent snowfall and blizzards.

Today was another cloudy day, and weak sunlight filtered through the gaps in the wood panels. The early risers were already up and about, preparing breakfast. Nobility and city dwellers didn't typically eat so early in the morning, but on a campaign, it was a necessity. Morning was one of the few times they could cook without much interruption.

Lansius's stomach growled, and he knew the wine from the night before would upset his digestion. Nevertheless, he needed a sip or two to warm up. Just as he was about to sigh, Stefi appeared with a bowl of stew she had received from the cook.

"You're awake?" she asked, offering him the bowl.

"Gratitude," he said, taking the bowl and sipping spoonfuls of the warm, savory broth.

*Smells burnt just as usual, but the warmth hits the spot.*

Lansius took another spoonful, while Stefi gobbled down a thick, round chunk of bread. They swapped the bowl for the bread and continued eating.

Stefi didn't bat an eye when they shared the bowl and spoon, partly because she was raised as a squire, but mainly because of practicality.

Most men carried a wooden plate and spoon, but washing them repeatedly in ice-cold water was a daunting task. One trick was to use a heated rock from the fireplace and dunk it in a bucket to warm the water, but even then, nobody wanted to do it repeatedly. Thus, sharing utensils was a common practice. However . . .

*Don't think about it—*

*But this is the same bowl and spoon . . .*

For better or worse, Lansius hadn't been close to a woman his own age in two years. But now, he and Stefi were practically inseparable. They marched, ate, and slept beside each other every day. Stefi, despite being younger, was knowledgeable and had taught Lansius the basics of survival during their journey, including what to wear, what was safe to eat, and how to prepare a tent.

As they traveled, they inadvertently shared some intimate moments, moments that Stefi seemed oblivious to. Once, cleaning and washing resulted in a skinny dip in the stream; another time, two straight days of steady rain meant they had to sleep half-naked in the tent. There had even been a spur-of-the-moment kiss from Stefi, not out of passion, but mischievously.

Lansius treasured the memories of these moments. Overall, he had managed to conduct himself well, earning Stefi's respect. Their camaraderie led others to tease them as a couple, which wasn't surprising given their closeness. Anyone who knew saw them as socially compatible and of the right age to marry.

As for themselves, despite her brash demeanor, Lansius admired her honesty and resourcefulness. Meanwhile, Stefi respected Lansius's educated background and his status as part of the young lord's retinue.

A pat on Lansius's shoulder brought him back to the present. "Time for some sparring," Stefi said.

"Right," Lansius responded as he followed her with a borrowed sword. The owner allowed anyone to use it for training, but it was old and dull. As Lansius unsheathed it, he felt surprised that it was so light, unlike what he had imagined.

"Show me your middle guard," Stefi instructed, preparing her own stance.

Lansius gripped the handle and pointed his sword at shoulder height, remembering where to place his thumb and not to death grip the handle.

"All right, parry mid, low, and high. En garde!" With a swift motion, Stefi thrust her sword toward Lansius's torso. It came like a blur, but Lansius parried it sideways. Stefi continued with a low slash. Lansius took a step back and defended with a block.

Stefi directed her sword upward. Lansius knew the routine, but instinct made him dodge backward. He felt it was more natural. However, she followed up with a swing that stopped inches from Lansius's neck.

"You need to parry it," she warned him before pulling back her sword.

"My bad," he said. "But it feels natural."

Stefi didn't acknowledge his excuse. "Again."

They resumed their stance. Repetition built muscle memory, and gradually the moves began to feel natural to Lansius, and he had less hesitation. Stefi had worked tirelessly to teach him the correct way. At first, he had been clumsy, but he was starting to get the basics right.

The two weren't the only ones practicing. Breakfast had ended, and more people were exercising and sparring. Many young first-timers practiced with their spears, but Stefi said that more spear training would be useless for Lansius. Since there was no word about Lansius's appointment, Stefi, as a squire, fell back on things she knew best, which was sword training.

Around midday, the barn turned into a chaotic work group. Some people searched for cracks in the walls to patch up, while others tended to the horses and mules. A few went outside, braving the knee-deep snow to relieve themselves in the adjacent hut.

When the sun was at its highest, everyone paused to bask in its warmth. Unfortunately, lunch wasn't very appetizing. The bread from the morning was blackened and soggy.

Lansius sat with his back against the wall, trying to munch the tasteless bread. A slice of ham, cheese, or pickles would have been a welcome addition, but those were reserved for the nobles.

"Still having trouble with the bread?" Stefi asked.

He groaned. "It's mushy and tastes horrible."

She chuckled. "My Master, Isolte, always said: Just be grateful it's still white. When things get hard, they use cheap grains, the same ones they used to feed the mules."

In shock, he asked, "How does that taste?"

"Horsebread? It's gross, smells, and tastes like dirt."

Lansius's terrified face made Stefi giggle.

"Finish your bread, and let's do some riding while there's still light," she said, rising.

Lansius followed and spent an hour riding slowly around the tight enclosure where they had cleared some snow while Stefi led the horse's reins on foot. She had taught him how to sit correctly on the saddle and what not to do when riding.

Even though he was just sitting on the saddle, it was tiring for someone who wasn't accustomed to the rocking motion, and the horse's smell was giving him a hard time. "Are you sure the saddle is all right?"

"Well, maybe it could have better padding, but . . ." She shook her head.

Lansius understood. Maintaining her gear alone was costly; boots needed new soles, coats needed mending, and horses needed fodder, to name a few. It was lucky that her old master used good bridles that still worked despite years of usage.

"Well, don't mind my ramblings. I'm already grateful that you are teaching me how to ride."

She chuckled. "Give thanks to Horsie. She's the one who carried you around."

The horse neighed as if she understood.

After a few hours, the sun began to set in the west. The temperature dropped and people begrudgingly donned coats and blankets. Despite daily exercise or handling animals, they rarely bathed, only doing so when absolutely necessary.

Lansius, too, adopted this practice to some degree, finding the hassle of bathing not worth the effort. When he did wash up, he used a bucket of warm water, a clean cloth, and firewood ash as soap.

Cleanliness was appreciated but difficult to achieve, so it was common to find cases of rashes and other skin disorders. Clothing was the only thing preventing an outbreak of body odor and putrid smells, as the many layers of fabric kept the unpleasant odors inside.

Lansius had a sensitive nose and avoided unpleasant smells when possible, but his introversion made him reluctant to say anything about his group. Eventually, Stefi noticed his predicament and moved them together to a group that stank less.

As a foreigner, Lansius often found himself at the center of attention, but he was cautious about revealing his origin, and only offered the new group vague answers about his birthplace. They did, however, eventually find out about Lansius's hair. Despite his attempts to always cover it up with a hood or traveling cloak, he couldn't hide it forever. It turned out he needn't have worried: nobody behaved differently. The men were interested in his foreign background, but largely unconcerned. Lansius began to feel truly welcomed.

The cold season seemed endless, and the troops did their best to entertain themselves with music, gossip, storytelling, playing dice, and preparing meals. When the sun went down each night, the barn would grow quiet except for the bubbling of the cauldron and the crackling of the fire.

The monotony continued for three weeks. During this period, some of the younger soldiers improved their weapon handling skills or picked up soft skills like reading and cooking. Lansius worked on his sword training, but made little progress beyond the basics. He instead focused on learning cursive writing with a wax stylus. A balding lieutenant with an arm tattoo, believing in Lansius's potential, offered to tutor him without charge, thinking that Lansius had potential and would go places.

One day, four men arrived and gathered the captain and lieutenant from Lansius's shelter. It was obvious that Lord Maurice had summoned them. Rumors of an impending attack spread like wildfire. Indeed, the weather had calmed down, and the snow was only ankle-deep.

When the captains and lieutenants returned, they confirmed the rumors. "Pack your gear. We march out tomorrow at dawn."

The shelter sprang to life as preparations for the journey began. Like Stefi, several of the group hailed from Riverstead. Driven out in the previous season, they were eager to return home.

"It finally happened," Stefi said to Lansius, who could only nod with a sense of uneasiness.

The next day dawned in Ceresia, with a drop in temperature and a fierce wind. The barn doors, which were usually closed, stood wide open, and lanterns and torches illuminated the inside. Dozens of men dressed in their winter gear were ready for departure.

Similar activity was taking place in neighboring towns and villages. After being cooped up in their shelters for over a month, the Arvena troops were finally returning to march.

The young lord assigned Stefi and Lansius to stay behind and take charge of the supplies. It wasn't surprising. They needed someone to guard the supplies and record them, and as squire and scribe apprentice, the two were fit for the task.

"Hope they win," Stefi murmured as the army received their order to march out. "Otherwise, we'll have to defend this place with only remnants and leftovers."

"How big is the opponent's army?" Lansius asked.

"Interested in war, are you?" Stefi quipped.

"Not really, just trying new vocabulary." He avoided the question, fearing that Stefi might use it as an excuse to train him harder.

"Well . . . hard to know. But ours should be bigger. I say two thousand versus a few hundred?" Stefi shrugged.

Lansius found their own numbers hard to believe, but he had some suspicion when he saw how many marched with him. He realized he had also been mistaken in his assumption about the scale of this world he found himself in. Although he had initially believed it to be similar to medieval times, he now saw that it was more akin to an imperial Roman civilization, one that had thrived into the medieval era.

*So, not just a lord, but more like a Roman governor with cohorts to command.*

"Ah, so it's likely we'll win," he muttered, more to himself.

Stefi shook her head. "Nothing is certain in a war. Securing the river crossing won't be easy."

Lansius had heard that the river between Ceresia and Riverstead was wide and had strong currents. There was only one narrow bridge, which was often damaged by flood. The forces who occupied Riverstead surely understood this bridge's importance and would be prepared to defend it.

*Looks like it's going to be a messy battle . . . Unless . . . if the river is frozen.*

He considered the possibility that if the river was frozen, the Arvenians could split their forces, cross the river, and attempt a pincer attack. However, he realized that he knew nothing about the Lord of Arvena's personality and whether he would gamble on such a risky maneuver.

"Stefi," he called as he approached and whispered, "is the Lord of Arvena bold?"

Stefi furrowed her brow and met his gaze. "Lans, we're campaigning in the middle of winter. If that's not bold, then I don't know what is."

Lansius felt foolish for asking. "Oh, right, of course."

Stefi crossed her arms in a relaxed way. "What's on your mind?"

"Oh, I'm just thinking, if the river is frozen, then—"

"Then it's going to be easy win at the crossing?" Stefi guessed.

Lansius nodded. "Yeah, something like that."

"Well, you're onto something. If it's frozen then it's only a matter of sending our strongest detachment to cross and attack their camp. However," Stefi continued, "it's not that simple. The river is wide, and it rarely freezes entirely. Have you ever walked on thin ice before?"

Lansius shook his head.

"Well, you never want to cross it in armor, and definitely not with a group of armored men," Stefi cautioned.

"I see, so it's possible—"

"But dangerous," Stefi said. "Lastly, if that's the plan then they'll need to move quickly."

"Why's that?" Lansius asked.

"The coldest time was several weeks ago. By now, the river may already be thawing," Stefi said with a sigh.

Lansius now realized that time was running out. With the weather unpredictable and the bridge likely fortified, the Arvenians needed to act fast. The fate of their campaign depended solely on their speed.

# CHAPTER 4

# TALL CLOUDS

Two weeks had elapsed since the Arvenian troops had set out. Lansius sighed from boredom, for what felt like the hundredth time. He had taken Stefi's advice to clean and maintain his equipment; his spare cloth was neatly rolled in his bag, the wooden bowl was scrubbed spotless, and he had even aired out the woolen coats and blankets until they were fluffy again. Still, he found himself with time on his hands.

*I really could use a book . . . I wonder how everyone is doing in Bellandia. I hope Tanya isn't overworking herself. It pains me to see her nails and fingers stained blue. And Mother Arryn, too.*

He exhaled yet another sigh.

*I wish I were with them . . .*

The relentless weather was the primary source of his gloominess. However, it hadn't always been this way. Upon the soldiers' departure two weeks prior, the weather had cleared, allowing Lansius to roam Ceresia without hindrance. It was then that they received uplifting news: the Arvena forces had triumphantly crossed the frozen river, secured the bridge, and opened up the road to Riverstead.

Regrettably, just as the Arvenians should have been advancing toward Riverstead to set up their siege against the occupier force, the weather took a sudden turn for the worse. A relentless snowstorm besieged the region, with no end in sight.

Sitting not far from Lansius, two elderly men in worn gambeson were patching holes in their bedrolls and blankets. "It's snowing again," one of them muttered.

His companion stood up, looking concerned. They went to the barn door and secured it tightly.

"I'm worried about our people," the second man whispered.

"They'll be fine. Riverstead is a four-day journey from here," his friend said, attempting to comfort him.

"But what about their supplies? They must be running low."

"Their provisions should suffice. There's no need to entertain such an ill-conceived thought."

Lansius couldn't help but feel a twinge of unease.

*We've captured the bridge, but maintaining a siege and taking a city is a different matter. Especially in a winter like this.*

Lansius, Stefi, the two old men, and two boys were in charge of a cartload of grains, small barrels of ale, cheese, and salted meat. They made up one of the many supply posts around Ceresia.

It wasn't much, but due to winter, moving them all to a dedicated spot was a logistical nightmare. Thus, instead of a well-guarded camp, the supplies were scattered with minimal personnel to guard them.

The main body of the army marched with as many supplies as they could manage. What Lansius and the other groups were guarding were leftovers that were too cumbersome to transport in the snowy conditions.

Linking them with the main army was a group of men and mules who would come regularly for supplies. But the last visit—and the last news—had been ten days ago, before the weather worsened.

*Keeping two thousand men from freezing with just medieval technology is almost unthinkable. Men need more than just food, tents, and blankets to survive the winter. Without a fire, nobody will survive at night. And firewood is cumbersome and not easy to get.*

His experience in Bellandia had taught him that firewood must be dried through the summer. A properly dried wood would make good heat with almost no smoke. Meanwhile, recently cut logs had too much moisture and produced less heat with lots of smoke.

With the path likely blocked by heavy snow, Lansius could only imagine the hardship that befell the men on the front line. The nobles could furnish themselves with charcoal heaters, but the common folks could only rely on foraging the snowy woodlands for fallen logs and dead branches. Meanwhile, the stacks of firewood in Ceresia lay unused.

*No use worrying about it.*

The dullness endured until the orange glow of the setting sun seeped through the cracks in the wooden walls. Observing this, the two elderly men enlisted the boys' help with chores.

The boys weren't particularly helpful, but the men appreciated their company. The youngsters were the same age as their grandchildren, and their lively chatter distracted everyone from thoughts of war.

As the pottage bubbled away in the cauldron, the food preparations came to an end. To fill the time before supper, one of the men chopped wood while the other taught the boys some winter crafts.

In contrast, Stefi seemed to snooze effortlessly, as if she hadn't a worry in the world. After sword training, a lunch break, and a bit of horse riding, she was indulging in a well-earned nap. To be fair, she had been eager for another round of training, but Lansius had declined, as his hands had developed painful blisters and calluses.

Stefi shifted in her sleep and faced Lansius's direction, and he caught himself staring at her.

*She does have a cute side. Without the fierce eyes, she looks innocent, even fragile.*

She had told Lansius that it was rare for women to take up arms. Many called her a shield-maiden, a term that harked back to an older era when men and women fought side by side in battles. Nowadays, as peace and civilization had advanced, it had become uncommon. While some women did become huntresses or knights, they were considered outliers, and their numbers gradually diminished.

His stomach suddenly cramped up, stirring him from his thoughts. He rubbed his stomach, to no avail. It was getting worse, but he didn't know why. He had been avoiding milk, but perhaps his habit of drinking wine, even when diluted with plenty of water, was causing discomfort in his unaccustomed stomach.

Quietly, Lansius resigned himself to the boredom and unease. He could try to strike up a conversation, but they had already exhausted their topics. Even Lansius, with his keen interest in the history of the Imperium, had grown weary of the old men's tales. What he wouldn't give for a visit from a wandering minstrel. *Or even the internet and some films.* He longed to learn more about the Ancients, the elves, half-elves, and dwarves. While this group, like most people, had some knowledge about their world's origins, they lacked the insights a wandering minstrel could provide. Though it wasn't always easy getting a minstrel to sing about what you wanted to hear.

The barn was suddenly filled with the sound of a creaking door. Lansius only managed a brief glance in its direction before Stefi sprang awake from her slumber.

*Sword?!*

Metallic flashes propelled Lansius into action. As Stefi rushed to the door with sword in hand, Lansius grabbed his sparring spear and ran after her. The two old men also scrambled for their weapons, but it was all for naught.

"Hello, boys," greeted a familiar bearded face as he opened up the barn door.

"Thomas!" shouted the old man behind Lansius.

"Please spare me the blade," Thomas said with a grin.

Stefi smirked and sheathed her sword. Lansius, too, recognized the man and lowered his guard.

Thomas was old enough to sport a full gray beard, but a protruding axe that hung on his belt proved he was still in his prime. Along with four other men, their horses, cart, and mules, they went inside to warm themselves.

Everybody asked about the frontline, but the newcomers just looked at each other with big grins and bright faces.

"Ah, damn it, just say it. We won," Thomas said in the most anticlimactic way.

Everybody couldn't believe what they heard.

"Did you—" Lansius tried to ask.

"We won!" somebody cut in, and the rest followed. A wave of emotion erupted as they realized that the war was over. Youngsters and old men alike jumped in joy and danced happily in celebration.

Spring of 4423 had yet to arrive when the Arvena troops successfully took back Riverstead City after a short siege.


It had been ten days since Thomas arrived in Ceresia, and they were now marching toward Riverstead. The trees were bare, their branches whitened by a layer of frost, and the road was still covered in ice. Despite the conditions, Stefi, Lansius, and the Ceresia supply group were in high spirits, as today marked the final leg of their journey.

Stefi rode her horse, while the coachman and the boys journeyed on the horse-drawn supply cart. Lansius, Thomas, and the others walked beside the mules laden with goods. By midday, they reached the outskirts of the city where they found a cobblestone road, significantly easing their travel.

Lansius was captivated by the grand city. The imposing towers and bridges of Riverstead were an impressive sight even from a distance. As they drew nearer, the view became even more remarkable, with rows of tall buildings with white plastered walls, their colorful roof tiles visible through the snow.

"Hehe, you like it here?" Stefi teased as they crossed the stone bridge leading into the city.

"This is awesome," Lansius admitted as they entered.

"Wait till you see the market when it returns to normal. They have everything."

Though currently sparse due to the war, the vividly colored shops and stalls caught Lansius's attention. He marveled at the city's advanced appearance compared to Bellandia.

"Come, let's report before dark," Stefi urged.

They said their farewells to Thomas and the rest of the supply group. Since they served the same lord and were stationed in the same town, they knew they would likely cross paths often.

Stefi and Lansius left their horse at the city stable and went in search of the captain. After asking several people, they finally found him supervising reconstruction efforts. Despite being well over fifty, he still possessed an imposing figure. He wore a thick woolen tunic in a rich yellow hue, layered over a padded gambeson for warmth.

Spotting Stefi, the captain gestured for her to approach.

"No mule is lost or injured, sir," Stefi reported.

*What the—that's not how to report?!*

The captain appeared annoyed, confirming Lansius's suspicions. "The goods, are they safe?"

Unable to answer, Stefi nudged Lansius, who pulled a parchment from his bag and presented it. "The supplies from the village of Ceresia are present and accounted for, sir."

The captain glanced at the parchment but dismissed it. "Keep it for the seneschal's men." Then, addressing Stefi, he said, "Make sure the animals are fed and rested. We're going to need them soon."

"Another battle, sir?" she inquired.

The captain snorted. "The northern bastard still refuses a truce or surrender. The lord is hunting the remnants as we speak."

"I see," she murmured.

"Will that be all?" the old man questioned.

Seemingly uneasy, she asked, "Mm, sir, any chance of payments?"

The captain shook his head. "You'll have to take it up with the marshal or his deputy. And they're both away."

She sighed. "Sir, what about him?"

Her question perplexed the captain. "What about him? A new scribe?"

Stefi grinned. "We're not sure yet, but the young lord personally recruited him."

Her statement surprised the captain, who took a closer look at Lansius.

"I'm Lansius, from Bellandia village, sir."

"Well, Lansius of Bellandia, what makes the young lord want you in his retinue?"

"I'm not sure—"

"Don't be modest," Stefi interrupted. "He can calculate real fast."

Lansius noticed the captain eyeing his darker hair peeking out from his hood, but the captain didn't mention it. "Did the young lord say anything more specific?"

Both shook their heads in unison.

The man sighed as he considered the situation. "It's not the first time," he muttered to himself. "Oi, fetch me the scribe," he instructed his squire.

After waiting, an even older man appeared, wearing a long blue tunic and brown robe. The captain dictated a brief letter and handed it to Lansius.

"Give this letter to the municipal office tomorrow morning. That'll be all." He dismissed the duo.

Lansius bowed his head, but Stefi had another question.

"Mm, sir, what about me?"

"Let me guess, as I predicted, you convinced no one to take you as their squire?"
She shook her head and feigned sadness.

"Oh, begone." He scolded her. "Just stick with this Lansius fellow."

"Eh, really, I can do that?"

The captain didn't elaborate and waved his hand to send them away.

The two walked away from the reconstruction site and headed into the main street.

"Well, I guess we're stuck together," Stefi said lightly.

"So glad that we're both employed," Lansius remarked.

She chuckled. "Come, let's head home before dark. I reckon there's a lot to be done."

That made him stop in his track. "Home? You have a house?"

"Of course. I lived here, you dummy. Well, it was my master's, but nobody threw me out when she passed, so . . ." she explained, carefree.

"Doesn't the city have a . . ." He tried to find the word barracks, but he couldn't find it in his vocabulary.

Stefi tilted her head.

Lansius seemed to realize that the word might not exist. "What's the building where soldiers sleep?"

"Guardhouse? That's reserved for guardsmen, and it's cramped."

"What about the other men-at-arms?"

"Oh, you mean billets. Yeah, the lord could ask the townsfolk to provide housing for his men, but I guess right now, Riverstead doesn't need one."

Most of the city was empty. Its people had evacuated when the war started last year. Some refugees had returned, but many would wait until spring or summer when the road was firm and passable.

The two walked down the cobbled path toward a lifeless, narrow alley. Not one in ten buildings had lights in their windows or smoke coming out from their chimney. They passed a tavern that was crowded with soldiers and city folks. The heavenly smell of grilled meat reached them. Stefi sniffed the air.

"Want to give it a go?" Lansius asked.

"We can't," she exclaimed and walked away.

He followed up and asked, "Is the place expensive?"

"Two copper, but we need to be frugal. Otherwise, we'll go broke."

Both of them sighed. Nobody expected the opponent to refuse a truce after defeat and keep up fighting. With the lord and most of his troops continuing the mop-up, nobody in Riverstead could pay them.

"Isn't Lord Arte in Riverstead?" he asked with hope.

"Lans, never ask money directly from the nobles. They'll get irritated. The ones who pay are either the seneschal or the chamberlain. Neither of them took part in the campaign, only their assistants attached to the lord or the marshal."

"I see . . ." Lansius took her advice to heart.

As they left the tavern behind, the sky above them transformed from a mesmerizing golden hue to a breathtaking reddish-orange, and a chilling wind whipped through the deserted alleyway. With empty pockets but hearts full of hope, Lansius and Stefi continued to stride forward, neither knowing what the future would hold for them.

# CHAPTER 5

# RIVERSTEAD

The growing darkness and looming snowbanks on either side of the road didn't hinder Stefi from finding her home. Lansius followed Stefi as she headed down a row of similarly sized buildings. She slowed down and stopped where the road ended. Lansius saw an empty two-story wooden house. As they stepped up to the door, they saw that the lock had been smashed open.

Lansius nervously turned to Stefi, waiting for her response. Stefi drew her sword, gave a confident nod to Lansius, and cautiously pushed the door inward.

The creaking of the frozen hinges heralded their entry, but no challenge came from inside. Stefi went in, and Lansius followed, drawing his knife.

The house wasn't large and was only modestly furnished, so they could easily see that nobody was inside. They checked the kitchen and the wet area but found nothing. Stefi dropped her bag and motioned upstairs. She ran up the flight of stairs and disappeared from view.

Lansius heard a door being flung open and then another. But then, there was only silence. Slowly, the knife in his hand felt insignificant. He stopped hesitating and went for the stairs, but the sounds of footsteps stopped him.

Stefi appeared from upstairs with an unlit candle. "All clear," she said with a faint smile.

"Anything lost?" he asked while sheathing his knife. It took two tries, as his hand was unusually tense.

"I'll worry about it later when I have time," she responded.

There were clear signs of looting or burglary inside, but there was nothing they could do about it. As darkness fell, Stefi placed a candle on the wooden table and began unwrapping a small pouch that contained a flint, a metal object, and small pieces of wood from the previous night's fire. She grabbed the flint and struck it against the iron, directing the sparks onto the pieces of wood. After several attempts, an ember glowed red, and she carefully used it to light the candle.

Lansius found a wooden plank lying on the floor, lifted it, and placed it into the corresponding iron bracket to secure the door.

"Come, let's head upstairs," she called, holding the lit candle in her hand.

The narrow wooden stairs creaked almost with every step. Upstairs, they were greeted by two doors.

"That's my late master's room," Stefi said, nodding to one of the doors. "You'd better not enter."

"I see. So where do you sleep?"

"My bed is beside hers," Stefi said vaguely as she led him toward the other door.

Lansius followed her inside to see a tidy study. "Umm, so where will I sleep?"

"Here." She lightly stomped on the wooden floor.

"At least it won't be cold," he responded, fully expecting to sleep on the floor.

"No, I haven't pulled out the bed," she clarified.

"Oh . . ." he remarked shyly.

That made her giggle. "Lans, you're my charge. I won't let you suffer."

The room was dusty and damp, so they did what they could with a broom and cleaning rags. Stefi found a dry rushlight on the cabinet and lit it up. Afterward, she went inside her room and dragged a bed out.

"You sure you can do it alone?" Lansius asked in between the screeching noises.

But with only a few tries, she managed to get the oaken bed frame out.

Out of curiosity, Lansius tried to move it.

*Oof, this is heavy . . .*

The bed refused to budge.

She chuckled. "Better do it together."

The two moved the bed into the study without an issue. Afterward, they returned downstairs only to realize that all the firewood was gone.

Lansius wanted to give it another look, but Stefi said, "Wait here." She lifted the wood plank on the door and headed outside. He followed and spotted her just as she entered an empty-looking neighbor's house.

*Did she just barge into her neighbor's house?*

He glanced around nervously, feeling like an amateurish thief's accomplice. Fortunately, Stefi returned quickly with two sizeable objects in each hand. She handed one to Lansius as she walked by, and the two hurriedly returned to their place.

"What are we going to do with these chairs?" Lansius asked her as they barred the door once more.

"They belonged to the jerk. He used to piss from his window at night, right onto my fence," she explained, lifting the chair and heading into the kitchen.

"What?" Lansius couldn't believe what he'd just heard.

"After my master passed away," she began, "this neighbor kept bothering me . . . One time, he even waggled his privates when I walked home."

Lansius was taken aback. "You let that go unpunished?"

She sighed. "I can't do anything. If I cause an incident, I might lose the house."

"How come?"

"It's a long story, Lans," she said, clearly not intending to elaborate.

After a brief pause, Lansius asked, "So, do you have a mallet?"

His question made her smile. Stefi didn't have a mallet, but she did have a small, rusty axe. Despite its bluntness, they quickly turned the chairs into firewood. Now, the wood burned brightly.

Stefi put the clean snow she had gathered into the cauldron and let it boil. Meanwhile, Lansius removed his coat and watched as Stefi arranged what they had left on the table.

"Lans, there's only gruel until I can get something from the market tomorrow."

"Let me pay for the food."

"Better save your coins. You might need better clothes," she said, pouring the grains into the cauldron.

"Ah . . . you think so?" He realized that all his clothes were shabby.

"You need to look the part, like the captain's scribe earlier. Let's visit some second-hand shops tomorrow."

The image of a long blue tunic came to Lansius's mind. "But don't I need to report in the morning?"

"Ah, it's fine. You can show up later. It's not like the captain would send a runner to inform them about you."

Lansius nodded. He knew he wasn't important enough to warrant that kind of treatment. Without things to worry about, he started to unwind. The comfort of the home felt luxurious after a prolonged stay in barns and tents.

He looked around and couldn't help but compare this place to his home in Bellandia. Almost every feature in this house looked better. Even in a lower-class area, the house had a sturdy construction and a separate living space. This way, the soot and stench from the kitchen area stayed below.

The cauldron made noises as it boiled. Stefi diligently stirred and added her last chunk of cheese, followed by a portion of salted meat from a waxed linen wrap. "It's almost ready."

Lansius picked up a bowl from his bag while Stefi grabbed one from the cupboard. The meal was a humble one, but the mood was uplifting and they still had their wineskin full of spiced ale. They had been sleeping rough for months, so the prospect of spending the night on proper beds was overwhelming.

As they ate, a curiosity dawned on Lansius. "Stefi, is it all right in the city for unmarried men and women to spend the night in a house together?"

"Of course not. If they're caught, they'll be forced to marry . . ." Her voice trailed off as she slowly realized what it was all about. "Oh, shit. We've been together for so long that I forgot about that."

Lansius exhaled deeply. Although they were technically still on a campaign, they were now stationed inside a city, which meant they could get in trouble with the parish laws. He had only recently learned about the restrictive and unreasonable rules that governed medieval society, such as the sumptuary laws that dictated what clothing, colors, fur, and jewelry were permissible based on a person's social status.

Worse still were the laws imposed on unmarried couples. If a man and woman were found alone together without a chaperone, the parish would levy a fine. If they were caught touching, the fine would be even heftier. If they spent a significant amount of time together, it could be deemed as adultery, a criminal act with its own punishment. In addition, the fines had to be paid when the woman got married, which served as a form of public shaming.

*I knew it. Something felt off with just the two of us.*

"J-just keep this a secret," she whispered. "Nobody needs to know, and no one will be the wiser."

He nodded. It wasn't like he could find another place to stay with the sun already setting. "I'll find somewhere else to stay tomorrow. It's getting late. We should get some rest."

Stefi took a deep breath and sipped her drink. "I'll help you out. There must be something I can sell around this house."

"Sell?" Lansius furrowed his brow. "No, I think I have enough to pay for rent."

"But you also need a new tunic for work," she reminded him.

Lansius smiled, appreciating her good intentions. "We'll figure something out tomorrow. Oh, go ahead and clean your room. I'll make sure the fire goes out."

"Right, I still need to do that. Good night then, Lans." She took her cup and went upstairs.

Lansius, left alone with his thoughts, couldn't help but imagine what would happen if they were caught and forced to marry. Although he couldn't remember his exact age, he felt that he was older than twenty. Meanwhile, based on her story, Stefi was nearing twenty as well. Both were considered old enough to marry.

*But would that work out? Hah, probably not . . .*

The smoldering of the fireplace interrupted his daydream. He approached the fireplace and knelt to light another candle from an ember. Afterward, he went upstairs to the study. Once inside, he realized he had the entire room to himself.

The newfound privacy relieved him like no other, but fatigue from days of walking and camping crept in quickly. He forced himself to arrange his bag and coat. Afterward, he blew out the wax candle, slipped into the bed, and pulled the blanket up.

Today had been full of new experiences for him. He had finally reached Riverstead and now looked forward to a new job. The feeling that he might just pull this off and help his family financially put his mind at ease.

The only thing nagging him was that he must find another place to stay the next day, and that might ruin him financially. The temptation to seek shelter in one of the vacant homes loomed large, but the risk of accusations of looting or theft was too great to ignore.

*Oh, I'll worry about that tomorrow!*

Leaving aside his worries, Lansius finally found peace and drifted into sleep.

# CHAPTER 6

# TWO SIDES OF A COIN

Lansius awoke to the sight of an unfamiliar ceiling, gradually recalling that he was sleeping in Stefi's house. As the events of the previous night flooded back into his mind, he took a deep breath, pushed his blanket aside, and rose to his feet.

The room was dark and cold, but a sliver of weak orange light streamed in through a slit in the window. Picking up his bag without bothering to change his clothes, Lansius quietly left his room. The house was silent, and Stefi's door remained closed. He carefully descended the nearly pitch-black staircase, feeling his way down and listening to the creaking of the wooden steps beneath his weight.

Reaching the bottom without a mishap, Lansius headed to the kitchen. There, he noticed more light seeping through the cracks of the door and front window. He approached the fireplace, where he had hung his old, worn shoes and socks. The lingering heat from the fireplace overnight had dried them out, freeing them from the previous day's mud.

Grateful for dry footwear, he pulled out a chair and sat down to put on his socks. While the wealthy could afford longer socks or *hose*, Lansius made do with short ones. The cheap wool was itchy, but it was better than the discomfort of rubbing against hard soles.

After putting on his socks and shoes, he thought to start a fire. Noticing that Stefi had left the fire-starting kit on the table, Lansius picked up one of the charred pieces of wood from the previous day and began to strike the stone and metal together to produce sparks.

Despite a couple of unsuccessful attempts, he persisted, considering this a valuable opportunity to practice his fire-making skills.

*Stefi*

Stefi yawned as she descended the stairs, wearing an off-white mantle and hood over her head. Her face was pale from the cold, her eyes unfocused, and even her lips lacked their usual pinkness. Surprisingly, a good night's sleep seemed to have actually made her drowsy.

She didn't even notice the crackling fire and was caught off guard by the warmth and light from the fireplace.

"Morning," Lansius greeted her.

"Lans, you made a fire?"

"Well, you taught me correctly. Turns out it's not that hard when it's dry," he replied with a hint of excitement.

Stefi chuckled, wanting to commend him but feeling too shy to do so. She approached the fireplace and knelt, basking in its warmth. Gradually, her pale face regained some of its healthy color.

Lansius offered Stefi a cup. Without needing to ask, she took it and drank slowly, aware that drinking too fast could provoke a cough since her throat was dry. After months stranded in winter, it had become routine to drink watered wine to keep warm. Soon, more redness returned to her face, especially her lips and cheeks.

"How's the weather outside?" she asked.

"Windy, with a bit of snow," he said as he sat near her.

She took another sip. "Have you had breakfast?"

"Not yet. I was thinking of waiting for you first."

She nodded, rose slowly, and approached the cupboard to find her small bag of grain. "How's your stomach?"

"Ready for some gruel," Lansius joked, as it was the only thing they had at the moment.

Stefi snorted and turned apologetic. "I'll cook stew tonight. I should be able to get something from the field kitchen."

"I'm not sure it's necessary," Lansius said in a serious tone.

Stefi looked at him, puzzled, and Lansius explained, "I'm going to rent a place tonight. Somewhere close, if possible."

"Ah," she muttered, clearly understanding his reasoning.

Her face turned a bit sad. Lansius, ever perceptive, noticed and asked, "You're good with that, right?"

"What? Oh, sure. I'm just thinking that I'm going to eat alone again," Stefi admitted, revealing more than she wanted.

*Eh, dang, why did I say that?*

Now, Lansius glanced to the side, seemingly perplexed before suddenly announcing, "All right, change of plan, I'm staying then."

Stefi almost jumped. "No, you can't," she said sharply. "Someone will see and start a ruckus."

He furrowed his brow in doubt and asked, "They'll do that, even after a siege?"

Stefi sighed and tried to explain. "Especially after a war like this when they're bored and without any entertainment."

Yesterday, they had seen several houses lit, evidence that many had stayed throughout the siege. Riverstead was populous enough, and many were affluent families of craftsmen and tradesmen; a siege wouldn't uproot them.

"I wonder what they'll gossip about us?" Lansius mused, a playful tone in his voice.

Stefi met his gaze, but Lansius quickly looked away, feigning ignorance.

Finishing her drink, Stefi placed the wooden cup on the table. "My knight master, Isolte, would've liked you," she commented without any particular intention.

Her cryptic remark seemed lost on Lansius. "Eh, come again? Why do you think Isolte would like me?"

Stefi's face softened, and she stifled a laugh as she recalled Isolte's eccentricity. "She was always unpredictable. She outwardly tried to push me into a marriage, but secretly, she always warned me not to because men are all not to be trusted."

"That's a bit confusing." He frowned.

"Indeed, she was like that. And it's not like I could afford it . . ." she quipped, the combination of an empty stomach and wine loosening her tongue.

"What do you mean?" Lansius asked.

"Well, the only thing I have is Horsie, and I don't intend to give her for dowry."

The thought of Horsie as a dowry amused Lansius, who burst into laughter.

"What's so funny?" She glared at him menacingly.

"No, it's just . . . Horsie as a dowry," he stammered between laughs, unable to provide a better explanation.

She misunderstood his reaction and stared at him, making him flinch.

Growing annoyed, she asked bluntly, "Lans, do you need some knockings?"

"Wait, no, no, hear me out," Lansius replied quickly, attempting to come up with an excuse. "I mean, in my . . . homeland, it's men who pay dowry!"

His explanation took Stefi aback. Her previous annoyance faded, replaced by curiosity as she nervously asked, "How much is this dowry?"

Trying to suppress his laughter, Lansius offered a number. "Probably more than three years of pay."

Stefi nodded, her brow furrowed, as she tried to calculate the sum.

*That's huge, definitely huge. They pay educated men more than common footmen or lowly squires.*

"How about it, suddenly interested?" Lansius teased.

*Only if they're well behaved, strong, but not brutish.*

However, Stefi soon realized that Lansius was the only foreigner she had ever seen in Riverstead. There were no other black-haired men around.

She paused to look at him and found him watching her so innocently with a faint smile. That made her wonder if this was his way of subtly proposing.

*Is he really into me?*

She couldn't help but think that marrying an educated man like Lansius would be a blessing for a dead-end, masterless squire like herself. And now he might even pay the dowry.

She also noticed that Lansius had become bolder since they first met.

*Is it because he saw me naked once . . . ?*

It was easy to tell that the man had no experience with women, but that only made her more protective of him. Despite how common it was, Stefi couldn't bring herself to exploit such an innocent, sweet guy. With so many thoughts racing through her mind, Stefi chose the approach she was trained for. She chuckled menacingly, alarming Lansius.

"All this talk about marriage so early in the morning. Maybe we're too drunk, and a morning training session is needed to clear our heads."

Lansius jumped from his seat, shuddering and shaking his head. "Wait, what? No, calm down. We don't have swords, and yours isn't dull."

Stefi grinned maliciously and threatened him. "Sooner or later, you'll need to practice against a real sword. Today is as good a day as any."

"Uh, ah . . . Oh, remember we need to hit the shop and buy some clothes!" Lansius said, trying to change the subject.

Stefi maintained her gaze, contemplating what they could use for sparring.

Lansius quickly added, "Maybe buy some breakfast too? I'll treat."

She blinked, her eyes softening a little. "Mm . . . bribery huh. I doubt you have the money, but I know just the place."

"All right, let's go then. I'm hungry," Lansius said, urgency edging into his voice.

Stefi could tell what he was doing, but decided to let him off the hook. "Let me change my clothes first," she replied.

Lansius immediately relaxed, clearly relieved.

*Lansius*

For over three thousand years, Riverstead had been a silent witness to the rise and fall of numerous kingdoms and all three Imperiums. This ancient city, having been resurrected multiple times from the ruins, was strategically nestled among three rivers that flowed toward the Great River.

Despite the rivers' presence, the surrounding land wasn't blessed with fertility, but rather with mineral wealth that had been mined since ancient times. As a result, generations of craftsmen had made their livelihoods here.

With access to the Great River, Riverstead maintained direct trade links with the Far East kingdoms and also served as a crucial trade hub for the northern provinces of the Imperium. Through the city, goods, particularly from the industrious province of Midlandia, flowed northward and eastward.

The city streets were paved with gray cobblestones, and the vastness of Riverstead was apparent, boasting hundreds, if not thousands, of buildings, including several multistory structures. Lansius found it fascinating that some of the buildings bore architectural resemblances to ancient Greek or Roman styles.

This morning, Lansius accompanied Stefi to the bustling market area, where they encountered open stalls teeming with people. Even in a city scarred by war, people needed to eat, and stall owners always found a way to make ends meet.

Stefi chatted with some of the stall owners who eyed Lansius and made comments about him. She either shrugged or waved them off, then returned with a wooden plate filled with various foods. One particular dish caught Lansius's attention—a yellowish-white, layered square.

Lansius took his knife, rubbed it on his inner clothes, and tried to get a taste, but he couldn't manage it. The food was slippery.

Seeing him struggle, Stefi used her spoon and thumb to pinch off a piece of the lasagna and fed it to Lansius. Once he tasted it, he found it to be similar to lasagna, with layers of pasta-like dough, and  salt and cheese, but without tomato sauce.

*Pretty good. I wonder if they have macaroni or spaghetti.*

As the two ate standing in the street, the city slowly began to stir. The market was still recovering from the war, but those stalls that were open were crowded.

"Fortune favors the brave," Stefi remarked, noticing where Lansius was looking.

Lansius nodded and commented, so casually, "Profit makes the world go round."

"So, you've heard the lore about the Ancients, huh?" she asked.

"What lore?" Lansius was intrigued.

Stefi furrowed her brow. "The round world?"

"You know the world is round?" Lansius asked, surprised, seeking confirmation.

She looked at him quizzically. "It's a children's story. Everyone knows that the Ancients transformed into dragons and soared around the world, outpacing the sun in a race. I suppose you foreigners don't have that tale."

Lansius shook his head. "Marc never mentioned it, and I've never heard a bard sing that song."

Stefi chuckled. "It's a children's story; bards don't usually sing those. Try asking a wet nurse next time."

"Wet nurse? What's that?" He was certain of his vocabulary, but nothing came to mind.

Stefi just laughed it off. "Come on, we still have things to do. Finding you a new tunic is a priority."

With that, she led him deeper into the market, where shops lined both sides of the bustling streets. As they browsed various cheap stores, excitement sparkled in their eyes. The day was still young, but things didn't always turn out the way they wanted.

# CHAPTER 7

# A MAN AND HIS TRADE

Lansius and Stefi continued browsing the quiet market, where only a few persistent vendors remained after the siege. They discovered a small shop tucked between two larger, shuttered establishments. Although there was no wooden sign, an assortment of colorful clothes hung gracefully from the second-floor window.

"Ah, the old grandpa made it through!" Stefi exclaimed excitedly, pulling Lansius by the hand and pushing the door open with the other.

Upon entering, they were met with the scent of well-worn fabric and leather. A tall, sharp-looking man with a thin beard and contrasting dark clothing rose from his seat, setting aside his needle and unfinished work. "Ah, Miss Squire, it's a pleasure to see a familiar face in Riverstead."

"Happy I'm not running from my debts, Keith?" Stefi teased.

Keith stifled a polite laugh, turning to Lansius. "How may I help you, tradesman?" He gestured toward the wares in his shop.

"I need a tunic, affordable but with a formal appearance," Lansius replied as formally as he could be, looking at the neatly organized racks of clothing, which included tunics, dresses, and cloaks.

"And for what purpose?" Keith inquired politely, albeit with a demeanor more akin to a soldier than a tailor.

"He's a scribe," Stefi chimed in.

"Ah," Keith murmured, turning to a neatly stacked pile of garments.

"Why not this one?" Stefi suggested, pointing to an already folded piece of clothing.

Keith glanced at Lansius, and Stefi assured him, "He's all right; he's with me."

Lansius quickly added, "I can keep a secret."

Keith smiled and explained, "The folded ones are likely looted from this city or nearby area. Lord Karius's men forced me to buy them. I've already bribed their officers, but they still demand more."

Stefi looked at them, found something she liked, and inquired. "Can't you sell them to us?"

"Let's avoid trouble. Those garments are tailored for nobles, and someone will recognize the original owner. If word gets out, we could all face consequences," Keith reasoned, pulling two tunics from the pile—one yellow and one blue.

Lansius immediately took a liking to the vibrant blue tunic, but he maintained a neutral expression and replied, "Don't you have something brighter? I don't want my employer to think I'm uneducated."

Keith chuckled, refraining from commenting on Lansius's accent, and returned to the stack, searching for a tunic that would suit Lansius's needs.

Stefi approached Lansius and whispered, "I like the blue one."

"If you're in a fight, do you show your intention to your opponent?"

Stefi was taken aback and understood his reasoning. "Good thinking."

"I'm not a teacher for nothing," Lansius quipped.

"Now, here's a brighter one." Keith pulled out a red tunic. Its color was faded, making it closer to a pink, but the intricate embroidery along the neckline and hem spoke of its former elegance.

Lansius had no intention of buying that one, but he put down his leather bag on the table and tried on the red tunic. The fabric felt soft and comfortable against his skin.

*Eh, linen can be this soft?*

"You can tell from the stitches that it's quality work, not too old. You can wear it until you're too old to work," Keith joked, promoting the tunic.

"What's the price for this one?" Lansius asked.

"If it were new," Keith said, employing his merchant skills, "the material, dye, and tailoring cost would make this tunic worth at least four silver."

Lansius softly sighed and said firmly, "Too expensive."

"You haven't heard my offer," Keith said.

Lansius removed the tunic and politely handed it back to Keith, saying, "If it's around forty copper new, then I probably can't afford it. Do you have anything else?"

"How about this Centurian blue tunic?" Keith suggested.

Lansius feigned disinterest. "How much for the yellow one, though it's a bit too big?"

"Don't worry about the size. I can tailor it for you."

Lansius smiled. "I believe that may add to the cost."

Keith chuckled. "Eleven copper for this fine yellow tunic, adjustments included." He then showcased its features. "Feel it, fine Midlandian linen, no patched holes, no frayed stitches. It will last you a long time. You can pass it down to your son and grandson."

"How about five copper?" Lansius countered.

"I can't do it for less than ten."

"Six, and I'll pay the adjustment fee."

"That's too low for a piece like this." Keith shook his head.

Lansius sighed and politely said, "Maybe some other time then."

"You won't find pieces like this anywhere else," Keith cautioned.

"That's precisely my problem. Your wares are too good. I can't afford them."

"That's most unfortunate. May I interest you in some less brightly colored tunics? I have quite a selection perfect for your size."

"Like that blue one?" Lansius asked nonchalantly.

"Yes, why don't you try the blue one."

Lansius tried it on and found it in excellent condition, with no stains on the hem, indicating it had been well cared for. It wasn't as soft as the red one, but it was undoubtedly better than the coarse ones he had acquired from Bellandia. "I don't like the color, but beggars can't be choosers," he quipped, much to the shop owner's delight.

"I like you, and since you're Stefi's friend, I'll give it a good price. Seven copper."

"Four! Even four is too much for blue dyes."

"I can't do that." Keith expertly positioned the tunic in the sunlight to reveal its deeper color.

Lansius didn't bother to look but instead focused on the seller. "I believe you still make a profit with four copper. What do you say? It's early, and they say good fortune to start the day is good for business."

Keith smiled and said, "Since you're a good lad. Let's make it six, that's—"

"Best I can do is five," Lansius pulled his purse and began fishing for five copper.

"Six is a fair price," Keith said, but Lansius ignored him, so he looked to Stefi, who smiled back at him.

"He's a good tradesman, Keith," Stefi remarked.

Lansius presented the copper coins, spreading them on his palm for Keith to see. "Five copper. We'll both profit, and this might be the start of a good business relationship."

Keith looked unsure, but Stefi delivered the coup de grace. "He's the young lord's newest retainer, you know?"

With his thumb and index finger, Lansius pinched the five coins and offered them to Keith.

Keith snorted, amused, and opened his palm. Lansius placed the five coins into it, and the deal was sealed.

"Gratitude, you drive a hard bargain. May I learn your name, tradesman?"

"I'm just a nobody. Call me Lansius."

"People call me Keith Senior, the tailor," he said, introducing himself. "If I'm not around, my son, Keith Junior, will be happy to help you."

"Nice meeting you, Keith."

"If you need a simple adjustment, I can do it for you, free of charge," Keith said.

Lansius proudly wore his new blue tunic as he stepped out of the shop, brimming with newfound confidence.

"Come here," Stefi beckoned, wanting to admire the blue tunic with its intricate orange embroidery along the neckline and hem.

"Lans, it looks good on you. Now you look the part," she complimented.

"Of course, it cost me five copper," Lansius quipped. "That's enough to buy food for a week."

Stefi giggled and elbowed him, knowing he had gotten it at a bargain.

"Oof, what's that for?" Lansius complained but couldn't help chuckling as he followed her.

"Next up is the sword," she announced.

"Eh, no, I'm a scribe. I don't need a sword," he blurted, fearing she was going to train him with a sharp sword for real.

Stefi paused and pondered. "All right, then let's just head there," she decided, leading him southward, toward a large building at the end of the market district.

"What's this place?" Lansius looked up at the tall stone compound with walls and large double gates for carts.

"Hopefully, your new office," Stefi replied.

Lansius was taken aback by the size of the municipal office. "But weren't we planning to do this tomorrow?"

"Well, it's nearby, and it can't hurt to try out your new Centurian blue tunic."

The two walked until they saw a small door just beside the double gate. A guard in brigandine lazily greeted them with a nod but didn't ask any questions. They entered through the open door and passed several other guards who watched them with similarly little interest.

Inside, they discovered a garden and a large, paved courtyard, with the towering three-story Riverstead municipal office building overhead. The structure had once been a proper castle, but now it served as storage and a taxation office.

Lansius marveled at the well-maintained medieval garden, filled mostly with herbs and a few blossoming flowers and plants protected by a fence. A carpet of grass and tall, old trees with roots spreading into the stone wall and buildings completed the picturesque scene.

The garden was so well taken care of that Lansius commented without thinking, "This would be a great spot for a picnic."

Stefi looked at him and asked, "What's a piknik?"

"Umm . . . eating out in the open on the grass?"

"Like when we're stuck outside on a campaign? Why would you want to do that again?" She rolled her eyes.

Lansius chuckled but refrained from explaining further.

They finally entered the building and observed its disheveled interior, a clear sign that it had been ransacked during the siege. The garden outside had survived, likely because it had been covered by snow all winter, but the once-orderly office, a symbol of Riverstead's administrative prowess, now resembled a war-torn relic.

The staff had made attempts to restore order, but it was a work in progress. Partially empty wooden cabinets lined the walls and the broken chairs, tables, and desks had been gathered, possibly pooled here to be repaired. Light filtered in through the shattered windows in the back, casting a gentle glow over the sorry scene.

Two servant boys were cleaning up, while a staff member in a gray tunic eyed Lansius and Stefi with suspicion, mistaking them for a merchant and his bodyguard. "My apologies, but didn't the guard inform you that the office is still closed?"

"We're not here for business. The guards probably can see that," Stefi clarified.

Lansius reached into his bag and pulled out a letter from the captain, displaying it to the staff member. "I'm part of the young lord's retinue. The captain sent me."

The staff member hastily wiped his hands on his sleeve before approaching Lansius. "May I see the letter?"

Lansius glanced at Stefi, who gave a nod of approval.

The staff member accepted the letter with a respectful gesture and skimmed its contents. "A new member?" His gaze flicked between the letter and Lansius, clearly taken aback. However, he decided it wasn't his place to question. "Please wait here. I'll inform Master Hubert."

# CHAPTER 8

# NOVICE

A tall, slender man with a slightly hunched posture from years of poring over documents and ledgers descended the stairs. His confident gait and footsteps signaled a healthy individual, despite his age.

His thinning hair, peppered with streaks of silver, was combed back and meticulously maintained, just like his sharp, vibrant blue attire with its extravagant contrasting silver embroidery. It made Lansius's second-hand tunic seem shabby.

Lansius gulped as the man exuded an aura of eccentricity. Unlike the predatory air of the noble, this man meant business.

"Well?" Master Hubert asked impatiently.

The staff member, not much older than Lansius, hastily introduced his master. "This is Master Hubert, the vice—"

"Current head clerk of Riverstead Municipal Office," Hubert corrected. "The old fool vanished before the siege, and we've been unable to bribe because of him. Lord Maurice should have listened!" he rambled and continued quickly, "Now, how may I help you?"

"The letter . . ." Lansius found his voice.

"Yes, I read it. But you're not trained in bookkeeping."

"I have been trained, Master Hubert, just not in the Imperium standardized bookkeeping style," Lansius countered with as much technicality as his vocabulary allowed.

Hubert glanced at Lansius and cast his judgment. "The Eastern style is not to be trusted."

"I'm not from the Eastern Kingdom. Indeed, theirs is not as advanced," Lansius clarified, standing tall.

Old Hubert let out a sharp sigh and extended his right arm. The staff member hurriedly placed Lansius's letter into the master's palm. Hubert gave it another glance and seemed to consider Stefi in her black gambeson, a color of wealth.

"I can't ignore the captain's wishes. So be it," Hubert said without even facing Lansius. He then quickly added to his staff, "Don't let him touch ink or paper. Get him into storage and see if he can help in any way."

"Thank you," Lansius replied sincerely. Though he hadn't recovered his memory from his past, he somehow knew this treatment all too well.

As Master Hubert climbed back up the stairs, Lansius was left with the same staff member who didn't mince words. "Are you a noble?"

"No," Lansius replied, knowing he would be at the bottom of the pecking order.

Before the staff member could nod, Stefi stepped forward. "He's my master, though, and a direct retainer of young Lord Arte. I'd be careful if I were you."

"There should be no problem between us. My name is Vince. I'm not very smart, but my family has been clerks here for generations." He extended his hand to Lansius.

Lansius grasped Vince's hand, saying, "Call me Lansius. I hope I can be of help."

"Hopefully so. We need lots of hands to clear this mess." Vince rubbed what little goatee he had. Lansius noted that the man's hair was neat and slick, a sign that he was trying hard despite his modest introduction.

"Oi, Jan, come here," Vince suddenly called for one of the boys.

A bright-looking boy stopped scrubbing and ran toward them. "Yes, Vince?"

"Take care of Lansius for me. Show him the empty quarters at the far end, so old Hubert doesn't see him," Vince added. "No offense."

"None taken," Lansius replied lightly, but then asked, "Empty quarter?"

"For your lodging, of course. You're a clerk now, not a scribe. We can't let new staff go in and out every day; there are too many risks involved. But don't worry, the dormitories are quite neat. You'll like it, unless you're from a much higher station than me."

"Ah." Lansius nodded and exchanged glances with Stefi, who was also nodding excitedly. They had just solved Lansius's housing problem, and he got it for free.

*I have to buy something for that captain. The man's a hero!*

Vince furrowed his brow, watching the duo's reaction, suspicious of their relationship, but continued. "As I said before, Jan will show you the room and then escort you to the storage. That's all, Junior."

Lansius chuckled. Vince introduced himself as a fool, but in the end, he asserted his seniority. "Yes, Senior Vince, I'll comply."

Vince looked pleased as he patted Lansius's right arm and headed out to the guardhouse, likely to lecture them for allowing a guest to enter without notice.

"Come, Master Lans, Squire. I'll show you the room." Jan happily motioned for them to follow him up the stairs.

* * *

Lansius and Stefi followed Jan to his new quarters on the third floor of the same building. The complex, while old and fortified with gray stones on the outside, boasted a more refined interior that was plastered and painted a pastel orange.

Despite the aging paint, the corridor remained neat and more attractive than most buildings Lansius had entered. The place was well ventilated. From the window, Lansius could observe the comings and goings at the building's gate.

Another window offered a view of the storage room entrance, likely designed for monitoring purposes.

The three walked past the row of rooms for the officials working there, noticing that only half were occupied since many hadn't returned to Riverstead.

"This is the place," Jan said as they reached the farthest end, pushing the door open.

Lansius noticed a layer of dust and a damp smell, but the room was adequate and showed little evidence of looting. The walls were plastered, and since they were on the third floor, the flooring was made of timber. The room also had a glass window, which Jan promptly opened, letting in a fresh breeze and sunlight.

*It's glass . . .*

This window was the first high-quality glass Lansius had seen in this world. It was lightly tinted but transparent, unlike the kind used in lanterns, which was only as transparent as parchment or fabric.

The room contained a proper raised bed with legs, a mattress without bedding, a small worktable, a chair, and a wardrobe.

"Do you like it?" Jan asked cheekily.

"I will, after I do some cleaning," Lansius replied.

Jan grinned. "I'll help you with it."

Stefi approached the wardrobe and discovered a selection of fine linen clothing. There was even a silk undergarment. "Is the owner not returning?" she asked.

Jan licked his lips and said, "The previous owner is unlikely to return. He's one of the few who ran before the siege happened, along with the stolen money."

Stefi nodded, reached into the drawer, and found several pairs of woolen socks; old and new, long and short. She picked the old ones and signaled for Jan to take them.

"For me, Squire?" Jan asked uncertainly.

She nodded and said, "I'm Stefi. It's nice to meet you, Jan."

Lansius understood the intention and added, "If we find more, we'll give you more. Would that be a problem?"

Jan shook his head. "Maybe someone will ask, so don't give them all away at once."

Stefi chuckled, glanced at Lansius, and remarked, "He's smart."

Pleased with the compliment, Jan bowed his head. "Oh, don't put your bag here yet. We should get the key first, but that has to wait until supper."

"Well, that can wait. Let's head down to the storage and see what my job looks like," Lansius said with a hint of excitement. After being stranded in a barn all winter, he was ready to put his skills to use.

*Ground Floor*

At Lansius's request, Jan led them to the ground floor, where they encountered three cavernous warehouses that made up the storage area. Each warehouse could accommodate three carts at once for loading or unloading.

After introducing themselves to the other staff, Lansius quickly surveyed his designated work area and found it a mess. His shoulders slumped as he took in the chaotic scene that resembled a campground in the morning more than a warehouse.

Sacks of grains and flour were piled haphazardly, wooden crates were scattered everywhere, and piles of leather curled from mismanaged storage gave off a strong odor.

Earthen jugs, likely filled with wine, were tied against the wall to an old wooden rack, while wooden or wicker baskets of various sizes held smaller jugs.

To make matters worse, dozens of wooden barrels blocked the way, making it hard to move around. Some of the unmarked barrels contained ale, while others were filled with goods like nails, fur coats, or blankets.

"The lord just won a tremendous victory at a fort near the Great River," Jan said proudly, referring to the battle that took place while Lansius was still traveling to Riverstead.

"I can see that." Lansius observed another unsorted pile near the warehouse gate, likely dumped after the valuables were recovered.

"This is going to take ten men and a week just to tidy things up," Stefi commented with stiff lips.

Lansius let out a sigh. He approached the mess, trying to figure out where to start.

"The workers are at your command if you need help," Jan informed him. "I can't stay for long, though. I'll be needed in the kitchen soon."

"For lunch?" Stefi guessed. "Will we get any?"

"Of course. Where do you want to take your lunch?" Jan inquired.

"Probably here," Lansius said, rolling up his sleeves. "I've got a lot of work to do today."

"This is just like Ceresia," Stefi quipped as Jan left the warehouse.

"Ceresia isn't plundered and pillaged like this," joked Lansius.

*That old fart, he named me a clerk but gave me manual labor . . .*

Lansius exhaled deeply. He had joined Lord Arte and traveled to Riverstead, enduring winter and war, with the expectation of working on something important. Yet, this didn't seem much different from stacking firewood. Slowly, he examined the crates one by one and sketched a crude map on a wax tablet, trying to come up with a plan.

As time passed, their efforts seemed to have little effect. Despite working through lunch, Lansius, Stefi, and a single worker had only managed to rearrange some of the items. The storage area now appeared even more chaotic, like a half-finished puzzle of misplaced pieces.

"This isn't working," Lansius mumbled, sitting on a crate, his blue tunic soaked with sweat.

"We only got one worker, and the rest just nod their heads when called, but leave as soon as someone else calls them back," Stefi replied, sweat dripping from her chin.

Lansius observed the workers in the neighboring warehouse and snorted, realizing their tactics.

*Whether working here or there, hard or not, the pay is probably the same. It's time to change the game.*

"Stefi," Lansius called.

"Yeah?" She noticed the shift in his tone.

"I need your help with something—something that might solve our problem."

Stefi looked around at the disorganized warehouse. "Show me your magic, Lans, because we won't finish this on our own."

# CHAPTER 9

# COMPATRIOTS

Lansius enjoyed his late lunch in peace, undisturbed by the shouting and yelling from the staff in the neighboring warehouse. He filled his thick bread with ham and cheese, then offered half to the worker, who graciously accepted it.

"Thank you, master."

"Eat well, my good man," Lansius said casually.

The man was baffled by the kind treatment but ate heartily.

Lansius took out Stefi's wineskin from his bag, poured a bit into his half-filled water cup, and offered it to the man. The worker didn't refuse the offer, as he was just trying to make a living. "Thank you, master," he said again, gulping it down.

Lansius wasn't trying to bribe him with food, as that would be impossibly difficult. Instead, he struck up a conversation. "So, how many years have you worked here?"

"Since the young lord was still a toddler," the worker recalled.

"Must be more than a dozen years. How much do they pay you?"

The man chuckled and rubbed his coarse facial hair. "Too little."

"A copper and two?" Lansius guessed.

His lips formed a small grin. "Master, if you know, why ask?"

"I don't. I'm new here, and they won't tell me anything," Lansius said and offered him two berries. "Tell me, how much does a staff member like me make?"

The worker took the fruit, looked at Lansius, and said, "I heard from a drunken staff member that he got four copper a day."

*About the same. Mine was six copper on campaign, probably four copper during peacetime.*

"And how much for a new staff that works in the warehouse?" Lansius inquired.

"Unfortunately, a lot less," he said apologetically.

*Not if I can help it . . .*

Lansius grinned. "Tell you what. I'm just here because the captain said so. I believe when things return to normal, I'll be recalled to Lord Arte's side."

The name drop shocked the man. "You're part of the young lord's retinue?" He sized up Lansius again, nodding his head as he recalled how Lansius was accompanied by a squire in a black gambeson. "I wish you fortune then, master. Your stay here might be unpleasant."

"Why is that?" Lansius asked.

The man looked around and whispered, "The one who runs this place is a bit odd in the head."

Lansius chuckled. "I have the same opinion."

The two laughed heartily.

Stefi appeared at the warehouse entrance and walked briskly toward Lansius, sweaty from her efforts. Lansius rose and quickly offered her a jug of water, which she took and drank gracefully.

The man grinned while admiring Stefi's appearance.

"Did you get it?" Lansius asked.

"Keith drove a hard bargain, but your note saved the day."

Lansius grinned. He had sent Stefi with two pieces of high-quality clothing from the wardrobe in their room to Keith.

Keith wasn't going to give them a good price easily, but Lansius had written a note stating that he still had a lot and would sell to another if the price wasn't acceptable. Keith faced a dilemma and gave an acceptable price of three copper per piece.

"He wouldn't give me socks as a bonus, but he gave me these." Stefi pulled out two head caps.

Lansius was amused. "Keith was a tough nut."

"But you cracked him good. I've never seen him give that much ground before."

Lansius gestured for Stefi to take a seat on the clean crate, and she did so, resting her legs from the return trip. Meanwhile, Lansius checked the head cap, finding it worn and yellowish, but clean, dry, and comfortable. He offered it to the lone worker.

"Monsieur, I can't accept this," he said, seeming half embarrassed and half fearful, perhaps because of Lansius's earlier announcement that he was part of the young lord's retinue.

"What's your name?" Lansius asked.

"Wade, master."

Lansius knelt and placed one of the caps in Wade's hand. "Nice to know you. I'm Lansius, but you can call me Lans."

Wade clenched the head cap. "Good to meet you, master Lans."

Lansius returned to the crate and sat as if addressing his subject. "Wade, I've been thinking about what you said earlier—about how things might be unpleasant for me."

Wade nodded, so Lansius continued. "I want to make my stay as enjoyable as possible. Can you help with that?"

"But how, master?"

Lansius smiled. "Tomorrow, bring a friend," he instructed while pinching another head cap. "If you bring more, I can always part with several iron coins if they're strong and they work hard and fast."

Wade grinned. "I have friends. I'll only bring the best."

"Tomorrow then. Now, let's wrap up and end the day."

"But it's barely past midday, master Lans," Wade said.

"It's useless with just us. I want you to be fresh tomorrow."

Wade nodded happily, grateful to find a benevolent staff member who wasn't stingy with his purse.

The following day, after a good night's sleep, Lansius arrived at his section of the warehouse to find five men already working. Stefi had yet to arrive, but he didn't mind.

"Morning, master Lans," Wade greeted him, while the rest bowed their heads slightly in respect.

"Morning, Wade. You're working early today."

Wade and the men smiled, charmed by Lansius's down-to-earth attitude, unlike that of the other staff. "Are these men enough, master Lans?"

"Only if they're as good as you said," Lansius replied. "I can give two irons per person, to be paid each evening. I'll allow you to return to your original post, so as not to offend the senior staff, but try to return when you can; otherwise, I can only give one iron."

The men understood and grinned knowingly.

Lansius continued, "Let's keep this a secret between us, lest the acting head clerk causes us problems."

"There won't be any," Wade said with confidence.

Lansius pulled a head cap from his bag and gave it to Wade. "Foreman Wade. Reward this to whomever you please."

With that, Lansius effectively established a hierarchy and command structure. While the ones who ultimately paid for the workers was the office, by using bonuses or bribes, he made them more inclined to work for him instead of the other staff. Afterward, things progressed smoothly despite the inevitable mishaps and snags that accompanied untangling such a large mess.

* * *

In just three days, the warehouse had visibly transformed. Master Hubert had heard rumors but couldn't be bothered to check until Vince brought him the record.

"Yes, I read that. Did you want more praise?" Hubert scolded his staff while remaining seated behind a large mahogany table.

"Master, a confession. I wrote that, but the calculation was the new clerk's doing."

Hubert's sharp eyes gazed at Vince, who didn't back down. "Are you implying that he works at noon and calculates records at night? Does he not need sleep?"

"Oh, I checked, master. The light in his room faded before midnight," Vince clarified.

"Then how is it possible . . . unless he's really good with numbers," mulled Hubert.

Vince nodded. "His writing is near illegible, but his calculations were spot-on."

"But why did you report this to me and not use it to your advantage?" the acting head clerk inquired.

"Because the new clerk is just too good, and now everybody wants to use him too."

Hubert chuckled. "And what are you proposing?"

Vince didn't hesitate. "Give him a chamber and put him to work. Let us be the only two who have access to him."

Hubert smiled. "Arrange it."

A few weeks had passed, and the frigid winds and snow that had held Riverstead City in their grip finally dissipated. Warmer air from the western sea quickly brought changes to the landscape. The snow thawed, rivers flowed once more, and the grasslands and tree lines sprang back to life.

Despite the muddy roads and persistent drizzle, refugees began to flock back to the city. The first week of spring saw Riverstead come alive with bustling markets and ongoing repairs throughout the city. There were even talks of spring festivals and victory celebrations.

As the city returned to normalcy, Lansius continued working alone in a small study. As he had planned, Hubert finally accepted him as a fully fledged clerk with all its benefits. He was assigned to the third floor, just at the far end from his room.

Hubert through Vince kept supplying Lansius with endless calculation work, ranging from minor purchases for kitchen supplies to various taxes received by the city. Dark shadows circled Lansius's eyes, and he yawned at random intervals. However, the cause of his sleep deprivation was not work-related.

While he feigned naivety around Hubert and Vince, Lansius was well aware that working too quickly could lead to exhaustion. Since he was paid by the day rather than by the task, he deliberately paced himself. Sometimes he would double-check his work, at other times he would study the documents on hand. However, his favorite diversion was reading books under the guise of studying.

The municipal office didn't have a proper library, but Lansius had discovered two old, leather-bound history books. While they read like children's stories—filled with tales of creation and heroism—he found them captivating. He was particularly intrigued by accounts of elves, dwarves, and half-humans, as well as their legendary deeds.

He also came across an old, incomplete report about the Mage Guild, which detailed its founding, headquarters, and objectives. This gave him something to discuss with his fellow clerks, usually Vince. From these conversations, Lansius learned that mages were rare. Even Lord Maurice only employed one.

Aside from mages, there were also saint candidates, said to possess the ability to heal. Lansius was skeptical, considering them to be physicians at best, if not mere shamans.

There were a lot of mysteries in this world, and he had to admit that he was rather excited with the possibility that magic was real. This fueled him to read as much as he could during the daytime, and by the dim light of his rushlight, he continued his reading well after sunset.

This passion for reading led to his peers respecting him, mistaking his haggard looks as proof of his hard work.

Just like any other day, Lansius was working in his chamber when a sudden knock on the door alerted him. "Who—"

Before he could complete his sentence, a woman in a black gambeson barged in. Lansius recognized who had entered and continued working as if nothing had happened.

Stefi took the only other seat and slouched. "Ah, it's much cooler in here."

"Well, it's the third floor."

She noticed a plate with a slice of spiced ham, beans, and hard bread on the table. "Oh, Jan has made his rounds?"

"Yeah, not long ago. Help yourself," he said, without losing focus on his parchment and wax tablets.

"They'll whip a squire like me if I ate before the master," she teased.

He chuckled but remained focused. Stefi took the only cup on the table and drank it straight. However, her simple act robbed Lansius of his focus.

*Her lips . . . on my cup.*

"Ah, it's refreshing!"

He banished his inappropriate thoughts, which had been triggered more often since they were apart. "It's just water."

"Well, it doesn't matter," she exclaimed and unfastened the lower part of her gambeson.

Lansius's eyes opened wide.

"There you go." Stefi pulled out a wrapped package and slammed it on the table.

"Oh, a gift?" he blurted.

"Hehe, a present for graduating from that warehouse."

Lansius chuckled as he unwrapped the package. "A belt! Oh, you didn't have to."

"Go on, test it," urged Stefi.

Lansius approached her and tried on the belt by wrapping it around his waist. However, he had never tied a sword belt before and got confused. Stefi assisted him and tied the ring belt. With her help, the sword belt fit snugly and correctly.

"So, this is how you wear one." He moved about to appreciate the look. "You're very good at this."

She chuckled at his remark. "Lans, I'm a squire. That's what I do for a living."

Lansius realized his error and grinned sheepishly. Indeed, a squire's primary job was to help their knight don their gear.

"Do you like it?" she asked.

"Of course. But are you sure it's not pricey?"

"Don't fret. You need it; the old one is worn out." She added, "Next is a sword and shoes."

He found her enthusiasm amusing. "I don't think a clerk needs a sword."

Stefi shrugged and poured another cup of water as Lansius returned to his seat. He then brought an earthen jar to the table along with a bronze goblet from the bottom cabinet.

"What's that for?" she asked, nodding toward the jar and goblet.

Lansius smiled as he poured the contents generously into the goblet. The rich aroma had a hint of honeyed sweetness.

"It's mead. Where did you get it?" She became excited.

"One of Wade's men broke an amphora, so all of them got their pay docked. I felt pity and helped out a little."

She whistled. "Must be expensive."

"Yeah, but I got this in return. So drink up and be delighted." He handed the goblet to her.

She gulped it with a big grin on her face.

Her reaction brought a smile to his face. "Hey, wanna go out for lunch?" Lansius asked.

"If you insist," Stefi masterfully quipped, putting a smile on Lansius's face. He wanted to visit Keith's shop again to look for gifts for Marc, Tanya, and Arryn. His campaign money was yet to be distributed, but that didn't deter his eagerness to browse around.

The day had turned dark. Even Lansius, usually awake late into the night with his reading, had succumbed to sleep when suddenly, the peace in his room was broken by a voice calling his name.

"Master Lansius! Someone called again from outside the room, urgency evident in the tone.

Lansius opened the door, peering out into the pitch-black hallway. Only the dim light of a servant's lantern illuminated their surroundings.

"Jan?" Lansius opened the door slightly wider.

The boy looked distraught. "Some people are leaving the city in a hurry," Jan whispered frantically. "Master Hubert and Vince too. Wade saw them packing goods onto a fast carriage."

Lansius's mind raced as he tried to make sense of why Hubert left, along with Vince.

*Embezzlement? No, the old crook is far too eccentric for that, and Vince collects wages for doing nothing.*

There was only one possibility left: war.

"Quick, help me pack my things," Lansius said, rushing over to the cabinet and flinging its contents aside. He knew he was probably too late, but he didn't need to outsmart anyone—just enough to get himself out of harm's way.

# CHAPTER 10

# CROSSROADS

The large glass window on the second floor creaked as Jan heaved it open. "Remember to climb down the bricks. It's too high to jump," the young servant whispered, opening the window to its fullest extent.

Lansius's heart raced. Earlier, Jan had convinced him this was the only way out without being seen by the guards. The municipal office was built like a castle and had just one exit.

"Can't Wade smuggle me out or something?"

"He can hardly even get out himself. Together with you, it's just not possible," Jan argued.

Slowly, Lansius approached the window and was surprised by his disheveled appearance in the incomplete reflection on the glass, but the chilly evening air rushed inside and demanded his attention.

"Which part of the garden is beneath us?" he asked, knowing the soft ground was his only safety net.

"The one at the far end, near the old tree."

Lansius hesitated. The darkness challenged him to jump.

"Master, please be quick, or someone will find out," Jan urged, as they were on the same floor as the staff's dormitory.

"Are you sure you don't want to leave with me?" Lansius asked.

"Who would feed me if I go? I'm a servant. I was here when the city was taken. They did little harm to me," Jan whispered.

Taking a deep breath, Lansius flexed his hands to test his grip and began to climb. He placed his hands on the stone window frame and pulled his body up. The night sky came into view, showcasing both beauty and terror. Fear would surely paralyze him if he could measure the height.

"Turn around," Jan urged him.

"I know. Just give me a moment." Lansius turned to face the wall and began to climb down. The earthy scent of moss warned him that the stone surface might be slippery, but he quickly found suitable spots for his hands and feet, securing solid footing.

*This isn't too hard.*

The municipal building was nearly ancient, having faced partial destruction and rebuilding several times throughout the centuries. Each time, only its entrance and courtyard received proper repairs, while the other sides remained rough and ill-finished.

"Good luck, Master Lansius."

Lansius looked up, but the creaking from the window signaled that Jan had already left. With no way back, he took a deep breath and continued his descent. Just two steps down, he couldn't find secure footing. Some stone bricks jutted out, but they were too slippery.

Growing frustrated after a series of failed attempts, his hands grew sweaty and raw. He paused on the last good foothold to catch his breath. At one point, he glanced down and saw the silhouette of a tree.

*This is only the second floor, right?*

An idea came to him. He carefully dropped his bag down, but the leather bag didn't make enough noise to reveal the height. Now, out of options and with hands throbbing from strain, he felt more inclined to jump.

First, he knelt, gripping the last jutting stone brick, and planned to lower his body down. However, he couldn't hold his weight and quickly lost his grip.

The fall was swift; he landed feet first and fell sideways. Despite the sharp pain in his ankle and back, adrenaline kept the pain at bay. In the darkness, he could see the silhouettes of trees and a line of bushes. He forced himself to run for cover, crouching behind the nearest bushes, and waited.

The building remained silent. Lansius felt relieved and sneaked to find his bag. It took several tries, as only faint starlight illuminated the area.

Once he retrieved it, he quickly left through the narrow path between two buildings. He made several turns and suddenly emerged onto the main street. He looked around to get his bearings.

"Master," someone called to him from the shadows.

"Wade?" Lansius whispered, and the man urgently motioned for Lansius to come closer.

As Lansius approached, Wade pulled back his hood and placed a small purse in Lansius's hand. "I gave the guard a hard bargain, only a copper to let me out."

"Keep the rest, Wade. You've earned it," Lansius said, proud of his men.

Wade grinned. "I knew you'd say that," he said, pocketing the bribe money Lansius had sent through Jan. "Are you hurt?"

"Nothing's broken," Lansius assured him.

Wade nodded. "So, where do we go next?"

"Stefi. We need to get her."

"Where does the squire live?"

Lansius racked his memory before recalling the location. "The old cobbler's alley."

"I know the way. Stay close." Wade looked around and led the way. Not wanting to attract attention, they walked close to the buildings.

The main street was deserted at this hour. As his adrenaline subsided, Lansius felt the pain from his fall in his palms, left ankle, and back.

Riverstead was almost pitch-black, save for a few establishments like the tavern that maintained lit lanterns in their front yards. As they walked, they came across a glowing orb that illuminated a large area.

The source of the orb was a giant glass lantern, adorned with a statue of a grotesque, giant lizard, marking an intersection.

Wade approached the low-hanging lantern and opened its small metallic window. The city had placed it there for wayfarers to light their lanterns if they went out.

Wade pulled a candle from his lantern and lit it. Then Wade led them into a dark, winding alleyway. After so many twists and turns, Lansius wasn't sure of where they were. The area was notoriously challenging to navigate, even at noon. Wade had to stop and study the building signs several times to make sure he wasn't lost. Then, he stopped.

"This is it, the old cobbler's alley," Wade remarked.

Lansius took the lantern from Wade. As they walked farther down, he noticed a row of similarly sized buildings and quickened his pace. With Wade following, they arrived at one of the houses, and Lansius began knocking on the door.

"Stefi! Stephania!" he called repeatedly while continuing to knock.

After a while, Wade stopped him and tried to push the door several times.

"Master, it's locked but not barred," Wade said.

"She isn't inside?" Lansius was horrified and surveyed the area. He was confident that this was the house.

Meanwhile, Wade examined the ground with his lantern and discovered footprints. "She's not here. Someone must've called her."

Lansius inspected the footprints in the muddy ground, kneeling to get a better look. There were indeed footprints, but he couldn't tell if they were fresh.

"We have to go," Wade urged. "She's most likely called to arms."

Lansius hesitated, but Wade pulled on his arm. As if pursued by ghosts, Wade led Lansius through the dark maze until they finally returned to the junction.

The grotesque lizard guarding the giant orb lantern greeted them again. Only then did they notice the roads growing livelier, with carriages now appearing.

As they neared the south gate, torches and lanterns illuminated the numerous horse-drawn carriages and carts. Most of the occupants were armed, with some even accompanied by cavalrymen.

A palpable sense of fear and anxiety permeated the atmosphere.

No one would take a clerk and his assistant seriously, but Lansius had no option. As they passed various carts and carriages, those inside eyed them nervously, their panic evident in the haphazard loading of their carriages.

It was unprecedented for a city to face another siege in such a short time. Everyone here had likely received a tip and was attempting to flee the impending siege. As Lansius drew closer, he overheard a heated exchange between the crowd and the guards.

"No men of arms are to leave the city," a man hoarsely argued with the crowd.

"I assure you, these are only my master's private household guards," someone in the crowd responded.

"We know you let a dozen carriages leave just moments ago," another accused, and the bickering persisted.

Judging by their elegant coats and fine garments, it was clear that the crowd came from a wealthy background.

Suddenly, a low horn sounded in the distance, followed by faint cries and shouts carried on the wind. The crowd froze, straining their ears to better identify the sounds.

As if confirming their fears, more windows lit up as the dwellers awoke from their slumber, alarmed by the same sound.

"We're under attack!" someone yelled in a panic. Men from the carriages surged toward the city guards at the gates, demanding they be opened. Overwhelmed, the captain finally relented, especially after learning that the danger approached from the north, while the southern approach appeared clear.

With a groan of iron and wood, the massive city gates began to swing inward. People hastily prepared their carts and carriages for departure.

The clinking of heavy chains signaled that the drawbridge was being lowered. When it finally settled, it revealed a path leading to a stone bridge and beyond, all shrouded in darkness.

Another low horn resounded from the north, stirring more residents from their sleep. People spilled into the streets, confused and fearful.

Three horsemen headed to the gate, carrying brass lanterns that barely lit the road ahead. They were leading a carriage out of the city, and others quickly fell in line behind them.

Before he knew it, Lansius found himself caught in the current of the crowd. Nervously, he glanced to the side and noticed that Wade had stayed behind. "Wade!" he called out.

"Take care, Master Lans." Wade waved back from the edge of the crowd.

Lansius was aghast. "You're not coming?"

"I can't. My family and friends are here," Wade replied, taking a step back from the fray. "Riverstead is home. No matter who the lord is, they'll need a warehouse worker like me."

Wade's expression was one of grim resolve. He had survived two sieges already; there was no guarantee he'd survive a third. Yet he knew little about the world beyond Riverstead's walls.

The crowd pushed Lansius forward, moving in one direction: out. The guards were keen to clear the area as quickly as possible so they could reseal the gates for the coming siege. Walking with the crowd, Lansius could see the faces of tired, nervous men all around him, illuminated by handheld lanterns.

The throng approached the drawbridge, and the cacophony of carriages, horses, and escorts filled the air. Soon, they passed under the grand arches of the city gate, leaving only the open night sky above.

Before long, they crossed the wooden drawbridge, then the stone bridge, and reached the open road. The walls of Riverstead now lay behind them, and an open field stretched out in front. And so, the crowd marched, intent on putting as much distance as possible between themselves and the soon-to-be besieged city.

Lansius stood alone near the stone bridge, still hesitating to leave the city and Stefi behind. He was contemplating running back when the echo of the gates closing reached his ears. Soon, the gates were shut, and the drawbridge was drawn up again after the last horse-drawn cart had cleared its way.

Now, there was no more going back. The guards certainly wouldn't lower the drawbridge for him.

"Out of the way!" the last cart's coachman shouted at Lansius.

Feeling that his chances were bleak, Lansius shouted back as the cart slowed down at the edge of the bridge. "I have some money. Can you give me a lift?"

The horse and cart sped up, ignoring Lansius's plight.

Lansius sighed, feeling foolish, and jogged to try and catch up with the crowd.

"Quickly," someone called.

Surprised, Lansius saw the coachman and several figures in the cart were waiting for him. He ran toward them.

Someone uncovered a lantern, producing a faint glow as Lansius approached.

"Ha! I know you," said the coachman.

"Huh?" Lansius couldn't see the man's face.

"To think I met you out here," the coachman muttered, grabbing Lansius's hand. He then called out, "Theo, help us."

The two helped Lansius into the back of the cart, where he landed between wooden crates. "I'm Theo, and this big fellow here is Max." The youth gestured to another boy.

Max groaned, wiped his blurry, sleepy eyes, and waved a little to Lansius.

"You said you know me?" Lansius directed the question at the coachman in front.

"It's Thomas." He removed his hood to reveal his bearded face.

"Thomas!" Lansius couldn't believe his eyes.

The old man smirked but hurriedly spurred his horses, and the cart sped up. Lansius noticed a figure clad in a traveling cloak, sitting next to Thomas.

"Did you happen to see Stefi?" asked Lansius.

"The squire?" Thomas asked without looking back.

"We traveled together from Ceresia, remember?"

"I hope she's in one of the carriages," Thomas replied weakly.

Lansius exhaled deeply, his hope faded. "What will happen to the city?"

"Another siege," replied the figure beside Thomas, her tone somber.

"Can the city hold out?" Lansius asked.

"Nobody knows, but Riverstead has never held against a siege," said Thomas. His words left Lansius feeling dejected.

"Try to make peace with it. I need you to stay alert," Thomas warned.

"Are we not safe here?" Lansius was alarmed.

"Sieges are always bad, whether you're inside or outside," Thomas cautioned.

"The horsemen may chase us for supplies and hostages," Theo added.

The cart became bumpier as the horses picked up speed. Riding in the dark, even with lanterns and torches, was dangerous, but everyone would rather risk it than be captured.

The sound of cracking whips filled the air as the coachmen urged their hesitant horses to run despite the darkness.

Lansius felt a crushing sense of loss as he kept his eyes fixed on the receding city. All he had wanted was a good job and a chance to improve his station in life. And now everything seemed lost.

*Stefi, Jan, Wade, please stay safe . . .*

As the dispersed crowd and convoy moved farther away, the glimmering lights north of the city became increasingly numerous and distinct. At first, Lansius mistook them for an eerie reflection of the night sky. But soon, the unsettling truth dawned on them: those weren't stars.

They were the glowing hearths of countless fires, illuminating a sprawling enemy encampment. The sheer size of the camp, visible even from a distance, suggested an army not in the hundreds, but likely in the thousands.

The realization that the defeated army—believed to be on its last legs—now appeared more formidable than ever sent a chill through the convoy. A palpable sense of fear and hopelessness settled over them as they left Riverstead to its fate.

# CHAPTER 11

# BRIDGE TO THE WEST

Last year, unwilling to wait for the Imperium's response, Lord Maurice mustered his forces and marched them to Ceresia on the eve of winter. There, he waited and launched a daring winter attack, which took Karius's men by surprise and turned the tides of war.

Lord Karius was swiftly dislodged from Riverstead and forced to flee, with Lord Maurice's men hot on their heels. However, even with the arrival of spring, the tensions remained unresolved. Lord Karius stubbornly resisted all offers of truce, seemingly engaging in negotiations merely to buy time.

Lord Maurice, out of an abundance of caution, secured a fortress to guard against any potential reinforcements. Despite his precaution, nobody suspected that an alliance had formed between Lord Karius and Margrave Gottfried.

The formidable margrave, ruler of four northern Brigandia provinces, had previously clashed with Karius, making their sudden alliance a surprise. The specifics of their agreement were unclear, yet one thing was certain: Karius had set a trap for Maurice.

Karius had successfully lured Maurice out of Riverstead, giving Gottfried and his formidable army the opportunity to cross the Great River and launch a devastating attack on the city. The situation rapidly escalated into a crisis for Maurice and his men, whose escape route was effectively cut off.

A speck of light glowed on the far horizon and the once dark sky slowly turned into bronze-yellow. The wind blew fiercely, as if hailing the birth of a new day.

Lansius felt someone pushed his shoulder. "Erm?"

"The sun is almost out," Theo, who slept next to Lansius, said weakly.

"A moment." Lansius fought the sleepiness off his head. His body felt stiff while his eyes were painful to open. He saw the underside of the cart and reminded himself not to get up like normal or risk smacking his head. He rolled his body to the right instead and immediately felt the cold sensation from the dew-covered grass.

He stood up and shivered. It was his second night, but nothing had improved. They carried no tent and slept underneath their carts as cover. It was better than sleeping out in the open, but cramped, smelly, and still cold.

Lansius lazily folded a sheet of canvas that he had used as a blanket. Theo appeared from beneath the cart. He looked equally miserable. The long and bumpy ride had taken a toll on all their bodies.

The horses, for certain, had it worse. They were moodier than ever and easily agitated by everything. Lansius, who had some experience with horses, took them to the patches of high grass and tied them to a tree as a precaution.

Lansius watched as Theo and Max headed to get water from a nearby creek. A strong breeze blew past, and he shivered again despite his gambeson. He took in the scents of the forest and pondered his decision to follow Thomas.

Despite the situation, Lansius couldn't shake off the lingering doubts and guilt about leaving Stefi and Riverstead. His rational mind, familiar with the horrors of a medieval town under siege, argued that escape had been the right choice. Yet, his heart disagreed, plaguing him with emotional torment.

Regardless of his internal conflict, Lansius recognized that his choices had led him here. Any chance he'd had for a life in a lord's retinue had probably vanished along with the likely defeat of their lord and the siege of Riverstead.

"Morning," someone said from behind.

Lansius turned to face Thomas. "Good to see you in high spirits, chief."

"Heh, you'd be just as spirited if you learned about this," Thomas teased.

"Learn what?"

"The scout said it's only half a day's journey till we reach the river," the older man explained.

"We're that close to Ceresia?" Lansius's mood indeed lifted a bit.

"Yep, with luck, we could be there before sundown."

"Chief, I hope you'll find a better place than that barn," Lansius jested.

Thomas laughed and slapped Lansius's back. "Hey, it's not that bad. It's spacious, and the roof is solid."

The morning went without a hitch, and the convoy departed in high spirits. As they kept riding west, the trees began to look different, taller, with fewer branches. The horses had to slow their pace as they traveled at a higher incline. Some carts even had their men get off and walk to ease their horses as they went uphill.

The cart Thomas commandeered wasn't heavy enough that anybody needed to dismount. It was a slow ride; the sky was cloudy and breezy. Max found the weather so irresistible that he dozed on and off. Meanwhile, Theo stayed on the lookout. The lad was dependable despite being only a year older than Max.

Compared to them, Lansius looked fragile. Unlike Max, who could sleep in an awkward position with his head unsupported and both hands gripping crates to keep himself from falling, Lansius couldn't make himself comfortable enough to fall asleep.

Unintentionally, he counted five carts and two carriages that made up the convoy. It was less than half of when they began. Too disheartened by war-torn Arvena, many had gone south into Midlandia, whose lord was on good terms with Lord Maurice.

The convoy Lansius was in traveled the same path he had taken last winter. Nobody questioned the decision. For them, it was only natural to return to the heartland. Like many, he was eager to return home and couldn't care less about the reason.

Since yesterday, Lansius had been dreaming of finally arriving in Bellandia and seeing his family. That thought kept him going despite the situation. Even the awful taste of the hard biscuits, which he had to soften with water just to make them edible, did little to dampen his spirits once he reminded himself that he could taste Mother Arryn's cooking in a few weeks.

He couldn't wait to play with Tanya and trade stories with Marc. On the surface, he felt happy, but the guilt of leaving Stefi behind was eating at him from the inside.

Lansius kept to himself more than usual. He didn't ask about Theo's or Max's background, nor did he inquire about the figure who sat next to Thomas. It was only because of their close vicinity that he overheard the boys describing her as a guard for hire, Miranda.

Miranda wasn't much of a talker, but had once mentioned how her only son bore a resemblance to Theo. She did little but maintain her prized crossbow every night, despite no apparent usage.

The cart slowed to a stop. Everybody but Max looked around to find the reason, but Thomas glanced back and shushed them with his finger. "Listen."

There were faint sounds of water moving rapidly.

"The river," exclaimed Theo.

The convoy needed to wait before they could cross the narrow bridge. The old wooden structure often had its support beams weakened by the strong current, and they needed to check it for safety.

The rest of the convoy dismounted as they waited. Most went to the river to sightsee, fill their canteen, or wash their face.

Lansius and Theo saw Miranda dismount, and they decided to follow. Thomas tied the horse to a tree and jogged after them, leaving Max sleeping alone in the cart. Lansius felt rejuvenated. The water's edge was picturesque, and the weather was lovely. Many sat on the ground or rested their back on the grass. A good respite from all the rough rides they had these past few days.

* * *

"Boss," Max cried from behind.

The tone made Thomas to jump into action. As he ran to the cart, Lansius and Theo followed. They watched as men from the other carts panicked and scrambled for the wooded area with just their weapons.

Miranda ran past Thomas and jumped to the top of the coachman's seat. Her face looked stricken. "Grab your spears and run to the trees."

The carts in front made a risky dash to cross the bridge, but for the rest of them, there was no choice but to run for the woods.

The smell of earth and decomposing leaves was everywhere as Lansius followed Miranda and Thomas deeper into the woods. The trees were tall but sparse. It wasn't nearly as easy to hide as he had thought.

Miranda found a hidden slope behind an old tree and signaled to take cover. "Stay away from the boulder," she instructed.

Lansius was too breathless to think, but Theo gave a questioning look.

"Any distinct spot like a rock formation is a landmark. Don't linger near them. The enemy will certainly look for you near there," she explained.

"Will they be chasing us?" Lansius asked as he sat behind the tree's giant roots.

"Calm down, lads. With luck they might just take the carts and leave us alone," Thomas said.

That gave some sort of relief, but soon the screaming and shouting dashed their hope. It wasn't possible to tell what was happening, but the situation wasn't promising.

"We need eyes," Thomas said to himself.

"I'll go. Your old bones might not be fit for the job." Miranda loosened her ring mail coif, put her sword and crossbow on the ground, then crawled out. She tried concealing herself while moving toward their cart.

As she went farther, the trees and vegetation hid her from sight.

"You three, wait here. I'm going to look for another spot." Thomas went deeper into the woods.

Theo looked at the other two. "Do you think we'll be safe here?"

Lansius had no answer, while Max let out a loud sigh and complained, "I shouldn't have listened. I never wanted to go to Riverstead."

The sound of leaves rustling alerted them. Theo went on the lookout. "It's Miranda; she's back."

She dashed toward them. Breathless and looking troubled, she hid behind the giant tree. "Thomas?"

Before anyone could answer, Thomas returned and crouched in front of her. "Not good," he reported.

"What did you find?" Miranda asked.

"Horsemen. They've cut off our escape."

"Damn it, they also have footmen encroaching on us. We're trapped. They want hostages."

"Or slaves . . ." Thomas added.

"So, what should we do?" Theo asked, his voice laden with worry.

They were trapped, with horsemen at their backs, a river to their left, and footmen blocking their path ahead. Their options were dwindling rapidly. A cold sweat formed on Lansius's back, and his grip on his spear tightened.

Thomas was silent. He knew the grim reality: their entire convoy consisted of only thirty men, most of whom were not fighters.

Miranda pulled her leather strap necklace. It connected to a small pouch she hid behind her ring mail. She emptied the content into her palm and revealed rings, jewelry, and gold coins.

Such valuables were so unexpected that they all did a double-take. For them, the value of such treasure was beyond their ability to comprehend.

"My job is to deliver this to Alba Castle," she began. "Sir Ian was wounded in battle. He's in no condition to ride, and chances are he'll get captured along with Riverstead. He wanted to send his signet ring and valuables to his son. That way, his son could either ransom him or succeed him if he perishes."

Miranda handed two decorated silver rings to Thomas. "Return these to his family and claim your reward."

"Why are you doing this? You should do this yourself," Thomas protested.

"Someone needs to lead them. I'll manage somehow," she said as she prepared her crossbow.

"Alone? It's too risky—"

"I can't let these boys be taken into slavery," Miranda insisted, and Thomas finally relented.

"The worst that could happen is to meet my son and husband in the afterlife," she murmured, more to herself than to Thomas.

Her words stunned the three, while Thomas looked grim as if remembering a bad memory.

Without wasting more time, she gave Theo a jewel-encrusted brooch and Max an ornamented buckle. Then she handed out half the coins to Lansius. "You're a scribe of some sort. Count it."

"Six gold coins and sixteen silvers."

"Good. Remember to return it to Alba Castle, or I'm going to find you and turn you into target practice," Miranda said to Lansius, who was older and not so naive as the boys.

Lansius nodded. It would be a simple task to find the only black hair in Arvena.

"Thomas, get them out safely. I'll cover you."

"Best of luck then," Thomas said and left with the trio.

Lansius took one last glance and saw Miranda fastening her ring mail coif. When she noticed, Lansius bowed his head in respect. That simple gesture made her smile.

Thomas led the trio to crouch between the vegetation and tall trees, hopping between slopes and taking cover behind irregular mounds. The sound of cracking branches and horses' heavy hooves alerted them.

The sound was getting closer. Thomas hid his head between shrubs while the other wouldn't risk getting seen. They waited in fear before a horseman in orange and black surcoat came into view. He was wearing a skull-cap helmet and ring mail, while his horse was without armor.

The horseman wound his way through the trees, clearly searching for anyone who might be hiding.

"Come out, you little dirty rabbits." The voice had come from another direction.

"Evnas, keep your mouth shut," came a distant response.

The banter between still unseen individuals made the orange and black horseman chuckle.

Thomas pulled back from his lookout spot and whispered, "I need to draw him away. Remember to keep walking with the river to your right. Find a shallow place and cross, but avoid Ceresia. The enemy will be there."

And then, without warning, Thomas climbed out of hiding and ran in the opposite direction.

"Halt!" the horseman cried as he spotted Thomas. "I found one," he declared to his comrades, and clenched his legs to signal the horse to speed up.

"Evnas, go assist him!" commanded the other person. But before the second rider could come, the rider in orange and black had given chase.

Meanwhile, Theo froze, but Max, who understood the situation, dragged his friend from the spot. Lansius followed without a word.

Thomas zigzagged between the trees as he ran, but the horseman kept his cool and trailed him from a distance. He couldn't run and hide forever. Out of breath, he slowed down. Before he stopped, instinct guided him to stand in the open instead of hiding behind the trees.

The horseman closed in with a drawn sword. The sound of hooves pounding the ground echoed through the air as he charged, intending to kill.

Thomas stood on his ground, his axe ready in his right hand. But the rider's approach left no gap, forcing Thomas to dodge roll at the last moment into the trees.

The horseman overshot his approach, trotted his horse around, and prepared for another pass. He could afford to play this cat-and-mouse game patiently.

One more pass and then another. The horseman kept harassing his prey to provoke them into making a mistake.

Out of breath and out of tricks, Thomas's attempt to bait the rider into a duel on foot had failed. Now, he risked meeting up with the footmen, or worse, the second horseman.

The horseman seemed to enjoy this and started another approach when a sharp, distinct sound echoed. It wasn't loud, but the rider staggered, dropped his sword, and moved about erratically. A bolt had penetrated his ring mail through the doublet and ruptured his lung. The rider soon suffocated as his lung became filled with blood.

Thomas dragged his tired legs, then attempted to deliver the killing blow, but before he could, someone rushed in from another direction and speared the rider.

The rider cried out in pain, but was unable to retaliate. His flailing causing his horse to panic. He fell backward, hitting the ground hard as the horse galloped away. The fallen man, decked in the orange and black surcoat lay motionless, either from the fall or his fatal wound.

"Ronan," Thomas called.

"Thomas, who shot the bolt?" Ronan asked as he pulled his spear from the dead body.

"It's Miranda. Where are the other guys?"

"Dead, tch—they even killed Ulrich . . ." Ronan's voice was full of anger and sadness.

"The lad? But he's no older than fourteen . . ." Thomas felt sickened.

"There's no reason to kill him . . . Unless they think we're hiding the young Lord." He grew frustrated. "Nothing good will come from this. Better run while you still can," he warned and walked away.

"Where you're going?"

"Swim."

"And lose all your gear?" Thomas asked.

Ronan turned to face him and opened his arms to signal, *what else can I do?*

Thomas reflected, but chose not to follow. Probably because he had no kids of his own, he wanted to save Theo and the rest.

Footsteps on his right surprised Thomas. He readied his axe, but saw Miranda and felt relieved. "Good shot."

Miranda pulled Thomas behind a tree and forced him to crouch. "Don't do that again!"

Thomas grinned. "Hey, let's bait another one."

"Are you an idiot? You'll be dead if I can't find a clear line of sight." Not wanting to hear his response, she added, "The footmen are closing in. Let's get out from here."

Thomas seemed to remember something. He took two rings from his pouch and threw them one by one to Miranda. "Catch."

"What are you doing?" She couldn't believe the Thomas she knew had turned suicidal.

"One more. For the boys," he said and went searching for the second horseman.

# CHAPTER 12

# AMERTUME FOREST

Tall trees with lush leaves and sturdy branches painted the backdrop as the trio ventured deeper into the forest. The undergrowth was teeming with bright green ferns, mosses, and shrubs that carpeted the forest floor. Max led the way, with Theo and Lansius following closely behind. Their only guide was to keep the river on their right.

Despite having trekked for some time, they had yet to encounter anything suspicious. This lack of threat emboldened Max to look for a shallow spot to cross the river.

Recognizing Max's intent as he steered them closer to the river, Lansius voiced his concern. "Max, I think we should walk farther before attempting to cross."

Max halted, catching his breath. "We'll get too tired if we walk farther."

"The sooner we cross, the better," Theo chimed in.

Lansius nodded. He didn't want to stall progress with a debate. Thus, they continued alongside the river until they found a suitable spot with jutting boulders.

Max was the first to wade into the water. He made steady progress initially but then suddenly found himself submerged up to his chest.

The other two could only exchange glances as a soaked Max returned. Taking over Max's bag, they continued their search along the riverbank. Before they knew it, they stumbled upon a potential solution.

Theo spotted a run-down hut not far from the river. Next to it, a piece of a canoe jutted out from overgrown shrubs. Hopeful, they jogged over to inspect the boat. It was old and decayed but, crucially, didn't have a gaping hole. Max and Lansius cleared the debris from the small boat while Theo investigated the hut.

Despite his efforts, Theo returned empty handed. "So, can we use it?"

Max looked at Lansius, who nodded and replied, "This might just do the job."

Together, they lifted the small wooden canoe into the river. Despite their panting and heaving, they were elated when the old boat floated without leaking much.

With help from the others, Max climbed aboard with an equally weathered oar, followed by Theo. The boat wobbled precariously.

"If we all get in, this thing will capsize," Lansius warned.

"What should we do then?" Theo asked.

"You go first with Theo and come back for me later," Lansius suggested.

"Okay, just wait here." Max began to row, unsteadily at first.

Lansius stood back and watched, a smile tugging at his lips as Max grappled with the oar. The boat drifted aimlessly at first, but Max was starting to get the hang of it.

The emerging sun cast beautiful reflections on the water's surface. Max was making good progress when he abruptly stopped and lurched forward. Theo quickly steadied his friend before shouting and waving at Lansius.

Lansius couldn't make out what Theo was saying due to the river's noise. He initially thought Max had grown weary from rowing, but then he spotted a blot of red on Max's tunic. He instinctively ducked and scanned the area in terror.

Confirming his fear, a silvery object darted again toward the boat, striking its side.

*Crossbowman?!*

Lansius scanned the area where the threat had come from, half expecting another bolt to be loosed in his direction.

"Get the boys, kill them. They might be Maurice's bastards!" a chilling voice echoed from the woods.

But the expected bolt didn't come, and Lansius saw no one. His survival instincts surged, and he abandoned his friends, sprinting away from the river-bank as fast as he could.

He had left his spear behind, but he didn't care. He ceased thinking and just urged his weary legs to keep moving. He slipped, crashed into a tree, then pushed off and continued to run. His left ankle twisted as it caught a tree root, sending him tumbling. But he got up and pressed on, delving deeper into the forest.

Lansius eventually came to a stop, collapsing in a fit of uncontrollable coughing. Exhaustion had finally caught up to him. He was drenched in sweat, and his body felt drained of strength. His limbs throbbed with every beat of his heart.

For a long while, he could do nothing but lie there, gasping for breath. He noticed the trees around him here were older, their bark a darker shade of brown. The ground beneath him was softer, the air thick with the smell of decomposing leaves.

The rustling leaves and branches above him created a serene soundscape, the sunlight and shadows dancing in a playful game. But all he could see were flashes of Max and Theo.

"Damn it . . ." he cursed, tears stinging his eyes.

He had known the boys for three whole days. They had traveled together, eaten together, slept side by side.

*To think they have to die like that . . .*

Overwhelmed by shock and grief, Lansius struggled to his feet. He was dizzy and in poor shape, but he had no other options. He clung to Thomas's advice: *Keep walking with the river to your right.*

So, he pressed onward, alone, farther into the heart of the ancient forest.

The chirping of birds stirred Lansius from his restless slumber. He woke to find himself chilled and crawling with ants and insects. Groaning, he rose, shaking off the tiny invaders and even beating his clothes against a tree trunk to dislodge them.

Afterward, he staggered to the largest tree nearby, draping his blanket over one of its branches and settling down on a protruding root. He was consumed by exhaustion, his sleep cycle disrupted. His nights were sleepless and filled with fear. To make matters worse, his empty stomach churned, making him feel as if he might vomit at any moment.

The lightheadedness persisted, so he occupied himself by massaging his legs. His left ankle throbbed painfully, and his right knee was sore from numerous falls and slips. Even his shoes were beginning to fall apart.

This morning marked the third day Lansius had wandered alone. As his heart worked to pump blood into his weary head, he pulled out his traveling bag and rummaged through its contents. One by one, he put its contents into his lap: a piece of hard biscuit wrapped in linen, a wooden bowl and spoon, a tin cup, two small purple carrots, and a peculiar red fruit he had found but dared not to eat.

In his determination to not leave anything behind, he shook the bag, and a pouch tumbled out onto his lap. It was the money pouch, which he had kept in his bag due to its significant value. He had forgotten about it, and out of curiosity, he emptied it.

Gold, silver, and copper coins formed a small pile on his lap.

He picked up one of the gold coins, inspecting it closely.

*How many months of work is one of these worth?*

It was a rhetorical question, but he found the irony amusing and burst into laughter.

*To think that I would die with six gold coins in my hand . . .*

His laughter only served to worsen his pounding headache. Dizzy and starving, he glanced at his meager ration of hard biscuit, but knew it was too dry to eat without water. He reached for his water pouch and took a few sips, then bit off a small piece of biscuit, chewing it like an awful tasting candy.

He had less than a third of his water remaining. He knew he needed to find the river or some sort of creek. The problem lay therein. The previous day, he had bet on finding another village if he kept following the river, reasoning that most settlements were located near a water source. Ceresia farmland was near a river delta, Bellandia had a large creek, and Riverstead was flanked by three rivers.

However, he had underestimated the terrain. The river had become increasingly difficult to follow on foot, frequently disappearing into steep ravines or similarly impassable areas.

Yet, Lansius could still hear the distant murmur of the stream, providing a glimmer of hope. He looked at the sun, steeling himself for another exhausting journey. He knew there was no turning back; he didn't have enough food to retrace his steps.

Now, it was either move forward or die trying. Aided by a walking stick he fashioned from a broken branch, he once again set out into the vast forest.

Lansius's stomach churned. He felt so weak and famished that he felt like boiling some leaves or mushrooms. His lack of tools to start a fire was now his greatest regret. It had cost him dearly. Fire would help ward off the chilly nights and kept insects from crawling over him. But most importantly, the absence of fire limited him to the wild berries he dared to eat.

Hunger was all in his mind. Yesterday, he had eaten the last half of his hard biscuit.

Now, only a leftover carrot remained, but even after chewing it, he found little respite from his hunger. To make matters worse, his waterskin was nearly empty, as he still hadn't located the river.

The sun was high on the horizon when he finally found the will to continue southward. His legs wobbled with exhaustion and fever seized him in waves, yet he trudged on almost mindlessly. He knew that if he didn't find a settlement today, surviving tomorrow would be near impossible.

The terrain was unforgiving, forcing him to mind his steps on the moss-covered rocks, fallen branches, and overgrown shrubs. There was never a direct path. He constantly had to adapt and navigate when the terrain became too treacherous.

By midday, his stamina had dwindled to the point that he needed to lean on a large branch for support. The dizziness persisted, and he slumped to the forest floor. He reached for the last piece of food he had, a fruit resembling a red mango.

With his left hand, he unsheathed his knife and inspected the short blade. But instead of using it to cut the fruit, the sharp edge seemed to beckon him.

After days of wandering alone in the wilderness, he questioned his own sanity. He tried to soothe his racing thoughts, but feverish images persisted.

*Stefi, Jan . . . Thomas, Max, Theo, Miranda . . .*

Lansius recalled their faces and exhaled deeply. Half of him felt so guilty that he contemplated ending it all right there, but the other half clung to a sliver of hope.

Before he knew it, he was overcome by shivers, and exhaustion claimed him. He managed to sheathe his knife before collapsing onto his side. He intended to take a brief nap, but half an hour turned into twelve.

Lansius didn't realize a new day had dawned when he opened his eyes. He felt surprisingly refreshed, and even his ankle seemed better. Oddly enough, he didn't find the usual insects crawling on his clothes.

There was nothing unusual in his surroundings, except for a plant with dark purple leaves and flowers near him. With nothing to lose, he took his knife and carefully excavated the plant, making sure to extract it complete with its roots. He wrapped it in leftover linen and stored it in his bag. Afterward, he checked his gear, took the last sip of water, and mustered his will for another trek.

Strangely, he no longer felt hungry. Unbeknownst to him, his digestion had slowed down as he'd barely eaten in almost a week. Now, his body pulled energy directly from his fat, and he became skinnier each day.

After what felt like two hours, he could hear the river more distinctly than before. This spurred him to continue.

Suddenly, his foot plunged into what felt like a puddle of water. He instinctively pulled it out, startled by the cold, wet sensation. On examining his surroundings, he found he had stepped on a hidden creek that was concealed by ferns, shrubs, and other vegetation.

This stroke of luck made him burst into laughter.

Suddenly, a loud neighing sound startled Lansius, causing him to jump sideways and land on his backside.

*A horse?!*

He could hear the animal's heavy breathing coming from somewhere behind the trees. He quickly filled his canteen from the creek and set off to find the horse.

He was concerned about the horse's rider, but after being alone for so long, he was willing to risk even a cell or a dungeon.

As Lansius peered between the trees, he spotted a brown horse with white spots. It was calmly drinking from the creek in the middle of a small clearing. The horse was saddled and had reins, indicating the presence of an owner.

Lansius scanned the surroundings, but found no one even after several minutes.

After some deliberation, he slowly approached the stream, doing his best to appear nonthreatening.

The horse neighed unhappily, but Lansius remained calm. He knelt by the creek to clean his hands and face, something he hadn't done in days. He continued to observe his surroundings and noticed saddlebags on the horse. Seeing them as a potential lifeline, he gathered the courage to approach.

He racked his brain to recall what Stefi had taught him about horses. He made no sudden movements, approached the horse indirectly, and stayed within its line of sight.

After a tense moment in which the horse moved several times and Lansius paused to give it space, he finally managed to grab the reins. As he took hold of the leather strap, the horse protested but didn't run or kick.

"Easy, boy . . ." Lansius patted the horse's head to calm it down before moving to the saddle. He wasn't planning to ride—his horse-riding skills were far too poor—instead, he opened the saddlebags and unloaded their contents onto the forest floor.

There were pouches, ropes, onion-smelling thing, linens, and various other items. On the other side, he found water pouches, a metallic flask, a black metal pot, and a sheet of fabric. The last thing he did was unstrap a sword from the saddle.

As the sword clattered to the ground, he first gathered the pouches and moved the items away from the horse, lest the animal trample them. Once done, Lansius let go of the reins.

"Go on, you're free to go."

The horse remained distrustful but eventually trotted away. He had considered keeping her, but he was too worried that her rider was nearby. He was also concerned that leading a horse might make him an easier target to track.

Loaded with goods, Lansius moved to find some cover. He continued until he found a cluster of gigantic trees with tall shrubs on either side, and then he began to unpack.

*Nuts? This is promising . . . and this is . . . ugh, moldy bread, yuck.*

He threw the bread away, along with some rotten salted meat to avoid attracting any carnivores. Without wasting any time, he popped a handful of nuts into his mouth, finding they tasted somewhat like almonds. He then uncovered thin biscuits and eagerly devoured them.

The biscuits were superb, better than any he had ever had. Next, he cut a chunk of cheese and ate it whole.

Curiosity led him to sample the ale from the engraved metallic flask. He coughed heavily as his throat burned, but he felt invigorated.

A metallic glint caught his attention. He had forgotten about the sword. He picked it up and drew it from its scabbard.

It was a fine-looking arming sword. Its blade had a fuller, the cross guard looked sturdy, and the pommel was rounded. The blade only had minor defects or imperfections. As Stefi had taught him, only the area around the tip was razor sharp. The rest of the blade was only as sharp as scissors and meant to be used against an armored opponent.

Feeling satisfied, Lansius sheathed the sword again and felt somewhat safer because of it. Not knowing how much time had passed, as the woods obscured the sun, he decided to push his luck further and continued his search for a way out.

*A horse, even a lost one, is a good sign that a settlement is near.*

With renewed spirit, he slung his newfound sword over his shoulder, along with his loaded bag, and set off again. His instincts told him to follow the creek, so he abandoned his search for the river.

The terrain became more challenging, with boulders scattered here and there. The sun changed its hue to a reddish-orange, and the trees began to thin out. This urged him to quicken his pace, and he noticed a spot where numerous beams of light penetrated the forest floor. Jogging toward the clearing, he hoped to find something, but what he saw left him speechless.

Vast meadows, two distant hills, a lake, and small rectangular shapes that could be farms or orchards.

It wasn't just a clearing; it was a way out. A warm wind greeted Lansius as he emerged back into the civilized world.

# CHAPTER 13

# A VILLAGE BY THE LAKE

Lansius sprinted through the woods until his better judgment stopped him. He surveyed his surroundings and concealed himself. Examining his bag, he realized he had items that could arouse suspicion. A clerk fleeing from war with a sword wouldn't go unnoticed, and carrying a large sum of gold coins would be unwise. At best, they could be confiscated; at worst, he could be robbed or jailed as a thief.

So, he scanned the area and noticed something gray. Lansius cautiously approached the spot, careful not to lose his bearings. As he got closer, he saw a large, half-buried boulder, which was easy to locate even from a distance—as Miranda had told them, perfect as a landmark but not for hiding. Lansius then spotted an old tree with dark-colored bark behind some shrubs.

He pushed through the surrounding vegetation and reached the tree. Sitting on one of its giant roots, he felt protected by the plants that concealed the spot. Lansius then noticed a gap in the tree roots and cautiously inserted his sword, still in its scabbard, to test its depth while praying he wouldn't disturb any snakes or spiders inside.

Finding the hole deep enough and undisturbed, he pulled out the sword and dug a small hole for his money pouch. He carefully placed the pouch inside, covered it with dirt, and flattened the surface using the scabbard. He then gathered several stones and plugged the hole, followed by a layer of dried leaves to conceal it further.

Satisfied with his work, Lansius checked his pockets for anything that might raise suspicion and found his purple plants. On a whim, he pulled out his knife and began digging in a clearing near the ancient tree. He planted the purple plants and sprinkled some water on them. Now, he was ready to meet the villagers.

Filled with anticipation and hope, Lansius retraced his steps to the gray boulder and then walked east toward the village beyond vast meadows and a clear, azure blue lake.

After an hour of walking, Lansius spotted an elderly couple in their orchard, staring at him. Lansius waved at them, and they quickly dropped their gardening tools and approached him. "Young man," they called.

Lansius stopped, his heart racing, as he finally met them.

"Young man, are you a merchant?" the elderly woman in gray gardening attire asked.

"Huh?"

"He isn't, Martha. Your eyes are deceiving you again," said the elderly man with a thin face but sharp eyes.

"I'm sorry, I'm not a merchant," Lansius replied. "May I ask the name of this village?"

They were stunned. "Are you lost? But Torrea is far from anywhere."

"I came through the woods," Lansius said, gesturing toward the forest.

The couple was taken aback. The elderly woman motioned for him to follow her, while the elderly man grasped Lansius's hand and led him away. "Come with us. The village chief will need to know."

Over two weeks had passed in peaceful monotony. Life in the village of Torrea was much like Bellandia for Lansius—slow and tranquil. The sun blazed on this day, but a cool, pleasant breeze persisted.

Lansius sat on a backyard porch bench as the village chief skillfully cut his hair. The old man with graying hair wielded his large scissors with ease.

"There, now you look the part," the chief said.

"Thank you, chief." Lansius then took a refreshing outdoor bath using water from the well, a quintessential summer activity.

"So, you're leaving tomorrow?" the chief inquired while sweeping the porch.

"Yes, in the morning."

"I see." The old man nodded. "I'll ask my daughter to cook breakfast for you."

"Gratitude," Lansius replied with a smile.

The chief waved his hand and went inside.

Lansius dried himself with a clean cloth and dressed in his work clothes. Though the summer sun would make him sweat soon enough, he didn't mind. He retrieved a wicker basket, a hemp sack, and a large, round hat from the shed.

Lansius routinely gathered firewood and wild berries, viewing it as both exercise and a way to contribute as a guest. He strolled leisurely along the path leading to the forest, waving politely to the people he encountered.

Serene and picturesque, Torrea featured fields and terraced farms that had recently turned a subtle shade of yellow, enlivening the landscape. Cicadas chirped, and birds flew freely around the lake, which teemed with life.

As usual, Lansius chatted with the elderly couple he first met in Torrea before excusing himself and heading toward the forest entrance. Ensuring no one followed, he made his way to a gray boulder. His recently purchased second-hand shoes were slightly oversized, but they protected his feet well enough.

Usually, Lansius would head directly to the half-buried boulder where he had hidden a thick piece of wood about the size of a sword. This piece was heavier than a real one, and he often used it for training after gathering firewood. Several trees had low-hanging branches that were perfect for this purpose. While he could have used the blade he had found, he didn't want anyone to see him in possession of a sword.

However, today was different. Upon catching sight of the gray boulder, Lansius veered right, heading toward the ancient oak tree. Pushing through the surrounding shrubs, he found a comfortable spot on one of its giant roots. The plant with purple leaves he had planted seemed to keep the area insect-free. Now, its small flower was blooming once again.

Lansius watered the healthy plant using his water pouch, carefully weeding out any other vegetation around it.

Through walking, carrying out small chores, and engaging in occasional training, he felt that he had recovered. He had gained weight, and the blisters on his feet had healed. His left ankle, however, never felt quite the same, but he accepted that there was little he could do to change that.

Birdsong from overhead reminded him of his task. Today, he didn't need to forage. Instead, he lowered his basket, knelt, and removed dried leaves from between the tree roots. He easily found the stack of firewood he had saved earlier. Afterward, he removed several stones between the roots where he had hidden his sword and money pouch.

Seeing no signs of spiders or snakes, he carefully reached inside and retrieved his arming sword. Even within its scabbard, the sword felt light. Resisting the urge to check the blade, he placed it inside a hemp sack and concealed it in a wicker basket, covering it with firewood.

Next, he dug a little deeper and pulled out his old money pouch. After confirming the contents of gold and silver, he placed it in his trusted bag. Lansius felt guilty for keeping these items a secret. The chief had been kind to him despite his dubious background and circumstances, but he couldn't risk confiscation.

The sun turned orange and bathed the clouds in gold-colored rays. Lansius packed his gear. His old fear of getting lost in the forest haunted him deeply.

He knew it was a close brush with death. The villagers told him that the river he had followed flowed westward into the Great Forest. If he had gone there, then he would have certainly died. There was no known path through, and it would take weeks to cross it. That is if he survived the rumored foul beasts and monsters that lurked inside.

Lansius looked at the purple plant one last time. Despite its special properties, he had no heart to pluck it for the second time.

He left the plant and oak tree behind. With hurried steps, he returned to the village.

Sundown came, and supper was served. The chief finished early as usual and left the two youngsters to clean up.

"I heard you're going?" Amelia, the chief's daughter, asked while cleaning the plates.

"Mm, yeah. While you were away, the land official returned with a travel permit," Lansius replied while scrubbing the cauldron.

"I see . . ."

The village of Torrea was so remote that it took seven days for the land official to learn about Lansius and to arrange someone to visit. When they finally met, Lansius shocked them with his report of war in Arvena. They forbade him from leaving until they could verify his story. As it turned out, confirming Lansius's story took another seven days, and an additional three days to find an official bound to Torrea so they could deliver his permit.

"Well, I understand why you want to leave," Amelia said in between cleaning.

Lansius stopped scrubbing. "How so?"

"This village, there's nothing in here but old couples and farm life."

He chuckled. "That's not true. Torrea has a lake, and freshwater fish are a delicacy."

Amelia giggled. "Too bad they're fishy and rot easily. Also, without salt, we can only grill them."

Lansius laughed. The two had talked about this topic several times. She was a few years older than him, but already a widow. Her much older husband had succumbed to an illness two years ago.

"Honestly, I like staying here. It's peaceful."

Amelia paused her work, turned around, and looked at Lansius. "Then stay." Her tone was serious.

Lansius exhaled. Even as dense as he was, he knew Amelia wanted him as a brother she never had, or as a substitute for her late husband. Torrea was surrounded by dense forest and lacked any trade routes, causing many young people to seek employment in neighboring villages with more opportunities. This led to a severe shortage of eligible partners for marriage.

"I wish I could," Lansius said. He had too much guilt to accept such an offer.

Amelia said nothing and returned to cleaning.

Lansius did the same. This was his last day, and he intended to clean as thoroughly as possible. While his hands worked, his mind wandered. The offer was a tempting one.

If he stayed, then his future would be set. As an educated man, he could apply for a clerical job in the nearest estate. Moreover, the chief's vast farming land would be his if he married Amelia. He wouldn't have to worry about anything. To top the list, Amelia had a sweet side and was dependable by nature.

"I'm going to prepare something for you tomorrow," she said when they were done.

"Gratitude," Lansius said politely, and the conversation ended that way.

As morning arrived, Lansius enjoyed an early breakfast. He had discarded his moldy gambeson, which was too conspicuous when not on a campaign. Instead, he traded it for a second-hand gray doublet that he confidently wore.

Carefully packing his belongings into a hemp sack fashioned like a duffel bag, he donned a felt hat to cover his hair. Unbeknownst to him, the chief had arranged for a donkey cart.

"I can't repay your kindness, chief," Lansius said, touched by the stranger's generosity.

"Don't get me wrong, lad. You've been a great help to me." The chief pulled an envelope from his coat and handed it to the coachman. "For the baronet."

The coachman nodded and kept it in his breast pocket.

Lansius smiled with satisfaction. The envelope represented his idea to initiate trade between Torrea and its nearest neighbor. Although Torrea lacked a prized commodity and wouldn't typically benefit financially from trade, Lansius believed the villagers should barter their harvest for salted meat.

While salted meat was expensive, this trade could help alleviate the village's salt shortage, which Lansius suspected had caused illness and deaths after the salt mine closed due to a lack of young miners. He also suggested the chief invite people who knew about the smoking process to preserve fish, potentially turning the underappreciated catch into a valuable commodity.

The chief bade him farewell. "Don't get in trouble again. Visit Torrea if you find yourself nearby."

"Thanks again, chief. Until next time." Lansius carefully loaded the hemp sack and climbed aboard the cart.

The coachman gently nudged the donkey, and the cart began to move.

"Visit us when you can." Amelia waved.

"I will. Take care, Amelia."

As Lansius left Torrea with the sun yet to shine brightly, he eagerly anticipated his return to the world outside.

# CHAPTER 14

# MIDLANDIA

For more than a thousand years, the Imperium stood as the largest human bastion in the Promissia Continent. Under its reign, the populace had seen unrivaled peace, order, and prosperity. However, its rule gradually fell apart.

The Imperium required vast resources just to maintain its territories. Burdened by an archaic bureaucracy, it consumed more than it could collect in taxes. As the treasury dwindled, the economy was strained and steadily worsened.

Since the turn of the century, the Imperium had found itself unable to maintain its borders. Strategic outposts were deserted; public buildings, roads, and bridges were left to ruin. Yet, the capital continued to siphon more and more wealth, leaving only crumbs for the rest of the populace.

Regions closest to the border suffered the greatest. Neglected, but pressured by harsh tax and labor obligations, many abandoned their birthplaces. All over the continent, there were signs of unrest.

The weakened border triggered a nomadic uprising in the west. To the north, the ever-tenacious northerners had defied the High Court and annexed regions with thinly veiled pretexts.

However, for the Imperium's elites, it was business as usual. Despite the deterioration, the status quo in the central plains remained unchallenged. Their grand festivals and lavish parties that they threw for all manner of ceremonies continued without interruption.

The summer of the Elven Calendar year 4423 arrived with tidings that shocked the Imperium to its core. Arvena, one of the provinces in the central plain, had fallen.

Ever ambitious, Margrave Gottfried had unified the rebellious northerners and led them across the Great River and into Arvena. His pretext was to stop a feud between a minor lord and Lord Maurice the Earl of Arvena. In the ensuing conflict, Lord Maurice, his descendants, and inner circle went missing, presumably killed, allowing the margrave to occupy Arvena.

A massacre of a member of the High Houses and a blatant takeover of an important region created a crisis. With the army held in the west against the nomads, the Imperium couldn't risk opening another front. However, everyone knew the margrave had crossed the line. Things wouldn't be the same anymore.

For the northerners, further conflict was a chance for revenge against their oppressors. For the ordinary folks in the central plains, this was a prelude to disaster.

After leaving Torrea, Lansius had been living on the road for two weeks. He rode open carts when they were available at a good price, usually when the cart was half empty. But for the most part, he traveled on foot. As much as he wanted to arrive faster at the eastern part of Midlandia, he knew money might be a problem, so he tried to balance speed and cost.

As was customary, he traveled in a large group with traveling peddlers, seasonal laborers, and people running errands. The group provided protection and the added benefit of someone who could cook in exchange for goods or money. Nonetheless, he was cautious about what he ate. The last thing he wanted was to fall ill due to diarrhea. Without access to medicine, stomachaches were not just an inconvenience but indicators of potentially deadly disease.

Despite resembling a guardsman with his doublet and sword hung on his belt, Lansius took precautions and sewed the gold coins into his doublet, blanket, and the inner part of his bag. He needed protection against thieves who might blend in with the group.

As he traveled, he learned about the province of Midlandia and its complex relationship with slavery. The Imperium strictly forbade the enslavement of its citizens. However, they allowed the sale of captured beastmen or nomadic people as slaves, who were mostly brought to the Eastern Kingdoms.

However, as the Imperium declined and increasingly relied on the lords to fight their border wars, they needed another source to fund their campaigns. As a result, they began to dabble in slavery, and the Imperium officials turned a blind eye.

This situation created a sense of urgency for Lansius as he worried about the people he left behind. He believed that if any captured people from Riverstead were to appear, it would be in Feodosia. However, time and money would be in short supply, as the Eastern Kingdoms were always hungry for more slaves.

Lansius thought about the gold coins. He knew they weren't his, but if he found Stefi or any of his friends, he would gladly buy their freedom and risk confrontation with Miranda or Sir Ian's House.

The sliver of hope that he might save someone motivated him to hit the road through the summer sun every morning.

Despite the heat, summer traveling was the norm, as the ground was firm and solid during the season. However, at midday, travelers needed to seek cover under shade or risk getting heatstroke.

Only after the sun waned did they dare to continue until sundown or until they arrived at a town or village along the way. But that wasn't much of a problem. Central Midlandia was bustling with towns and villages surrounded by farmlands and orchards.

These places were busy, large, and industrious. Carts and carriages filled the roads, while the markets were full of traders with their goods and wares.

The towns had shops and workshops that offered all kinds of products. One, in particular, caught Lansius's attention. After much deliberation, he traded his shoes for new, better-fitting boots. While the soles were hard, they served him well in lessening the heat from the road.

*Just one more village to go.*

Lansius walked with a determined stride. Today was a lovely day, but the sun was merciless. It was so hot that the birds stopped chirping. Lansius walked alone, as safety wasn't an issue when the road was so busy with carts and carriages.

Since his escape from Riverstead, more than a month had passed. There was a growing fear that should his friends have been captured, the slaver could sell them before he arrived. This propelled him to travel faster, even if it meant traveling alone.

Lansius had upgraded his hat to a larger one, but the summer sun still burned into his back and tanned his hands and any other exposed skin.

The occasional breeze was his only respite, while the sound of cicadas provided the only distraction from the maddening heat. When the cobbled stone was too hot even for his new boots, he walked on the roadside where the grass was cooler.

As midday approached, the road became less crowded. Most travelers had stopped to rest, but Lansius kept going for an extra mile.

By chance, he heard a squabble on a speedy horse carriage that was moving toward him.

*A couple's quarrel?*

He was ready to dismiss it, but the rising voice and the harshness of the tone signaled that something was off.

"No, no, don't, that's dangerous, watch out!" the coachman yelled.

Lansius looked at the speeding cart that barely passed him. His eyes widened as he saw long golden hair fluttering in the wind. Mesmerized by it, he failed to notice anything else.

"Oof," Lansius cried. The area around his face suddenly felt warm. Something heavy had smacked him and sent him falling backward. He landed on the ground with a thud and hit the back of his head. The impact nearly knocked him out and left him dizzy and confused.

Lansius groaned weakly. He didn't know what had happened and could only see stars spinning with his closed eyes. Worse, throbbing pain came from his head, chest, and back.

"Oh, so sorry," said a concerned woman with a lovely voice.

*A girl? From where?*

Lansius tried to see, but it was all blurry and painful. The metallic taste grew stronger in his mouth, so he spat into the grass.

"So sorry . . ." She kept apologizing and grabbed Lansius's hand.

His knees felt powerless, so despite her help, he could only sit on the ground. With head still felt like spinning, he asked, "What happened?"

"You fell pretty hard. Does your head feel all right?"

"Do you see what hit me?"

"Mm . . . more or less."

"Can you tell me? If it's a wooden crate or barrel, I might need a bandage." He gently rubbed his pained head.

"No, you should be all right. I'm not that heavy," she said, while pulling her straw hat down slightly.

"Y-you fell into me?" Lansius, for the first time, managed to open his eyes and glanced at the lady. He was awestruck by the sweet-looking face, blue azure eyes, and gorgeous golden hair.

"Oh no, you're in shock," she said, panicking.

"Eh, no no, I'm . . . thinking . . . about— er . . . I'm just preoccupied, that's all," he stammered.

"Lemme check." She moved beside him and checked the back of his head. "There's no blood—oh, my, what a lovely hair color."

Lansius was stunned and pulled his hat firmly down over his ears. "Please, it's all right. I'm fine, my lady," he added as he just remembered that blond hair usually meant nobility.

She giggled. "Relax. I'm not a noble." Again, she offered her hand.

Her smile swayed Lansius to take her hand.

She helped him to get up with a smile and whispered, "It's all right. I saw nothing."

Lansius flustered and nodded quickly. "A-anyway, are you okay? I mean, you're jumping from a running cart."

"Seems that way . . ." She looked at her left and right side. "Just some light bruises." She showed him her reddened elbow.

"To get away from a speeding cart with just bruises. That's truly good luck."

"Hehe, my friends always called me lucky. I guess I am," she said with the most radiant smile.

Lansius's heart skipped a beat. He turned his face around and noticed the cart was coming back. "I apologize for minding your business, but why did you jump?"

"Ah, the jerk lied to me," she said sharply. "He said just a minor detour before heading to Feodosia, but here we are, almost a city away. He also wouldn't stop to let me down."

His eyes lit up. "You were kidnapped?"

# CHAPTER 15

# FORTUNA

**B**eneath the sweltering summer sun, Lansius found himself in the midst of an unexpected encounter on his way to Feodosia. He had come across a blond stranger who appeared to have been kidnapped, and now she stood her ground, boldly facing the approaching cart that might have been involved in her abduction.

"Do you need help?" Lansius asked as the cart slowed down.

"Nah, I'll take care of it," she said confidently and stood firmly.

Lansius watched by her side as the coachman parked his cart. The man immediately rushed to her, and yelled, "Why did you jump like that?"

Lansius cleared his throat, catching the coachman's attention. He noticed how Lansius looked like a guardsman and had his hand resting on the hilt of his sword.

"Why are you lying to me? You're not heading to Feodosia, but away from it," the lady stated.

"Miss, you're mistaken. I'm merely taking a slight detour to fetch my goods," he argued.

"Detour so far in an opposite direction? How absurd. I'm done with your words," she said firmly.

"But you agreed to pay," the coachman said, fuming.

"I said I'm done. I'd rather walk," she replied as she turned around and walked away.

"But, miss, it's a long way," the man protested, about to follow her.

Lansius stepped forward and blocked his path. "She has spoken. Please leave."

The coachman's face turned sinister. "Don't interfere. You'll regret this."

The tone triggered Lansius, who drew his sword in an instant. He pointed the sharpened steel at the coachman. "Remove yourself," he said in a low, cold voice that he didn't know he had.

The coachman took a step back. He muttered curses under his breath, but turned and walked away.

The lady peeked from behind Lansius. "Did you get agitated easily before?"

"I-I don't know . . . It's actually my first time pulling a sword at someone," he whispered and sheathed the sword again.

She grinned mischievously. "I really need to take a better look at your head."

"Please don't, I beg you," he said meekly. His hair was obviously dirty from all the dust and sweat.

The lady giggled. Afterward, the two of them quietly watched the cart until it went out of view.

"Any chance you're a minor noble?" she asked as they resumed their walk.

"Eh, no, if I were a noble, I wouldn't travel on foot."

"Ah, true . . . Too bad neither of us are noble," she said cheerfully.

Lansius felt something was off about her: She was too casual with a man she had just met. He also noticed that she looked upper class from her attire, not like someone from the villages. Even her straw hat was painted white.

*Not a noble, so a bastard? And why is she so friendly? She saw the hair too . . .*

Lansius felt uneasy about her friendliness. "Umm, are you sure you want to walk beside me?" he asked.

"What do you mean?" she replied, holding her straw hat as the wind blew past them.

"I mean, I'm a vagrant. If you need someone to watch over you, I can follow you from behind."

She giggled. "The heat has gotten to you. Come on, let's not stay under the midday sun any longer." She wandered off the road, and Lansius had no choice but to follow her.

The two of them walked through the grassy area and into a nearby cluster of trees, finding a small grove with several old, withering trees. She sat under the largest one, which unfortunately had only half its branches full of leaves. The sparse shade they provided left Lansius with no good place to sit away from the sun.

"Come sit beside me," she said, tapping the grassy ground beside her.

Normally, he would shy away from the offer, but the midday sun was relentless, so he gladly accepted. They sat side by side, resting their backs against the old tree.

Without any hesitation, she unlatched her shoulder bag and pulled out a wrapped item. Unwrapping the linen, she revealed a slice of meat pie. She broke it in half and offered a portion to Lansius.

"You don't have to," he said.

She insisted, so he reluctantly took the pie and gave it a bite.

*Mamma mia, this is fantastic!*

Lansius hid his reaction to avoid being ridiculed. He then took out the bread he'd bought that morning, broke it in half, and offered it to her.

She smiled but shook her head.

"It's just plain bread, think nothing of it," he insisted.

She accepted the rye bread. "Oh, silly me. We haven't introduced ourselves. My name is Felicity. I'm . . . nobody's daughter." She chuckled at her own jest.

"I'm Lansius, also nobody's son," he responded with a chuckle.

"Call me Felis. Everybody does that."

"So, Felis, why are you heading to Feodosia?" he asked.

"I work there. Well, it's more like I live there now. But occasionally, I still need to go home to check on my parents."

"I see . . ." Lansius wanted to ask about the slave market but hesitated. It wasn't a topic he wanted to discuss with a newfound friend.

The sun was at its zenith, and there was nothing the two could do but stay under the shade and rest.

As they rested, Lansius noticed that Felis was his complete opposite. She wasn't shy or timid and trusted others easily. Earlier, she had said she wanted some rest, folded her cloak like a sleeping rug, and just like that, she fell asleep.

*I did help her a little, but still . . .*

There was no one around but the two of them as far as the eye could see.

*How can a girl be so careless like this? Even I, given the chance, could turn into a . . .*

As if teasing him, Felis opened her mouth slightly, revealing her alluring lips, which disrupted his train of thought.

Lansius gulped. The sight of a young woman sleeping so close was a huge temptation. He noticed her chest rising and falling with each breath. He averted his gaze and let out a sigh. Somehow, the sight made him think of Stefi.

He shook his head, trying to erase the sudden gloom, but the guilt had resurfaced. He felt terrible sitting so casually beside a pretty blonde while Stefi might be enslaved or dead. The occasional breeze offered some comfort, but Lansius could only look downcast.

As the midday sun finally waned, the travelers continued on their journey. Felis had awakened, and together with Lansius, they marched eastward. After three hours of walking under the sun, they arrived in the village of Pozna.

"Pozna, I'm back again," Felis said bitterly. She had been here earlier that morning before the cart fiasco.

"Well, what's your plan now?" Lansius asked, glancing around the new village.

"I'm going to report that guy first." Felis stormed toward the stable master.

The old man was grumpy because of the heat, and he grew even more irritable when he heard Felis's story. "It's crazy that this happens so often these days."

"What would have happened if I had been kidnapped?" Felis asked boldly.

"Well . . . they'd have taken you somewhere remote in the next province and assigned you some work. They wouldn't let you return unless you paid them an exorbitant sum for transport, food, and lodging."

Felis remained unfazed, while Lansius felt disgusted.

*It's not slavery, but it's still very much evil.*

Felis provided the coachman's description so the stable master could warn other travelers. She left the place with a satisfied expression.

"I'm guessing we'll stay the night here?" Lansius asked.

"Yup. As much as I want to return to Feodosia, there's still half a day's walk ahead."

Unfamiliar with the area, Lansius chose to follow Felis's suggestion. However, she showed no sign of stopping in Pozna. "We're not staying in Pozna?" he asked as they passed the village limit.

"Oh, there's a nearby inn I'm used to staying at. If I'm lucky, maybe I can still use my room from last night." Felis led him toward a large intersection. There on one side stood a two-story building with white plaster, glass windows, and several chimneys. It had an adjacent stable where a carriage and at least two carts were parked.

She entered through the front entrance and effortlessly pushed the mahogany door open. The clean hallway and high ceiling gave the place a classy appearance.

*This is so different from the cheap ones . . . I bet they have separate rooms, not a shared floor for everybody.*

At this point, Lansius didn't dare to tell Felis that he used to sleep in the corner of a barn or on people's porches if he had to.

"Back again so soon, mademoiselle?" a man with a rounded belly, vibrant colored clothing, and a work apron asked Felis from behind the counter.

"Yes, there were some circumstances. My previous room, please, and another one for my friend," she said to the innkeeper, pulling a silver coin from her purse.

Before Felis handed over the coin, Lansius whispered, "Umm, you know, I can sleep in a servant's quarters or a warehouse corner. Don't spend your hard-earned money on me."

"Don't worry about it. Take it as a thank you for helping me out. Besides, I enjoyed your company." Felis smiled.

Hearing praise like that, Lansius couldn't help but smile.

The innkeeper smiled warmly as he received the silver and produced eight copper as change. "Supper is included."

A teenage boy led them to their rooms. Lansius's small room was furnished with a bed, a window, and a small desk. Compared to Lansius's usual spartan arrangements, it was luxurious.

*It's also clean . . .*

Lansius felt the urge to clean himself. As expected, he found a water basin on the table and a bucket in the corner. He washed his face first, then his hands. Next, he changed his clothes so as not to look out of place in the establishment.

His doublet wasn't too dirty, but the tunic underneath was yellowing from sweat. Thus, he pulled his only spare tunic from his hemp sack and put it on.

The clean linen felt good on his skin. The tunic had stitches in several places from when he had ventured deep into the woods. He almost reminisced but pushed the thought away.

Now clean and proper, he sat on the bed and found it comfortable. He leaned back and found bliss. He knew he should wash his clothes. There should be a well near the inn, but after two weeks of rough sleeping, the bed was irresistible.

*Maybe I could take a short nap.*

Felis eventually knocked on the door after half an hour, and they went downstairs for an early supper. Lansius didn't dare to leave his belongings in the room, so he brought everything.

They chose a corner table with an open window. Nobody offered them a menu. It wasn't necessary. The inn would serve their guests a plate of whatever they cooked that day. Anything more, like ale or wine, would cost extra.

"This inn is famous for its roast meat," Felis said.

Lansius's nose agreed. The aroma was rich and savory. "The meat pie we had this afternoon was also good."

"You liked it? I got the pie from here too. Two slices for a copper."

"Reasonable price. It's delicious." Even as thrifty as he was, he had to admit it was a good deal.

A servant boy brought two cups, a pitcher of water, and a smaller pitcher of ale.

Felis filled their cups with ale. "Let's toast to a good meeting."

"Cheers." The two raised their cups and drank. The ale tasted fruity and malty, with a hint of bitterness.

*Oof, this is stronger than what I usually get.*

"Ah, need to dilute this, otherwise I'll be tipsy in no time." She giggled.

The cool breeze, the inn's well-maintained wooden furniture, and Felicity, who looked like a goddess, made this supper an exceptionally pleasant experience for Lansius.

Outside, the sun had lost its luster, but sundown was still a good one or two hours away.

More people were coming to the inn, and the dining hall was halfway filled. From the look, Lansius guessed the customers were tradespeople, local yeomen, and maybe even a member or two of the lower nobility.

Three more people entered the premise. Two looked like guardsmen, in bright brigandine, while the third was much older, in a fancy, colorful doublet. Lansius thought nothing of them. For travelers, guardsmen equaled safety and protection against bandits.

However, the man in fancy clothing saw Lansius and stood in silence as if struck by something.

It was odd enough that Lansius caught the act out of the corner of his eye. Lansius glanced at him, but dared not to see his face for too long. He didn't recognize the clean shaven and neatly combed man.

*Probably just gawking at Felis.*

He calmly asked Felis about the man, but she shook her head.

The man stormed toward Lansius. "It's you!"

"Y-yes?" Surprised, Lansius replied warily. He never caused a problem in Midlandia, so he quickly assumed this was some trickery or scheme.

"Oi, what's the fuss?" One of the young guards, who was built like a bear, approached.

"Anci, this is the guy. We found him," the man said to the guard, who looked at Lansius with ferocious eyes.

Lansius could see the smirk and sadistic eyes radiating from the big fella toward him.

*Oh, shit, what did I do wrong?*

His brain went into high gear and recalled an entrapment like this. The group he had been with taught him that the best way out was to challenge them to reveal his name. If they couldn't name him correctly, then he could rally the other guests to intervene.

Before Lansius could open his mouth, Felis said innocently, "Is there a problem with my friend Lansius?"

Lansius was sweating bullets. Felis, unknowingly, had thrown him under the cart.

# CHAPTER 16

# BINDING CHAINS

The sun was halfway to the west, and the weather had turned pleasant. More travelers showed up in cheap inns around Pozna after a day's journey. But the better part of the society headed straight to the crossroads where a well-known inn, the Swan, was located.

While most inns offered a communal hall to sleep, the Swan offered cleanliness, separate rooms, and lavish meals. Right now, the atmosphere in the hall was perfect to wind down, with comfortable chairs, excellent ales, and cool, airy halls, made possible by the inn's high ceiling and multitudes of windows.

Whiffs of rich aroma from the grill complemented the scene, but for Lansius, it just turned into a dilemma. One old man in fancy clothes and his guard had flanked him for reason unknown. He had nowhere to hide, and Felis, unknowingly, had given his identity.

"God-damnit, it's really you, Lansius," the old man said, getting chummy with him.

Lansius felt cornered. He was sure this was some sort of trickery.

"My lady, please excuse us," Anci, the tall and muscular guard, said. Despite looking like a musclehead, he seemed educated.

*Can I talk myself out of this?*

Before Lansius could try anything, the old man kept arguing. "Lans, it's me. How could you not recognize me?"

"Apology, but I don't know you," Lansius answered, as polite as he could.

The old man chuckled. "It's me, dammit. It's Thomas."

The name struck Lansius. He did a double-take, but the clean shaved and neatly combed person looked so different. Only now he noticed the similarity. His jaw dropped, and his eyes widened unconsciously.

Thomas laughed, watching Lansius's reaction, and slapped the man's back.

"Ouch, what'd you do that for?" Lansius winced, but couldn't resist grinning. He was relieved to see Thomas and also gladdened that nobody actually tried to con him.

Felis and Anci chuckled softly.

Thomas straightened up and adopted a more formal demeanor, turning toward Felis. "Please forgive our behavior, my lady."

Felis shook her head gently. "No need to apologize. I'm not of noble birth. I'm sorry if I gave you that impression." She bowed her head respectfully.

The second guard overheard the discussion as he approached. "Mademoiselle, your blond hair and blue eyes would make a high noble-born envious."

Felis smiled at the flattery. "Please, call me Felis."

Anci elbowed the second guard, who gasped in pain before returning the favor with a good punch to the guts.

Thomas shook his head as the twenty-something lads traded friendly jabs at each other. "Guys, knock it off."

They quickly stopped and allowed Thomas to ask Felis, "Mademoiselle and Lans, would you care to join my table for a chat?"

Lansius shot a questioning glance at Felis. She nodded, and the two followed Thomas to a bigger table.

"I better introduce ourselves. I'm Thomas, and this is Anci, and Hugo. They are Sir Peter's squires." And then to the squires. "Boys, this is Lansius, the clerk whom I befriended in Riverstead."

Despite the lack of introduction, Anci bowed his head to Felis first, before giving a weird grin to Lansius and offering his hand. They clasped hands, and Lansius found his grip to be firm and strong.

Hugo, the lean-looking squire, followed afterward. "Nice to see another Arvenian."

As they sat together, Lansius asked, "Thomas, how did you get here? Isn't Arvena occupied?"

"We went the long way round through Tiberia and Elandia," Thomas explained. "So, what happened to you in the river crossing?"

The topic turned heavy. Despite not being prepared for it, Lansius told them everything, including what happened to Theo and Max.

As his brief story came to an end, Felis patted Lansius's arm to console him.

In a span of a story, Thomas looked older with wrinkles and eyes that lost their luster. He exhaled deeply and said to Lansius, "Don't blame yourself."

"It's clear that the margrave intended to massacre the entire House of Arvena. They even murder kids based on some rumors." Hugo didn't mince words.

"If only the High Court wasn't so spineless," Anci grumbled.

"Is it true that the young lord is missing?" Lansius asked. He had heard gossip about it on the road.

Thomas reluctantly nodded. A servant boy interrupted their discussion as he brought them a pudding, which to Lansius looked like a tart cake.

Without anyone's objection, Anci took a slice, followed by the others. Lansius only took a small portion, fearing it may contain milk. Meanwhile, Felis took a big chunk and ate merrily by hand.

*Erm . . . Well, who am I to judge?*

The sweet treat changed the mood for the better. Everybody seemed pleased and ate happily.

Thomas cleaned his knife and sheathed it again. "You're lucky to make it this far safely. The road and the cities aren't as safe as Arvena."

Lansius nodded. "Indeed. Just today, we had brush with a kidnapping."

That didn't seem to surprise anyone. "Midlandia may look prosperous, but many turned poor from the growing industries. It's good that you got yourself a sword," Thomas remarked.

"I felt safer with it around, but I haven't train—" He abruptly stopped. "Thomas, have you seen Stefi?" he blurted out.

Thomas shook his head. "Sorry, lad. We've found a few remnants and survivors, but . . ."

Felis patted Lansius's arm again, her grubby finger accidentally smearing a bit of pudding on his clean blue tunic.

Despite the stain on his only clean clothes, Lansius appreciated her good intention.

"Boss, there's still some light outside." Hugo carried a serious tone.

Thomas nodded. "Mademoiselle, may we ask Lansius out for a bit for a chat?"

The pudding was gone, but they had yet to finish their supper, as roasting meat in the fire pit was a lengthy process. Lansius felt something was off, but he trusted Thomas.

Felis cleaned her hands on the yellowing tablecloth and declared, "I'm coming too."

The five of them went into a small wooded area. Anci stood guard at a distance against eavesdropping. Felis seemed to read the situation and stuck with Anci.

Hugo went farther, but he too gave a wide berth for Thomas and Lansius.

"It's far enough." Thomas stopped and turned himself to face Lansius. "Lad, you got something from Miranda."

Lansius's heart raced. He knew this would happen. "Can I say a few words beforehand?"

Thomas looked at him sharply. "Speak up."

"I'm going to use it to free Stefi if the slavers got her. If I can't find her, then I'll return everything."

"No, no . . ." Thomas shook his head in disbelief. "You were entrusted with it. It's not yours to use."

Thomas's flat out rejection surprised him. "Give me a chance. I'll pay it back. I carried it this long. You can't just appear and grab it away."

"Lans, it wasn't given to you." Thomas refused to listen.

"I almost lost my life in that forest. It was me who saved this money, so whoever owns it, they owe me that much. I didn't go this far for nothing," Lansius exclaimed, unintentionally raising his voice. He knew there wasn't much logic to his argument, but he was at his wit's end.

The outburst forced Thomas to gesture Lansius to quiet down. "Are you out of your mind? Those guys are Sir Peter's!"

"What's this got to do with Sir Peter?"

Thomas exhaled. "Sir Peter is Sir Ian's son."

Lansius took a step back. Only now he realized how Thomas had got his fancy clothing and two squires. "Are you here to help the escaping Arvenians or to hunt me down?"

"It's not like that . . ." Thomas knitted his brows. "Sir Peter is making a war band, and it needs money."

Lansius became conflicted, but said stubbornly, "I can't go to Feodosia empty-handed."

"Lans, the squires will cut you down if you run with the money," Thomas warned.

Lansius exhaled sharply and glanced around. The wooded area was sparse and had the markings of men: pathways, cut-down trees, and no old branches on the ground. He hated the forest, but he knew this was far from that ancient forest. He could survive here easily.

"Don't do it." Thomas read him easily. "You may outrun me, but not the squires."

Lansius hesitated, and Thomas said nothing, giving Lansius time to rethink.

"Help me," Lansius pleaded. "There must be another way . . ."

Thomas sighed as if giving up. "Even if I let you—even if I help you. The two of us can't take them. Maybe I could stall Hugo, but not Anci. That lad is a monster."

Lansius's shoulder slumped. Since the first time he saw Anci, his instinct had screamed not to mess with him.

"Look, I understand your cause and I don't want to lose you like I lost Theo and Max. But there's no other way." Thomas's voice was tired and sore.

The mention of the two jolted Lansius, making him pause. Yet, the thought that he might find Stefi and Jan but be unable to free them tormented him. He couldn't think of another way. His friend's safety depended on the money he had hid. His muscles tensed, but his mind didn't know what to do.

Then he realized just how good Thomas's clothing really was and found a slim opening. "The prize. Miranda mentioned a prize. You got that nice clothing and certainly more. What would I get?"

Thomas was taken aback. He went into thinking and exclaimed afterward, "Fine, take the silver."

Lansius wasn't going to give up. "It's only sixteen silver. I can't free a slave with just that?"

"Ah, fuck it, Lans. I'm not some charity." Despite Thomas's harsh words, he reached out for his inner pocket, pulled a money pouch, and fished some coins. He grabbed some and gave it away.

Lansius counted seven silvers. "Much obliged." He knew it was far from enough, but that was probably the best Thomas could do.

"Ready the gold. I'm calling Hugo."

"Wait—" Lansius scrambled to open the sewn gold coins in his doublet, blanket, and inner part of the bag.

Thomas watched, his face showing surprise at Lansius's ingenuity.

"Here." Lansius showed six gold coins. The amount could buy two cottages, or a well-built two-story house in a friendly neighborhood.

Thomas didn't take it, but whistled to signal for Hugo.

The laid-back squire, in a light blue brigandine, approached them. He saw what was on Lansius's hands and received it politely. "On behalf of Sir Peter, I offer you his gratitude."

The problem seemed to be resolved for Hugo and Thomas, but Lansius still had one concern.

"Umm, can I get a receipt?" he asked.

Hugo and Thomas were dumbfounded by the request, and Thomas couldn't help but be amused. "Well, he's a clerk. What can I say?"

Hugo and Thomas laughed, and Lansius chuckled along.

Hugo offered his right hand to Lansius. "If my signature is good enough, you shall have it."

Lansius gladly clasped hands with Hugo.


The sun turned orange when Lansius, Thomas, and Hugo headed out.

"So, tell me about the war band?" Lansius asked.

Hugo bent a low-hanging branch so they could pass easily. "Not much to tell. We got less than a hundred, but mostly too young and without weapons."

"I see . . ." Lansius paused for a bit. "Well, call me crazy, but have you ever considered rescuing slaves?"

"Rescue?" Thomas scoffed. "That's ballsy, but foolish."

Watching Lansius's reaction, Hugo filled him in. "The Lord of Midlandia tolerates our presence, but he'll kick us out if we try something funny with the slave trade."

Lansius reluctantly nodded. He had heard rumors that the Imperium sanctioned the slave trade to appease the two Eastern Kingdoms that grew powerful, but only now did he have an indirect proof.

*So, not even the Lord of Midlandia dares to go against the slave trade.*

"The local lords are especially jittery about the presence of armed men in their regions," Thomas commented about themselves.

"But I heard that Midlandia is on our side. Can't they intervene at all?"

Hugo glanced at Lansius. "Only if it benefits them. This means we need the young lord. As the rightful heir, he could claim Arvena. If we have him, then Midlandia will gladly assist in exchange for a hefty compensation."

"More likely a debt so large that Arvena could never repay," Thomas sneered.

"Aye," Hugo agreed. "This is why we can't rely on Midlandia too much. With the Imperium like this, certainly Midlandia wants to carve out pieces of Arvena for themselves too."

"And us as the henchmen." Thomas swatted an insect that flew too close to his face.

Lansius tasted the hopelessness, but pushed forward. "Umm, if we found the young lord, would he do something about the Arvenian slaves?"

Hugo spared him some hope. "Well, those are his subjects. I think he'll try to free them one way or another."

Lansius noted the subtle change in Hugo's voice but nodded at the false hope.

They trekked the short distance toward the edge of the wooded area and met with Anci and Felis.

"So, what are you guys talking about?" she asked.

Hugo looked at Lansius. Felis was an outsider.

Lansius nodded, but had another thought. "She's from here. Maybe she could help."

"Help with what?" Felis was intrigued.

Hugo mulled, but Anci nodded at him.

"Well, why not," Hugo said. "We're looking for a noble from Arvena. You might've heard about him, young Lord Arte. Light brown—"

"Light brown hair, beautiful jawline, charming, and speaks candidly like a bard? And oh, also a scar on his left eyebrow?" Felis sent rapid questions at Hugo.

The men stopped with eyes opened wide. "Y-you saw him?" Hugo nervously asked.

# CHAPTER 17

# NORTHERN HILLS

Lansius and the three squires could hardly believe what they had just heard. Felicity had perfectly described Lord Arte's features: light brown hair, a charming demeanor, a beautiful jawline, and a small scar on his left eyebrow. This could only mean that Felis had met Lord Arte.

"Where did you see him?" Hugo inquired cautiously.

Felis's excitement grew. "I knew it! He's not just some wandering minstrel. He has a different aura about him."

"Was he alone?" Anci interjected impatiently.

"He was when I met him. He introduced himself as Archie, perhaps a disguised name," Felis replied.

"And where and when did this happen?" asked Hugo.

"Pozna, just yesterday," Felis replied with a smile.

The expressions on Thomas, Hugo, and Anci were a mixture of disbelief and relief. They had searched fruitlessly for weeks, even venturing to Feodosia in the slim hope that Lord Arte might have been captured and sold as a slave without being recognized. Now, it seemed that luck was on their side.

"Did you talk to this Archie?" Thomas probed.

"Only by chance. We met at the stable while waiting for our carriages. He introduced himself and made a humorous remark when I asked him a question."

"Funny?" Thomas furrowed his brow.

"He said he was going to whore himself out to save his friend," Felis giggled.

Her response left Hugo and Thomas dumbfounded. They now had more questions than answers.

"Where is he heading?" Lansius asked at last.

"North," Felis replied with certainty, then added, "I don't know if you'll believe me, but I fear your friend intentionally headed there to meet with the slavers."

"Slavers? Aren't they supposedly in Feodosia?" asked Lansius, his brow furrowing.

"Those are the Imperium-approved ones, Lans. There's also the illegal kind, you know?"

"Illegal slavers?" asked Lansius again.

Felis nodded unenthusiastically. "Unfortunately, there are people who trade slaves within the Imperium."

Lansius recalled the rumors he had heard on the road. There had indeed been several mentions of it.

Noticing Lansius's puzzled expression, Felis elaborated. "It's an open secret that despite the law, many powerful men keep slaves to work on their vast, secluded estates."

Hugo and Thomas exchanged thoughtful glances. The news did not sit well with them. A group audacious enough to operate against the Imperium's law would likely be powerful and have ties with the local strongmen. However, their loyalty demanded they attempt to rescue their lord.

Despite their silence, the squires were already considering how many men they could gather before storming the location. They were trained for violence; it was their primary instinct. The idea of trying to negotiate their lord's release or attempting to purchase his freedom crossed their minds, but their lack of funds, as well as their pride and honor, prevented them from uttering such thoughts.

Lansius observed them; he had a different idea. While Lord Arte was his master, he didn't know him well on a personal level. More significantly, he had other priorities at the moment.

Anci broke the silence. "I'll head north and scout around. There should be only one road, so we can easily find each other. You can gather men and follow when you're ready."

Thomas agreed. "A few simple markings should be easy to spot."

Hugo nodded. "All right then, Thomas and I will head west to gather our men. You and the clerk should go north."

Lansius was taken aback and protested. "I beg your pardon, but I must go to Feodosia."

His response elicited stares from Hugo and Thomas, with only Anci remaining indifferent.

Lansius hurried to explain. "I cannot fight; I am dead weight. You have my purse, so let's part ways here. I need to find my friend in Feodosia before she's sold to someone else."

Thomas looked away. He knew Stefi and understood Lansius's motivations.

Anci snorted, seemingly amused by the turn of events. "There's no need for him to come along. I can handle it myself."

Hugo sighed, understandably offended that a retainer wouldn't prioritize his master's safety. "Let's return to the inn. We'll depart at first light tomorrow."

Before they could move, a lady in a pale blue gown chimed in. "Do you need fighters?"

The group looked at her quizzically.

"You're not suggesting yourself, are you?" Hugo asked.

"Well, I'm part of the package," Felis said casually, then added, "I know capable fighters in Feodosia. Men-at-arms looking for contracts."

This was welcome news for Hugo, who would take any offer in their current situation. "I need brave stout men, not kids or old men in armor."

"Of course, I'm talking about duelists, watchmen, and thief-takers," replied Felis.

Hugo nodded. "How many can you find and at what cost?"

Felis smiled brightly. "Well, I might be able to gather nine or ten if I can reach them all, but probably less if you need them quickly. As for the price, let's discuss that later at the inn." She paused and glanced at Lansius briefly. "We'll need to borrow paper and ink, and then Lansius can handle the paperwork for us."

"Why me?" Lansius was taken aback by the sudden mention of his name.

Felis gave Lansius a smug look. "I want this contract in writing, and I'd like to secure downpayments as well."

Hugo glanced at Thomas, who shrugged. "All right, let's do it your way," Hugo conceded. With the arrangements settled, they made their way back to the Swan.

Despite their dire circumstances, the squires found solace in the feast before them. Their table was strewn with empty dishes and empty earthen jugs. Even Hugo seemed to be enjoying himself. The unspoken consensus among them was that they might die in a few days, so they ought to savor life while they could.

The squires knew little about their adversaries, but rumors circulated that the illegal slavers were influential and powerful, with enough sway to undermine the Imperium's authority. Engaging them in battle would likely be suicidal, which perhaps explained the group's merry demeanor.

Beneath the soft glow of tallow candles, a wandering minstrel played his stringed instrument. The crowd requested a lively, humorous melody to lift their spirits. Meanwhile, the servers bustled about, providing more ale and food, their work clothes stained from a long day's labor.

Thomas had passed out, his head resting on the table. The old man seemed to carry a heavy guilt that he kept to himself, unwilling to share.

The atmosphere grew rowdier when five women entered the inn. Most of the guests became boisterous at the sight of them, with some making bold advances. Hugo was among those flirting, focusing his attention on a woman in a dark green and white gown, her full lips and long, wavy hair capturing his interest.

Lansius, however, felt hollow and disconnected. His guilt prevented him from enjoying the festivities, even in the presence of the beautiful blonde, Felis, who sat beside him. It didn't help that his evenings were usually quiet, wary about who might be sharing the communal sleeping space.

Noticing his gaze, Felis smiled. "Pozna wenches. They're shy compared to the ones from Feodosia," she commented.

Lansius simply nodded.

Felis leaned in closer. "Don't you want to join in? I could help you pick a good one."

Lansius knew she wasn't teasing but politely declined. "Maybe next time."

Felis giggled and took a sip of her ale. She had to raise her voice to be heard over the clamor and music as she turned to Anci, who sat at the next table, and tapped his back gently.

Anci craned his neck and gave her a questioning look.

"Come, let's head outside. I need to talk to you about something," Felis said.

Anci furrowed his brow. "About what?"

"About things that'll involve you too," she replied cryptically.

After a moment of contemplation, Anci stood. As he did so, Felis gestured for Lansius to follow. They stepped outside, not far from the entrance where two large lanterns cast a warm glow. Another lantern swayed gently near the wooden fence by the road, replacing the sounds of music with the chirping of crickets.

"What do you want to talk about?" Anci asked, guarded, while Lansius remained silent.

"Well, I want you to talk some sense into your friend here," she began.

The two men were intrigued. "What do you mean?" Lansius asked.

"Well, you're looking for your friend, right? A female fighter," asked Felis.

"A female squire, yes. Why?"

"Lans, I doubt she'll make it to Feodosia," Felis said bluntly.

Lansius felt alarmed.

She continued. "I've never seen female fighters in Feodosia. They're popular and in high demand as guards for harems in the Eastern Kingdoms or as bodyguards."

Lansius's suspicion arose. "Isn't that a contradiction?"

"No, listen," she insisted. "Female fighters are in demand, but we never see them in Feodosia. From what I've heard, someone always recruits them first—and it's not traders from Feodosia."

Lansius and Anci exchanged glances.

"Who is this someone?" Anci asked.

"It would be a lie if I said I knew for certain, but it's most likely the same group you're going up against. Between here and Arvena, I doubt there are two groups operating so close together."

Lansius drew a deep breath. "You want me to go north?"

Felis nodded. "You might not trust me, but that's my suggestion. You'll have a better chance of finding her there than in Feodosia."

Lansius hesitated before a large, rough hand patted his shoulder.

"The way I see it, if your friend's not there, then she'll be in Feodosia. However, if she's there, then you won't see her in Feodosia," Anci said, flashing his predatory grin. "Looks like you're coming with me, clerk."

"Felis, are you absolutely certain?" Lansius asked, urgency coloring his tone.

"Without a doubt," she responded with conviction. "I may not look the part, but I'm well-acquainted."

Lansius sighed in resignation and later whispered, "But don't you need company to Feodosia? Hugo just gave you a downpayment, remember?"

Unfazed by the extra silvers in her purse, Felis giggled. "I'll persuade Thomas to accompany me. It shouldn't be too difficult; after all, I could easily disappear with all your coins," she teased.

Her voice took on a serious tone as she noticed Lansius's reaction. "Even if you go to Feodosia with me, you'll need a proper introduction and then wait for days before receiving a formal invitation from the slavers. It's not as if you can just have a look around . . . So, what will you do? Will you wait in Feodosia, and risk missing her, or will you take a quick detour to ensure that doesn't happen?"

Anci stifled his laugh while Lansius gazed at the night sky, uncertain about the consequences his decision would bring. His head was still processing just how many things had happened in this single day. There were so many chance meetings and lucky coincidences that astounded him.

*It's as if someone, or something, is pulling the strings . . .*

The following morning, as the first light broke, the Arvenians, one Midlandian, and a foreigner gathered. As agreed upon the night before, Thomas would accompany Felis to Feodosia, so they parted ways at the inn.

As Thomas's horse-drawn cart headed east, Hugo, Anci, and Lansius set off west toward Pozna. Upon arrival, they quickly marched to the stable, where Hugo paid a deposit to rent a horse.

"Take care. I'll meet you in two days," Hugo said after testing the horse just outside the stable.

"You know my patience. Don't take too long," Anci half-threatened.

Hugo laughed heartily. Despite his eyes still being reddened from the previous night, he exuded confidence.

Anci approached the horse and gave it a firm pat, urging Hugo to leave. He set off at a brisk pace, racing west to gather fellow Arvenians.

After Hugo's departure, Lansius followed Anci on foot as they set off to the north.

And so, the trio separated, and their plan was set into motion.


The hill range separating Midlandia and Rhomelia was teeming with birds flying freely. Despite being in the middle of summer, the land remained lush and green, dotted with ponds and marshes in the lowlands.

Lansius and Anci had traveled on foot for a day to reach this hill, where they spotted a suspicious manor surrounded by a palisade wall on the adjacent hill. They spent the remaining daylight constructing a crude tent. Neither was skilled in craftsmanship, so the shelter was poorly built.

After a fireless supper, Anci took the first watch. Nothing happened during his watch, so he woke Lansius, and they took turns watching like this until dawn. The night was quiet, too quiet for Lansius's taste.

At dawn, as the wind blew, and the fog dissipated, Lansius could see the walled manor house perched on the hill, surrounded by farms and cottages. Even at a glance, he could tell that it was fortified. Aside from the palisade wall, it had guards and even an outer gate.

With spare time on his hands, Lansius drew a map on the ground using sticks and pebbles, depicting the manor's defenses.

*It looks like a mini fortress . . . walls on each side, fences, patrols, and checkpoints.*

Attacking such a place would be suicidal. But knowing the Arvenians, Lansius felt they would most likely attempt it anyway. He sighed, pondering the possible outcomes.

# CHAPTER 18

# COLD STEEL

The sun rose, and the day grew warmer. Anci stirred from his slumber, roused by the sounds of birds and rustling leaves. Their crude makeshift tent was far from ideal, but it had served its purpose for the night.

"Can't believe we traded the inn for this place," Anci complained as he munched on yesterday's bread.

Lansius sighed, thinking of the inn's comfortable bed. "At least we had the roasted meat," he said.

"Oh, that finely seasoned and juicy meat," Anci said.

"So tender," Lansius commented, and they shared a laugh.

"So, what's your story with that blonde?" Anci asked, changing the subject.

Still groggy from his night watch, Lansius paused. "Felis? We barely know each other. Why do you ask?"

Anci stroked his chin. "Well, she's not an ordinary girl, you know."

"What do you mean by that?"

"Mm . . . should I tell you, or should I not?" Anci teased.

"Forget it. I can always ask her myself."

Lansius's defiance made Anci laugh. Despite their differences, the two bonded easily. Anci, born Archibald, came from a family with a history of serving as squires. He told Lansius his grandfather had been a knight, but his father never earned the title. Anci himself barely made it as Sir Peter's squire due to his imposing physique.

The sun continued to climb, but nobody entered or exited the manor. Nevertheless, the two continued their scouting mission. The area was remote, with only a handful of hamlets within a day's journey, so the road was practically empty, with only the occasional birds flying and circling around.

Lansius fell asleep after breakfast while Anci kept watch for any signs of danger.

* * *

"Oi, oi . . ." called Anci.

Lansius wearily opened his eyes and crouched beside Anci. "What did you find?"

"A carriage." Anci gestured in its direction.

Lansius looked toward the lone incoming carriage.

"Well?" Anci asked impatiently.

"Well, what? I don't think that's our reinforcement."

Lansius had expected tens of men and several warhorses, especially considering the six gold coins he had given.

"Oh, that's one of the slavers, all right." Anci grinned wickedly.

Lansius squinted, trying to follow Anci's train of thought. Meanwhile, Anci withdrew deeper inside their shelter and retrieved his broadsword.

"What are you going to do with that?

"Information gathering." Anci laughed and strolled out in a relaxed manner.

"By the ageless." Lansius scrambled to tie his sword to his belt, grabbed his bag, and hurriedly followed Anci. When he found him, Anci was already standing in the middle of the road, blocking the carriage. Though not particularly tall or big, he was muscular and as intimidating as a bear.

The two horse-drawn carriages stopped as they saw Anci blocking the road. The coachman looked at Anci wearily, and shouted, "What do you want?"

"Just some questions," Anci said while shouldering his broadsword.

"Go on," the coachman replied.

"Do you know anything about *slave trade*?"

Anci received no further answer. Three men descended from the carriage, weapons in hand. The burliest of them, clad in ring mail, led the assault.

"My, my, so impatient," Anci jeered at them.

Anci stood defenseless as one of his attackers lunged at him. At the last possible moment, he executed a slash so swift it was almost invisible. The resulting clang echoed loudly through the air. The assailant's grip wavered, and he only just managed to regain his balance when Anci launched into another swing with effortless precision.

The man attempted to parry, but he misjudged Anci's speed. His blade failed to meet Anci's, which landed with a faint metallic echo, followed by a dull thud. Anci's broadsword had broken through the burly man's upper arm bone and didn't stop until it had cracked several ribs. Only a few rings of the man's armor were damaged, but the impact sent him to the ground, gasping for breath.

The remaining two men were both terrified and enraged. They launched their attack in unison.

Anci managed to parry the attack from the slimmer assailant, but he intentionally engaged in a blade-lock with the larger man's sword. Utilizing his strength, Anci wrestled and positioned the larger man in such a way that his back obstructed the slimmer man's advance.

The larger man, confident in his superior strength, attempted to force Anci's sword in his direction. Instead of further contesting the brute force, Anci cleverly redirected the man's sword downward while delivering a swift knee kick to his groin. The move was executed so rapidly that the man could only gasp in surprise before his eyes rolled back, overcome by the sudden shock.

Without waiting for his final ally to crumple, the slimmer man launched a desperate attack. Anci blocked the thrust with a solid parry and deflected it aside. The man, seemingly blinded by desperation, attempted another strike. However, his stance was sloppy, his movements ill-coordinated. Anci's heavier sword swung faster, its blade slicing through the man's gambeson and burying itself into his right shoulder.

"I yield! I yield!" the slim man shrieked as he knelt with his right arm dangling. A deep gash and blood soaked his layered fabric armor and tunic.

Lansius was Anci's backup, but he only stood in awe. He was glad that Anci was on his side.

Anci heard his opponent's plea and snorted. "That's why you should introduce yourself, so I'll know whether to keep you for ransom or to end you."

"Money, I have money, take it." He scrambled for his money pouch with his left hand. "J-just let me live—"

A horse's neigh alerted them.

"That can wait," Anci said and then to Lansius he said, "Keep them down. I'll be back soon." He casually ran after the speeding carriage.

Lansius, with a drawn sword, watched over the man who sat on the ground whimpering from his injury. Lansius pitied the man. "Cut some of your cloth and press it on the wound. That'll stop the bleeding. Otherwise, you'll be going cold soon."

The thin man nodded in fear and tore some of his cloth to dress the wound.

Meanwhile, Anci chased after the slowing carriage as it ascended the hill. He climbed from the back, and soon enough, the coachman flew overboard and tumbled onto the dirt road like a sack of wheat. He groaned loudly from his injuries, but Anci wasn't feeling generous. He turned the carriage around and pursued the man until they came to a stop near Lansius.

The coachman collapsed to the ground with battered breath and bruises covering his body, pleading for mercy. "Please, forgive me. Do no more harm. No more," he rambled.

"I know you," Lansius said to the coachman, then turned to Anci. "He's the one who tried to kidnap Felicity."

"Please, have mercy. I won't do it again," the coachman begged.

"Oh, I'll give you my mercy," Anci declared as he jumped down from the carriage and held out a bloodied surcoat for Lansius to see.

Lansius recognized the heraldry of a river and a small castle. "Riverstead," he exclaimed.

The coachman trembled with fear as he realized he was dealing with Arvenians.

"Lans, you better climb up. There are kids and women."

Lansius hurried toward the crude-looking carriage and climbed up. Inside, he discovered scattered baskets of clothing, along with three frightened women hugging two children. He didn't recognize any of their faces, but it did not matter. "Don't be afraid. We'll get you out of here."

After midday, Anci and Lansius, with some help from the women and children, had pulled the carriage to the side and hidden it from sight. All of the captured men, fainted or not, were tied up. The burly man might not make it, but there was nothing they could do but turn him on his side so he wouldn't drown in his own blood.

Just as they finished, the promised reinforcements arrived. Hugo led thirty men, most of whom were in their teens. They also had three warhorses and four additional horse-drawn carts.

Lansius informed them about what had happened, and they went to meet the coachman. The man confessed that he was a smuggler, who dealt with everything from contraband to slaves. Today, he was sending a fresh batch of slaves from Arvena.

Realizing his safety depended on cooperation, the coachman-smuggler glossed over his role in acquiring slaves from Arvena, focusing instead on details about the manor complex. "The Den is fortified. They have lots of men, a hundred, if not more."

*A hundred, no way . . .*

That surprised everybody. Normally, a baronet could only muster a dozen men or two, while a knight would only have himself, his son, and his squire. Only a baron could command such a number.

However, Hugo didn't let that fact bother him. "Why do you need to keep them there?"

The coachman looked like he might snigger at such a question, but Anci had slapped him once, which broke one of his front teeth and made his cheeks swell. "T-the slavers wanted to keep the price high. They keep the slaves there and only sell a few."

"Isn't slave trade legal? Why bother with hiding and smuggling?" Lansius found it hard to grasp.

"The goods bound to Feodosia are bad batches. The too old, too sick, crippled. They're only good for the Eastern Kingdoms," the man reluctantly explained. "The young, healthy, and those with skills, they command a high price. The purveyor will secure them before Feodosia's slaver arrives."

"And then sell them to who?" Hugo asked.

The man looked left and right before answering meekly, "Anyone with money. The barons, baronets, knights, even rich city folks."

"In Midlandia?"

He nodded and added, "Also Rhomelia, Elandia, Nicopola . . ."

The smuggler's answer triggered a murmur among the men. Many felt sickened that fellow Imperium subjects bought slaves.

"Lies! No men would take slaves under his household!" one of Hugo's men said from behind, followed by a ruckus of support.

"The Eastern Kingdoms are human too, but they used slaves for everything," the smuggler said and unintentionally silenced the place.

"All right, that's enough. Anci, get the men to rest and arrange for scouts," Hugo commanded.

Anci whistled and waved his hand. It was enough to direct the men outside.

*At least they're listening to command easily . . . but thirty against a hundred?*

Lansius felt that victory was slipping away.

As the surrounding area was being emptied, Hugo asked the smuggler again, "Do you know anyone named Archie?"

"I never ask their names. It's better that way . . . less guilt."

Anci knelt beside the smuggler and whispered, "Try to remember."

The man nodded fervently, out of fear. Hugo gave him Arte's description, but the coachman shook his head.

"Are you the only one transporting slaves to this Den?" Lansius asked.

"Of course not. I'm merely a middleman. They got others as well." Sensing the opportunity, he drove the point home. "I think your Archie friend must be with one of them."

The interrogation gave no concrete evidence about the young lord's whereabouts, but stopping wasn't on their mind.

Hugo checked the knots on the man's wrist, nodded to Anci, and strolled out. Afterward, Lansius approached the smuggler. "A female squire with fierce eyes. Have you seen one?"

The man hesitated for a moment. "I recall taking one into the Den, but she never opened her eyes."

"What happened to her?" Lansius asked, his voice laced with a chilling edge.

The coachman swallowed hard, his eyes darting nervously between Anci and Lansius. "I don't know. She had a bandage wrapped around her head. The men carried her both in and out. That's all I know."

Lansius let out a weighted sigh, leaving the coachman behind as a flurry of mixed emotions began to consume him.

*It could be her . . .*

The decision to follow Felis's lead was starting to appear more justified. Instead of wandering aimlessly in Feodosia, he found himself in a place where the prospect of rescuing his friend seemed abruptly within grasp.

# CHAPTER 19

# DUCERE

A horse-drawn carriage, trailed by two canvas-covered carts pulled by pairs of mules, approached the hill leading to manor that Lansius now knew was called Sabina Rustica. Anci, on lookout duty, recognized Thomas and Felicity. Swiftly descending from his vantage point, Anci waved at them and guided them to the camp where the others awaited.

As promised, Felis was accompanied by seasoned men in their late thirties or early forties. These duelists, watchmen, and thief-takers formed an intimidating group, some sporting proud mustaches while others were clean shaven. Dressed in gambesons or brigandines, they were ready for battle, and their carts were loaded with poleaxes, swords, helmets, and shields.

Felis introduced the seven men-at-arms for hire first, then presented their leader and his assistant. "This is a special friend of mine, Calub, the alchemist, and his assistant, Jardin."

Calub was a tall, tanned man with short curly hair, and he wore a milky-white leather coat. He offered a slight bow, followed by Jardin. While Calub had the appearance of a scholar, the shorter Jardin exuded an imposing presence, his beard and muscular arms evoking the image of a living dwarven statue.

"Fire grenade." Anci's eyes flashed.

Calub heard the comment and smiled in response. Lansius guessed the two would become fast friends.

With little daylight remaining, they proceeded to discuss their battle plan. Together with Felis's group, they had around forty men, but they had yet to decide on a course of action.

"Palisade walls with almost no gap. Armed men, patrols, even stables," Anci reported.

"From the smuggler, we learned that the compound houses at least a hundred men, possibly more," Hugo informed the newcomers.

"Looks rough," Jardin commented.

No one spoke for a moment, so Anci took the initiative. "It's within our strength. I say let's storm them from two sides." He used both hands to illustrate a pincer attack.

Calub shook his head. "You may have the numbers, but not the age or experience."

Hugo and Jardin nodded in agreement.

"Indeed, many are too young," added old Thomas.

Lansius wanted to suggest a different approach, but his background as a mere clerk weighed him down. He even felt that he didn't have the right to be there.

Meanwhile, Felis seemed eerily comfortable. "We only have five crossbow users, including me."

Lansius noticed that Hugo looked slightly uncomfortable. He suspected that, like him, others also doubted Felis's ability, but they couldn't risk offending her and her associates. They also needed as many hands as possible. "The spear and shield will do just fine," Anci remarked. "The men have met the women and children I rescued earlier, so their morale is high."

No one contested Anci's words, leaving the decision to Hugo.

Among the three, Thomas was older but had only recently become a retainer. Before that, he was merely the equivalent of a foot soldier. Anci, on the other hand, was younger and had less experience than Hugo.

"Anci, take Thomas and twenty men. I'll take another twenty. You'll attack first and draw them out. Keep them preoccupied while I attack from the west side and stage a rescue." Hugo then looked at Lansius. "We'll leave the younger ones in your care. Just wait here. If we need help, we'll come to you."

*By the ageless, that's only a bit better than Anci's plan.*

Lansius glanced at the rest of them, but nobody said a word.

*Where in* The Art of War *do forty go against more than a hundred with half-baked plan like this?*

Thomas, Felis, and Calub turned their backs, signaling the end of the discussion.

A wave of panic washed over Lansius. His memory was a mess, yet he had glimpses of spending countless hours online, honing and perfecting his strategy and tactical skills. The time and effort he had dedicated as *username: Lansius* must have been immense, as some of it still lingered in his head. He could feel that he had made plans and led hundreds of players in guild wars, with thousands on the battlefield. Looking at the current situation, he was sure a disaster was brewing. His heart pounded hard, and an inner voice screamed that everybody was going to die.

"Do you mind if I share my thoughts on this attack?" Lansius spoke up.

Everyone paused. Calub looked at Lansius and asked, "You're what, a scribe?"

"A clerk," Lansius corrected, "but I have also studied warfare."

Hugo and Thomas contemplated Lansius's suggestion. Felis gave him an encouraging smile, while Calub nodded once to show his openness. However, it was Anci who broke the silence. "Meh, we've heard the slowpoke's, might as well listen to the clerk."

Lansius knelt down and quickly drew a rectangle, a series of lines, and a circle on the ground using a stick. Hugo, Thomas, and Calub immediately understood his intention and knelt down as well.

"This is our target, the manor on the next hill." Lansius pointed to the rectangle. "And this is the only road from there leading to us."

Calub followed the crude map, nodded, and asked, "And what is this circle in the middle?"

"There's a lake between us and our target, just beside the road," Lansius explained.

"The lowlands," Anci remarked from behind.

Lansius continued. "My plan is not to attack them at their strongest point, but to lure them out and fight them at a location of our choosing."

Thomas glanced at Hugo, who nodded. "And how do you propose we beat them once they're out?" Hugo asked.

Lansius placed three stones on the map, saying, "We'll bait them here, and then one team will hold them while another team flanks them from behind."

Lansius's basic plan began to make sense and captured everyone's attention.

"My men and I can stage a defense. Even with a small force, we could easily hold off dozens of men if the terrain is suitable," Calub offered.

"A bait and ambush might work better than just a surprise attack," Anci commented.

Hugo seemed to like the plan.

"But first," Lansius warned them, "this can only work if we eliminate their horses." He knew all too well that fighting on foot was at a great disadvantage against cavalry. They needed a way to counter this.

An elderly man reclined in solitude beneath a large tree near the manor's palisade gate. Though the sky was overcast, the summer heat was still relentless. He had hung his doublet on a nearby branch, allowing the breeze to cool him down. Since morning, he had toiled to maintain discipline among his men, resolving minor quarrels and ensuring order in the newcomers' dormitory.

The sounds of steady plowing and weeding bore witness to his efforts. Everything was well organized, just as his master had demanded.

Following the Arvena war, Sabina Rustica Manor, also known as the Den, experienced an influx of "newcomers." They were assessed like commodities;

those with potential were further cultivated to garner a higher value, while the mediocre were assigned to work in the shops or on the farm.

Contrary to popular belief, female slaves did not fetch high prices. What drew a premium were skilled individuals. Unprincipled nobles would pay handsomely for laborers, carpenters, or scribes. Laborers were employed on farms or orchards; carpenters for private construction projects or concealed rooms on estates; and scribes to handle confidential dealings and transactions.

There was minimal risk of leaks, as slaves were bound to their masters. This loyalty made them ideal candidates for sensitive roles, such as serving in the inner chambers where family affairs were talked about openly.

Not all requests were malicious. Occasionally, a secret adoption would be arranged. There were other specialized roles, such as female bodyguards, as opposed to eunuchs. Nonetheless, it was indisputable that these slaves would never experience freedom again.

At the heart of this illicit operation was Bogdan, an old veteran of the northern uprising. As the caretaker, he directed his laborers to expand their fields. He had ambitious plans to enlarge the complex, which already included an additional farm, dormitory, and vineyard.

For Bogdan, the manor symbolized his reward, sustenance, and retirement, all in one. Though not the owner, his role as caretaker granted him near ownership. Sabina Rustica afforded him a life far superior to what his social standing would otherwise permit.

This advantage extended to many of Bogdan's accomplices, including the elderly man who now enjoyed his tranquil private garden. The day was far from over, yet he was already contemplating his evening meal, a game of dice, and spending time with his mistress.

As he swatted flies away from the festering wound on his right hand, he was reminded of the incident two days prior, when he had been careless with an Arvenian woman. While punishing her, an unexpected guest had arrived, and Bogdan needed him to bolster security.

A sly smile crossed his face as he pondered the retribution he would exact upon her once the guest had departed.

*Clang—Clang—Clang!*

As if doused with icy water, the old man sprang to his feet, scanning his surroundings before focusing on the sentry atop the manor house.

The sentry finally noticed him and yelled, "Three horsemen!"

This revelation alarmed the old man. The Den was only expecting a carriage from Arvena sometime this week, but no one had mentioned horsemen. Hastily, he donned his doublet, grabbed his poleaxe, and sprinted to the gates. "Does anyone know about this?"

"No, boss. No one heard any . . ." one of his men replied.

He clicked his tongue, sensing something amiss. "You lot. Come with me."

Four men groaned as they emerged from the wooden gatehouse. The heat was oppressive, and they had been secretly drinking.

"Where'd these horsemen come from? I thought the boss bought off all the local baronets and knights," one queried.

"Maybe they're just the guest's men?" another suggested nervously.

"I didn't sign up for this," a third grumbled.

"You signed up for rape, loot, and arson, but not fights?" the fourth taunted his comrades, inciting a commotion.

"Silence or I'll cut off your noses!" the old man barked.

The five men stood and waited until the three horsemen were close enough to shout at. They could see the horsemen wore brigandines and ring mail, but bore no banners.

"I'm Archibald, a champion from Arvena. Prepare to die!" the lead horseman declared.

"What did he say?" The men glanced at each other. Their instincts told them to flee, and so they did, legs pumping at the first sound of hoofbeats.

The old man readied his poleaxe, but he knew he stood no chance. He, too, sprinted away, yelling for support from behind the gates. "Crossbows, crossbowmen!"

The three horsemen thundered after the fleeing men, who desperately cried for their allies to open the gates. The horsemen easily caught up and attacked ruthlessly. Three of the fleeing men collapsed in an instant.

"Crossbowmen!" The old guard made his final plea before a lance pierced his back.

Fulfilling the old man's dying request, a meager two shots were fired from the slits near the gate. Both missed their marks.

The horsemen laughed as they cut down the last man, who went limp before his face hit the ground.

Two of the horsemen dismounted, dragged the victims away, and stripped them of their gear. "Wow, look what I found—a gold ring and a necklace. These guys are loaded!"

Anci laughed and turned his attention back toward the gate. "Is there no one with manhood inside?"

The sentry above hammered the iron bell again. The sound drove everyone into the gatehouse. They had yet to learn what had transpired when they heard the sound of shattering glass from outside. Suddenly, the left side of the gate erupted in flames.

"Fire!" The guards panicked and backed away from the gate.

"Get the buckets! Tell the slaves to fill them!"

It took several moments, but they eventually extinguished the fire with buckets of water. That was when Bogdan arrived on the scene. "What are you waiting for? Get the riders out!"

Black smoke still billowed from one side of the gate as the heavy wooden door swung open. Eight riders brandishing swords and lances galloped out in pursuit of the three horsemen.

Seeing the new threat, Anci led his two comrades in a hasty retreat.

## CHAPTER 20

# SABINA RUSTICA

The eight riders from the Den relentlessly pursued Anci, charging downhill toward a picturesque glade where the dense forest met the tranquil waters of a large pond. The unsuspecting pursuers, focused solely on their quarry, failed to notice the strategically positioned men hidden among the trees. As the riders entered the glade, a group of determined men armed with spears and swords burst forth from the woods, catching the riders off guard.

"Ambush! It's an ambush!" the riders exclaimed among themselves. They slowed down and attempted to wheel around.

The men from the woods hurled rocks at the riders, while another group of spearmen moved to block their exit.

"Have courage!" the leading rider urged his companions. However, he failed to notice Anci, who had turned around and was now closing in on him from behind.

A gasp echoed as Anci's lance pierced the leading rider's ring mail. The rider fell from his horse, a section of the lance still embedded in him. The unsettling scene caused the remaining riders to grind to a halt, their faces reflecting panic and fear.

"Yield, or I'll do the same to you, slavers! Decide now!" Anci threatened, while his allies regrouped by his side.

In spite of the threat, three riders made a desperate dash for the exit.

"Spear in front, keep formation!" Lansius commanded as the three riders galloped toward them.

Eight men readied their spears or polearms. In addition to the eight spearmen in the front row, Lansius had only four crossbowmen and Felis in the second row. He prayed that he had enough forces to deter a cavalry charge.

"They won't stop!" Felis remarked cheerfully.

*What kind of girl is she?*

"Pick your targets," Lansius directed the crossbowmen. At this range, he didn't need to question their accuracy. "Loose!"

The four crossbowmen around him and Felis pulled their triggers. The sounds of bowstrings and wooden prods snapping back into place filled the air, followed by the whistling of bolts.

Two steel-tipped bolts found their targets. One struck a rider, while the other hit a horse. Both veered off course.

Small cheers erupted from Lansius's ranks.

"Not yet, one more!" Lansius moved to the front row to fortify their under-manned wall of spears. Standing shoulder to shoulder with the other men, he planted the end of his spear into the ground like a stake and held it firmly.

The lone horseman, less than forty paces away, continued to gallop, appearing mad enough to force his way through.

Lansius wanted to rally his men, but the words wouldn't come. Others clenched their jaws or ground their teeth as they stared at the approaching terror. The charging horse made each of them feel as if it were targeting them personally.

*This isn't going to work, we're too thin . . .*

Doubt and fear dawned on him as the ground shook from the thundering hooves of the warhorse. Taller than a man and weighing more than nine of them combined, the warhorse alone was a formidable opponent.

Its large black nostrils flared as the beast went against its instinct to keep away from the column of men. It continued galloping, leaving a trail of dust and dirt in its wake.

Lansius's fingers turned white from gripping his spear tightly. The other men trembled, cowered, and braced themselves for the inevitable.

Suddenly, a deafening yet familiar sound came from behind. Lansius hesitated to turn, his focus locked on the horse in front of him. He noticed the sudden shift in the horse's movements as the powerful beast slowed, its gait becoming unsteady, seemingly rejecting the idea of continuing its charge. With a sudden swerve, the horse changed course while its rider slumped lifelessly in the saddle.

"Oh, I got it," Felis declared, her tone dripping with casual confidence.

Only then did Lansius look back and see Felis, who had clearly fired the last shot. The other crossbowmen were still busy reloading.

Realizing they were out of danger, the men cheered exuberantly. Many could barely stand straight, and the ground reeked of urine, but they raised their fists in the air and taunted their opponents.

"Great shot!" Lansius shouted to Felis, amid a chorus of compliments from everyone else.

Felis chuckled but didn't celebrate. "Compared to running goblins and the labyrinth's foul beasts, they're nothing," she muttered quietly to herself.

Lansius took a deep breath. They had stopped the riders from breaking through, but the battle wasn't over. In the distance, he saw another rider challenging Anci.

"Anci's horse seems tired," one of the crossbowmen observed.

Lansius squinted his eyes.

"Nah, he'll be all right. The man is a natural," Felis reassured.

"You can tell?" Lansius inquired.

"The way he controls the horse. He's not relying on the reins, as the nomads do," Felis explained.

*Ah . . . Indeed, nomads used bows on horseback.*

Just as they had predicted, Anci bested the final challenger without any drama. Afterward, the remaining riders finally threw down their weapons. Witnessing this, Thomas, Calub, and a few other men rushed from the far side to capture the riders.


Anci and Thomas's men secured the captured raiders, who had surrendered their weapons and horses. Anci dismounted, checked his horse for injuries, and patted the mare when he found none.

Thomas approached with a waterskin. "I can't believe this actually worked."

Anci took the water, drank some, and offered the rest to his horse. "Your friend has a sharp mind."

"I never knew he was more than just a clerk," old Thomas admitted.

"Maybe you never asked?" Anci suggested.

Thomas chuckled.

Calub approached the two and said, "Sorry to interrupt, but I think we should send a messenger."

"No need, the marshal is right there." Anci gestured toward the line of spearmen who had yet to move.

Thomas followed Anci's gaze and saw Lansius in front of his men. Thomas laughed while Calub tried to understand the humor.

In Sir Peter's retinue, Hugo had always acted as if he were in charge, much to Anci's annoyance. Despite Hugo's laid-back attitude, he was rather bossy. Seeing someone else in command now gave Anci a great deal of satisfaction.

"So . . . ?" Calub wasn't sure what to do next. There wasn't a clear chain of command in a ragtag war band like theirs.

"No need for a messenger. I'll speak to Lansius myself on my way up," Anci said.

"You're going up again? Oh . . . the second, or is it the third step?" Thomas asked, half-guessing.

Anci tried to count on his fingers.

"First step is the baiting. Second is luring them here. Now, it's the third," Calub clarified. As an alchemist and part of the educated class, he easily understood Lansius's seemingly complex battle plan.

The other two nodded in agreement. Having tasted a minor victory, they were eager for more. Their success was proof enough that they could trust Lansius's plan.

With renewed confidence in their strategy, the group started planning the next steps. Anci and his fellow riders took a short break, giving their horses a chance to recuperate before continuing. After the rest, Anci observed his horse panting heavily, so he affectionately patted the horse and switched to a more rested one.

With the sun on their back, Anci proceeded at a relaxed pace alongside four other men, while five footmen joined them, each guiding one or two horses. As they came into view, the manor complex came to life with the sound of metal hammering and shouting.

Unfazed, Anci paraded the horses they had acquired from the riders. "I thank you for these lovely horses. Anything else you can offer?" he taunted in a loud clear voice.

This time, the slavers responded boldly, with the gate swinging open as armed men poured out. "Charge, punish these fools!" Bogdan, clad in bright brigandine, commanded.

Anci surveyed the scene, noting seventy men lining up against him, with another thirty emerging from a hideout on the far side of the complex. Surprised by the wide front, Anci hesitated before retreating in disarray, losing two captured horses in the process.

Sensing panic in Anci's retreat, the slavers threw their full force into the pursuit. One hundred men charged downhill, with Bogdan leading them all in. He was suspicious after the eight riders he had sent earlier never returned and didn't want to risk another piecemeal attack against his opponents.

As the slavers descended, their line became stretched out. The front group kept pace with Anci's men and reached the glade in the low ground, where they discovered four horseless carts blocking their path.

Anci and his horsemen rode past the carts, which were guarded by a group armed with spears and swords.

Confident of their numbers, the slavers charged headlong into a direct assault. A fierce battle ensued, with the defenders using the carts as makeshift barricades. Slavers attempting to climb the barricades were met with brutal resistance, being hacked down, pelted with stones, or shot by crossbow bolts.

Undeterred, Bogdan directed his fresh men into the narrow gap where Anci had slipped through. The bulk of the fighting took place in the tight space, with both sides thrusting and raking with spears and polearms, each struggling to gain or maintain their ground.

Casualties started to pile up on the slavers' side, but that didn't faze them. Their morale remained high. After all, they had a hundred fighting men, a significant force their opponents could not match.

Even if the neighboring baronet and knights combined their forces, they could only muster around thirty fighting men. This was a fight they could not lose. Their opponents had merely poked a hornet's nest.

Fresh blood and gore stained the grass as the fighting grew more intense.

Suddenly, desperate shouting and screams erupted from the slavers' rear. Bogdan looked back and saw their rear ranks under attack by a swarm of men who had seemingly descended out of nowhere. "What's going on? What are our men in the back doing?"

"Two dozen men or more attacked our rear," one of his aides hastily reported.

Bogdan realized that his hundred men had been stretched thin as they marched through the narrow hill path. However, he never expected that the enemy had enough numbers to pull off such a deception.

*Indecision breeds disaster,* Bogdan thought. "On me, on me! Boys, that's where the bastards are hiding. Time to give them a warm welcome!" He rallied his most trusted men and led them toward the source of the trouble.

Old Bogdan knew he could still salvage this situation. The enemy was cunning but lacked experience.

# CHAPTER 21

# BURNING SANDS

Hugo and his men had been hiding on a secluded trail that branched off from the hill path. They had waited and watched as the slavers' one hundred men charged downhill.

The hill path that connected the manor to the low ground was narrow and in several parts no wider than a cart's width. Such terrain formed a natural bottleneck and forced the slavers to make an elongated formation like a snake.

Hugo wiped the sweat from his forehead and noticed Jardin's glance.

"Now?" the alchemist assistant asked.

"Do it," Hugo said.

Jardin puffed a smoke from his clay smoking pipe and grabbed two glass bottles from a nest of hay inside a metal container. He pulled out their corks, jammed waxed linens into them, and lit one using the ember from his pipe. Once it was lit, Jardin looked at Hugo.

"That section over there and there." Hugo pointed his hand toward the two narrowest sections on the hill path.

Jardin lit the second bottle using the fire from the first bottle, loaded the first one into his leather sling, and then whirled it over his head several times. At the right moment, he released one of the cords and the bottle flew with an astounding accuracy. Before the first one hit the ground, Jardin had loaded and let loose the second one.

The glass bottle crashed without an explosion, but the liquid turned to mist on impact and readily caught fire from the linen wick. It burst into a fireball and the flame spread over a small area.

The fire stunned the slavers' rear formation. Several men got caught in it and caused panic. When the second bottle landed with another fireball, the slavers abandoned their position.

"For Arvena!" Hugo led his men to attack. Lansius had instructed him not to attack at the very end of the slavers' formation, rather in the middle, to sever the rear from the main body.

The fire and surprise attack had scattered the slavers, but they soon re-formed into several large groups to defend themselves.

Jardin launched another bottle and successfully prevented two of the largest groups from joining. That would be his last assist as melee fighting broke out between the two sides.

Knowing the element of surprise wouldn't last, Hugo had concentrated his best fighters at the front. With spears and polearms, they hacked and slashed the slavers' rear, who were lesser fighters compared to their vanguard.

Against slavers, with slim chances of encountering highborn, the Arvenians ditched formalities and went for the kill. Today, they were not in the mood to take hostages.

The fighting turned brutal. Patches of red and dark gore stained the grassy ground. Meanwhile, fires kept blazing through the dried grass.

The slavers' middle and rear combined had more than forty men, but the narrow terrain negated their numerical advantage. The gap in skills and resolve caused the slavers to lose men rapidly. It didn't take long before they feared their opponent.

Hugo's small but hardened party whittled down the slavers' number and secured a footing on the hill path. As planned, they split in two. One chased the rear section; the other, led by Hugo, continued their fight against the middle section. This move further strained their small number.

However, the slavers had it worse. They were in disarray. Not wanting to die for nothing, many pushed and jostled against their allies to avoid fighting. However, those who stood and fought were no slouches. One tall man answered Hugo's halberd thrust with the swing of his sword.

A thin metallic sound rang as the man tried to rush Hugo. However, Hugo raked and locked the man's sword using his halberd's axe. He tried to yank it out, but Hugo was ready for a follow-up. However, unseen by Hugo, his ally to the right blocked a vicious attack from his opponent, lost his footing, and bumped into Hugo.

Their lapse freed the tall man's sword, and he roared while launching a thrust into Hugo's chest. The sword came too fast, and Hugo parried it poorly. The steel sharp tip stabbed Hugo's brigandine, dented the thin metal inside before slipping harmlessly into the shoulder.

Staggered, Hugo took a step back and raised his weapon just in time to block a cut aimed at his neck. Unflinching, Hugo grabbed his shaft closer to the tip, and lashed it out against the opponent's arm. The halberd's axe bit the opponent's left elbow, and the tall man groaned. Despite the gambeson that extended to his wrist, he was in so much pain that he went on defense.

Hugo was out of breath but continued to swing his weapon. He saw an opening and hooked the halberd upward into the tall man's face.

"Gahh!" The tall man winced as the halberd's axe struck his chin and made a deep gash. Pain and shock made the man lash out blindly with his sword.

Hugo sidestepped and countered with a thrust. The jolt felt squishy as the halberd's point plunged into the man's abdomen. The man shrieked before kneeling down powerlessly.

Hugo kicked the dying man aside and pulled his halberd. He didn't celebrate, but breathlessly recovered his stance. The fight to his right immediately demanded his attention. He brazenly approached and made a quick thrust when his ally parried.

The unexpected attack scored a clean hit. The opponent dropped his weapon out of shock and gasped for breath. He then stared at the halberd, which jutted out from his stomach. His breath became erratic as he gazed at Hugo with blood-shot eyes. He ground his teeth and pulled the halberd's tip out.

Hugo brandished his halberd again. His ally was also ready, but the wounded man turned pale. He took several steps back only to collapse, never to stand again.

"Look, they're running!" A wave of emotion erupted from behind. Breaths of relief and some chuckles quickly followed.

Hugo realized he had slain the last opponent. Despite praise from his men, Hugo felt humbled. The battle had played out exactly as Lansius had predicted.

The fighting on the hill path was practically over. The slavers' middle section had ceased their struggle and fled to their main body. Uphill, Hugo's split group had routed the slaver's rear, who fled to the manor.

The slavers were just local troublemakers. Even strengthened by a percentage of men-at-arms, they weren't qualified for war. They were paid to guard slaves, not to fight a pitched battle.

Hugo spat before drinking from his waterskin. Afterward, he looked at his allies, whose faces were full of sweat, dirt, and blood. "Don't celebrate yet. Wash the blood from your hands. There's still another fight upon us."

The fighters nodded in solemn anticipation. They had taken the hill path, but the slavers' main body on the low ground was still intact. And now, even without squinting their eyes, they could see the slavers marching toward them.

Led by Bogdan and reinforced by their best fighters, the re-formed slavers' column looked solid and intimidating.

"I believe it's my time again?" Jardin asked Hugo as he arrived at the front.

Hugo snorted. "Do as you're told, but nothing extra. We're a little tight on the purse."

The response tickled Jardin's nerve who chuckled and replied, "Most certainly."

* * *

The sun was searing hot despite the multitudes of clouds. Bogdan's men slowed their march just before the hill climb as exhaustion piled up. Bogdan let his men catch their breath before the big push. This was not a race. They needed the stamina to fight.

Made up of mostly veterans, their morale was high. Their earlier failure against the four-carts barricade didn't dampen their spirit. In their eyes, they had forced the main perpetrator out, and now things would be resolved quickly.

Hugo's men had arranged themselves six men wide and three ranks deep. They were similarly exhausted after the last fight, but they had time to catch their breath and were in a better position.

In terms of numbers, Bogdan commanded more than fifty, of which half were his veterans. Meanwhile, Hugo had less than twenty. However, the Arvenians looked every bit intimidating as they stood their ground and brandished all their spears and polearms.

Led by Bogdan, the slavers resumed their march, but suddenly a small object flew in their direction. It cracked like clay and burst into flame when it landed at the center of their formation. The attack caught several men's cloth armor on fire and terrified those in the formation.

"Push forward, let nothing stop you!" Bogdan commanded. Whatever the cost, he needed the assault to happen quickly.

Another clay object flew into their front and shattered, fire blazing just like the first one. However, this time, they were ready and only two got caught in the fire. Both fires fizzled surprisingly quickly and left a plume of white smoke.

Bogdan capitalized on the enemy's apparent failure. "See those men in front of you? They're nothing but thieves and robbers. Your wealth, your money, they're going to take it all from you! Are you going to let that happen?"

Bogdan's words pumped his men, and they clamored for battle.

"So, what are you waiting for? Make them pay!" Bogdan raised his sword.

Emboldened, the men yelled their battle cry. Their distance was less than two hundred paces away from Hugo's men.

"Onward!" one of the lieutenants shouted, but a wave of screaming from their ranks alerted everybody. They looked around and saw panicked men trampled left and right to get away from the white smoke. The smoke was clearly unusual. They noticed everywhere the white smoke passed, men immediately suffered.

The men avoided the smoke like a plague and left the formation in shambles. Indeed, it was hazardous. It contained a fine white powdery substance that reacted with moisture and caused burns.

A person engulfed in the white smoke would feel their eyes, nostrils, and throat burning. It blinded them and filled them with immense pain. Even breathing felt like swallowing a burning charcoal. Many scrambled toward the large pond to douse themselves from the pain.

The white smoke had only caught less than a dozen, but it shook the column. Bogdan had shouted at the top of his lungs to keep control. Just then, ten horsemen and a score of Arvenians appeared behind them.

With a wall of spears in front, the threat of more white smoke, and now, cavalry appeared at their back; the slavers were beginning to panic. "This is madness. We can't win, not like this," one rambled.

"There's no hope. We should run and meet back at the manor!" another tried to convince their comrades.

Many nodded and fled as the horsemen advanced closer.

Watching his men fleeing, Bogdan eerily kept his calm. Instead of running, he dismounted and gave the horse to his aide. He was too old to lick boots. Moreover, he had no child of his own and little love for his concubines.

Together with twenty like-minded allies, old Bogdan re-formed the column, and they readied themselves against the cavalry charge.

Anci led his horsemen into a wedge formation. Instead of galloping, he opted for a trot to better aim their lances. The horses showed some resistance at first, but eventually they charged directly into the slavers' position.

The column of men and horses clashed. In an instant, many fell by the lances while the warhorses tore, trampled, and crushed whoever stood in their way. It wasn't clear how many died, but the remaining slavers frantically disengaged and ran.

Anci wheeled his riders and gave chase to prevent the opponent from regrouping.

While Anci went on a chase, Lansius arrived at the scene. Thomas, Calub, and Felis were at his side, together with eleven men whom almost all had wounds. They had given their best just to march and keep standing.

Lansius looked around with deep concern on his face. Many took it as reading the battle, but in reality, the scattered corpses, blood, and gore mortified him. He took a deep breath, but the distinct smell of blood made him nauseous.

Calub took notice. "You okay?"

"I'll be okay when this is over," Lansius replied.

The white smoke had dissipated from the field. As Calub had warned them, the area wasn't ideal. There was a strong wind coming from the hillside, and thus the smoke could only last for a minute or two.

Still, it got the job done. Without the burning sands, their casualties would be higher. An evenly matched battle was the worst in terms of casualties. They were lucky that Felis brought the alchemist, who spared them from that fate.

Calub and Felis, in turn, were grateful for Lansius's uncanny understanding of the alchemist's tools and how he could integrate them into his plan.

Thomas stepped forward. "I'll take some men to round up the survivors."

Lansius nodded. "Try to link up with Hugo."

"Aye, will do." Thomas was about to walk away when Lansius grabbed the old man's arm.

"Be very careful . . . no ransom is worth our men's lives," Lansius said.

Thomas gave a warm, fatherly look. "We'll avoid danger as much as we can."

Thomas went with just four men and scoured the battlefield. The other seven quickly lost their composure and dropped to the ground. Their role as reserve luckily wasn't required.

"Don't drink if you have deep wounds. Dab some water on your lips to keep them from drying." Lansius watched the men and was reminded of the few he had left behind in the four-carts barricade. He looked at the bright sky momentarily and shook his head to keep away the feeling that he was responsible for the dead.

*I did my best. Nobody should blame me.*

But the plan wasn't flawless. Originally, two of the carts should have been burned to keep the attackers away. However, the small amount of fire bottles had failed to burn the carts. Thus, their severely limited number had borne the brunt of the attack.

Lansius knew that was his mistake. He had miscalculated and made Calub assign most of his stock, including both of the burning sands, to Jardin.

*If only Calub carried one . . .*

As Lansius had witnessed, even a single bottle of burning sands was powerful. If it had been used on the barricade, it would certainly stopped the attack on the carts and saved many.

"Tsk." Lansius chastised himself. He had downplayed the technical side and incorrectly assumed that the dry wood would catch fire easily. However, the carts' thick wood proved to withstand the small douse of benzene from the fire bottles.

"Good job, Lans."

The sudden praise took him by surprise. He turned around and saw Felis. Her smile and blue piercing eyes almost made him blush.

"Hey, be proud. This is a significant accomplishment," she said heartily.

Lansius felt guilty, but the verbal pat on the back felt so good that he let out a stiff smile.

*Maybe this isn't all bad.*

Felis tilted her head at Lansius's lack of reaction. "You looked concerned. Is something wrong?"

"Nah, it's just that . . . it's time to finish the job."

**CHAPTER 22**

# LUPULUS

The sun had yet to turn orange when the Arvenians secured the battlefield. Anci had returned and sent a few riders on patrol. Hugo took the captured men for interrogation. Meanwhile, the Arvenians looted the dead for better gear and trinkets. They collected all they could and surrendered the more valuable ones to Thomas for safekeeping.

Sitting on top of a big rock, Lansius was busy mending both of his hands. Something had smashed his right thumb during the fight and caused the nail to cave in. He wrapped it tightly to help with the throbbing pain. At least he could address that one. His left palm had gotten some wood splinter that went too deep.

*Darn it! Wish I had a tweezer, even a flimsy one.*

Done with the interrogation, Hugo met up with Lansius and gathered the rest. "Bogdan, the caretaker of the place, is among the dead."

A wave of relief was on everyone's face. They felt victory was within grasp. Thus, all agreed to storm the compound. Despite the risk, the fear that the slavers might retaliate against their loved ones drove them to attack.

Lansius knew that Anci and Hugo would storm the manor regardless of his decision, for the two were looking for a far more important prize, the future Lord of Arvena. This made him wary. "Thomas, get the wounded somewhere cool and safe. Start a fire and boil some water. Treat their wounds if you could."

Thomas nodded lightly. He cared for the men and was happy to oblige.

Next, Lansius looked at Calub. "Can I ask you to go with Thomas?"

"I need to warn you that my knowledge of medicine is limited," Calub said.

"We have no one else. I'm only asking for a bit of cheap wine to clean the wounds, clean linen to wrap them, and some honey for treatment."

Lansius's explanation caught Felis's and Hugo's attention. They were familiar with the treatment, but Lansius's confidence was rather unusual.

Calub smirked and asked, "So you're also well read in medicine?"

"Just a bit . . . oh, and promise me, no bloodletting. Even if they have a fever, don't draw blood," Lansius warned sternly.

The alchemist's grin grew wider. "I'm not a barber-surgeon. Anything else?"

Lansius offered his hand. "Just wishing you a good luck."

The two clasped hands. "You too. Stay safe." Afterward, Calub departed with Thomas.

Anci, who had stood there patiently, finally stepped forward. "Are we done with the preparation?"

"Pretty much," Lansius answered.

"So, what's next?" Hugo asked in anticipation.

Lansius looked him in the eyes. "The men are well rested, yes?"

Hugo, Anci, and Felis looked at each other. "I think the men are ready," Felis answered.

Lansius looked down momentarily. Nothing was amiss, he thought, and he involuntarily nodded. "Let's move to the summit and claim the prize."

Anci chuckled and gestured to his riders to saddle up. Meanwhile, Hugo turned to his men and shouted, "Gentlemen, time to free your sons and daughters. Let's move out."

Only twenty-three Arvenians were in shape to fight, but they responded with a fierce battle cry.


Taunts and screams echoed across the courtyard of Sabina Rustica. The Arvenians had cleverly used a cart and inclined wooden poles as makeshift ladders in their assault. The defenders rushed to contain the breach by sending their best group of fighters.

Even being leaderless, the slavers zealously defended the place and almost succeeded if not for their disunity. Despite their heroic attempts, too many had left through a hidden back door with their gold and silver. The lack of men finally turned the tide for the Arvenians. The fight turned sporadic, but quickly died down as the slavers fled to the manor proper, the only stronghold left standing.

The manor's usually clean courtyard was now littered with blood and gore. The last few continued to fight inside the main hall and storage area. Only after they had nowhere else to run did the remaining four yield. The thud of their swords on the wooden floor marked the end of the slavers' resistance.

However, another party existed.

"Drop the sword!" demanded Anci, whose broadsword was dripping blood to the wooden floor.

"Easy, we're not related to the slavers," said one of the three men in red brigandine.

Despite the declaration, the Arvenians who had stepped foot on the manor's second floor and the three guards kept staring at each other.

"Tch—" Anci spat to the side. He looked around for threats before hollering down the stairwell. "Get Hugo. We got company."

At his behest, a few rushed downstairs. They passed the call and not long after, hurried footsteps echoed against the stone stairwells.

Hugo appeared with a bloodied face and hair.

Anci snorted. "Someone got you good."

"Fuck off, 'tis just a scratch," Hugo retorted and then gazed at the men in red.

"We're not hostile unless you threatened our master," the most senior of them replied.

"Who's your liege and what're doing here?" Hugo asked.

"We're accompanying our master, the baronet of Brunna."

The name drew Hugo's attention. "Tough luck, it seems that we got your master with his pants down."

"I'm sure we can—"

"It's a walk to the gallows for slavers. It's not a path you should follow," Anci cut in.

The three looked stressed and gave no answer, but continued to stand in front of the guest chamber.

Hugo gestured to his men to lower their weapons. And then to the tree he proposed, "Yield, and we'll promise the safety of you and your master."

"Will you hold us for ransom?"

"Nothing substantial for you three. Two goats or one if you're poor."

One of the guards snorted. The joke came out of nowhere. "What about my master?"

"I can't decide for a baronet. We'll let the nobles decide."

The three looked at each other before lowering their swords. "Fair enough," the senior guard said and presented his sword to Hugo. "We yield on the conditions that no harm befall our lord and the three of us."

"I, Hugo, on behalf of Sir Peter, accept."

That brief ceremony marked the end of the conflict in Sabina Rustica. Now, Hugo and Anci were free to roam the second floor for their biggest prize, Artc of Arvena, but his whereabouts remained elusive.

"Nothing here but marks of looting. You sure there's no hidden cell downstairs?" Anci asked as they searched the master chamber.

Hugo exhaled deeply while patting his forehead with a clean linen he had found. "There's nothing in the cellar or storage . . . Must be outside. There are several suspicious buildings—"

"Wait, we haven't checked the guest chamber." Anci marched out.

Hugo ran after him and they watched how the red guards called their master, to no avail. "No answer?" Hugo asked.

The senior guard shook his head. "No luck. We explained it's safe to get out, but . . ."

Anci snickered. "Is he dead?"

The guard sighed and lowered his voice. "I hope not. I have a family to feed."

"You," Anci called for one of his men. "Get me an axe."

"Umm . . . how about a poleaxe?" A rather young-looking man offered his weapon.

Anci grabbed the poleaxe and found it solid. He smirked. "This will do."

Inside the guest chamber on the second floor, things remained calm. The room had seen better days, but the plaster on the wall still retained its bright color. A cool breeze rushed from a fully opened decorated glass window on the far side. Lacquered furniture completed the fancy look.

Nowadays, guests rarely used the chamber anymore. Decades ago, a potential customer would need to travel to see the wares, but nowadays the slavers had bribed enough that they could smuggle their wares directly to the customers. Thus, there was seldom a reason for a visit.

However, three days ago, a valued customer, no less than a baronet, had traveled on a whim. He just had a new company, an effeminate wandering bard from the looks. They wanted to browse the wares before deciding on a purchase. Their host was just too happy to oblige. But now their trip had come to an abrupt end.

A muffled roar from outside followed by a violent smack shuddered the room. The oaken door creaked while wood splinters flew. A dozen more powerful bashes followed until the edges of the door frame gave up. Despite the layers of tallow, the metal hinges had rusted.

"Jam it into the gap—"

"We need a chisel!"

"Stand back! Yeaaarrggh!"

The hinges burst while the iron lock slipped. Anci, one of the ones who brute-forced it, sneezed loudly as wooden and plaster dust gathered around. The room was too quiet to his liking, but that didn't stop him. "Yield," he demanded while brandishing his reddened broadsword.

"You're too loud," came the answer.

The tone and the sight dumbfounded Anci.

An effeminate young man sat naked on the bed. His shoulder-length light brown hair swayed by the wind as he filed his fingernails calmly. To his side, a grotesque man lay exposed in an awkward position with mouth foaming.

"Oi, what happened?" Hugo asked from behind. He impatiently shoved Anci aside and saw the young lad. "Who're you?"

"I'm just a guest here. You must be looking for this big arse?" The naked lad gestured his hand at the grotesque man. "He's a slave buyer all right, but not the owner."

The heightened tension and heat caused blood on Hugo's head to start dripping again. He wiped it off as he approached the bed. Suddenly, his eyes went wide. "That's the baronet of Brunna."

"A baronet?" the lad asked.

Hugo nodded while ascertaining that the baronet still drew breath.

"Oh, to be taken advantage of by a baronet," the lad said as if in a play. "I thought he was at least a baron in disguise."

"Brunna is a wealthy estate. He's as powerful as a baron." Hugo felt compelled to explain while he took a piece of cloth and dabbed the reddened sweat from his eyebrows.

"You better get that checked—" He was cut off by the appearance of a lady at the door.

Felis held her crossbow in her arms as she went inside. "Oh, my." She noticed the naked lad and gawked at the beautiful yet masculine body.

"Please pardon my uncouthness, my lady." The lad jumped from the bed after he had noticed the blonde and made a gentlemanly bow, all without trying to cover his groin. "A most unfortunate circumstance just befell me."

"Not at all. Please, I'm not a noble," Felis corrected him. "But . . . you're Archie, right?" She saw through the heavy makeup.

The name forced Hugo and Anci to do a double-take. As mere squires, they rarely saw Lord Maurice's son in person. Only now, they began to see the resemblances.

"Ah . . ." The lad's surprise turned to smile. "You're the lady from three days ago. Such a good fortune to be blessed with your presence again. But tell me, for what purpose, my lady, are you here in such an unpleasant place, and are these your men?"

Felis smiled. Before they could interact further, someone intruded from outside. "What's happening? Is my master all right?"

"Oh, he's fine. Just a bit drunk." Anci blocked the way and passionately guided the guard out. "Listen, there's personal stuff happening, totally unrelated to your master. So, grunts like us, we better wait outside."

Hugo breathed a sigh of relief at Anci's quick thinking. Afterward, he approached the naked lad and took a knee. "My Lord, I'm Hugo, Sir Peter's squire. We have come to rescue you."

"My, to be found by my own retinue. 'Tis so unexpected." The lad, no other than Arte of Arvena, stood taller as he straightened his back like a seasoned fighter that he was.

To their side, Felis gathered the scattered clothes and offered them to Arte.

"Gratitude, my lady. And pardon for the sight."

"Not at all, my lord. I heard it's a sign of nobility when one isn't ashamed of their own body."

Arte chuckled at Felis's flattering while Hugo readily assisted him to don his clothes.

"Squire, tell me about your master."

"My master is Sir Ian's firstborn son."

"Ah, the old baronet. It seems that the Ancients' light has not forsaken me." Arte closed his eyes to gather his thoughts. "I'm indebted to you and your master, but for now, let's drop the formality. I'm in a poor state, and there are likely assassins coming after me . . . Until I can stand on my two feet, call me Archie, a knight from Arvena."

Hugo bowed his head and then asked, "Sir Archie, may we ask what happened and why you're here?"

"It's a long story. Maybe for some other time." Archie looked at the man in the bed. "You only need to know that I used this poor excuse of a man to hide from my pursuer. Unknowingly, he kept me safe. But there's always a catch . . ."

Hugo nodded diligently. Outwardly, he appeared content to serve his newfound lord, but inside, he knew the story didn't add up. However, there was no reason for a lowly squire like him to pry further.

"So, what did you do to him, Sir Archie?" Felis innocently asked.

"Well, how should I explain . . . this sorry man enjoyed my company, so it's only prudent to return the favor, no?" Archie let out an innocent smile.

Felis unexpectedly giggled. Meanwhile, Hugo found it hard to digest. "He's passed out from that?"

Archie laughed but didn't offer an explanation. "More importantly, now you've rescued me. What is your plan?"

Hugo's back tensed up. He knew it was best to consult with a certain someone, but this was too good an opportunity to pass. "Sir, I think it's best to head out tomorrow at the first light."

# CHAPTER 23

# MISSING

Nightfall descended on the newly liberated Sabina Rustica, the sky awash in hues of dusky purple and blue. The manor was now under complete Arvenian control, but there was no sign of celebration in the air. They ended the day with only a small feast. Despite having a cellar full of alcoholic caskets, only bitter pale ale was available. This wasn't due to self-restraint, but a need for preservation.

Exhausted and weighed down by wounded men, the Arvenians also faced the risk of a counterattack. The slavers could return with fresh accomplices and stage a night attack. Thus, the feast started abruptly and ended just as quickly. They knew they needed their rest before their rounds of night watch.

Meanwhile, freed slaves and captured men drank wine merrily, an absurdity that was actually a calculated gamble. The Arvenians were trying to calm the slaves while simultaneously robbing them of their fighting abilities. With the slaves' loyalty in question, the Arvenians couldn't take any chances. They simply didn't have enough eyes to watch everyone.

Despite earlier hostilities, the Arvenians provided their captives with meals, blankets, and linen for bandages. It was a stark contrast to what they used to have, but they could only drink their sorrow. The only thing that kept them from the sword was their labor. After all, there was no rose garden after the war, only piles of dirty jobs. It fell to the defeated to dig burial pits, bury the dead, and wash looted articles.

The victors fared only slightly better. The care for the wounded was taxing and oftentimes ill-fated. As the night fell, the remaining uninjured Arvenians barricaded themselves in the manor, gatehouse, and dormitory. Inside the manor's main hall, injured personnel were being tended to. The atmosphere was heavy and riddled with whimpering, whining, and sobbing. However, on the second floor, an altogether different scene was unfolding.

Clean and serene, the private hall was filled with small chuckles and lively discussion. A number of peers were waiting for a ceremony. The air was scented with the fragrance of incense wafting from a censer.

Inside the master chamber, Sir Archie prepared himself by donning a fresh, clean tunic. Today, the Arvenians had won a brilliant victory against an opponent thrice their size. He should be ecstatic, but he remained dispirited. Truthfully, he had gone to Sabina Rustica not to hide, but in search of a servant boy who was like a brother to him. The two had gotten separated when they escaped Riverstead. Ever since that day, Archie had been on the lookout. Unfortunately, he couldn't find him, not even at the Den.

Archie remembered their times together and let out a sigh. However, he did not dwell on it. He was the Lord of Arvena, and his men needed a leader, not an emotional youngster.

Two knocks on the door alerted him. "Enter," he said without hesitation.

An old esquire named Thomas appeared. "Sir, we're ready for your presence."

Archie strode out from the master chamber, into the adjacent hall where a big mahogany chair stood in the center. He sat on it and looked at the guests arrayed before him. Some looked like Arvenians, some were not, but all were equally unfamiliar to him.

Squire Hugo was the first to approach, and he knelt down in front of Archie and formally stated his deeds in an embellished manner. Originally, this was a herald's job, but the only one they had had been injured. After Hugo finished, Archie offered a praise and bestowed three gold coins, a share of the loot, and a promise of sizeable arable land in Arvena.

Hugo rose and returned to his colleagues, and Anci stepped forward to play the jester and embellish his merits to an extreme degree, causing a riot of laughter. The unexpected entertainment helped him win a bigger prize. Valor and courage alone weren't enough; one needed to promote oneself to gain a reward.

Next, Thomas stepped forward, delivering his performance solemnly and politely. For his efforts, he received one gold coin and a promise of two horses. Felis and Calub were then called forward. Sir Archie praised them for their assistance, giving a sizeable pouch of looted riches as payment.

The ceremony ended quickly, and they got down to business. Hugo started with the information about the slavers. "We stumbled upon a powerful group who surely will try to exact revenge on us."

Archie pondered the new threat. "Nothing we can do about it but to proceed carefully . . . anything else?"

Since the time they had found him, Archie had been a constant relief to his retinue. He lost his father, his closest colleagues, his loyal entourage, and the whole province, yet he remained steadfast.

Thomas coughed once to draw attention. "From what we gather, this Gottfried bastard and his northerner barbarians have captured the entirety of Arvena except the western area."

"The reinforcement from the Duke of Tiberia forced Gottfried to withdraw. Even he couldn't act brazenly against them," Hugo added.

Archie nodded, but didn't say anything.

A haunting memory gushed into Thomas's head. "These barbarians are no better than animals. They kill and chain whoever they cannot use in their army, even children—"

"The margrave will pay," Archie stated with cold and loaded voice.

Satisfied that his pleas were heard, Thomas bowed his head deeply.

"If nothing else . . ." Hugo looked at the other and then at Archie. "Tomorrow, we'll move out with ten riders to Selene Manor."

Archie looked perplexed. "Selene? Shouldn't we head for Lubina Castle?"

"Sir Peter is a guest at Selene Manor, but more importantly, it's Lord Bengrieve's summer residence," Hugo explained.

The name made Archie nod easily. While only a seneschal and not the Lord of Midlandia, Bengrieve held the actual power. If Arvena was to survive, he needed that man's support.

"How about the rest of us?" Anci asked.

Hugo recalled the conversation he had with a certain someone. "Thomas will lead the men to Pozna. Remember to pillage this manor before leaving; otherwise, brigands will use it. If you have trouble, consult with Calub, or lady Felis."

"Isn't it better to ask Lansius?" Calub suggested with a faint smile.

"Lansius? The name seems familiar," Archie remarked.

Hugo's heart raced as he hastily responded, "He's just a clerk from Riverstead."

The room fell silent. Hugo shot a look at Anci and Thomas, who reluctantly nodded their heads in agreement, having previously discussed and agreed to advance their own interests over some unknown foreigner.

Archie's eyes narrowed, and he leaned to one side in his seat with a face devoid of any expression. The tense silence in the room deepened.


While his colleagues were being rewarded for their merit, Lansius was facing harsh complaints from fourteen freed slaves inside the dormitory. Instead of being grateful, these women vehemently refused their newfound freedom.

*Something about opportunity?*

*Can't return home? Really . . .*

He tried to listen, but his mental capacity had reached the limit. Outwardly, he only looked slightly tired with bags under his eyes, but deep inside, he was in pieces. He had risked so much, yet he couldn't find the one he sought.

*Damn, my fingers are all blackened. Is this toxic?*

Lansius worried about his injured thumb and palm, now covered in coarse soot from the torches he had used during his searches. The torches also left a strong tallow scent on his padded coif.

Suddenly, the sole remaining Arvenian attached to Lansius, a young man, couldn't hold himself back and exclaimed, "You want to be sold as slaves?"

"And what's wrong with that?" a woman snapped back.

Their exchange triggered an avalanche of heated accusations, with the young man pitted against fourteen angry women.

Lansius watched the verbal melee with contempt from the sidelines. Only when it reached a fever pitch did he intervene, saying, "Now, now, everyone, please calm down." He also signaled to the young man to step back.

"I apologize for the sisters' outburst. My name is Leda," said one woman in gorgeous blue traveling attire. "It's just that you don't know our situation. Where we came from, there's only backbreaking labor waiting for us."

"Or death in childbirth," another woman hastily added.

Despite their attempts to explain the situation, Lansius's lack of response deterred the women.

Leda continued. "Some of us come from Nicopola and Lowlandia, but we're mostly Rhomelians. We're born poor. The land was hard to cultivate. Even with children working in the field, there's only food for a person or two, not the whole family."

"Raids from the east are becoming more frequent. If we stay, we're going to end up as slaves either way," added another woman.

Lansius tried to understand their situation. "I get it, but now you're free from this place. Isn't that a good thing?"

The women exhaled or let out a sigh, but the woman in blue calmly said, "Can't you see our clothes? Can't you hear the way we speak? Sabina Rustica gave us education and a chance at a better life."

Lansius suddenly realized that these women, who were born in villages, spoke and behaved like city folks. They were obviously educated, and it showed in their confidence.

*This place is a school?*

"We don't mind being sold to the highest bidder. They're more likely to give us a better life than if we stayed in Rhomelia," one of the women said, and the others shared their tragic stories one by one.

"Two of my sisters died young. One in childbirth. Another beaten by her drunken husband."

"My mother died from hunger, and my auntie's family, who raised me, got sick with the black rye plague. I watched as her fingers rotted away. They sold me away to spare me from the same fate."

"Anything is better than staying. If you think whoring is bad, you haven't seen the brothels in Rhomelia where women are treated akin to seasonal meat to be discarded before winter."

Lansius raised his hand. "I-I get it . . . I was not aware of your plight. I apologize."

A wave of relief greeted the response. "Can you do something to help?"

Lansius exhaled deeply. "I'm not a slaver, so I can't help you with that."

The group of women clicked their tongues or sighed.

"Can't you go to Feodosia and sell yourselves?" The ill trained and undisciplined youngster couldn't resist a taunt.

The boy's comment was met with a chorus of jeers from the rest of the group.

"All right, enough," Lansius rebuked the youngster. "Just take it easy, and let me handle it."

The youngster stubbornly looked away.

"Hear me," Lansius started slowly. "You can't expect us to sell slaves . . . However, if you have a quill pen, ink, and paper, I may be able to help."

The women frowned, puzzled by the request.

"Please wait a moment," Leda said, gesturing to her sisters, who sent the youngest among them to gather the necessary supplies.

Lansius took a seat in the nearest chair facing the long table in the dormitory hall, and the rest of the sisters followed.

"What do you need the supplies for?" Leda asked as she handed them to Lansius.

"I'm going to write your name, age, place of origin, and skills you have," he said while resting his back on the stiff wooden chair.

"And then?" she inquired.

"I'll report to my superior, and then we might find a solution."

Leda looked confused. "Pardon me, but will it really help?"

"If what you're saying is half true, then some of you are bookkeepers, scribes, musicians, or bakers."

The sisters realized what Lansius had in mind and grew excited.

"I promise nothing, but at least this is legal." Lansius sharpened the quill pen and looked at the women. "Now that I've helped you, it's time to return the favor."

"What do you want?" Leda asked with reddened cheeks. "Companionship for the night?"

Lansius paused but shook his head. "Nothing like that. Any of you know anything about a female squire from Arvena?"

Leda's shoulder stiffened. "Are you looking for Thilde?"

Lansius shook his head as he remembered the woman they discovered at the small wooden cabin on the far side of the vineyard. "No, we already found her. She's not the one I'm looking for."

Many of them drew a breath of relief. "Thilde was new," Leda commented.

The youngster fidgeting with curiosity. "So, what's her story? Why's she in a cell?"

"Thilde's background story is different from ours," Leda reluctantly explained. "She was born an esquire and only recently taken from her family's estate. Naturally, she wishes for her freedom back. A senior guard took a liking to her. We don't know what happened, but they got into a row, and she bit a chunk of his flesh."

"No wonder." Lansius felt disgusted as he recalled the wounds on Thilde's limbs.

*So it was torture . . .*

"Unlike us, she never faced hardship and famine," said another sister with pity on her voice, followed by nodding from the rest.

Lansius kept a stern gaze on the youngster on his side to keep him from throwing a stupid comment. The male raised his palms in protest.

Leda clapped her hands to gain everyone's attention. "So, the master's original question, do any of you know anything about a female squire from Arvena?"

"Sharp eyes, short hair, good with swords," Lansius added.

No one answered.

"None of you?" Leda confirmed, before turning to Lansius. "I'm afraid your friend isn't here. We oversee this dormitory, and we'd certainly know if someone special like her was inside."

"Special?"

"Sword trained, short hair."

Lansius felt utterly hopeless. "No chance you missed her?"

"I'm sure. For certain, we got nobody with short hair," Leda clarified.

"I see." Lansius sighed as his heart pained.

Leda sympathized with him. "I'm sure she's in a better place. There's a good chance that your friend is free somewhere out there."

"The Den rarely accepts combatants. If your friend was caught, she would likely be sent to Feodosia," another suggested.

Lansius felt torn. He had spent several precious days here, all for nothing but a cruel detour.

*There's no hope in this. I'm just fooling myself. She's—*

Leda sat down next to him and spoke in a soft, concerned tone. "You appear exhausted, master. Perhaps you should consider getting some rest."

Moved by her sincere offer, Lansius exhaled sharply and reached for the coarse, thick parchment. He carefully dipped the quill pen into the ceramic inkwell and asked, "Your name and training, please."

As Lansius began writing a list, a knock on the door interrupted them. They turned to the source and saw a man in a milky white leather coat accompanied by a stout but shorter man. The door had been left ajar, so this was either out of courtesy or urgency.

"Master Lansius, they require your presence," said the stout fellow.

Lansius felt a twinge of unease.

# CHAPTER 24

# ARMS BEARER

The main hall was somber, with eerie shadows flickering on the walls as if the lanterns and chandelier breathed life into them. The Arvenians had taken the hall as their quarter and had acted accordingly by arraying their temporary beds across the floor.

Despite their numbers, the place was devoid of life. There were only faint whispers and weak groans. The floor was littered with piles of dirty linen bandages, also buckets that reeked of blood, piss, or vomit.

There were no medical staff besides the volunteers who had also had their fair share of fighting today. They were mostly driven by a sense of camaraderie to care for their unfortunate allies.

Some had lost limbs, while others had lost a friend or family member. With only alcohol to ease the pain, many were lost in their own thoughts.

The cold evening air blew in as the night watch pushed the door open.

Footsteps echoed as Jardin, Calub, and Lansius entered the hall. What greeted them was dampness, the smell of blood, and the rancid wine they used as antiseptics. Lansius immediately noticed a few gazes wandering toward him, so he kept his eyes low. If he had to guess, he would say that the looks were directed at him in resentment or hatred.

With this many injured and dead, Lansius couldn't shake the feeling that he had let them down. However, Calub, the alchemist, seemed unfazed. Led by Jardin in front, they kept walking briskly toward the end of the hall where a stone circular staircase was located.

As the shadow from the staircase fell over him, Lansius exhaled deeply. "What does the lor—"

Calub, who had barely ascended several flights of stairs, raised his hand. "He's just a knight for now."

Lansius had heard that they found someone named Archie and deduced that Hugo found what he was looking for. However, for the young lord to use another disguise was surprising. "And why does the knight want to see me?"

"Better ask that directly," Calub replied as they reached the second floor.

The spacious, illuminated room and the scented air felt a world different from downstairs. As he entered, Lansius noticed that the conversation had stopped and grew wary of the nature of the summons.

He wasn't sure what to do when Calub turned to face him and whispered, "Be mindful that now they've found him, there's no need to carry out another attack."

Lansius's eyes widened.

*Just what did he imply?*

He had yet to get an answer when Felis approached. She feigned friendly greetings while speaking softly. "Only ask for money. Your goal may lie in Feodosia."

Despite how normal-looking their exchange was, it still grabbed everyone's attention.

"Better present yourself," Calub said openly to allay the room's suspicion.

Felis smiled and motioned Lansius to follow her. Meanwhile, Calub and Jardin made their way to the side.

Lansius noticed the stares from Anci and Hugo. While Anci eventually flashed his teeth, Hugo simply closed his eyes and feigned ignorance.

*Something is indeed wrong . . .*

"Now, go." Felis smiled and then proceeded to bow her head slightly toward the chair in the middle, where a man sat idly to one side. It was the same person Lansius had met in Bellandia. His hair was longer now, and he was wearing a much plainer outfit.

"It's been a while." Archie addressed Lansius first. "Come closer. You can call me Sir Archie," he instructed plainly.

Lansius swallowed his fear and knelt near his master. "Your servant is gladdened that Sir Archie is well." An eloquence Lansius never knew he had flowed from his lips.

"You seemed well yourself." Archie's face looked bored or annoyed. "So, tell me, oh servant of mine. Why didn't you report your deeds to me?" he said without even looking.

The tone made him uncomfortable. "I-I'm just a clerk, sir. I only partook a little in the fight."

Archie moved his gaze toward Lansius, and after a few moments of thoughtful silence, said, "I know you're a foreigner, so maybe they do things differently where you're from. But here, you need to claim your merit. Else, you're going to be a deadweight."

Not knowing where this conversation was going, Lansius could only play it safe. "My apologies, but I only helped a little."

Archie scoffed. "I remember our meeting. Back then, you acted like this too . . . Too shy for your own good."

Embarrassed, Lansius quipped before he could think. "My good sir, do you wish for an ambitious retinue?"

It was almost a rhetorical, yet Archie responded lightly. "And what if I do?"

The answer surprised Lansius, and he quickly regretted it.

Archie watched Lansius's expression and chuckled. As his mood improved, so did the tension in the room.

As a lowly clerk, Lansius usually put up with humiliation, but today he felt exposed. The wound from his failure to find Stefi was still fresh. So, uncharacteristically, he fumbled in his bag and retrieved a scroll. "May I approach?"

With a finger, Archie motioned Lansius to come closer. "What's this?"

*No shame in trying . . .*

"A gift for my good sir's freedom."

Archie read the parchment, and his lips turned into a sinister grin. "Clerk, why do I see names and their professions?"

"Sir, I'm sure you'll need them to rebuild your forces."

"You offer me slaves?" Archie balked.

"Sir, we're not enslaving them. We're recruiting them."

Archie snorted as he found the suggestion to be funny. "And how will you explain when the Imperium sends their agents?"

Lansius could've stopped there and excused himself as a foreign fool. However, his wounded pride wouldn't let him. "Sir, they could inquire all they want. I made no trickery. It's the freed slaves who wanted this. They begged me for this chance."

The answer made Archie lean forward in his seat. "Is this not a jest?"

"Sir, if you wish to find out, you may ask the alchemist," Lansius said, naming a third neutral party.

All eyes were on Calub, who serenely enjoyed the limelight and proclaimed, "The clerk spoke the truth. I overheard that the enslaved Rhomelians wanted to join. They refused to return, as their homeland was rife with constant raids, famine, and extreme poverty."

Archie shook his head and massaged his temple with one hand. "I have yet to ascertain whether you are the ones responsible for today's battle. And here you are bearing a substantial gift. Lansius, what kind of man are you?"

"An ambitious one, sir," stated Lansius nervously.

Archie couldn't hold himself and burst into a fit of laughter. After he laughed his heart out, he exclaimed, "So why do you refuse to claim the highest honor?"

*Refuse to claim? The highest honor?*

Lansius was clueless, but felt obligated to honor the men. "Sir, I'm just the one making plans. It's Anci, Hugo, and Arvenians who bleed for you. I dare not to claim the honor."

"So you don't deny making it?"

"Indeed, sir. I made the plans, but they're not even worth mentioning."

"To beat a hundred and fifty with just forty, and you say it's not worth mentioning," Archie said with a dry chuckle, and then he suddenly proclaimed, "Enough! You shall not make fun of me any further."

Like a storm in a daylight, Archie's wrath was so unpredictable. Lansius almost begged for a pardon, but Archie stood over him and asked, "Tell me oh clerk, what is thy desire?"

*Is this a trick . . . ?*

Cold sweat ran down his back. Then what Felis had said flashed through his mind. "Money," Lansius said and quickly added, "I want to free an enslaved friend in Feodosia."

The answer seemed to be correct, as a stiff smile was on Archie's lips. "People fight for their own interests. A man who asks for nothing cannot be trusted," he imparted to Lansius.

Lansius absorbed the words and saw the change in his master's expression.

Archie gazed upon Lansius with renewed interest. "Lansius from Bellandia, from this moment on, I take you as a squire of the tent."

The sudden declaration was met with a clamor from the room.

*What the! What kind of job is that? I don't even like tents.*

"As for the money." Archie reached for a small wooden chest and showed its contents. The bottom part was filled with valuables. "One part for my House, another for the troops, and this shall be yours." He grabbed a fistful and opened his palm for Lansius to see.

The emotional roller coaster made Lansius speechless, but he was so thrilled by the golden reflections.

Archie dangled the prize from his hand, so Lansius crouched with a raised hand to accept his reward.

The small coins and two heavy rings trickled into his hands. A few hit his bandaged right thumb, but the adrenaline dulled the pain.

Lansius stared at the five gold coins and two rings in his hands. It felt surreal, so he clenched them tight, then opened his palm to see the soot, ink, and blood staining the coins and rings.

*It's real . . . they're real!*

Filled with gratitude, Lansius exclaimed ecstatically, "All hail, Lord Arte of Arvena!"

Archie guffawed and slapped his thigh.

*All hail, Felicity, my goddess of luck.*

Lansius had received a substantial reward, and it would be foolish to ask for more, yet he couldn't betray his conscience. "My Lord, may I ask another thing on behalf of the wounded men?"

Archie looked at him cautiously. "Speak."

"The men are in danger from fouled bandages. One man's blood shouldn't make contact with another's. It would be so kind to provide them with clean linen. They need it more than their share of loot."

"Is it true?" Archie beckoned to the others in the room, all of whom turned their gaze at Calub.

The alchemist bowed slightly. "Indeed, Sir. This Lansius fellow seemed to know a thing or two about medicine."

"Then it's settled." Archie rose from his seat. "Thomas, pick the worn-out and faded ones, and ensure that enough is distributed for their needs. I need men to fight wars, not clothes."

The next day, the sky was clear and cloudless, displaying warm shades of pink, orange, and gold. Lansius rode in a slim cart, drawn by two swift horses, accompanied only by a coachman.

Lansius had taken the ride from Pozna. Instead of spending the night there like the rest of the Arvenians, Felis had persuaded him to press on. It was costly, but she deemed it necessary. Lansius went with her suggestion and rode with just a few hours of daylight remaining.

At first, he was doubtful, but the slim cart, with its sleek and light construction, proved to be fast and nimble. With nothing onboard but Lansius and his bags, it easily maintained high speed through the bends and corners.

The summer sunset was breathtakingly beautiful. The fields all around them were illuminated by the last rays of the setting sun, casting long shadows over the rolling hills and tranquil hamlets dotting the verdant landscape. For a moment, Lansius forgot about his troubles and simply basked in the peaceful beauty. It was a rare chance to escape from the harsh reality of medieval life, so he savored every minute of it.

His new brigandine, looted from the manor, felt comfortable despite the steel plates inside. It was a finely crafted piece that fit his body perfectly. Even the backing felt soft and supple. He might not find what he was looking for, but Sabina Rustica had made Lansius a wealthy man. His pouch was laden enough to free a slave, buy a farm somewhere, and live peacefully.

Driven by his newfound wealth and status, he dared to dream about living carefree with his family from Bellandia. He also fantasized about living together with Stefi.

A sudden realization hit him.

*Hang on, when did I look at her like that?*

The memory eluded him, while the cart overtook another horse-drawn cart along the cobbled road. "This feels like a race."

The coachman let a chuckle. "Worry not, maester. You're in good hands."

The wild and jerky ride continued eastward. Soon, they started to see the outlines of the city of Feodosia, with its ancient, derelict, gray stone wall.

## CHAPTER 25

# AUTUMN STREAM

*Arvena, One Year Earlier.*

The sun shone brightly that day, and the warm weather was a welcome change. The sky, visible through the forest canopies, was a brilliant shade of blue. It contrasted greatly with the reddish leaves of the late fall season.

It was the tenth day after their departure from Bellandia. The Arvenians had crossed several hamlets and villages along the way, but only the lords, knights, and their retinues could stay for the night. The rest of the troops had to make do with their simple tents pitched in the fields.

Last night, they had camped just outside the forest, in a clearing where they built a large campfire and a field kitchen. The site wasn't ideal, but the woods provided them with easy access to firewood and opportunities to forage for wild berries and eggs.

After breakfast, Lansius and Stefi began packing their belongings. The strong morning sunlight made the situation rather hectic, as some had decided to march earlier than usual. Several men with their spears and shields were already forming groups and waiting on the dirt road.

This far from the frontline, they marched at their own pace. While it seemed lax, the rearguard who marched behind would ensure that nobody was deserting.

Stefi had taught Lansius how to pack his gear, and after more than a week of living on the road, he had mastered some simple tasks. Stefi untied the ropes while Lansius carefully pulled and wiped them off with a dry rag.

Ropes were costly, so care was needed to maintain them. They were literally the thing that held the roof over their head every day. Without ropes, the tent would turn into a large poncho. Made from braided natural hemp fibers, they were coated with wax to protect against mold and decay.

As Lansius worked with the ropes, Stefi gathered the bowls, spoons, and waterskins and said, "Pack them all up. I'm going to the stream."

"Don't take too long. Everyone is already on the move," Lansius warned.

"No worries. We have Horsie, remember?" And then she left.

Indeed, she was right, Lansius admitted. He initially thought that only the rider would benefit from a horse, but he was wrong. As it turned out, having one benefited the entire group.

Tents, battle gear, and foodstuffs were especially burdensome to carry. A pack animal could easily carry them, allowing the group to march faster and farther.

Lansius continued to dry wipe the remaining ropes. Once he was done, he gathered them all and approached the horse carefully. After a week of traveling together, Horsie was already familiar with him, but Lansius was wary of the big animal. He approached from the front and only proceeded to the saddle once he was sure that the horse's demeanor remained unchanged.

Although he winced at the horse's strong odor, he put the ropes into the saddlebag and left gracefully with a relieved face. He repeated this process several times with the bedrolls, blankets, and their lantern.

Finished with it, he noticed Horsie nudging toward a patch of tall grass, so he pulled out his knife, cut it, and brought it to her.

As the horse ate, Lansius noticed more movements on the road. He saw that the usual group he had marched with had started their march. Even the traveling peddlers that followed their column were preparing to move.

Lansius patiently waited, but after a while, he couldn't ignore it any longer. So, he rose, took his and Stefi's bag, and tightened Horsie's reins to ensure that she wouldn't wander on her own.

Before leaving, Lansius took a good look at his surroundings to ensure that no one was eyeing the horse and their belongings. Satisfied that nobody was nearby, he made his way to where the stream was supposed to be, guided by its faint sound.

"Stefi," he called, but there was no answer, so he tried again, louder. Still, there was no answer.

Realizing he had no other option but to descend the steep and possibly slippery path, Lansius cautiously checked the surroundings for any signs of danger. Despite being told that there were rarely any beasts in Arvena other than the occasional highland wolf, he took no chances. He was aware that what was considered a monster by humans like him might be seen as a mere animal or beast by people of this world.

Lansius hesitantly began his descent as he found no evidence of danger.

*At least there's no goblins.*

He remembered how Stefi had assured him that she had never heard of green-skinned monsters who walked like a human and used weapons.

As the path became steeper, he grabbed onto branches to steady himself. Halfway down, he looked up and grew wary of having to climb back up again. When he looked down, the vegetation obstructed his view.

"Stefi!" he called again, but the sound of the stream was loud enough to muffle his voice.

Lansius's worry urged him to continue. He carefully descended the treacherous path, holding on to branches for support. Finally, with sweaty and reddened palms, he reached a flat area near the stream.

The ground was covered with gray river stones and black sand. The stream turned out to be wider and deeper than he expected. Lansius glanced up and marveled at how the lush trees had concealed the place.

Next, his eyes wandered at the stream that glimmered with the sun's reflections. However, he spotted something. His eyes opened wide as he realized what he was looking at: a young woman, waist-deep in the stream, her bare skin glistening in the sunlight.

Their eyes briefly met, and Lansius quickly recognized her and her strong gaze, but then his eyes drifted toward two finely shaped round objects, which were normally concealed behind a black gambeson.

"I-I didn't mean to," Lansius finally snapped back, turning around with a reddened face.

Stefi said nothing but calmly rinsed her hair once more before wading to the banks. She walked toward a large boulder where she kept her clothes, grabbed her breaches, and turned away. "Sorry, did you wait for too long?"

"S-sorry," Lansius stuttered.

Stefi chose not to respond, but silently dressed up. Once she was done, she asked, "So, why are you here?"

Lansius turned to face her. "I . . . oh, everybody had left."

Stefi ignored Lansius's slightly reddened face and said, "I probably took too much time . . . The water wasn't cold, so I was tempted to wash myself."

Lansius nodded. "Can't blame you. It's been days."

Stefi motioned for Lansius to pass her bag. As he did so, Stefi gave him his waterskin. "Better drink some."

Lansius took a sip but hesitated to drink more, worried about the raw water. He typically made excuses to boil the water or mix it with wine to, hopefully, kill any pathogens inside.

Stefi put the utensils she had cleaned inside her bag. Afterward, she fished out a clean cloth and used it to dry her hair.

"Umm, shouldn't we hurry?" Lansius asked.

"Before we leave," Stefi said sharply, and Lansius sensed a scolding was coming. "Lans, it's best to keep this between ourselves."

"I understand. Again, I apologize," he said remorsefully.

Stefi shook her head. "I don't blame you. It's just that I had a friend who saw a village woman's thigh by accident. She reported him, and he was forced to marry."

*Yikes* . . .

"At first it was funny, but it didn't end well for them," added Stefi ominously. "Also, if that happened to us, everybody would say that I'm taking advantage of you as my charge."

Lansius bowed his head. "I swear, I'll never mention it to anyone."

"Well, let's get going."

Leading the way, Stefi showed Lansius an easier path upward. As she began to climb, she suddenly asked, "Say, since you saw mine, what should I do with you?"

Lansius shook his head and replied meekly, "You know I don't have that much coin."

Stefi looked at him. "Who said it had to do with money?"

"Eh?" Bewilderment was written all over his face. "You want to see me naked?"

Stefi giggled. "I'm a squire. I see men left and right, so that's not a good bargain."

"Then what?" Lansius was intrigued.

She motioned for him to come closer, as if to whisper something in his ear. He leaned in, eager to hear what she had to say. But before he knew it, Stefi had her hands on either side of Lansius's face and was pulling him in for a kiss. It was sudden and unexpected, but he couldn't help but feel a rush of excitement as her lips met his.

As abruptly as it began, she pulled away, a mischievous grin on her face. "I stole yours, so now we're even!" she said, and nimbly climbed up.

"How—how did you know?" Lansius anxiously asked, but all he heard were faint giggles coming from her direction. He was confused by the mixed signals, but the big grin on his face didn't lie.

# CHAPTER 26

# SPECTER

A month had passed since Lansius arrived in Feodosia, and the sharpness of his appearance had faded into a haggard weariness. He seldom left his room, save for a quick stroll to the baker at noon or for supper.

Lansius sat on the edge of his straw mattress, his back hunched and his gaze fixed on the floor of his dimly lit room. He wore his faded blue Centurian tunic, a garment that stirred memories of his friend. Clinging to these memories offered him a bitter form of comfort.

A half-empty small jar of wine and an empty bucket lay on the floor near his feet. He had attempted to drink his sorrows away, but the taste of undiluted local wine was too bitter, even for his desolate mood. Outside, the final hour of sunlight cast a reddish-orange glow through the open slit in the window. Lansius noticed the warm hues and let out a heavy sigh.

*Another day wasted . . .*

He ached for the familiar comforts of home and family. Yet, he knew the perils of returning to his home in war-ravaged Arvena far outweighed his longing. For sure, the journey was fraught with danger, with northern men known to detain travelers without cause. Lansius's distinct dark hair, a clear mark of foreigner and the fact that he came from Midlandia direction would made him a clear target of suspicion. The risks were simply too great.

Lansius's thoughts turned to the fruitless search he had undertaken and how it slowly turned him into a recluse. Day by day, he had waited for good news that never came. And each day, the cowardly decision he had made in Riverstead had come back to haunt him.

His stomach growled again, and the nausea returned. Lord Arte had granted him status, wealth, and the privilege of exercising his own will, but Lansius had squandered it all with his own irresponsibility.

With a heavy feeling, he fought the urge to lie down. He planted his feet firmly on the floor and took a few wobbly steps toward the table.

*Guh . . .*

He quickly took hold of the table to steady himself. Despite the proof of intoxication, Lansius stubbornly refused to acknowledge it. Rather, he attributed the weak knees to prolonged sitting.

Without meaning to, Lansius's gaze drifted to the table. Although it had been pristine upon his arrival five days ago, now a thin layer of dust covered its surface. Yet, the dust was the least of his concerns; sitting next to a jar of water and a wooden cup was an unassuming paper scroll.

The men he had hired were competent enough to submit a written report after their search. However, just like his own search, they had found nothing.

*"There was no slave that fit the description." "Most likely she perished in the war."* Lansius recalled the last conversation he had with them.

Anger sparked within him, but not because of the failure. He felt ashamed to maintain such a feeble and foolish hope for so long. The likelihood of finding Stefi alive was always grim. Before he had hired anyone, Lansius had visited the slave merchants in Feodosia. They could only offer their sympathies as they couldn't find her either in their place or in their logs.

As Lansius reached out absentmindedly for the cup, he took a small sip of water and winced at its stale taste. Putting the cup down, his attention was drawn to the empty seat in front of him.

"Hey, if you're dead, why don't you tell me and save me all the trouble?" he blurted out at the empty space.

There was no answer but the darkness that crept in as the sun inched closer to the west.

"Hmph, you're probably floating freely and laughing at my misery," he continued, but this time, the alcohol in his blood whispered an imaginary answer.

"Guilt? But what can I do in Riverstead? I'm no swordsman . . . To die at your side, is that what you want of me?" His heart pounded as he finally spoke some of his burden out loud.

"You're not special. There's nothing between us." He denied his own feelings. "I've seen you naked once, but that's nothing. I've seen plenty of naked girls before. Where? The internet. You don't know? Hah! See . . . you know nothing about me."

This time, there was no answer to his ramblings, only silence. Frustrated and ashamed at his monologue, Lansius retreated to the bed and held his head in sadness. Not even amnesia could erase the deep yearning he felt for a companion, and Stefi was the closest he ever had.

*   *   *

The last faint glow of the setting sun finally ebbed.

Lansius let out a long, tired sigh. Despite his misery, he couldn't ignore the encroaching darkness. His earlier outburst had pumped so much blood into his head that he felt slightly sober. He grabbed his bag and lantern, and pushed the iron bolt lock open.

The corridor of the timber and stone inn was dimly lit, with only a single lantern casting a feeble glow near the stairs. The sound of creaking floorboards echoed as Lansius made his way downstairs.

Lansius quickly entered the dining area next to the kitchen. The innkeeper and her two kids were too busy to greet him. That was perfect. The last thing he wanted was for somebody to judge him by his looks.

For that same reason, he liked to come early. Today, there was just one guest in the corner. Keeping his head down, Lansius went to the small table by the window. As he was about to sit down, the man in the corner raised his cup. Lansius thought it was just a greeting, so he waved back.

"Lans, my man, you look unwashed."

The man's words sent a jolt down Lansius's spine. He looked at the man and recognized the facial features along with the milky white leather coat. "Calub!"

The alchemist raised his cup even higher as a smile formed on his lips.

Ignoring his suspicion, Lansius rushed to meet him. He had changed inns twice and used an alias, but a friendly face was something he yearned for. Truthfully, he was worried about staying alone in Feodosia, especially with a sizable amount of money.

Calub carefully kicked the chair in front of him, and Lansius gladly took it. "So, how's Feodosia?" the alchemist asked.

"Better than what I expected," Lansius replied cheerfully, concealing his issues.

Calub smiled. "It's a small town but passed through by many trade routes. You can find almost anything in here—" He abruptly paused. "Ah, what am I saying? Please pardon my ramblings."

"What for . . . ?" Lansius grew suspicious and asked carefully, "You've heard?"

The alchemist's response was solemn. "Lansius . . . I'm saddened that you can't find what you're looking for."

The mood turned heavy, and Lansius didn't give an answer.

"I have some connections who informed me about it," Calub explained. He poured spiced ale into another cup and offered it to Lansius.

Lansius took the cup, but sipped only a little as his stomach didn't feel well.

Calub didn't push for an answer, so Lansius pondered his situation. Meanwhile, the kitchen next door bustled with activity. Lansius's senses were awakened by the sound of crackling fire, the clanging ladles on the metal cauldron, and the rich aroma from the meat puddings being cooked.

"So, how is Lady Felicity doing?" Lansius asked after he remembered just how much he owed her.

"She's fine. She runs a tavern, you know. We should visit her, but perhaps not tonight," Calub replied, and glanced at the innkeeper. "Can we get one bowl of porridge, please? For a hangover."

"That'll cost extra," the innkeeper replied without looking.

"Make it tasty then," Calub said without asking for the price.

Lansius could only watch in silence. After some hesitation, he finally asked, "Calub, am I chasing a ghost?"

"Don't say such a thing," Calub uttered, but he didn't elaborate.

A rather plump lass no older than fifteen arrived with two bowls of stew, a small lump of blackened meat pudding, and warmed up bread. Lansius hadn't ordered, but each guest got the same meal.

"You better wait for the porridge," Calub suggested while stirring his stew.

Lansius nodded. He was grateful for his concern.

The stew was steaming hot, so Calub broke his bread and dipped it before taking a bit.

"Mm, how's Sir Archie doing?" Lansius asked.

"Now you're talking." Calub dipped another piece. "It's good that the squire is thinking about the master."

Lansius exhaled sharply from guilt. He had accepted the honor as squire, but ended up like this. "He gave me freedom of will."

"I'm sure it doesn't include wasting your life away," Calub said, gazing at him. "Lans, shouldn't you return to your master's side?"

Lansius couldn't challenge that notion. "Since you're here . . . does it mean you've come to fetch me up?"

Calub shook his head. "Last time was a contract, but I'm not joining the Arvenians."

Something didn't add up, Lansius thought. "But then, why are you looking for me?"

Calub paused for a moment. "Well, it wasn't easy, but as I've said before, I have connections." He pulled a thin brown leather wrap from his inside coat pocket and put it on the table.

"What's that?" Lansius asked.

"An invitation."

The answer puzzled him, but the contents might hold an answer. "May I?"

Calub motioned him to do as he pleased. Lansius proceeded to open the rugged leather and reached out for a thick envelope inside. He noticed the purple wax seal that bore a crest of a regal-looking man riding a horse.

Lansius didn't recognize the crest, but he knew that good quality paper was expensive. He looked up at Calub. "Is this for me?"

Calub nodded, and Lansius carefully unsealed the wax, pulling out the paper.

He saw neat handwriting on the letter with distinctly legible and glossy black ink, clearly the work of a skilled scribe. Although it was an invitation, Lansius felt more like he was being summoned by the noble who sent it. "What does this baronet want?"

"I haven't the faintest idea." Calub exhaled sharply. "Nevertheless . . . I thought it would be beneficial for you. That's why I accepted the task of delivering that letter."

With too much weighing on his mind, instead of responding, Lansius tore off another piece of bread and dipped it into the stew. He and Calub were comrades, but Lansius hardly knew the alchemist well. The fact that Calub now brought an invitation from a baronet in Midlandia was unsettling.

*Who is he working for?*

Calub didn't press for a response and instead quietly ate his stew. The plump serving girl returned with a bowl of gruel and placed it in front of Lansius.

"Gratitude," Lansius said to the girl, who bowed her head before leaving. He stirred the gruel with his spoon and noticed pieces of cheese and salted meat swirling around. Feeling somewhat calmer, he turned to Calub and asked, "What is this invitation about? Can I decline?"

"Of course," Calub reassured him. "It's not a summons. But why don't you meet them first?"

Lansius hesitated, so Calub went on. "It's clear that they have an interest in you. Midlandia's nobles may be ruthless, but they're also fair."

Upon hearing that, Lansius stopped stirring. "But I'm a squire to Sir Archie."

"That's exactly why you need to meet them. Your master needs Midlandia's support. You'll do well to build a relationship with a baronet to help Sir Archie's cause."

Lansius couldn't find fault in his friend's logic, but he remained indecisive. "I need to consult with my master first."

"By all means," the alchemist remarked lightly.

"If I accept the invitation, will you accompany me?"

Calub smiled and replied, "I could, but I shouldn't. They are only interested in you, and we wouldn't want to make a rude gesture."

Despite the questions, Lansius didn't feel like accepting. He had a carefree life. Why would he risk it for something vague? He had tried hard to improve his station in life: working as a farmer, teacher, workhouse clerk, forest survivor, and squire—all in a single year—but all had led to nothing.

Fate had a way of pushing him back to square one, leaving him feeling powerless. He felt like a dry leaf caught in a whirlwind of conflicts.

This year, Lansius had witnessed more violence and desperation than most men experience in a lifetime. The traumas from Riverstead and the

Amertume forest never left him. Because of this, he was reluctant to even hold onto hope.

Yet despite his emptiness, a faint ambition began to kindle within him. His eyes sparkled as he pondered whether there was still something—or someone— worth living for. Though he had lost Stefi, the thought of his family in Bellandia gave him pause for hope.

*Perhaps this'll pave the road to return home.*


One week had passed since Lansius began his journey to Toruna. Today, the sun rose over the medieval countryside, casting a warm glow on the landscape. A refreshing breeze swept through the fields, carrying with it the unique aroma of ripe crops ready for harvest. The narrow path meandered through the golden fields, the stalks gently swaying in the breeze.

The sound of hooves echoed against the dirt road. Lansius rode in a horse-drawn cart laden with goods, sharing the space only with the old coachman sitting up front.

Before he left on this journey, Lansius had consulted Sir Archie, who recognized that the baronet of Toruna was an influential man in his own right, and also close to the powerful Seneschal Bengrieve. Because they needed all the influence they could muster, he agreed to send Lansius on his first errand as a squire.

"There." Suddenly, the coachman pointed to the south after they passed over a hill.

Following his hand, Lansius spotted a manor beside a small river, flanked by recently harvested farms, orchards, and a nearby village. "Is that where the baronet of Toruna lives?" he asked.

"This is Toruna," the coachman replied with a thick foreign accent, seemingly struggling to make small talk.

Lansius allowed himself to become fully immersed in the breathtaking beauty of the harvest season, a reminder of the bountiful fields of Bellandia. After a month of seclusion in Feodosia, he felt rejuvenated, his old self having returned.

"Always, good harvest. Land is blessed," the coachman added proudly.

Lansius politely nodded. The land was indeed prosperous, with a good population, and looked well-governed.

It took another hour before they reached the manor. The coachman drove the cart through the vast courtyard and up to the entrance of the manor.

Lansius grew anxious, worried about his first impression. He saw two armed men accompany them from the gate, but they kept their distance.

"Go on. Go down," the coachman instructed.

Lansius carefully dismounted from the cart and gazed up at the imposing three-story structure that loomed before him. Though not a castle, it radiated an air of authority and grandeur. The walls were built with smooth, large gray stones, while the wooden parts were painted white, creating a striking contrast. At a glance, there were no vines or moss, making the entire building appear immaculately maintained, as if it had been constructed only recently.

*Now, this is a manor.*

Compared to this, Lansius thought, Sabina Rustica was aptly named a rustic villa.

A surprised pageboy approached Lansius. "Oh, we expected a delivery, not a guest," he complained innocently.

Lansius couldn't resist a smile. "It's all right, I can wait outside." He pulled out a letter, showing the crest on the purple wax seal.

"Gratitude, maester, please wait here. Don't go anywhere," the boy said and ran inside. His footsteps echoed inside the cavernous hall.

# CHAPTER 27

# HENCHMEN

Lansius stepped inside the medieval manor house, his senses filled with awe. The great hall was immense and filled with long wooden tables and benches that may accommodate thirty or forty people with ease. The high ceiling made the air feel clean, not stale, dusty, or moldy.

At the hall's far end, Lansius saw a raised platform, likely the high table where the host would sit. However, it was the big glass window upstairs that caught his attention the most, letting in warm, sunny light that filled the great hall with a gentle glow.

As the page boy led him farther into the manor, Lansius noticed a group of servants moving about their daily tasks, too preoccupied to take notice of him. Behind them, two guardsmen trailed them from a distance.

Soon, the page boy escorted Lansius into an antechamber, a place where a guest could wait or rest. "The steward will be here shortly—please make yourself, mm . . . comfortable," he stammered. "Oh, there's water in the basin and a washcloth." The pageboy tried his hardest to deliver his line.

"Gratitude, I'll be waiting here." Lansius smiled and the page boy hurriedly left.

Lansius saw the bench, a small table, and the stone basin.

*Better to clean up.*

Custom dictated the guest wash their face and hands before meeting a respectable host, but Lansius wanted to go above and beyond to show that he wasn't a country bumpkin. After all, he was Lord Arte's squire. Disguised or not, he needed to keep a good appearance, not tarnish his lord's name.

With that in mind, he changed out of his traveling clothes and into a deep blue doublet he had taken from Sabina Rustica. Although it was a little loose around the waist, he could easily fix that with his belt.

He wrapped the sword belt around his waist and suddenly felt nostalgic for his long-lost friend, but he quickly dismissed the sentiment. Today wasn't the time to reminisce about the past.

Just then, a servant knocked and entered before Lansius could reply. A young boy appeared and bowed deeply. "Maester, I'll clean your boots."

Lansius was taken aback. He had never had this treatment before. "Um, what should I do?"

"Just stand there, maester," the boy replied energetically as he scrubbed Lansius's boots with a horsehair brush.

Lansius couldn't help but feel uneasy about the child labor, but the boy looked happy, with chubby cheeks, clean clothes, and good manners.

*He probably received an education and a better job than most Arvenians . . . probably also sleeps in a comfortable bed.*

Lansius briefly pondered the morality of it, but shook his head. He wasn't here to judge.

The boy quietly left, closing the door behind him after finishing his task.

After enduring a grueling two-week journey by cart and foot, Lansius finally found himself alone in the waiting chamber. He let out a deep sigh as he lowered himself onto the bench, feeling the weight of exhaustion settling heavily upon him. With a tired hand, he took out his waterskin and took a long swig of water before settling in to wait.

As the sun began to set, the manor sprang to life with bustling activity. Lansius, now cleaned up and refreshed, could imagine that a feast was taking place in the great hall, as was customary for feudal nobles.

The lord of this manor may have been just a baronet, but it was clear to everyone who saw it that Toruna was a rich, fertile land. It beggared belief that someone who wasn't a baron could own such a grand estate. Meaning, the baronet of Toruna was either a rising star at Midlandia's court, or old money.

A much older gentleman appeared at the door. "Excuse me, maester. The baronet requests your presence at dinner."

Lansius rose from his seat. "Please, call me Lansius. I'm just a clerk turned squire."

The old steward smiled warmly, but remained silent as he led Lansius up an elegant staircase and through a series of corridors that eventually brought them to a private dining hall. It was smaller and more intimate than the great hall, but no less impressive.

Though they were on the second floor, the ceiling was high, and two beautiful chandeliers illuminated the space with an unflickering white light that was brighter than any candles Lansius had ever seen. The walls were plastered evenly and painted bright colors.

At this time of year, the room was furnished with colorful tapestries depicting scenes of battles and hunting. One in particular intrigued Lansius, a small green tapestry that illustrated what looked like dwarves and their underground citadels.

Regrettably, he couldn't approach the tapestry out of respect to his host. Nevertheless, he marveled at the room's other features, including murals, painted statues, and two gorgeous suits of armor.

The steward gestured for Lansius to take a seat on the far end of a long, exquisite table. "The baronet will arrive shortly."

Lansius sat and found the air pleasant, filled with the sweet scent of fresh flowers or fruit. Ironically, such a lovely place might hide a dangerous threat, like the lair of a dragon. He noticed two guards standing by the exit. From their demeanor and discipline, he could tell that they had proper training.

One piece of advice from his long-lost friend rang in Lansius's head: be prepared to not go home when a noble has summoned you.

*Tonight it's either a comfy bed or a dungeon . . .*

There were stories of nobles summoning lowborn, only to accuse them of a crime they never did and throw them in the dungeon.

*Why did I even bother showing up?*

Before Lansius could get cold feet, the sound of marching footsteps outside announced the arrival of the master of the house.

Lansius stood and made sure not to gawk at his host as he entered. To his surprise, the baronet was an athletic man dressed in a red silk outfit.

Following the baronet was a lady in a dark gown and veil that covered her face, as well as a squire and a page boy.

"Just sit wherever you like," the baronet said as he took his seat at the opposite end of the table.

The lady seemed bothered by Lansius's presence and just stood there.

*Why is she so tense? Don't tell me I still smell.*

"Audrey, you're not going to sit?" the baronet addressed her.

"I will not take part in this scheme," the lady blurted out, catching everyone's attention.

*A scheme . . . ?*

Lansius's throat felt dry. Meanwhile, the baronet merely laughed at the lady's words and turned to his guest with a faint smile. "My name is Stan, and this lovely lady here is my lovely sister," he said, emphasizing the last two words in a peculiar way. "And you're here because the seneschal ordered me to invite you on his behalf."

*The seneschal? Lord Bengrieve!?*

The stakes were getting higher, and the situation was spiraling out of control. "Sir, my apologies, but I'm just a clerk turned squire. I'm hardly important." Lansius tried to reason with him.

"It doesn't matter. Let's talk over dinner." The baronet nodded at his steward, who signaled the servants to bring out the food.

But his sister refused to be ignored. "What does he have to do with this? He should leave now!" the lady demanded.

Lansius felt a sting of offense, his self-esteem knocked down a notch.

"Audrey, he's a fellow Arvenian, like you," the baronet said, as if patronizing her.

*A fellow Arvenian?*

The lady clicked her tongue in protest and approached the baronet's table hurriedly.

Lansius froze as he tried to make sense of what was going on. It was then that he realized the reason for the lady's black dress and veil.

*She's in mourning! Oh, no . . . did she lose someone in Sabina Rustica?*

Cold sweat ran down Lansius's back. He could already taste the rotting dungeon, the stench of piss and decay.

The two bickered in private, leaving Lansius standing nervously as if waiting for his judgment. They were still at it when the three servants arrived with silver platters.

The servants brought a variety of appetizing dishes. Lansius spotted roasted meat, aromatic stews, sweet and tasty puddings, and an assortment of freshly baked bread. One of them also poured him a generous amount of pale ale in a beautiful silver goblet.

With his fate uncertain, Lansius decided to eat and drink as much as he could before rotting away in the dungeon.

"My guest!" the baronet yelled suddenly, making Lansius's heart skip a beat. "We have reached a consensus."

"Y-yes, my good sir," Lansius steeled his heart as the baronet in red and the lady in black watched his every move.

"On behalf of Lord Bengrieve, I'm going to give Lady Audrey to you," the baronet guffawed at his own silly joke and jumped from his seat. He was just in time as the lady picked a handful of green grapes from the table and threw it at him.

"That's not how it goes!" the lady complained as Sir Stan dodged the grapes. She snatched up a nearby cup of wine and hurled its contents at her brother, who was surprised but stayed put. He seemed to accept the splash, but before the wine could hit him, a gust of wind blew out of nowhere.

The baronet smirked in triumph as he saw the wine spray back onto the lady, drenching her as if she were a cat caught in a downpour.

*Magic!*

Lansius was uncertain of what to do or say, but he slowly scanned the room, taking in the scene around him. He had heard of mysterious individuals, known as mages, who wielded magical powers. If someone like Sir Stan could employ one, it meant that he held great influence despite his low rank.

The guards and the servants were struggling to suppress their chuckles, while the steward and squire appeared uninterested. However, Lansius could not spot any visible signs of the mage. He felt foolish; he had been expecting to see someone with a long beard, wielding a staff and wearing a pointy hat. In truth, he had no idea what a mage looked like.

"Fine," the lady spat, after her humiliation.

Sensing the tension in the air, the baronet attempted to defuse the situation. "Lady . . . let's be civil," he suggested. When it didn't seem to have the desired effect, he added a gentle threat. "Or else I'll have to confine you to your room . . . without alcohol."

"Drop the pretense, we're not related!" she snapped back, before pointing her finger at Lansius. "Let him out, or hand him over as my retinue, and we'll call it even."

Lansius squinted his eyes at this new development.

"Are you going to hurt him?" Sir Stan asked playfully.

The lady merely grunted in response.

Upon hearing this, the baronet clapped his hands twice and exclaimed, "Deal!" before quickly adding, "Now, let's eat."

Merriment erupted on his command. The troubadours took center stage, playing a lively tune. The baronet, as if famished, dipped a pretzel into the stew and devoured it. Ironically, despite his command, only the lady in black and Lansius were joining him at the table. The others in the room were merely in waiting.

Meanwhile, Lansius repeated the words that had been echoing in his mind.

*Did I hear that right? Hand me over . . . is this some kind of feudal employment, but on what grounds?*

Clearly, Sir Stan's earlier comment about giving the lady to Lansius was in jest. However, their final decision for him didn't seem like one. Nonetheless, Lansius's limited understanding of noble etiquette meant he couldn't be certain and needed to seek advice before reacting. Otherwise, he could offend them.

The lady in black, after having some assistance from a maid, approached Lansius. "Eat," she commanded coldly.

"Yes, my lady," Lansius answered despite the many unanswered questions in his mind.

"I'll meet you after," the lady announced, making it clear she wouldn't be partaking in the dinner. With those words, she pivoted and departed, her veil swishing behind her, radiating an air of determination.

**CHAPTER 28**

# THE LADY IN BLACK

The feast hosted by the baronet of Toruna was delightful. Lansius would've never thought that the baronet was a natural party maker. Sir Stan even hand-fed morsels from his own plate to the troubadours, danced with them, and poured ale for his subordinates.

Lansius felt privileged to witness these supposedly private moments between a lord and his closest retinue.

The harvest season brought an abundance of grains and vegetables, sparing Lansius from some of the more unique dishes he dreaded, such as roast hedgehog, brain jelly, or viper soup. He was always anxious about being expected to eat something or potentially offending someone.

Fortunately, Sir Stan had an uncanny, relaxed attitude toward the men beneath his station. He didn't even try to make small talk, but motioned for Lansius to dig in and enjoy the merriment. This put Lansius at ease.

As with any other lowborn, Lansius wisely feared the noblemen, as offending them could result in flogging or a trip to the dungeon. Thus, seeing the noble behaving so relaxed was a revelation.

Despite the ongoing confusion about the nature of the summons, and the issues with the lady in black, Lansius found his appetite. He had yet to learn about why he was here, but food was food. After living as a farmer for two years, he was too grateful for any opportunity to eat good food.

And he ate with a clear conscience. After all, food was in abundance around harvest, so this wasn't a privilege of the rich. Lansius ate well and enjoyed the feast.

The meal was the best he ever had, with no salted meat in sight, meaning it was freshly cut. He could taste ginger, pepper, and possibly cloves, which were a rarity.

Surprisingly, Sir Stan mostly ate brown bread and vegetable stew with only a few slices of meat. For dessert, they had a sweet pudding made from milk, egg, and day-old bread, topped with cinnamon and honey.

The music ended with a round of applause from everyone, including Lansius. The troubadours bowed elegantly while Sir Stan walked away after his last cup of water. A cool breeze entered the chamber as if signaling the end of the feast.

Lansius felt this was his only chance. He dared to approach the baronet and asked, "My good sir, I thank you for the hospitality, but I still don't know what is to become of me?"

Sir Stan paused, unexpectedly reached for Lansius's shoulder, and patted him firmly. "For better or for worse, you have caught the eye of a powerful man. My advice to you . . . play to his tune."

"But sir, I am Sir Archie's squire." Lansius couldn't reveal his master's true identity.

"Oh, the Arvenian lord," Sir Stan mused, which shocked Lansius. However, he ultimately refused to give counsel. "Well, that's hardly my problem, but I'm sure someone will sort it out. Now, if you'll excuse me."

With a vigorous stride, the baronet left, leaving Lansius to wonder about his fate.

The old steward called out to Lansius, "Maester squire, I believe you have a place to visit." He then motioned his hand toward a tall guard and said, "He will escort you there."


Lansius was surprised by the interior of the manor. Instead of a gloomy castle, the corridor was fresh and lively, with bright lanterns on the sides or hung above the staircase. The white plastered walls reflected the light, creating a welcoming ambience even on the darkest of nights.

Led by the guard, Lansius arrived at the parlor, reserved for confidential discussions. Before knocking, the guard looked at Lansius, cautioning, "The lady has been injured in recent conflict. She's prone to emotional outbursts. If you require assistance, just knock on the door."

Lansius didn't get a chance to inquire; the guard had already knocked. A maid appeared, bearing a tray covered with a linen cloth, and without a word, she left the room. "Come in and close the door," a voice beckoned from within.

Now, without anyone's interference, something about her voice stirred a vague sense of familiarity within him. Yet, Lansius couldn't quite place it, and there was little he could do but walk in as instructed. Upon observing a lady elegantly clad in a black gothic gown, he gently closed the door behind him, isolating himself with her and leaving the guard stationed outside.

Just as the door closed, she raised a finger to her lips and beckoned him closer with her other hand.

Something didn't feel right, but Lansius cautiously followed her instructions. He had only taken a few steps when the woman suddenly lunged at him.

"What are you—" he started, attempting to raise his hand in surprise, but she tackled him harshly, knocking him off balance. He felt himself falling backward, and suddenly everything went dark.

Lansius groaned in pain, the sensation jolting his consciousness back to the present.

"Be quiet and stay still," a woman's voice commanded.

Recalling her attack, Lansius scrambled to his feet.

"Lans, stay still," she repeated coldly, showing him a dagger.

But, she didn't really need to. Suddenly it all clicked. The way she called his name, her voice . . . He turned around expecting Stefi but found instead a figure shrouded in a black veil.

"We don't have much time. I apologize for attacking you, but—"

"Show me your face." Lansius couldn't help it anymore. He knew he recognized the voice and dared to risk the consequences.

The woman sighed. Without a word, she lifted the black veil from her face. It was more akin to a wedding veil than a typical coif or headscarf.

Lansius beheld a complexion of unnatural paleness, a result of makeup, contrasted by two piercing brown eyes that seemed fierce enough to make children weep in fright. Meeting her gaze, his eyes reflexively widened, his muscles tensed, and for a moment, he forgot to breathe. He could only stare at the face he yearned to see for so long.

"It's me," she said somberly. "But now, you shall address me as Audrey of Toruna."

"But—"

She raised a finger to her lips. "Answer me first, why are you here?" she asked.

*Did she suspect me of betraying* the *Arvenians?* Lansius wondered.

"I was invited here."

"Invited? Why?" she asked.

"I'm just as clueless as you, but I have the letter in my bag. That'll prove my innocence."

She slowly reached for his bag, and rummaged through its contents, pulling out a letter. After reading it, she shook her head.

"Stefi, how did you end up here? I was—" He stopped.

The mention of the name seemed to trigger something within her.

"Don't call me that," she protested as if in agony.

Lansius approached her. "I'm sorry. Are you hurt?"

Audrey gritted her teeth, a sign that something was terribly wrong. Then, it dawned on him.

*The veil . . . could it be concealing a head injury?*

"Never mind me," she said, clutching the dagger firmly in her hand. "What happened with the rest of the Arvenians?"

He suspected it could be post-traumatic stress. Lansius took a deep breath to compose himself. Using a softer voice, he assured her, "You may not believe it, but Lord Arte is safe. He's in Midlandia."

"The young lord escaped Riverstead?" she asked, the suspicion in her voice dissipating.

Lansius nodded. "We rescued him from the slavers' den." He tried to sound cheerful to sell his story.

Audrey's face betrayed the turmoil inside her.

"It's me. You can trust me. Why do you look pained? Tell me where it hurts," he said, concerned.

She shook her head, gradually regaining her composure, then slowly sheathed the dagger and tucked it away.

"If you're comfortable, tell me all your worries; let me help shoulder them," he offered gently.

She looked at him, her lips forming a pout. "The Lansius I knew wasn't this bold," she remarked, her tone lighter.

"Things happened . . ." Lansius replied. Memories of the events that led him here flooded his mind, including the Amertume forest. Emboldened by these thoughts, he took her hand and said, "Love, I have been looking for you. I've searched everywhere." He paused. His own words surprised him.

*When . . . ?*

He hadn't even realized it before, but the pain he'd felt when he couldn't find her, the pain that drove him to drinking—now all of it suddenly made sense. He loved her. She was more than just a comrade to him.

Audrey stared at Lansius. Her gaze seemed more intense than before.

He looked away and felt Audrey move closer. She sat beside him, resting her head on his shoulder and muttering, "I'm glad you're safe."

"So am I," he agreed, holding back tears of joy.

*I thought I lost you . . .*

The heavy lump in his heart, the one not even alcohol could manage to erase, was beginning to feel lighter.

For a moment, they sat in silence.

"Why didn't you recognize me earlier? At supper?" he asked.

"Your appearance surprised me, but I tried not to show it."

"Why?"

"Lans, we're not in Arvena anymore. It's better not to let them know that we know each other." She then added, "I don't know these guys. The last time I—" Pain flashed across her face.

"You don't have to think about that." Lansius was worried about her memory from the last war.

"I can't recall much. It always gives me a headache. But I woke up here, which I believe is far away from Riverstead. They treat me well. But they never explain anything to me."

Lansius found it hard to believe but chose to reassure her gently. "You are you; nothing has changed."

She looked at him with softer eyes and whispered, "You're probably here because a Midlandian nobleman wants to use you."

"Lord Stan wanted me?"

She shook her head. "He's just another pawn. The mastermind is Lord Bengrieve . . ."

The name made Lansius's heart skip a beat. "Why does he need me? For what?"

Audrey exhaled sharply. "How could I know that? I don't even know their plans for me."

Lansius scratched his head. "Could it be related to Sabina Rustica?" he ventured, more to himself.

"Sabina what?" She furrowed her brow "I'm not familiar with Midlandia. I hope that's not a brothel."

"No, no, well . . . sort of," Lansius admitted awkwardly.

Her sidelong glance held an intensity that made Lansius falter. "Is it just me, or has that look in your eye grown fiercer?" he asked.

"The veil does also help with that," she hinted cryptically.

"So, you have no idea why this powerful man wants me? I doubt he's interested in a lowly clerk or squire like myself."

Audrey pondered for a moment. "I'm not sure, but perhaps it has to do with your origin."

"Origin?"

She glanced at his hair, and Lansius instinctively realized she meant his black hair, the mark of a foreigner.

*A foreigner, huh? Indeed, having a foreigner could be useful if they need a scapegoat, especially one with clear, undeniable proof.*

Lansius let out a long sigh. His black hair continued to become a blessing and a curse in one. Despite his newfound worries, he felt a burden had been lifted from his chest. "At least I found you. That's what matters most."

She pouted again and looked away, a response Lansius was all too familiar with.

"Why did you change your name?"

Audrey abruptly stood, masking her emotions as she moved to a seat across the room.

In that moment, a realization dawned upon Lansius. Despite her present state, Audrey had likely been a captive, possibly even sold into slavery. He once read that in the Imperium, the stigma of slavery was so profound that freed individuals would adopt new identities. The old name was seen as unlucky or even cursed.

He followed her, taking a seat opposite hers. He finally asked the question that had been gnawing at him. "What's happened to you? That fine black gown, everyone referring to you as a lady, even the baronet calling you his sister . . . Did you marry someone?"

Audrey stared at him, disbelief etched across her face. "Why would anyone want a female squire with no lands or titles to her name?"

Lansius could only nod in understanding, choosing not to press further. He was well aware of her tendency to become stubborn under pressure.

Over time, she slowly began to open up. "At first I thought they needed a female squire for some reason, but they haven't assigned me to protect anyone."

Lansius pondered this, trying to determine whether the Midlandian nobles were allies or potential threats.

"We're mere pawns in their grand game," Audrey murmured with a grim acceptance.

"Let them try," he retorted, his face stoic and his voice determined. "One way or another, I'll find a way out."

Her gaze held a glimmer of admiration. "To be the master of your fate is a dangerous idea . . . Remember the wine that soaked me earlier?"

Lansius's eyes widened with sudden comprehension. "Magic?"

She nodded. "One of his retainers must be . . . Sir Stan is Lord Bengrieve's most trusted henchman. Having a mage under him is not that far-fetched."

The thrill from his close brush with magic still lingered, yet Lansius had something else on his mind. "What about us?" he dared to ask.

"Us . . . ?" Audrey echoed with surprise.

"I'm now Squire to Lord Arte. Am I not good enough?" He tried a line he had picked up from traveling minstrels.

She blinked, clearly taken aback. "Lans, do you realize what you're saying?"

Lansius could only offer a small smile. "My feelings are sincere."

Audrey shook her head. "Why would you want me?" she muttered, more to herself than to him. "I am just a sword maiden. And a broken one at that." She turned slightly, sweeping her hair aside to reveal a scar on her head.

Lansius felt a surge of emotions: anger at whomever had harmed her and an overwhelming urge to care for her.

She continued. "Sometimes, even in daylight, I feel as though I'm walking through a nightmare. I even assaulted you. I fear . . . I'm not the same person you knew."

He took her hand and held it tight. "All the more reason for me to stand by you."

Audrey broke a smile. "The hurried hare falls prey to the waiting hound," she recited.

"What does that mean?" Lansius questioned, puzzled by her sudden adage.

"It's what my master used to remind me," she began, her voice dipped in nostalgia. "Haste leads to unpreparedness and danger." She took a deep breath, meeting his gaze. "We need to focus on surviving now. Afterward, we can talk about us."

Understanding dawned on Lansius, and he nodded, appreciating the pragmatism behind her words. "Promise?" He sought assurance, offering his hand.

Audrey took his hand, her grip firm and steadfast. "I'll renew my oath to you. No matter the circumstances, I'll protect you."

Outside, the gentle whisper of the wind caressed the night, offering a deceptive tranquility in this idyllic, rustic corner of the world.

# CHAPTER 29

# A LADY NAMED AUDREY

A gentle breeze swept through the mansion's private yard adjacent to the garden. The sun was still cool, and the cold breeze was abundant—a perfect time for training.

Inhaling deeply, Lansius filled his lungs with the earthy scent of the changing seasons. He drew his blunt training blade and lunged at the lady dressed in a black gambeson. She parried his thrust, but it lacked finesse, leaving her open for a follow-up attack.

However, she had already anticipated Lansius's next move. Taking a step forward, she sidestepped his thrust, guiding his blade aside with her protected underarm. With a swift motion, she tapped the pommel of her sword against the left side of Lansius's head.

"You're dead," Audrey said, her tone full of disappointment.

"It's still too early," Lansius said, offering an excuse.

Audrey sighed. "You went into battle with just this?"

"I used a spear," he countered.

"That's no excuse. Again!"

Lansius retreated a step and raised his sword. He knew Audrey's teaching style was brutal.

As he had feared, Audrey lunged forward with a thrust. Lansius moved his sword to parry, but as their swords connected, the lack of force behind her blade signaled that it was a feint.

*Oh, crap!*

He instinctively raised his left arm to shield his head and took a step back. His guess was correct: his wrist took the brunt of a blow from her left fist.

"Ha! Guessed it right!" he proclaimed, only to feel something poke his gambeson-protected stomach.

"You blocked a fist but missed the sword. Lans, you're getting worse. You're unfit to be a squire!" Audrey chastised.

The words were a blow to his ego. He offered a faint smile but gripped his training sword's hilt more tightly.

"That's more like it. I see anger in your eyes. You said you wanted to protect me? Back up your words with steel," Audrey challenged.

Lansius grinned and sidestepped to the right. Audrey adjusted her position accordingly. They moved almost as if they were dancing in a circle.

*There!*

Lansius noticed exactly where the sunlight was hitting the stone floor most intensely, and he lured Audrey into that spot. The moment she blinked against the sun's glare, Lansius quickly stepped forward.

Audrey heard his rapid footsteps and took several steps back. Once her eyes adjusted, she saw that Lansius had closed the distance and launched a horizontal cut, which she blocked.

A metallic clang filled the air as their swords met. A faint smile graced her lips. "That's more like it."

Suddenly, she turned the clash into a grapple, both of them half-swording as they tried to overpower each other. Lansius sensed that Audrey was not putting her full strength into it. "Are you injured?" he asked.

"I've been injured for weeks, maybe months. And they won't let me train."

"So this is your first training in months?"

She flashed a grin. "Yep, and I intend to enjoy it to the fullest."

Lansius swallowed nervously. In a deft move, Audrey shifted her weight backward, disrupting his footing and balance. As he struggled to regain his poise, her piercing gaze forced him to momentarily close his eyes.

*SMACK!*

Audrey laughed, withdrew her sword, and ran. She had just slapped Lansius.

Lansius froze, feeling a stinging sensation on his right cheek. "Why did you do that?" he shouted.

Audrey, however, was laughing as if she were thoroughly enjoying herself. "I couldn't help it. You were too close and too unguarded!"

"Come here," he retorted, chasing her into the wooded area outside the garden where servants usually collected firewood.


Two figures observed the events in the garden through a window inside Toruna Mansion.

"Stan, are you sure it's okay to let them roam free?" asked a female servant with long brown hair. Her tone lacked the usual deference.

"It may sound crazy, but I trust that man. He seems level-headed and reasonable," replied the baronet, still clad in his flamboyant red silk robe.

"I hope so. I've put in a lot of effort to heal that woman. It would be a waste if she escaped."

Sir Stan chuckled. "You'll be compensated either way."

"Certainly," she said without doubt. "I'm just curious about why Lord Bengrieve wanted to save her."

"It's best not to question our master's motives," Sir Stan said, smiling.

The servant nodded quickly. "Right. I trust that you have guardsmen on standby?"

"Of course, they're keeping watch and have horses ready," Sir Stan reassured her.

Moments passed before she ventured, "Stan."

"Yes?"

"Can I stop doing this? I'm tired. I wish to return to my own life and live carefree."

The man chuckled, completely disregarding her pout. "Hannei, you're too valuable to our master. Just be grateful he stopped pressuring us to marry."

"Eugh," she groaned and shuddered. "You should abandon your life of debauchery and marry someone more suitable. Just stay away from me."

Stan grinned, flexing his toned arms and abs, which were fully visible as he wore his robe loosely. This annoyed the servant, who muttered something under her breath. Suddenly, a cold breeze blew toward the baronet.

"All right, all right, cut it out. You're making me want to pee!" Stan barked, comically shielding his crotch with his hands.

The servant sighed at her friend's antics, waved her hand dismissively, and left.


Lansius chased Audrey into the wooded area and found her out of breath. The long confinement had ruined her stamina. Still, she turned around with her sword drawn. However, Lansius dropped his blade and approached with open arms.

With a ragged breath, she looked at him and questioned his gesture. "What are you doing? We're still training!"

"Hugs?" Lansius quipped.

"We don't have that kind of relationship," she retorted, her cheeks reddening slightly.

Lansius chuckled and dropped down onto the dew-wet grass, leaning against a tree. He unbuttoned the top part of his gambeson to cool off. "Ah, it feels nice to sit down like this."

Audrey rolled her eyes but followed suit, sitting down in front of him. They sat in silence, catching their breath and listening to the rustling leaves and the gentle breeze. The ground was still cool from last night, while the sun was still far in the east.

Lansius noticed that Audrey's mood had vastly improved since the day before; the suspicion and coldness were gone.

"Lans, I apologize for the slap," Audrey began, interrupting the silence.

Lansius glanced at her. "Hey, it's training. I bet you were aiming for another punch."

Audrey pouted and crawled toward him. "You can slap me back if you want," she offered.

She then closed her eyes, looking nervous, as if waiting to be slapped, and it sent Lansius into a stifled laugh.

Hearing Lansius's reaction, she opened her eyes and furrowed her brow.

"Not fair," he complained. "How could I hurt someone I like?"

The atmosphere grew awkward as both averted their gaze. Lansius had spent the night reflecting on their situation, but he knew her oath to her master prevented any thoughts of marriage.

She exhaled deeply. "I also apologize for yesterday."

Lansius caught her gaze and saw guilt written all over her face. "You were just confused by my sudden appearance. I get it. Apology accepted."

Audrey sighed a breath of relief.

"Considering how things went yesterday, I'm surprised Sir Stan allowed us to spar so readily," Lansius mused.

Audrey glanced around, ensuring no one was within earshot. "I'm not sure why, but I'm grateful for the opportunity to train. My arms feel sluggish."

Lansius nodded. "How's your injury?"

Her hand reached the top of her head and rubbed it. "Sometimes it feels itchy, but the headaches are just painful."

"Isn't there any medication?" Lansius asked.

"Sir Stan offered me some, but it dulls my senses. I'd rather not."

The chirping of birds interrupted their conversation. "A love song," commented Lansius.

"I didn't know you speak bird," Audrey quipped.

"Oh, I know many things," Lansius shot back, making her laugh.

"We should get back to training before anyone becomes suspicious," Audrey suggested as she stood up.

"Wait, tell me more about your name change first," Lansius urged.

Audrey stiffened. "I told you about it already. What more do you need to know?"

Lansius also stood and said, "Easy, you only have to tell me if you want to. I'm not forcing you to do anything."

She nodded, so Lansius continued. "You did explain it yesterday, but I'm a foreigner. I don't fully understand."

Audrey looked away and said, "Don't call me by my old name. Anyone who falls into slavery is considered dead, and their name becomes cursed. So, if you survive you pick another name."

Lansius sighed. He had liked that name and felt sentimental about it.

Audrey's reaction was also a contrast to that of the slaves he had liberated in Sabina Rustica.

*I guess there's a different culture even inside the Imperium.*

"You would do well to like my new name. None other than Lord Bengrieve gave it to me."

"He did what?" Lansius was stunned.

Audrey shrugged. "I was told that's the case. And then I was adopted into this baronet family. Can you believe it?"

Lansius shook his head. "Unbelievable," he muttered.

Audrey shook her head and said, "They won't give me a straight answer, so I'll have to rely on you for that."

Lansius picked up the training sword and swung it twice to shake off the dew. "What do they want from Arvenians like us?"

"Lans, we're not even Arvenians. I'm born in Centuria, and you're not even from the continent."


The fall season arrived in Midlandia, ushering in a bountiful harvest. While the inhabitants reaped the fruits of their labor, other regions of the Imperium found themselves in the throes of a threatening famine.

The grave situation worsened with the intractable nomadic incursion in the west, escalating beastmen attacks in the south and the northern provinces breaking away from the Imperium.

The Elven Calendar year of 4423 was shaping up to be the most challenging year the Imperium had faced since its inception. As for Lansius and Audrey, despite the joy of their reunion, they found themselves in a precarious situation.

"Lord Bengrieve wanted me because I'm a foreigner?" Lansius asked, having just been briefed.

"That much I can tell you," Sir Stan replied. "But officially, it's me who wanted you. Best not to mention our master's name outside this study."

Lansius pondered a little, while Sir Stan sat comfortably in his padded chair with a smug look on his face. The two of them were alone in the luxurious chamber.

"But why does my background matter so much?"

"This is only between you and me," warned Sir Stan. "We're going on a campaign."

Lansius was intrigued. "To Arvena?"

"No, to the south."

"South?" Lansius was surprised.

"We need to secure our rear before heading north."

Lansius nodded. He didn't know much about the political situation in the region.

"I'll have someone brief you about the south, but in the meantime, you need to study and train."

"Will I be involved in battles?"

The owner of the manor chuckled. "Lansius, technically you're a squire under me. Act like one."

Lansius straightened his back. "Yes, sir."

"Good. Since your lord has temporarily transferred you to my house, I'll start paying you. There will be a bonus for confidentiality."

Lansius wasn't surprised. Lord Arte really needed to curry favor with Midlandia, and lending him out wasn't a big deal. Recalling Audrey, he decided to risk a question. "What about Lady Audrey? Why was she adopted?"

Sir Stan grinned. "For that, you'll have to ask Master Bengrieve. I'm sure he'll summon you next season or so. But . . . it's better not to inquire about Lady Audrey."

Lansius furrowed his brow.

"You can ask, but he'll likely give you a false answer. So, a piece of advice, squire: learn to live with mysteries."

Lansius nodded hesitantly.

Just as Sir Stan had told him, Lansius and Audrey spent the ensuing months training, preparing for their roles as pawns in Midlandia's grand scheme.

Outside of Toruna and Midlandia, the world was changing rapidly. Throughout fall and winter, Lord Arte gathered support from the Midlandian nobility, solidifying his status as a shrewd politician. He talked and finagled his way into becoming a favorite at court.

When winds from the eastern sea blew inland, news arrived: Calub had successfully recruited a small band of followers at Sir Stan's behest. Upon their arrival in Toruna, Calub, and his recruits caused quite a stir. The alchemist's influence was strong enough to persuade Sir Stan to grant Lansius permission to meet with the mage.

## CHAPTER 30

# THE MAGE

A spring thunderstorm was howling outside. Inside Sir Stan's manor, the servants began to light the chandelier. The thunderous booms could be felt despite the manor's sturdy stone construction.

Lansius cleared his throat. He wasn't in good shape. His face and body were bruised, and both of his palms were bandaged from training. His buttocks remained sore after continuous horse riding, even during winter.

*I should've carried a flask or something.*

He wasn't thirsty, but his throat felt bad. He wanted to get something warm, but he couldn't possibly pass up the opportunity to meet the mage.

Sir Stan had just granted his permission after receiving Calub's recommendation, and Lansius feared the baronet might reconsider his decision. So, he patiently waited just outside the chamber, waiting for a summons.

His thoughts returned to the alchemist. Calub turned out to be more influential than he initially thought. The way the two conversed made it clear that Calub was well-acquainted with Sir Stan and was even trusted enough to vouch for Lansius regarding the mage.

The man was either humble or simply concealing his status as an agent of a powerful noble.

At first, Lansius felt deceived, but he soon understood that secrecy was paramount in their circle. In exchange for such treatment, he gained access to a wealth of knowledge. The old Imperium history book he had read in Riverstead paled in comparison to the volumes the manor possessed.

In one manuscript, Lansius discovered detailed lore about the Ancients, the first beings to roam this planet. They were nearly immortal and, through their guidance, nascent species such as the elves and dwarves reached their peak during the Ancient Era.

During his time off from training, Lansius was currently engrossing himself in reading about early humans. These beings, the Grand Progenitors, were said to have lived even longer than the elves and were depicted much like the demigods from Greek mythology, complete with heroic deeds and epic tales.

However, there was one big caveat. One of the last Great Progenitors still walked the halls of the Imperium. He was known as the Ageless One. The reigning emperor.

While Lansius had heard about this before he read the books and manuscripts in Toruna, the grand figure was shrouded in great mystery. Everybody talked about the Ageless One as if he were a constant, much like the sun or the sky.

Only recently did Lansius understand there was more to the stories than just an immortal being.

The creaking of the heavy oaken door alerted Lansius. Audrey, decked in her usual gothic attire, stepped out from the chamber. Compared to last autumn, she had recovered some of her muscles.

"How was it?" asked Lansius as Audrey closed the door behind her.

"Ah, nothing. She—the mage is just curious about my eyes."

"She? The mage is a woman?"

Audrey let out a sigh. "Turns out to be." They had been suspicious about several guards and the squire, but never one of the maids.

"What about your eyes?" asked Lansius.

"She said she wanted to invite a colleague of hers, a Hunter Guildsman, to give them a check."

Lansius nodded nervously. He knew something was abnormal about those eyes, but he never thought it was something serious. "Are they magical or something?"

Audrey couldn't hide a faint smile. "I wish that were the case . . . Now go on, the mage wants to meet you."

Drawing a deep breath, Lansius was about to enter when Audrey whispered, "She seems trustworthy."

He paused in front of the door, their eyes met, and he whispered back, "How can you tell?"

"I trust my instinct."

Nodding, Lansius cautiously opened the door.

"Come in," came a female voice from inside.

Lansius entered and saw the mage in person. She wasn't much older than Audrey, wearing servant attire, but was relaxing on a comfortable-looking couch like a pampered lady.

"Please sit." She pointed at one chair in the corner where the desk was.

"Now that both of you know about me, I don't need to be in disguise anymore," she mused, as Lansius approached the chair.

The mage undid her off-white headscarf and pulled out her brown hair, which turned out to be a wig, revealing long, blonde hair beneath it.

The sight of her hair shocked Lansius. "Please excuse my curiosity, are you, my lady, a noble-born?"

"Even a dull blond catches the eyes. Eh?" she scoffed. "Hardly, but I get that a lot." She scratched her head with little regard for Lansius. The casualness of her demeanor emphasized their status disparity. "So, you asked to meet me. Why?"

Lansius had thought about this so many times that his heart almost burst. "I want to learn about magic."

"Learn about magic? Well, I suppose I could find you a book."

How easily she agreed didn't bode well for Lansius. "No, I read a book about the history of magic. That's not what I seek."

She paused to glance at Lansius momentarily. "Good, I hate books. The Imperium's alphabet is driving me nuts."

*She can't read the common tongue?*

Lansius tried again. "I want to learn magic. Can you teach me?"

"Oh, it's the same as that girl before you," she said flatly, with a hint of boredom.

"Eh?" He couldn't believe what he just heard. "Audrey wanted to learn magic too?"

The mage found the reaction to be funny and chuckled. "She didn't tell you? How quaint. I thought you two are a couple."

Lansius was rather taken aback. "Well, we still have our secrets."

The mage smiled judgmentally.

"Um, so can you teach me magic?"

She picked a comb from her pocket and began to comb her hair. "I can't teach. Magic is a talent anyway. Some have it, most don't."

Lansius pushed on. "At least you should test me."

"Test . . . ? Oh that test, so you did your homework. Well, I suppose I could."

"Great, then what should I do?" asked Lansius excitedly. Despite knowing about the test from the history of magic, the book didn't say anything about the procedure.

"Cast a fireball or something," she mused, almost laughing.

"How?" Lansius asked, brimming with anticipation for instruction.

The mage was stunned. Even the dumbest men in Midlandia knew that conjuring a fireball or any element was impossible. "Aren't you supposed to be smart? Even Calub vouched for you."

"Err . . . what does a fireball have to do with me being smart?"

"Because it's impossible!" she responded, a hint of tiredness in her voice.

"Oh, uh, right . . ." Lansius felt dumb.

The mage exhaled deeply in her seat, muttering, "*C'est pour ça que je déteste les gens.*"

The words sent a tingle through Lansius's ears, stunning him. They sounded like a foreign language he had once studied, likely in school. He nervously asked, "*Parlez-vous . . . français?*"

The mage jumped from her seat. Her eyes went wide as she hid herself behind the chair as if fearful of Lansius.

"No way," Lansius commented with his mouth agape. His suspicion was confirmed.

"What are you?" she challenged, wielding an ivory comb as her weapon.

Lansius rose and answered, "I-I'm from Earth."

"The fuck, why did you say it like that? Are you an alien or something? Where are you from?" she snapped.

"I can't remember. I lost most of my memory," Lansius tried to explain.

Unconvinced, the mage's eyes darted to Lansius's hair. "Are you Asian?"

"I don't know, but I guess so." He shrugged, uncomfortable under her intense gaze.

She squinted at him, clearly evaluating his appearance. "But you don't look Asian."

Lansius replied weakly, "Really, I don't remember anything. I could be from anywhere."

As the mage gathered her thoughts, the earlier tension slightly dissipated.

Breaking the silence, Lansius asked, "So, how?"

She lifted a hand. "Quiet, I'll do the asking."

"At least tell me your name," Lansius asked in frustration.

She hesitated for a moment. "People call me Hannei."

"That doesn't sound French."

"Fuck you!" the mage retorted passionately and with expertise.

"Okay, calm down," Lansius said, trying to de-escalate things.

*Great, she's got an even shorter fuse than Audrey!*

"Prove to me that you're . . . from Earth," the mage responded.

Lansius chuckled. "Like how? As if I could pull a smartphone from my pants."

"Smart phone . . . ? That sounds dumb. Are you fooling me?"

*She doesn't know about smartphones . . . ?*

Lansius's eyes widened as he processed the implications. "No way. You got into this world before the year 2000?"

Hannei gasped, her hand flying to her mouth in shock. "You reached the millennium?"

Lansius nodded. "A good two decades," he revealed, watching her carefully for her reaction.

Hannei shook her head in disbelief. "No way! But I've only been here for ten years."

Lansius frowned, his mind racing as he tried to make sense of their differing timelines. "That doesn't make any sense . . . unless time here moves slower than on Earth?"

She paused, looking visibly perturbed. "Ugh . . ." she grumbled, the theory not sitting well with her. But after a moment, her curiosity seemed to take over. "Tell me about Earth before the millennium then."

Lansius sat back in his chair, grateful for the change in subject. He was so happy to have met another Earth-born that he momentarily forgot about magic. "Well, what do you want to know?"

Hannei looked at him intently before asking, "Tell me about *Olympia*?"

He tried hard but almost found nothing. "The mountain in Greece . . . ?"

"What? No, it's a ship. Try to remember, it's a big, big action movie," she clarified.

"I don't remember . . ." Lansius paused and then something hit him. He slowly asked, "Do you mean *Olympia*, the sister ship of the *Titanic*?"

"Titanic, what's that?" replied Hannei with a furrowed brow.

Lansius was shocked. "Tell me who won World War II?"

"World War? Do you mean the Great War? Are you joking with me?" She shot her strongest gaze at Lansius.

Lansius didn't even blink. Compared to Audrey's eyes, any eyes looked cute. "The Great War is the First World War," he began. "There's another one, the Allies against the Axis: Nazi Germany, fascist Italy, and Japan, you don't know any of that?"

Hannei shook her head and asked, "Why are you using that word? It's Deutsches Kaiserreich."

Lansius gulped. "You mean, in your year 2000, Germany, is still ruled by a Kaiser?"

"Is it not the case in your world?" replied Hannei nervously, and both drew the same conclusion. Somehow, they were coming from different Earths.

*A parallel world? Just unbelievable . . .*

Lansius slumped in his seat as he tried to gather his thoughts. Meanwhile, Hannei returned to her seat, looking devastated. However, she found some solace and commented, "Well, at least, we're still from Earth."

Lansius nodded. They should have more in common with each other than with the rest of the Midlandians or Arvenians. "Do you watch TV?" he asked.

"Yeah, and also cinemas," replied Hannei.

"Shampoo?" asked Lansius.

"Oh, how I wish I had it."

The atmosphere was growing friendlier. Thus, Lansius dared to ask, "So, can you tell me how you learned magic?"

She bit her lip. "No, I can't. As much as I want to, I just can't."

Not giving up so easily, Lansius tried again, "Can't you test me or something?"

"The test is only to check the potential. Even if you have it, magic isn't something any mage can teach."

"Well, no harm in checking—"

"I just told you . . . I'd rather not," Hannei raised her voice.

Lansius tried his best to persuade her. "Please, I've come to this place without anything, not even my memory. At least can you check it?"

Hannei let out a long sigh. Without saying a word, she rose from her couch and walked toward Lansius. "Just stay still," she instructed, placing her palm over Lansius's forearm.

She then recited, "*Gloire au Père, au Fils et au Saint-Esprit. Comme il était au commencement, maintenant et toujours, pour les siècles des siècles.*"

Lansius didn't recognize the prayer; his French was not that good.

Being close to her, he began to realize that Hannei's eyes weren't entirely brown, but a bit golden. The prayer stopped, but all Lansius felt was the warmth of her palm. "So?"

Hannei pulled her hand away, took a step back, and simply shook her head.

Lansius chuckled and used his hands to cover his face. "Oh, I thought I had it, you know. Being summoned to this world and all," he rambled, embarrassed.

"Don't sweat it. Magic is rare unless you're an elf," Hannei consoled him. "Although your mana is exceptionally low . . ."

"Is that bad?"

"Not sure. It could be a treatable injury, but I'd rather not give you false hope."

Lansius nodded. "Why did you recite something in French?"

"It's just something to attune me to my source."

"Source?" Lansius blurted out.

Hannei drew a deep breath. "Enough. I gave you what you wanted. Now leave."

"Wait, we still have a lot to talk about."

"You're too nosy for your own good," she retorted, returning to her couch. "While I'm not a member of the Mage Guild, the craft is still a secret. I've told you things I shouldn't have. So zip your lips."

Then, with more urgency, she added, "If you want to live longer, keep the Earth thing between us. Don't tell anyone about our origin, not Sir Stan, not Lord Bengrieve, not even your lover."

## CHAPTER 31

# BANNER OF THE UNKNOWN

Spring of the year 4424 arrived in earnest, and finally, Lansius received the summons he had been waiting for. After a three-day trip on horseback, Lansius and his escorts found themselves in a beautiful castle, grander than anything he had ever seen before. The towers were imposingly tall, the archway grand, and the gates majestic—however, since it was late, he was ushered in speedily and had little time to marvel.

The next day, Lansius was bathed, given a fresh set of clothes, and served a small meal as he waited. He waited for hours until suddenly, guards and servants came. They escorted Lansius through a dizzying array of corridors, stairs, and hidden pathways until a maid opened a great lacquered door that led to a luxurious study chamber.

The maid gestured for silence, while another servant gently shoved Lansius in. The door closed, and Lansius found himself before the renowned Lord Bengrieve, seneschal of Midlandia.

There was little doubt of the identity of the man now sitting calmly in his comfortable-looking padded chair, reading scrolls on his elegant, small circular table, completely unbothered by Lansius's entry.

*The most powerful man in Midlandia . . .*

The chamber was occupied by only him and Lansius. Remembering the maid's gesture, Lansius could only wait anxiously for his host to address him.

He knew his status too well to even try to cough or draw attention. To Lord Bengrieve, he was just a nuisance.

Releasing tension from his weary legs, Lansius took in the tasteful design of the room. Absent were grandiose furniture or gaudy art pieces; instead, a single painting complemented the clean, lily-white plastered wall, and sleek marble floors added to the room's elegance.

A large glass vase filled with freshly cut flowers lent a pleasant floral scent to the airy chamber, and the most striking feature was the natural light streaming in from the adjacent open garden, connected by a series of large folding windows. However, a towering metallic statue, the size of a giant bear and painted in a deep, glossy blue, stood as an oddity, clashing with the otherwise serene surroundings.

*Is this supposed to be artwork?*

The silence was punctuated only by the occasional chirping of birds outside, and despite the fully opened window to the garden, there was no chilling spring wind coming in.

He couldn't shake off the feeling that the temperature was being controlled by a mage. It was strange to think that the high nobles employed these rare, powerful individuals like glorified bodyguards and even portable air conditioners.

*To use them like this when they're needed the most in the fight at the border. Isn't this decadence?*

Lansius wanted to ask Lord Bengrieve many things, such as why he saved Stefi, why he wanted him, and whether he would release them. Unfortunately, he was merely a henchman, and it was not his place to ask.

The fact that Lord Bengrieve didn't bother to dress up and remained in his black silken robe conveyed the gulf of status between them. Although this realization made Lansius uncomfortable, he knew better than to let his pride get in the way of his duties.

The sight of the recently blooming flower garden gave him some much-needed respite. The garden was highly decorated, complete with its own fish pond, working fountain, and even a mini waterfall.

*Pipes and pumps, or is it magic?*

"Lansius, why are you here?" the host finally spoke after throwing his last scroll down to the table.

It was not a casual greeting, and Lansius quickly replied, "I'm here to serve you, my lord."

Lord Bengrieve gazed out into his garden, his eyes seeming lost in thought as the sweet chirping of birds filled the air. After a moment of silence, "Lansius, what is thy desire?"

"My lord, I wish to fulfill your order," Lansius replied despite the growing tension.

The host turned his head and gazed directly into Lansius. "Lansius," he repeated slowly, as if savoring the name. "What is thy desire?"

As if hypnotized by the sharp eyes, Lansius suddenly remembered a rumor that Bengrieve did not forget anything that was spoken to him. A powerful man with a perfect memory. "To save myself and the people closest to me," he nervously admitted.

"A selfless guardian," the host remarked disinterestedly. "To whom have you directed this protection?"

"To Lady Audrey, the girl you saved, and for my family in Bellandia."

The lord's expression was unreadable, and he turned his gaze to the garden once again. After a moment of thoughtful silence he said, "Prove your worth, and I'll arrange for my men to escort your family out of Arvena before the war begins."

*Did I hear that correctly?*

"Yes, my lord." Lansius trembled as he bowed his head deeply. Never in his wildest dreams did he expect something like this to happen.

In just a few words, Lord Bengrieve had gained Lansius's allegiance.


Lansius returned to Toruna and saw the increased military presence around the area. He knew enough to realize that war was imminent. After his meeting with Lord Bengrieve, Sir Stan and Calub entrusted Lansius with more information.

One piece of news was Felicity's betrothal. Calub broke the news: Felis had gotten her wish to become a noble. Lansius was utterly surprised, but gladdened. In Felis he hoped to find a reliable ally, so he wrote a letter to congratulate her.

Another revelation was the campaign to the south. Instead of marching directly north to Arvena, Lord Bengrieve had unexpectedly launched a campaign against a small barony in Lowlandia.

Sir Stan explained that the plan was to secure Midlandia's exposed flank before committing to a major push against Lord Gottfried in Arvena. While the southern campaign against a small barony looked like an uneven battle, Midlandia couldn't afford a prolonged siege or to waste men and supplies. They needed a quick and decisive victory.

The problem was the presence of a powerful viscount in Lowlandia. Although the province was fragmented, the viscount had backed most of the baronies in the area to maintain his regime's status quo. These small baronies acted as a buffer, separating his region from Midlandia.

For this campaign, Sir Stan would be accompanied by Lansius, Audrey, and Calub. However, they would separate from Sir Stan and the main army. Midlandia needed someone to lead a diversion, and that person turned out to be Lansius, along with Toruna's ragtag band of misfits.

Lansius suspected that he was selected because he was a foreigner, which provided a convenient scapegoat should he be captured. Initially unsure, Lansius accepted the mission after Calub convinced him, citing his victory in Sabina Rustica as proof of his commanding ability. Despite having only a season to train and equip his troops in Toruna, he chose to embrace the risk. Under the guise of a raiding mission, Lansius's small band of poorly trained troops embarked on what seemed, in all respects, to be a suicide mission.

*Lowlandia, Summer 4424.*

It had been a full year since the fall of Arvena, and nine months since Lansius first set foot in Toruna. The relentless passage of time mirrored the unceasing winds that swept across the Great Plains of Lowlandia.

The Lowlandia province, far to the south of Midlandia remained desolate despite the approaching harvest season. There was no abundance of golden crops or orchards full of ripe fruits. Instead, only endless fields of yellowing steppe grasslands stretched as far as the eye could see, with little signs of life.

Lowlandia was sparsely populated and economically poor, with limited farmland scattered across its vast landscape. The Great Plains, vast but lifeless, separated the province's two viscounties and eight baronies into eastern and western parts.

The western part bordered with two other provinces via a treacherous mountain range that effectively served as a natural boundary. The eastern part shared a border with Midlandia, along with one of the two human Eastern Kingdoms.

Despite being a part of the Imperium, Lowlandia was closer to a lawless province. The local lords had quarreled and warred against each other for centuries, with the High Court paying minimal attention and unwilling to get involved as long as tribute was paid.

From time immemorial, the Imperium had seen the region as unimportant. The province was largely infertile, and its only other feature was the border with the deadly Great Marshland to the south. However, for the local lords, the place was ancestral, and they would eagerly defend it with their blood.

*Viscount Side*

Lord Robert, the Lion of Lowlandia, once again took to the field. A ragtag troop flying an unknown banner had raided his land. Despite his advanced age, his eyesight hadn't failed him. He calmly surveyed the opponent's formation arrayed across the open plains.

"Our right wing and left wing are ready, my lord," Michael reported as he gently reined in his horse. The excitement in the youngster's voice was evident as it was his first battle as the marshal.

The viscount didn't share his enthusiasm and remained silent. No bite, Robert observed. He had moved both of his wings as bait, but the opponent's formation remained unchanged.

Robert's passiveness unintentionally caused unease among his men.

"My lord?" the marshal asked again after a while.

"I heard you the first time, Michael," Robert said to the marshal who was also his future son-in-law.

"Our men are eager to fight. Would you give us the order?" Michael feared the opponent might try to flee.

Robert weighed his decision. Unlike Michael, who was in his prime, Robert was full of wrinkles and grayed hair. However, he had what the younger man lacked: experience. Michael was like a set of armor that had never seen battle, pristine and without a scratch. Robert, on the other hand, had fought in over twenty battles.

"Michael, retreating doesn't necessarily mean an army is weak," Robert warned.

"But that's all they've done since invading our lands, my lord," Michael replied.

Robert's warning fell on deaf ears, but he acknowledged that Michael wasn't completely wrong. Ever since Robert had assembled his troops and given chase, the invaders hadn't attempted to fight. Instead, they simply ran from every engagement. This behavior puzzled Robert and made him timid, while Michael saw it as weakness, which made him grow bolder.

"What do the scout reports say?" Robert asked.

"My lord," Michael said proudly at his preparation, "I've sent riders in three directions. They reported no sightings, only empty plains."

Robert took a deep breath. It was against his guts, but he felt that his men needed the confidence of a war leader, not a superstitious old man. "Very well, since the enemy isn't taking our bait, marshal, you may lead the center column. Keep the two cavalries to guard your flanks. And I'll hold the reserve with a hundred cavalry."

The trumpets and bugles rang out, signaling the march. Banners unfurled at the front of the formation, fluttering in the wind. The captains rallied their troops, and one thousand soldiers advanced in polished armor and helmets that glistened under the sunlight.

Robert watched as the column marched past him, his highly decorated armor and fierce-looking warhorse adding to his lordly presence and inspiring his men. Yet, the armor was just for show. In reality, he was too frail to fight.

Before the sun rose higher, the center column had successfully rejoined with its two wings, which had earlier tried unsuccessfully to provoke the opponent.

In total, there were approximately one thousand men, bolstered by two hundred cavalry, thrown against an opponent with no more than four hundred.

Despite the three-to-one advantage, Robert felt uneasy. He wondered why the enemy had chosen to fight that day. After pondering for a while, he concluded that something unexpected must have happened, forcing the opponent to engage. "I suppose I overestimated our enemy," he mused.

"You're being cautious, my lord," a senior knight beside him responded.

"Let's follow our center." Robert spurred his horse, and his entourage of knights, squires, and servants followed closely behind.

CHAPTER 32

# THE DIE IS CAST

They're coming!" Audrey pulled the reins of her mount and came to a stop.

Before her stood Lansius, the leader of their ragtag army. Though many dismissed him as a no-name exiled noble from a distant kingdom, Audrey trusted him enough to join his seemingly suicidal offensive.

"Listen up! Everyone waits until we're within crossbow range, then we pull back to the trenches," Lansius ordered.

His command did little to ease the fear in his men, but Lansius paid no heed. He looked at Audrey and spoke. "Lead the cavalry and make the breakthrough as planned."

Audrey stared at him with a cold, piercing gaze that could easily frighten children and adults alike.

"I'll be fine. Go, move as planned," Lansius answered, almost cheerfully. He knew Audrey well enough to understand the meaning behind her stare.

"Good luck then," she replied.

"You too. Let's get some drinks after this is over," he said, despite the overwhelming odds.

Audrey went to her cavalrymen and rallied them. Soon, fifty riders moved out against the opponent's right wing.

*At least she's with the cavalry*, Lansius thought while suppressing a sigh of relief. He knew that if the worst happened, Audrey would have a good chance of escaping. Two seasons had passed since their fateful reunion at Toruna Manor, yet here they were, facing yet another armed conflict. Lansius felt a sense of despair in their new lives as henchmen.

Lord Arte, who was busy gathering followers and currying support from Midlandia's nobility, had given his approval for Lord Bengrieve to employ Lansius. Now, Lansius had assumed a fake identity as an exiled knight from the Mercantile Kingdom. If he were found out, he would surely lose his head.

While Lansius was lamenting his situation, fear continued to haunt his troops' rank and file. Even with their cavalry riding out in strength, they were hardly convinced.

The Midlandians had enlisted for what they believed would be a simple raiding party, not a pitched battle. They saw Lansius as an exiled noble from a foreign kingdom, with no reputation or standing to claim a fiefdom, and so no one had expected him to start an open war.

Yet here they were, facing off against the Lion of Lowlandia, the biggest name in the region. The sight of the viscount's banners, fluttering boldly in the wind, sent chills down their spines.

Many muttered curses under their breath, their eyes darting nervously between the enemy's imposing formation and their own ragtag troop. The thought of fleeing to save themselves constantly crossed their minds.

Although Lansius had treated them well, nobody wished to die for someone else's cause. Many felt betrayed, like sacrificial pawns led to a butcher's shop. The thought made their stomachs churn.

The only thing that stopped them from killing the black-haired bastard and breaking formation was desperation.

It was clear to all that their situation was beyond hopeless, with flat grassland stretching in all directions for miles, leaving nowhere to hide. Whoever fled would be easily chased and slaughtered, or captured as slaves.

Their fear drove them to quietly follow Lansius, who had yet to show signs of panicking.

Unbeknownst to his men, Lansius himself was inches away from a nervous breakdown.

*Am I really doing this?*

Watching the lines of men in formation moving toward him made him second guess. However, Lansius had bet everything on his reckless plan. He had spent his money on recruiting more men, horses, and equipment, risked the trust of his benefactors, and even jeopardized the love of his life, who stubbornly wanted to participate in this madness.

Lord Bengrieve and Sir Stan's initial plan was simple: Lansius was to create a diversion, allowing Midlandia to freely siege another barony to secure their back line.

The root cause of this conflict was a bitter relationship between the prosperous Midlandia and the poor lords of Lowlandia, who secretly supported raiding activities on their vast border. Now, with Midlandia poised to fight a major war against the unified northern people, they needed to secure their weakest border.

To ensure victory, Midlandia was willing to sacrifice hundreds of men to prevent the Old Lion from learning and sending a relief force to their besieged neighbor. However, despite their apparent hostility, Lord Bengrieve still wished to maintain good relations with the powerful viscount.

Thus, Lansius, the foreigner, was the perfect candidate. Even if he and his command were caught, there would be little evidence that could be traced back to Midlandia's court.

Externally, Lansius went along with this plan. It was a simple plan. His job was to take this cheaply recruited company as a decoy for as long as possible, before their eventual capture and demise. Lansius was to escape with the cavalry and abandon the rest to their fate.

However, he couldn't bring himself to sacrifice the men. The troops under him might be nothing but the unfortunates, the lowlifes, and the rowdiest scumbags in all of Midlandia, yet they were still his men.

But mercy wasn't the main reason why Lansius had reneged on the plan. For he had seen a sliver of hope. And ever since learning of the possibility, he had been torn between risking everything for a chance to win big, or playing it safe by sticking to Lord Bengrieve's plan.

Only now, as he faced the enemy, did Lansius begin to feel truly at peace with his decision.

*If you lot are destined to die, then let's test our fates against the heavens.*

Since Lord Bengrieve had already written off the fate of Lansius's troops, this gamble presented no extra risk or cost to him. For Lansius, however, securing a victory would mean tremendous merit. It would be a lie to claim he wasn't motivated by personal gain. His daring decision was also driven by the desire to bring maximum reward to his master, quickly proving his own worth.

Thus, trusting his instincts, twelve days prior, Lansius had ordered two hundred men to establish a camp and dig three horseshoe-shaped trenches. The first trench was the longest, followed by two other smaller trenches behind it. This would serve as the main combat line, while the smaller trenches behind it would act as support and reserve.

Lansius had chosen this location because the ground was soft and could easily be dug. The scouts had learned that the area was occasionally flooded when the monsoon came, which made it easy to get clean water by digging crude wells. Because of this, they were able to prevent some of the rampant disease and its effects, such as deadly diarrhea.

While Lansius and his men began their work digging the trenches, Sir Justin, a surviving Arvenian knight turned mercenary in Lord Bengrieve's service, had led fifty cavalry and two hundred men deep into Lord Robert's territory to raid and lure him out.

Things seemingly advanced as planned; however, they had badly underestimated Lord Robert's forces.

* * *

Calub, the alchemist who had also joined Lord Bengrieve's mercenary company, jogged over to Lansius's side. He gestured for Lansius to speak in private. The two moved away from the rest of the troops, and Calub whispered, "The scouts weren't making it up. It is a thousand."

Hearing that, Lansius felt a knot of dread in his stomach. While he had prepared to face an army twice his size, these overwhelming numbers made his already high-risk plan even more precarious. "How in the world could a viscount muster a thousand men?"

Calub brushed aside Lansius's complaint and asked, "Can we still win this?"

Lansius saw the concern on Calub's tanned face and avoided his gaze. He needed time to think.

*Four hundred of our ragtag army against a thousand of the best Lowlandians? We're doomed . . .*

Calub exhaled deeply and massaged his temple. He then looked around at the advancing enemy troops in the distance and changed the subject. "Is Audrey with the cavalry?"

Lansius nodded weakly. "Yes, why?"

"Good. She should be able to make her escape. Then I'll pack." Calub turned away.

Lansius caught Calub's arm and asked, "You're leaving?"

"You're not?" Calub was in disbelief. "Lans, this whole thing, your plan is breaking apart. We should flee while we can and continue with master's original plan."

Lansius defiantly shook his head. "They're more numerous than expected, but that doesn't mean my plan won't work. Let's give it a chance."

Calub muttered under his breath, but remained indecisive.

"They're getting closer!" one of the lookouts cried out fearfully.

Lansius strained his eyes as their cavalry formed a wedge formation, while the viscount's right wing across the field took shape in a line formation.

The sight of hundreds of galloping horses across the green grassland was a spectacle. Massive, colorful flags flew from the bannermen, adding to the stunning visual display.

"By the Ageless." Calub turned away, his voice filled with dread. "Have you forgotten about those days in Feodosia?"

"That's why the big boy is with her." Lansius nervously wiped the sweat from his forehead as he watched the two cavalries on a collision course.

"Him? That's . . . not entirely promising," Calub said with an equally nervous smile.

"Lances down! They're lowering their lances," the lookouts cried out, drawing everyone's attention.

The vibrant spectacle came to a sudden halt as the two sides clashed in a brutal head-on collision. Lances shattered and pierced through flesh with sickening thuds. In mere moments, cavalrymen were thrown off their horses or impaled by steel-tipped lances, reducing many valiant men to mere casualties.

The gruesome spectacle left everyone feeling sickened.

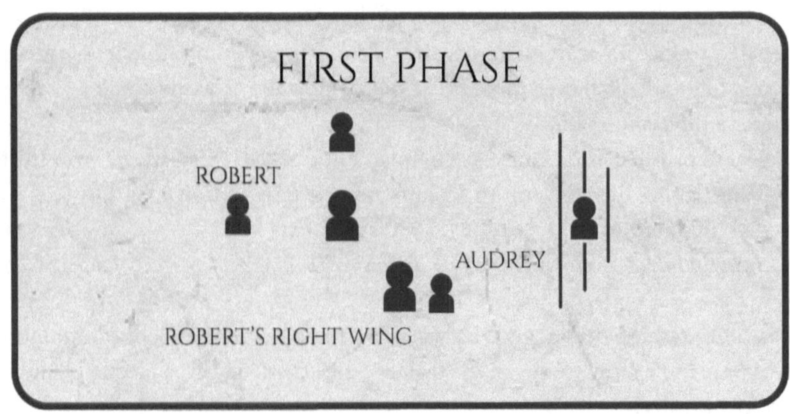


Watching as Audrey courageously led her cavalry, gave Lansius a much-needed mental slap to the face. She trusted him enough to put her life on the line. He clenched his fist and felt his blood slowly boil. There was little time to observe her fight as the enemy's main group had closed in on Lansius's position.

"Sound the signal. Move to the trench," Sir Justin, one of the few who had plate armor, ordered.

In response to his order, three hundred men started to descend into the trenches, where another hundred stood ready.

The men looked pale, and a few were already quivering.

Lansius let out a sigh, but knew that they were the only ones available to a no-name upstart like himself.

Sir Justin approached Lansius from his post whistling a carefree tune as he walked with a relaxed gait. His familiar-looking squire followed behind.

"Sir Justin, Hugo," Calub addressed them.

Hugo bowed his head to Calub. Fate had played a cruel joke on him by reuniting him with Lansius as a subordinate. They had buried the hatchet and now Hugo tried to win Lansius's trust, but he ended up in this suicidal plan. He lamented his luck, and like the rest, desperately wanted Lansius's plan to work.

Sir Justin nodded at Calub before turning to his squire, Hugo. "Protect us," he commanded.

Hugo dutifully placed himself between them and the enemy and raised his shield.

Lansius saw the knight's gaze shift to him. "Commander, last chance," Sir Justin said, giving Lansius the option to retreat or prepare for battle.

Lansius, drenched in cold sweat, summoned his courage and responded, "I think I'll risk it. Sir, can I count on you?"

The older gentlemen nodded. "I'll give it my best."

"Gratitude, sir." Lansius bowed his head slightly.

"Don't feel too indebted. If things go awry, I only need to discard half my armor to run. My horses are fast, and my men are strong enough to escort me out."

The honesty of the former knight, now mercenary, elicited a chuckle from Lansius. "Sir, please call me by name. I'm hardly your superior."

Sir Justin grinned. "I'm pretty sure they made you the commander."

"Men will follow someone they respect," Lansius remarked.

The knight seemed happy, and he turned his gaze toward the advancing enemy. "Lord Robert has good troops."

"Indeed. Meanwhile ours . . ." Lansius couldn't resist comparing.

*The poor and unfortunate, also the scum of every town and village. They are every bit unfit as soldiers. More like a bunch of bandits . . .*

The knight snorted. "What we got might be not as good or well equipped, but at least they'll follow orders."

"That's true . . ." Lansius admitted as he watched their last group of men descend into the trenches with a mixture of gratitude and guilt.

*Surely, following me was a big leap of faith for them, especially when I employed such an unknown strategy that involves digging a series of ditches in the middle of nowhere like here.*

"I better go," Calub suddenly announced.

"Calub," Lansius called out. "Next time, remind me to double-check our opponent's strength."

Calub let out a deep breath. "If we make it out of this alive." Then he turned to the knight. "Sir, may I ask, why did you agree with this plan? You must have known that Lord Robert is a good warlord."

The knight chuckled. "I've always wanted to see the Lion in the field."

Calub let out a sigh. "Lans, I hope your plan works."

"If it doesn't work . . . see you in the afterlife?" Lansius joked, finally pushing past his fear limit.

Calub chuckled and made his way toward the trenches. He was needed on the far right where the fighting was likely to be the fiercest.

"We need to move," Hugo interrupted urgently. Just then, the sound of an arrow slicing through the air reached their ears.

"Right, right . . ." Lansius took a final glance at the enemy formation before quickly making his way to the ladder.

Sir Justin and Hugo followed suit, with a few crossbow bolts whizzing above their heads as they descended. Finally, at the bottom, the smell of earth and humidity greeted them.

One of the aides handed Lansius his crossbow, and he proceeded to check how the string felt. The dampness in the trenches could affect the string, but he felt that the tension was all right. Next, he checked the bolts in, two quivers on his belt, each with twelve bolts.

Sir Justin secured his poleaxe while Hugo fetched his bascinet helmet and assisted him in fastening it firmly.

Lansius finished up by wearing a sallet helmet. Its layers of linen padding felt comfortable. It wasn't a full-face but had a retractable visor. Now, after a lot of doubting and second-guessing everything about his own decision, he finally felt a sense of clarity. With everything in place, he knew it was time to face whatever lay ahead.

# CHAPTER 33

# NOISE BEFORE DEFEAT

The newly dug trenches were still relatively fresh, the earth around them moist and sticky despite the summer heat. Several men trudged through the trenches as they prepare for the impending battle, their boots covered in red mud.

Lansius tapped his sallet, and the reassuring metallic ring echoed through the air. Then he pulled down the visor to test it. The helmet limited his view, but he knew he needed protection for his head.

Lansius surveyed his surroundings, taking note of his men's dirt-stained gambesons and emaciated faces. The weeks of marching and sleeping rough had already weakened their bodies, and common maladies such as colds had further sapped their strength. The air was thick with the stench of their sweat and urine.

Sir Justin had taken the rowdier men to his part of the trenches, leaving Lansius with this group to manage.

He lifted his visor and locked it in place. Now, he could feel the weight of their stares, their silent anger for sending them into a battle where they stood little chance of survival.

They feared they would be slaughtered like helpless livestock. Four hundred poorly equipped men stood no chance against Lord Robert's veteran vanguard.

*I better address this lest they rebel at the last minute.*

"Gentlemen," Lansius called out, his voice wavering slightly with apprehension.

Now, all of their attention was directed at Lansius, whose introverted side was screaming for him to back down, but he steeled himself. The trenches weren't wide, so he climbed the ladder halfway up to make himself more visible.

"Most of you know that I'm a poor rider," Lansius began, his tone light. "I can't outrun anyone on a horse, and I'm not much faster on foot. So, if things go wrong, I'm probably not going to make it."

A few cracked their lips at his dark humor.

"But don't worry," Lansius continued. "I've staked my life on this earthen fortress we've built. It's a well-known strategy in my homeland. Great kings and generals have used it against formidable foes, whether human or fell beasts."

The men murmured among themselves, some nodding in agreement.

Lansius noticed a warmer expression as he spoke again. "Our opponents are unaware of this strategy. We have the upper hand and an abundance of weapons, and we know this place like ants know their burrows. So, are you with me?"

The men responded with nods and a growing wave of enthusiasm.

"Gentlemen, look around you. Are they not your fellow kin? Do you not trust them? I'll tell you this: if you cover their backs, they'll cover yours. And I'll do the same. We're in this together. So, do we fight, or do we give up and accept the chain on our necks?"

Hugo stepped forward and shouted, "I say, let those bastards have it!"

The men cheered and clamored in agreement. That effectively rallied them.

Lansius was thrilled. Although he knew he was lying, he had no other choice. "Ten silver coins for every man who fights valiantly today!" he proclaimed. "Fight with all your might, and I promise to personally reward you even more!"

The trenches echoed with a resounding cheer. Lansius had won over the soldiers' hearts and minds. It was true that the lure of money could make even the most perilous and unimaginable tasks bearable.

*Viscount's Side*

Robert observed as the center column closed in on the opponent's line, anticipating a fierce battle. However, something unexpected occurred. In response, he promptly dispatched a scout to investigate. While it seemed trivial, Robert knew that morale was a finicky matter. Surprised men could flee despite having an overwhelming advantage.

While they awaited the scout's report, their attention was drawn to the ongoing cavalry skirmish on their right flank.

Finally, the scout returned with the news. "My lord, as you suspected, the main enemy force has moved into a ditch."

This news ignited a debate among the command staff, with each member offering their opinions.

"Is it really just a ditch?" Robert interjected, hoping to clarify the situation.

"My lord, it appears to be deeper than a man's height. At least two men could walk side by side. They also have crossbowmen. One even fired at me," the scout answered.

Robert grew restless. He sensed that this wasn't a mere ditch, but could it be a distraction?

"Did they purposely make it? But for an earthwork of that size, enough to cover hundreds of men would require a lot of preparation." The senior knight who rode beside Robert offered his counsel.

Robert massaged his chin and said, "You're right. Send—"

Suddenly, the knight on the lookout cried out, "Riders ahead! Riders ahead!"

Everyone was caught off guard as dozens of riders broke through their right wing and charged toward their position. Their right-wing cavalry was in pursuit but lagged behind.

"Clever bastards!" exclaimed the senior knight. "Our knights in plates can't catch them. My lord, with your permission," he asked, more of a formality, and shouted to his men, "Fifty knights, on me!"

The remaining horsemen hurriedly escorted Robert in the camp's direction.

"But the main battle," Robert protested, but his men were having none of it. Protecting their lord was paramount. Nothing else mattered.

Despite this temporary setback, they remained confident in their main troops and believed that the opponent's cavalry charge was a one-trick pony. With that threat now thwarted, they saw this retreat as merely a noise before their ultimate triumph.


"What the hell is going on?" Michael demanded answers from his staff, who were just as puzzled. They just saw the enemy launch a desperate cavalry action, but now the enemy's main formation slowly disappeared into a ditch.

A senior staff rode his horse farther to get a better look, but still couldn't find an explanation. As far as they knew, a ditch or moat was meant to impede or block movement, not to hide troops. The rank and file began to speculate on this oddity, attracting a lot of attention.

Uncertain about what to do but feeling the pressure to take action, Michael ultimately ordered his crossbowmen to test the enemy.

Over a hundred crossbowmen marched onto the field, but they were without their helpers or large pavise shields. They had to rely on whatever cover they could find or some assistance from other units. The ensuing shooting exchange was brutal, but it quickly became apparent that their side was badly outmatched. The enemy had better cover inside their ditch and could fire with impunity.

The sight of their retreating crossbowmen disturbed the entire column. They had been confident with their three-to-one advantage and expected an easy battle, but now fear began to seep in.

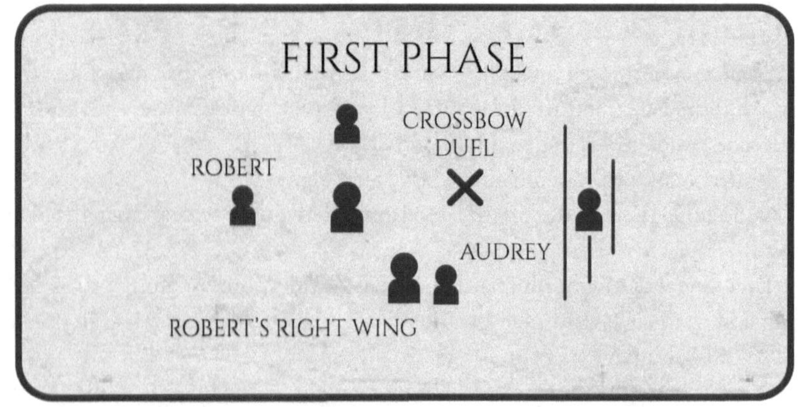



"Marshal, it's time to attack," urged the staff.

"Very well." Michael took a deep breath. "Signal the men." He knew that further delay would only worsen the troops' morale.

Five hundred of their hardest fighters took to the field while Michael and his staff stayed behind with the remaining three hundred.

The vanguard, clad in plate armor and shields, marched forward in loose formation and soon endured a hail of crossbow attacks. Bravery was present that day. They held their formation and only charged when they were within a stone's throw from the enemy's ditch.

Michael lost sight of the vanguard as they fearlessly descended into the ditch. Behind them, closely following, were the men-at-arms. They may have been less equipped than the vanguard, but they were equally eager for violence and recognition.

However, despite their numerical superiority, they were withered by relentless crossbow attacks. The noise of the bolts' high-pitched sounds as they sliced through the air continued to scream at their ears.

"Where are they coming from? Why do they keep coming?" Michael vented his frustration as the enemy showed no signs of being distracted, even under assault.

His senior staff tried to divert Michael's frustration by pointing out a group of brave men who made a defensive line with shields. However, their defense was short-lived and collapsed under the enemy's ceaseless ranged attacks.

The amount of ammunition required to maintain such a constant barrage was tremendous, and it made Michael feel queasy. Doubt began to form in his mind. Was he falling into a trap?

A scout was spotted galloping toward them, his horse kicking up dust and dirt as it approached. As he drew closer, he pulled up sharply and quickly dismounted. "Marshal," he said, catching his breath. "There's more than one ditch. At least two more behind the first one."

Michael winced while his staff looked at each other in shock and disbelief. They had been outmaneuvered and outwitted. The realization hit them hard, and Michael felt a sinking feeling in his stomach. Only now did they understand why the ranged attack didn't lessen at all.

As they had already committed to the attack, Michael and his staff could only watch in horror as their comrades mercilessly fell victim to the ranged attacks. The scene was both humiliating and heartbreaking. They had relatives and friends among the assault force who were now fighting for their lives. But there was nothing they could do. The assault must succeed at all costs.

Not surprisingly, the assault began to falter. Several groups had seen enough blood, broke formation, and retreated.

"Round them up," Michael ordered his staff, fearing that the retreat could turn into a rout.

Before they could do anything, a rider emerged from their right galloping toward Michael. The rider pulled up abruptly after he found Michael. "Marshal," he said breathlessly. "The enemy cavalry has broken our right wing. They're aiming for Lord Robert's position."

Michael instinctively pulled the reins of his horse, ready to rush to his lord's side. However, a knight grabbed his arms and stopped the young marshal.

"Marshal, you are needed here," the knight said sternly.

"But Lord Robert is under threat," Michael stated angrily.

The knight's grip on Michael's arm tightened. "You can't leave this spot or else our entire formation will collapse!"

Michael tried to compromise. "I'll leave my banner—"

"The men will still recognize you," said the knight firmly.

Michael groaned but remained in his place.

"Lord Robert is a skilled fighter, and he has capable knights with him," the knight tried to reassure him.

Michael took a deep breath and surveyed the battlefield. "Then tell me, what's our next move?"

"I believe we just need to focus on winning what's in front of us," the knight replied.

Michael looked at his staff and made his decision. "All right, send the rest of the troops forward."

"Marshal, I believe we're the only group left," his staff reported.

"Then we shall commit ourselves," Michael said resolutely and dismounted.

Word that the viscount was retreating spread like wildfire, but before anyone could react, a general attack was ordered.

Michael and his staff joined the remaining men-at-arms and marched with their shields raised. Behind them, the levied troops followed. The latter were trained peasants with little armor and weaponry. Their inadequacy was only remedied by their sheer size. At their rear, a score of cavalry remained vigilant to deter anyone from desertion.

However, the Lowlandians showed their mettle today. Michael and his comrades were ready to give it their all, and as they charged forward, the barrage of crossbow bolts began to dwindle. A path opened up to them. With great cries that echoed across the field, they fearlessly plunged toward the trenches, and the battle descended into chaos.

# CHAPTER 34

# THE BLOODY HARVEST

The thunderous sound of clashing metal and the piercing cries of combatants filled the hot summer air. Blade and lance sliced through the air, striking helmet and armor with bone-crunching force.

A knight was thrown from his horse, crashing to the ground with a sickening thud. Blood gushed from his mangled helmet, splattering the polished surface of his armor. In contrast to the unmoving master, the riderless horse bolted out of control.

Anci, the victor, proceeded without care. He had just bested another knight. Decked in white brigandine and bascinet helmet, he pressed his mount to pick up the pace.

The cavalry skirmish was a swift but brutal exchange of blows, with riders passing each other in quick succession before circling back for another round. However, Anci's objective today wasn't cavalry supremacy but to capture the enemy leader.

Driven by the promise of a large bounty, his Midlandia-trained riders had bravely clashed against the opponent's right wing. Against all odds, their fifty light cavalry prevailed and were now aiming for their opponent's rear, where Lord Robert's personal banner was spotted.

This turned the fighting into chaos as half of Lord Robert's reserve scrambled to block the invader's cavalry advances.

Anci smiled at the opponent's reaction. He relished the opportunity for more fights. Officially, he had only agreed to join this mission because Lansius had pleaded with him to come. The former clerk, now a fake knight, had convinced him that there would be a great battle, complete with knights to capture. Lansius had said he needed Anci to co-command the cavalry.

However, even for a glory-seeker like Anci, jumping into a fight in Lowlandia wasn't an attractive prospect. He regarded Lowlandia with a healthy dose of skepticism. Its knights were generally poor, and a fight without the potential for ransom held little interest for him.

What ultimately persuaded him to join were Lord Arte's wishes for him to make a name for himself, his own innate love of violence, and the sizable payment that Lansius had offered him to safeguard the commander.

The rhythmic pounding of the horses' hooves echoed across the open plain. Shouting through his visor, Anci ordered, "FORM UP ON THE COMMANDER!" He had spotted Audrey, the one individual he had sworn to protect.

Anci's riders obeyed and tried to re-form. Anci urged his mount forward. Its powerful muscles rippled beneath its glistening skin.

In the distance, the enemy cavalry loomed, a dark, foreboding wall blocking their path. The air was thick with tension and filled with the sound of clinking armor as the two similarly numbered sides charged toward each other.

But equal, they were not. The Midlandians had spent their lances against Lord Robert's right wing. Their horses were tired, and not all of them had emerged unscathed.

Meanwhile, Lord Robert's reserve was as fresh as ever, clad in their polished plate cuirasses.

The Midlandians' side was also disorganized. They had yet to fully establish a cohesive formation. Despite all this, they fearlessly charged into the opponent's deadly embrace. However, at the critical moment, Audrey led her fifteen riders to execute a sharp right turn.

It was so masterfully done that the enemy's heavier cavalry failed to catch her move. As they turned to intercept her, the enemy left their right flank vulnerable, and that was when Anci's riders joined for an onslaught.

"Nyahaha!" A sickening laughter was followed by a flash of a metallic object that cleaved through the wind in a giant, powerful swing. With a loud metallic clang, one knight crashed to the ground after Anci's broadsword connected with his arms and pauldron.

The hardened iron skin was merely dented, but the victim's arm was mangled, and he struggled to crawl himself to safety.

Audrey's riders had deftly dodged the enemy and lured them into Anci's trap. The alpha of the pack grinned devilishly at Audrey's success, as his riders wreaked havoc upon the enemy's ranks. Anci moved on to new prey, an astute rider who happened to cross his path.

The marked man, a stalwart knight by appearance, noticed Anci's approach and reacted accordingly. Within seconds, they closed the gap between them, fate dictating that they would pass on their left side. The knight raised his lance without hesitation, preparing to strike. Meanwhile, Anci kept shouldering his broadsword confidently.

When they were but a lance's distance apart, Anci leaped into action. He put all his weight on the left stirrup, extended his body to the side, and with a lightning-quick motion slammed the incoming lance with his broadsword.

The lance wobbled out of the way but didn't break, sending splinters flying between them as the knight and his steed struggled to balance themselves.

Anci's horse swerved, nearly throwing him off balance as he came alongside his opponent. They locked eyes from their visored helmets. In jousting, this would have marked the end of the round, but Anci wasn't finished. In that brief moment, the young squire wrested control of his sword, twisted his body to face the passing knight, and unleashed the sharp metal into the knight's back.

A dull clang rang through the air as the tip of Anci's sword made contact with the knight's back plate. Though the knight's back plate wasn't broken, he was not entirely immune to the impact. The knight continued to ride as if unharmed, but astonishingly dropped his sword and crouched lifelessly in his saddle.

An additional dent had been etched on the tip of Anci's sword. He had been using them hard like a blunt mace. His horse made noises as if complimenting his master's latest win. He grinned and patted his horse while suppressing tremendous pain from his torso.

*Bah, I shouldn't twist it that much!*

Groaning, Anci scanned the surroundings and found no immediate threats as the enemy was turning around wide to give chase. He counted his riders and found only twenty-seven, including himself and Audrey; the rest were either injured, dismounted, or dead.

Even Anci, an excellent rider by anyone's standards, had been dismounted during the early battle. But as any seasoned cavalryman knew, being dismounted was far from the end. He simply whistled to call his horse and rejoined the fight.

Including the last one, Anci had bested eight riders, but not without paying the price. Part of his brigandine had been torn by a lance, and his left shoulder was swollen from the fall. His right arm was lacerated, and the coat of steel plates inside his brigandine couldn't protect him completely from the lance's attack. Even without penetration, he was sure he had a broken rib or two, making breathing painful.

He lamented about not purchasing a cuirass, but he had an eye on something else. As Anci continued to press forward, Audrey began to slow down.

Anci caught up with her. "Change of plan?" he asked, opening his visor and slowing down to a trot.

"Anci, we've done it," Audrey exclaimed.

"Huh, isn't the goal to capture the viscount?"

"Not necessarily. Lans said if we forced the Lion out, then it's already a win for us."

"Ah, f'kin good!" Anci grinned widely. "I'm still in shape, but my horse needs rest. Then shall we?"

Audrey nodded. "Yes, let's pull back and regroup."

Anci let out another groan as he unconsciously twisted his injured torso to reach for the saddlebag. After a few tries, he finally found what he was looking for: a brass circular object. With a gentle nudge of his foot, he coaxed his horse to turn around.

Lifting the mini buccina, Anci blew into the mouthpiece, producing a distinctive sound that he repeated twice. Instantly, every surviving cavalryman began to move in one direction.

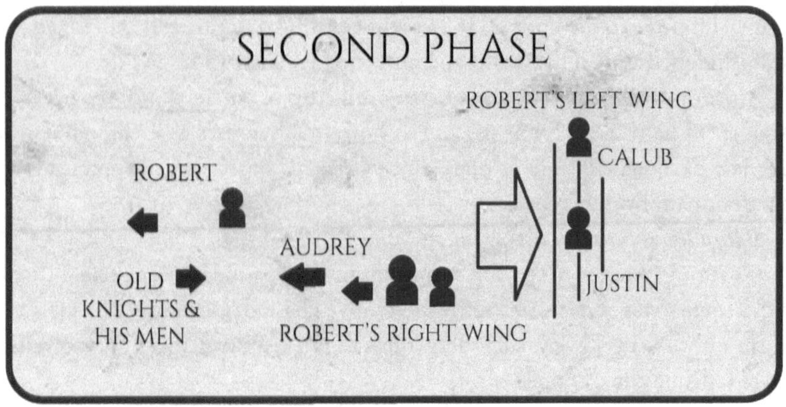


The opposing cavalry was in pursuit but weighed down by their heavy plate armor. Their horses were exhausted and unable to keep up with Audrey's forces, who were lighter.

Equipped only with ring mail, brigandines, and a few cuirasses, despite having less expensive warhorses, Audrey's cavalry was able to outrun the enemy.

This had been their tactic from the start. Initially, Audrey and Anci committed their cavalry to battle, only to then switch to evasion, tiring the enemy's heavy cavalry into a chase. Their light cavalry was controlling the tempo and maintaining the initiative.

Meanwhile, the main battle between Michael's center column and Lansius's ragtag army in the trenches raged on.

*Banner of the Unknown*

The sound of fighting was deafening in the trenches. A messenger shouted repeatedly to get Lansius's attention, "Sir, a message from Master Calub."

"What did he say?" Lansius yelled back.

"Traps are working. We're holding," the skinny messenger reported.

"Do you have anything from Sir Justin?" Lansius asked as he put his weight on his right foot to keep the crossbow's metal stirrup down while he drew the string with both hands, effectively priming the mechanism.

"There's so much fighting. We haven't been able to," he reported while kneeling behind Lansius.

"You hear that?" Lansius yelled at Hugo.

"I'm a bit busy here!" Hugo replied as he fended off a knight with his sword. Earlier, his poleaxe had been broken in a vicious fight.

Lansius faced the messenger. "Go to Sir Justin. Tell him we're holding."

"That's all, sir?" he asked in between the sounds of swearing and frequent metal-to-metal clashes that echoed through the underground trench.

"Go," Lansius confirmed, loading a bolt into his weapon and taking aim.

"Left, left!" he shouted to anyone in front of him. Meanwhile, the messenger disappeared behind his men and into the other side of the trenches.

Hugo quickly ducked to the left, and Lansius squeezed the lever trigger, causing the string's release to echo violently in his hands. The wooden shaft hurtled toward its target, exploding upon impact against the knight's breastplate and sending wooden shrapnel flying.

The victim staggered and fell backward, a steel-tipped bolt protruding from his breastplate. His side attempted to evacuate their fallen comrade, while another knight squeezed to take his place. However, the narrow and confined trenches made movement difficult, particularly in heavy plate armor, and the slippery red clay ground only made it worse.

Hugo got up from his kneeling position. He had been shielding his face from being peppered by wooden shrapnel, some of which had lodged in his ring mail. He charged at the unprepared opponent alongside another squire and made a bloody result.

In contrast to the attackers, Lansius's men had come prepared by tying ropes onto their footwear, providing them with much-needed traction for work and fighting in trenches. Meanwhile, the knights in their sabatons struggled to move without slipping on the slick, clay-like ground.

With all this advantage and preparation, Lansius's smaller force had miraculously managed to hold their ground against the larger, better-armed opponent, but they were left utterly exhausted, unable to press for dominance.

As the bitter and bloody struggle continued, everything hung in the balance. The slightest shift could tip the scale in either side's favor.

# CHAPTER 35

# THE MISFITS

Following the initial assault, Lansius's first trench was no longer able to use crossbows as freely anymore. It became mainly a melee affair. But the crossbows, as planned, had done a great job in blunting the initial assault.

Moreover, Lansius had put the bulk of his crossbowmen in the second trench, where they could fire freely at any incoming enemy on the surface. These ranged attacks became Lansius's best defense against the enemy's onslaught, preventing them from being slaughtered from the top like animals trapped in a gutter.

Lansius's side didn't have a monopoly on crossbows; their opponents had tried to use them as well. However, they were unprepared. Anticipating a melee, Lord Robert's men had failed to bring a sufficient number of crossbows into the trench.

Meanwhile, Lansius had amassed a large stockpile of bolts, enough to last an hour. He had also trained more than half of his men in the use and maintenance of crossbows. Bows took ages to master, but crossbows required only two days to learn the basics and two weeks to become proficient enough for battle.

While Sir Stan had equipped the troops with spears, polearms, and a few dozen crossbows, Lansius allocated more of his war fund to acquire a hundred more crossbows, even going so far as to spend his own personal five gold pieces—equivalent to 100 silver—to buy forty additional crossbows.

Still not satisfied, Lansius borrowed thirty heavy arbalests from Toruna's armory, along with a large supply of bolts. To further bolster their arsenal, he sold some of their surplus supplies to purchase additional ammunition.

All these preparations enabled his troops to maintain a high rate of fire against their opponents. This proved especially effective against the enemy's transitional armor, which was primarily ring mail rather than proper plate. Lowlandia was a poor province, and despite its involvement in multiple conflicts, its men-at-arms lacked the best equipment the Imperium could offer. Its plates made from mild iron offered little protection against Midlandian steel-tipped heavy bolts.

But now, the battle had entered a new phase.

Steel clanging echoed as Hugo exchanged blows with the new opponent. At one point, the knight turned it into a sword grapple. However, Hugo was a tad faster and slipped his sword into a thrust. The steel tip dug deep into the knight's unprotected inner right elbow, causing him to recoil in pain.

Despite not being the greatest fighter, Hugo's agility and sure-footedness, helped by the rope trick, gave him an advantage in the close and confined space. Hugo wrestled the opponent down with that advantage, but another fighter intervened.

Hugo took a step back, and another knight in engraved plate armor wielding a shield and mace took the spot easily. The other fighter also faced difficulties with his opponent and was saved only by Hugo's intervention.

This unnerved Lansius. The opponent was getting better at this game.

Despite their initial setbacks, the Lion's knights and men-at-arms had slowly adapted and regained their edge. There was no more hurried attack or halfhearted assault, only cold precision and a steady push.

Exhausted, Hugo signaled for a replacement. Lansius and his crossbowman seized the opportunity to fire at the enemy. However, the knights were prepared and readily shielded their upper bodies, making the bolts thud harmlessly upon impact.

Another pair of fighters bolted to the front. Meanwhile, Lansius reloaded his crossbow and realized he could hear heavy breathing coming from the enemy's direction.

The hot and humid conditions underground made it difficult for anyone in full-face helmets to breathe through their small vents. As a result, many of Lansius's opponents had their visors open, despite the risk of getting hit by stray bolts or deadly shrapnel.

Lansius suddenly rallied his men. "Keep it up! Once we stop the vanguard, the rest will fall." Upon hearing his words, the new pair of fighters charged forward with their poleaxes.

The rest of Lansius's men behind didn't respond verbally. Having borne the brunt of the assault, they were exhausted, but their eyes showed renewed determination.

However, determination alone was not enough to win the fight. Despite their best efforts, the new pair of fighters struggled in their fight and continued to lose ground against the more-skilled opponents.

Hugo looked at Lansius, who nodded, agreeing to another swap.

Despite the advantage, the opponent did not rush. They were acting like a cat playing with a mouse in their grasp. When they spotted another swap, they were so accustomed that they readily raised their shields.

Watching them, Lansius deliberately withheld from firing his crossbow. Instead, he aimed it around threateningly to give his men some breathing time. The trick worked, and his fighters retreated without problems.

At this range, and in the absence of wind, everyone knew that not even plate armor could provide invulnerability. However, the problem still persisted: a crossbow would not be very effective against a shield.

A bearded man stepped forward. He wore a sallet along with a heater shield and an axe. From his looks, he was eager to fight.

"Careful, don't get cocky," Lansius warned the bearded guy.

Thomas chuckled. "No worries, I got my beard back."

The man could have an easy life in Midlandia, following Lord Arte and Sir Peter on their political tour, but Thomas decided to follow his guts. Out of respect, Lansius had put him in reserve, but the man yearned to fight.

Thomas and Roger, a younger man who had paired up with him, approached the opponent's line calmly. The mace-wielding knight suddenly lunged at Thomas. Thomas dodged a blow from a mace and countered with a ferocious axe attack.

The knight blocked with his shield and felt a jolt in his arm and shoulder. Thomas kept hacking at it, but a shield bash took him by surprise.

Thomas stumbled back as the knight swung his mace. He raised his shield to block, crouched low, and lunged at the knight. It was such a short distance that the knight failed to react.

The knight lost his footing as Thomas launched a series of blows. The knight immediately fell, and Thomas pinned him down, ready for the killing blow, but a halberd greeted him from the front.

The axeman released his prey and took several steps back. Two knights assisted their fallen comrades readily. One dragged the guy back; another kept brandishing their halberd.

"Thomas!" Lansius shouted.

Old Thomas barely ducked when two bolts screeched through the air and landed at the two who tried to evacuate their friends. One got hit in the thigh and groaned in pain, another was unconscious from a big dent in his helmet.

"On me!" Thomas charged into the opponent's confused line while Roger tried his best to contain the other knight from interfering.

Hugo sprang into action and joined the fray while Lansius frantically reloaded his bolt, hoping this might be the break they were waiting for.

Thomas, Hugo, and Roger fought admirably with tenacity. However, despite the golden opportunity, they were facing the best of Lord Robert's men-at-arms. The knights soaked the damage and re-formed their line.

In this confined space between the two red dirt walls, there was no place for flanking, and Lansius men's momentum stalled. They took two for ransom and injured several, but failed to make the breakthrough they desperately needed.

Just then the fighting stopped as both sides took breathing room.

"Get down," the crossbowman beside Lansius yelled, as he thought he had found his chance.

Already anticipating the attack, the men ducked. The bolt flew straight but narrowly missed the knight's helmet. Lansius, too, fired his crossbow, but the bolt got deflected at the other knight's pauldron and flew harmlessly into the earthen wall.

After they had spent their ranged attack, the opponent suddenly charged forward.

*Fuck! They were waiting for this.*

"Fall back," Hugo screamed as if reading Lansius's mind. Thomas and Roger acted like a rear guard and tried their best to defend against the charging knights.

Lansius's men retreated, more panicked than orderly. Suddenly, one of the guys in front screamed. Lansius stopped and saw Roger's shoulder pierced by a spear. Blood was gushing through his gambeson.

Lansius tossed his crossbow to his assistant and dashed back. "Lend me a hand," he cried as he dragged the wounded guy as fast as he could.

Hugo and Thomas were close to their limit, answering multiple attacks at once. The opponents clad in plate fearlessly rushed like raging bulls.

A spear slipped and nearly impaled Lansius. It made him slip into the red mud. A female in ring mail moved past them, pushing them, and used her shield as cover.

"Carla, don't get reckless," her friend warned her from behind.

"Mind your business! If they fall, then we're also going to die," Carla said defiantly.

"That's more like it," Lansius commended while redoubling the effort to drag Roger. There was not enough space for two, but a few hands reached out to them to help.

Carla eventually took the front after Thomas got hit on the side of his helmet. Afterward, they picked up the pace, where suddenly the width along the trenches got wider.

They finally reached a place that Lansius named the gatehouse. It was not only wider, but it was also separated by a wooden fence with a functioning gate.

As they passed the wooden fence, Lansius, Hugo, and the rest just dropped to the ground. Red sticky soil was the least of their problems.

A few men who were in charge of the gate, less experienced but protected behind the fence, readily brandished their spears and fired their crossbows against the incoming knights and men-at-arms.

After a short skirmish that felled several of their members, the Lowlandians lost their momentum and retreated, seemingly into the far end of the trenches.

Lansius slumped with his back against the reddened wall. Hugo and Thomas were next to him. Despite being wider than the rest of the trench, it was still only enough for four people to stand abreast.

Fresher personnel passed between them to reinforce the gate. The fighting grew quiet around them, so Lansius could hear crossbow bolts being fired overhead.

"Fighting still rages top side," Hugo commented after watching Lansius looking upward.

Lansius nodded. He knew that it meant that the opponent still had more men coming. However, this was all within expectation.

Looking at his men working hard to survive made him breathe a sigh of relief. His biggest gamble had paid off. From the beginning, Lansius's problem wasn't only the enemy, but also his men's willingness to fight. Truthfully, they were nothing but misfits, poorly recruited and motivated only by raiding and looting.

Exacerbating the problem, Lansius had no reputation. Despite all his fair treatment, no Midlandians would trust him with their lives. Thus, he had deceived them. He had led them to a place where they couldn't possibly run, so their only option was to fight for their lives. This trench strategy was essentially that.

Lansius gambled that, even without divine rights, beliefs, or ideologies, men would always fight for survival. And once again, he had proven the assumption to be correct. His men were exhausted, bruised, and battered, but still motivated to fight. And the Arvenians gladly showed them the way.

Ever more experienced, Hugo began skillfully reorganizing his men. In a short time, a fresh group of thirty men sallied out. Their rallying cries pumped everyone's morale as they exited the gateway.

"Tough lads," Hugo commented as he noticed Lansius gaze at the men.

Lansius nodded. "Any words from other sectors?"

Hugo searched around and called, "Oi, messengers."

One perked up and headed toward them.

"What're the words from Sir Justin and Master Calub?"

"Sir Justin and his men have captured a dozen. Several fell, but they steadily gained ground. As for Master Calub, his traps worked; the enemy was kept in check."

Hugo looked at Lansius, who nodded, satisfied.

*Anything other than getting wiped up is good news.*

While the battle raged on, they could afford some quick treatment. A barber who followed them was their designated healer, as was the norm for this era.

The barber cleaned Hugo's small wounds with wine and wrapped them with a clean linen cloth. Meanwhile, Thomas had a cut on his cheek and had lost a lump of hair from a narrow slash. Part of his beard was reddened with blood.

Lansius took a deep breath. The realization that these men bled for him was overwhelming.

Suddenly, the wooden fence came alive again. The second group was being pushed back, and the knights were hot on their tails.

Thomas put his sallet back while Hugo took a crude-looking halberd from one of his men. Lansius, too, rose up, ready for the finale.

# CHAPTER 36

# YOUNG MAN'S GAME

The air was thick with the sound of thunderous footsteps and rallying cries as Lord Robert's men-at-arms charged toward the wooden fence. Though their stamina was failing and the enemy's tactics unpredictable, their pride burned fiercely.

In the confined space, they hurled themselves against the sturdy gates with all their might, using their weight in place of a battering ram.

But the defenders were well-prepared. Armed with polearms and crossbows, they pushed back the attackers and made them pay a tremendous price.

Despite the sacrifices of eleven of their bravest, the two-meter-tall wooden fence remained seemingly impregnable. Bloodied by a persistent stream of crossbow bolts, they could only drag the wounded along with their retreat.

Deep in the trenches, they licked their wounds and prepared for the inevitable.

The wooden gate groaned as it swung open. Many of its posts were bent or pushed from their spots. The chipped and splintered wooden fence stood as a testament to the relentless assault of their opponents.

Lansius emerged from the gate in his battered gray brigandine, accompanied by his men who surveyed the scars of battle with him. "Hugo," he called out with a weary yet resolute voice.

Hugo rested his crude halberd and replied, "Yes, boss?"

"Pick your best men," Lansius commanded.

With a sigh of relief, Hugo turned to his men and rallied them. "Come on lads, for the finale."

With Lansius and Thomas behind, Hugo led a contingent of his best men into battle. They quickly located Lord Robert's exhausted troops and offered battle. An intense melee ensued, but it soon became clear that the opponent's men-at-arms were on their last leg.

The once fearsome troops were reduced to a sorry lot. Their best fighters lay wounded or dead on the ground, leaving only the inexperienced ones to carry on. Their breathing was ragged, and their movements sluggish as the stifling heat and humidity drained them of their last bit of strength.

Trapped in the trench, with Lansius's crossbowmen positioned to cut their escape, Lord Robert's side had no choice but to surrender.

The deputy commander knelt before Lansius, casting aside his helmet adorned with a great plume. He offered his sword as a token of surrender. It should have been the marshal doing this, but word had it that he had lost an eye to shrapnel.

"I accept your surrender and guarantee the safety of your men who lay down their arms." Lansius reiterated the words whispered by Sir Justin, who had just arrived from his front.

His men clamored as Lansius finished the words. They shouted victory in loud emotional voices and threw their fists in the air. Many of them looked at Lansius intensely and made him uncomfortable.

"VICTORY!" The word was repeated and echoed, spreading through the trenches like wildfire.

Eventually, the fighting ceased in all the trenches. The defeated had accepted their fate and surrendered their weapons.

Sir Justin conversed with the deputy commander, while Hugo, Thomas, and their men ensured security. Guarding numerous hostages wasn't easy, but they were like assets waiting to be cashed in.

Lansius stood with Carla, his temporary adjutant, away from the limelight. Suddenly, the sound of hooves followed by a large shadow loomed over them. Carla instinctively drew her sword and readied her shield, but soon recognized the figure of a cavalrywoman on the ground level.

*She must've trotted along the trenches until she found me.*

Lansius pulled his sallet off.

"So you survived?" Audrey asked as she opened her visor.

"You seem to be displeased?" Lansius retorted.

That made Audrey laugh so hard that her visor fell in a comedic manner, causing Lansius and his men to burst into laughter as well.

Before the laughter subsided, Lansius ordered Carla to fetch back the ladder. They carefully flew their banner first to avoid getting shot by the other trenches by mistake. Audrey was already present, so there was a low risk, but Lansius insisted just to be safe.

Lansius climbed up after Carla and took in the sight of the battlefield, littered with casualties. Across the grassy plains, many were groaning in pain. Some writhed, while a few calmly waited for the slow coming of death. The aftermath was always a sad scene.

In the distance, the enemy's retreat had turned into a rout. The decisive factor had been the great show of force by Audrey's cavalry they had made by forming a wide line, even though in truth, they only numbered twenty-seven riders. However, to the remaining enemy, their presence was evidently too much to bear.

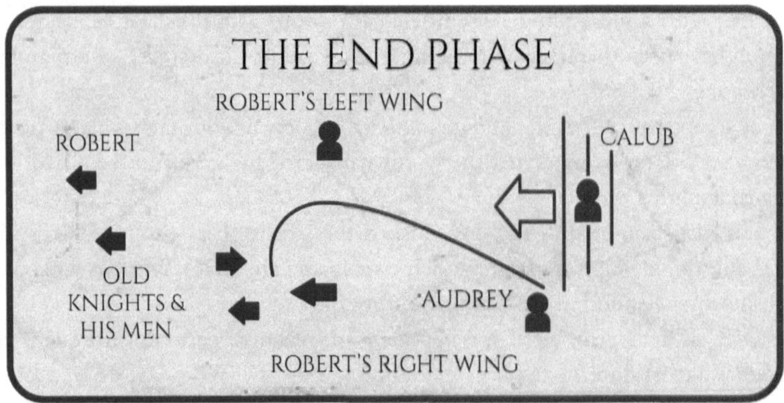


On the other hand, Robert's cavalry had left the field, unwilling to risk themselves by going near the trenches.

Lansius expected the rout, given the isolation of the enemy commanders and vanguard. The remaining levied men and armed villagers had little motivation, and the few knights and remaining men-at-arms had no choice but to retreat. Now, they no longer flew their banners.

"Get me Sir Justin," Lansius said to Carla.

Sir Justin emerged from the trenches. "What do you need, Commander, a party?"

Lansius chuckled. "That can wait. Sir Justin, I see all those beautiful horses and knights. What do you think we should do?"

Sir Justin laughed and shouted down to his men, "Time for a ransom hunt!"

The knight's words were greeted with fierce jubilation from his men. Quickly, they made their way to the back trench, where they had hidden their horses.

Lansius saw Anci approaching. He looked mauled, but still alive and kicking as usual. "Anci, go nuts," he said to encourage him.

"Haha, easy," Anci replied. "Come, Hugo, don't be a slowpoke," he taunted Hugo, who had just climbed up.

"Fook you and your blasted horse," Hugo cursed, drawing laughter from the troops. They knew Anci and Hugo had grown up together as squires to the same knight.

Then something occurred to Lansius. "Audrey, let them surrender and arrange for talks if you could."

With her visor returned to its place, Audrey threw a hard glance at Lansius before nodding once and spurring her horse forward.

*Viscount Robert*

In the aftermath of the rout, the enemy's smaller yet fiercely motivated riders pursued Robert's fleeing troops, scattering his other units from the battlefield. The only remnants of Robert's forces were those who had sought refuge within their camp.

They attempted to barricade the camp, but they lacked sturdy walls for protection, and many had abandoned their posts, taking their mules or carts with them. In this dire situation, Robert's loyalists urged him to flee. However, he knew his slow-moving baggage train would be easy prey for the enemy. When that happened, it would be a lost cause.

Right now, he still had the numbers to force the enemy into the negotiation table. However, Robert suspected the enemy held numerous hostages, enough to make his own nobles turn against him. Many of these captives were sons, uncles, or husbands of influential families.

Even if Robert managed to escape and secure himself within his castle, he would face internal conspiracies. The families of the hostages would be driven to overthrow Robert's rule to ensure the safe return of their captive kin.

This precarious situation meant that a large number of Robert's still numerous men and cavalry were reluctant to fight, fearful that their actions might endanger their relatives.

The enemy had triumphed, a fact Robert was forced to acknowledge. Believing that bravery was not only demonstrated in victory but also in defeat, he sat beneath his tent, patiently awaiting a negotiation while his men valiantly organized a final stand.

However, a group of riders acting as messengers arrived, bearing an offer of negotiation from their leader. Robert welcomed the opportunity for dialogue, and a truce was swiftly declared. The hostilities halted on both sides.

As both armies tended to their wounded and collected their fallen, a large ivory tent was erected between them, a symbol of forthcoming discussions.

As the victor's cavalry patrolled the vicinity and stood guard at the site, the Lion of Lowlandia made his appearance, exuding an air of calm dignity. A small retinue of knights accompanied him as a protective entourage.

Despite the sweltering heat and his evident fatigue, Robert remained clad in his armor, resolute in leveraging every potential advantage in the forthcoming negotiations.

His adversaries welcomed him readily, though ironically the ivory tent was his own, one of many things he would lose in the aftermath of this conflict. Yet even in the face of defeat, Robert maintained a straight-backed posture, wearing an expression that suggested he was relishing every moment.

However, Robert mostly maintained his silence, allowing a trusted aide to handle the negotiations. To his surprise, his counterpart mirrored his approach.

There was no gloating in the adversary's leader's face. The man named Lansius sat quietly in his seat, observing the proceedings without interjecting. Both leaders exchanged several glances but refrained from direct conversation.

The first topic of discussion was the status of the hostages. A knight was dispatched to verify their condition and reported back that they were safe, kept in separate pits throughout the trenches as a precaution. The knight also confirmed that Marshal Michael had survived, though likely at the cost of an eye.

Robert drew a deep breath and nodded to his knight, his silence conveying his relief.

The second issue raised was the fate of Robert's baggage train. Given their distance from the nearest settlement, supplies would be precarious. Fortunately, while the victors insisted on confiscating all wealth, they were reasonable enough to leave almost half of Robert's food supplies intact.

This was more than sufficient for their march back home, and Robert was appeased. With the two main subjects addressed, Robert turned his attention to the opposing leader. To Robert, this Lansius was an intriguing figure. Not because of his black hair that marked him as a foreigner, but due to his lack of the pride or entitlement typically flaunted by the nobility.

The discussion soon hit a deadlock when the subject of land rights was broached.

"I beg your pardon, but your side lacks a valid casus belli against my lord's domain. While we acknowledge your military superiority, you cannot lay claim to White Lake without risking intervention from the Imperium," Robert's representative argued with conviction.

Sir Justin scoffed at this. "Stop this nonsense. It's common knowledge that the lords of Lowlandia have been competing and seizing lands not rightfully theirs for generations. The Imperium has never intervened."

"We are not brutes! My lord only engages in battle when his rightful claims are threatened," retorted Robert's representative.

"Says the one who didn't send an envoy this morning and launched an assault without even a parley," Sir Justin shot back.

Robert's side reeled from the statement, but chose to ignore it. "In the last conflict, Viscount Jorge pledged Korelia as payment for a joint attack on the Southern Alliance. When Lord Jorge reneged on his promise, my lord was justified in reclaiming what was rightfully his."

The crux of the matter was that Lansius held no legitimate claim to Robert's domain. In reality, Robert would capitulate due to his defeat, but Lansius couldn't legally retain Robert's domain without the appropriate justification.

If Lansius forced his way, it would be seen as taking White Lake hostage, a move that would invite all the lords of Lowlandia to attack.

Robert was curious to see how this young man would navigate this messy issue of casus belli.

# CHAPTER 37

# CESSATION

*Lansius, Leader of the Banner of the Unknown*

When the question of casus belli was raised, Lansius shifted his posture for the first time, drawing the attention of those around him. "Let's put that problem aside for now," he suggested, his tone pleasant and friendly. "What if this has all been a misunderstanding?"

Robert's aide looked at him in confusion, and Robert turned to Lansius with a hint of disdain. "A misunderstanding?" he challenged.

Seated comfortably, Lansius simply nodded. "I want you to continue ruling White Lake as you always have."

Surprise flickered briefly across Robert's face before he countered, "That must be a jest! I'm a defeated noble. Why would you make such an absurd statement?" His response was roundabout, seemingly designed to provoke Lansius into revealing his true intentions.

"My lord, I assure you I'm not jesting. I am extending an offer for cooperation between us," Lansius replied resolutely, deliberately addressing Robert as his lord in an attempt to placate him.

"There's no cooperation between the victor and the defeated. The relationship is between the conqueror and the subjugated. Why resort to pleasantries?" Robert retorted.

"I never intended to conquer you, Lord Robert," Lansius responded with patience. In truth, he had nothing to offer that would impress Robert, but his ambitions lay elsewhere, and he might still have a chance to achieve them without relinquishing too much of his spoils.

Taking a deep breath, Robert asked, "Then how do you explain today's battle?"

Lansius paused before answering, "Let's consider it a mock battle."

"A mock battle? For what purpose?"

"To bring about change," Lansius declared enigmatically. "The realm south of Midlandia has been stagnant for far too long. I wish to change that."

*Viscount Robert*

Robert was momentarily stunned by Lansius's declaration.

*Does he intend to unite Lowlandia?*

The feuds among the Lowlandian nobles were older than the third Imperium itself. The ambition persisted, but nobody openly expressed it among peers.

Yet, Robert found it hard to dismiss Lansius's statement, given the astounding victory his ragtag group had achieved over Robert's larger, seasoned force. Many of his men were veterans Robert had personally recruited, trained, and led for more than two decades.

A blind bravado had been his undoing, but Robert felt the need to credit Lansius for creating a near-miracle victory. That made him ponder what he could accomplish with someone like Lansius serving as his marshal. Perhaps even the unification of Lowlandia was within reach, he mused.

However, he quickly dismissed that notion and instead asked, "Please indulge me? What exactly is your plan?"

"I wish Lord Robert to continue his rule, with a few beneficial changes for both of us," Lansius clarified.

Suppressing a mix of skepticism and hope, Robert nodded. "Please, continue."

"I propose military protection in exchange for a strategic castle as a base, and a portion of your income. The funds would be used to purchase food and other supplies from your domain, allowing wealth to circulate locally and preventing you from becoming any poorer than before."

Lansius's rough use of the language suggested a lack of noble upbringing, yet his innovative ideas were intriguing.

"So, a mercenary company?" Robert ventured.

"Not quite. A mercenary is hired to fight someone else's war. That's not my intent," Lansius clarified.

"And what about rebuilding my forces? Would you permit it?" Robert asked, half in jest.

"Certainly, we are not your conquerors. You may do as you please."

Robert's gaze narrowed. "You're not afraid I might betray you?"

"There's always a risk. But I believe in time, you'll see the larger picture and choose to ally with us," Lansius stated firmly.

Robert stroked his small goatee. Despite the absurdity, he found himself warming up to Lansius. He wasn't as polished as many noblemen, but his voice held a note of genuine empathy. Moreover, his demeanor was devoid of ill will and even suggested humility.

His instincts told him to trust this young man. The decision wasn't difficult. As a defeated noble, his options were limited: capitulate and be sent somewhere remote as a hostage, or take a long journey to the old capital in Centuria, besieged by wars with the western nomads.

Accepting Lansius's plan offered a way to retain his position, albeit with reduced power and wealth. It was an enticing proposal.

"Before the battle, I heard reports from the villages your men visited," Robert reminisced about the scout's remarks several days prior. "I fully expected to hear about damage or looting, but to my surprise, there were none. Instead, the village chiefs reported your men purchasing food at fair prices. Why?"

Lansius smiled, seemingly flustered. "I may not look the part, but I'm not a robber."

The old viscount chuckled for the first time as a hunch dawned on him.

*He purchased those goods to garner public support. He knew he would likely triumph in battle. How audacious!*

Robert was amused, for in a war such a strategy seemed impractical and offered little gain. Yet he admired a war leader who refrained from looting the poor. "Perhaps you're on to something," Robert muttered as he considered the offer. "Would you also permit me to run my court?"

"That's my intention. Let's make this into cooperation. I'll handle military affairs, and my lord shall take care of politics. This way there's no need for a casus belli."

Robert glanced at his aide, who nodded in agreement. Even they found the proposition appealing.

However, propelled by curiosity, Robert asked further, "Why all the complications? Wouldn't it be more straightforward for you to rule the region yourself?"

"No, that would invite too many problems. I don't want to get entangled in court politics," Lansius declared, his true intentions remaining a mystery.

The victor and the vanquished set off toward Robert's domain to orchestrate the transfer of power. Their pace was slow yet steady, their ranks weighed down by the wounded. The baggage train was also heavy with the confiscated armor and weapons from the defeated. They also had prisoners to consider and ransoms to secure, necessitating careful progress to avoid unnecessary risks.

Sir Justin led the troops while Calub tended to the wounded. In this era, medical care was scarce. The best they could do was to dispatch the gravely wounded to the nearest village for basic care.

Lansius wished for more comprehensive care for them, but Robert refused it as the situation hadn't yet stabilized. The threat of conflict still loomed, as Robert's allies might attempt to intervene.

Ironically, they remained on a war footing until they could safely escort Robert to his castle to exercise his authority. This was the very reason Lansius had set up camp deep within Robert's domain, effectively holding him and his commanders hostage.

Nevertheless, the transfer of power eventually occurred without a hitch. Only then, Lansius sent word to his benefactor, explaining his victory and his reasons to ask for Korelia as a base of power in the region.

In the letter, Lansius expressed his wish for Lord Bengrieve to send him a replacement commander and contingent, so he could return to Midlandia. However, when Lord Bengrieve replied, Lansius was surprised at his benefactor's reaction.

Following Viscount Robert's disastrous defeat, the Lion of Lowlandia carefully ceded Korelia to the victor, an unusual arrangement that led many to assume a secret agreement had been made.

Regardless of the truth, Korelia was no longer under Lord Robert's control. Although a small fief with limited resources, Korelia held strategic importance as a middle ground between the western and eastern parts of Lowlandia.

The town could serve as a gateway to unify the province under one's rule, but its lack of arable land posed a problem for supporting a larger population.

Beyond the small castle town, there were only several villages spread to its eastern side. With little arable land but grassland, its population was small and mostly composed of herders.

Despite being a humble fief, the transfer of Korelia disrupted the balance of power in the region. Adding to this tension was the fall of Orniteia Barony to Midlandia after a siege. Now, every neighboring lord was plotting their moves. They knew conflict was inevitable.

*Fall of 4424, Korelia. Two Months After Lansius's Victory*

Lansius, the temporary officer of Korelia, was awed by the sight of the cloudless blue sky above him. It was unlike anything he had ever seen before, with a seemingly endless expanse of grass stretching out as far as the eye could see. It felt as if Korelia was the only human settlement in this part of the world, surrounded by the vast emptiness of a nomadic steppe.

*Have I ever visited Mongolia?* Lansius asked himself, but his memory offered no answer. While he could remember movies, books, or even games, he had a hard time remembering personal details of his life. He couldn't even recall his nationality or origin, but that didn't bother him anymore. Now, this life was all he had.

Sitting under a rectangular field tent, Lansius contentedly watched the building project he had envisioned for Korelia taking shape. The gray-colored canvas flapped in the breeze as the sun rose higher on the eastern horizon.

Several hundred men dug trenches on the west side, while another hundred worked on the southern side of the town. They were making trenches for city defenses.

He hated trenches, but there were not enough woods to construct a palisade even for just one side. To compensate for the lack of defense, Lansius had ordered his men to make picket fences and stakes using whatever wood was available.

Usually, this kind of work was frowned upon by the population. Unless they were exempted from annual tax. But, instead of the usual forced labor, Lansius was offering wages, much to people's delight.

While Lansius believed in treating people fairly, his real intention was to prevent sabotage or dissidents. Moreover, he theorized that paid labor worked faster and was generally more reliable.

Just this week, Lansius's view was vindicated. Aided by Lansius's goal-oriented payment, the workers managed themselves efficiently. The defense work began to take shape right on schedule.

Another factor that contributed was the quick harvest time in Korelia. The area didn't have much farmland, and after the festivities ended, Lansius had the full labor of the farmers at his disposal as well.

A billowing cloud of black smoke caught Lansius's attention. It was the blacksmith Calub had invited from out of town to produce nails and bolt heads for their side project. Though the local smiths couldn't produce swords or armor, they could handle simple repairs and maintenance.

Lansius had wanted Calub to head another project to build workshops. They wanted to employ craftsmen, artisans, and volunteers to produce crossbow parts.

As Lansius watched the project progress, a sudden horse's neigh drew his attention. He glanced up and saw a friendly silhouette approaching.

"I see that you're well enough to go outside today." A hint of a smile was on Audrey's lips as she approached closer and covered him with a fur coat.

"Ah, thanks." Lansius felt the warmth and found it pleasant.

Audrey noticed how windy it was. "Mm, perhaps you shouldn't be out here for too long."

"Do I look that pale?" he asked.

"Well, prevention is always wise," Audrey remarked smugly.

"You sound like Calub," he chuckled. "Lemme check your forehead for a fever."

His jest was shot down by a cold stare. "Not funny. You've been bedridden on and off for almost three weeks. Everybody is terrified."

Lansius's chuckle died down quickly. "I know. I'm sorry to make you worry."

Audrey kept staring, and Lansius could only look down.

She let out a soft sigh before tenderly patting Lansius's shoulder. He caught her hand with his own, savoring the warmth of her touch.

After a moment of comfortable silence, she asked, "I heard about the letters."

Lansius exhaled deeply, awash in a mix of emotions. His recent victory had set off a chain of unexpected events, many completely beyond his control. And nothing could have prepared him for the response from Midlandia.

The triumph he had fought so hard to achieve now seemed to be pulling him further from his desires and closer to the chaos of war. On the other hand, it had also opened the door to great opportunities.

# CHAPTER 38

# LORD OF KORELIA

A gentle autumn breeze brushed against the gray canvas of the field tent, causing the edges to flap lazily in the morning sun. Standing at Lansius's side, Audrey looked stylish in her tailored black dress. It was barely a few months old, a gift from Lord Bengrieve, their benefactor. Contrasting that, a worn belt adorned her slim waist, the same one that she had worn when they first met last year.

Lansius thought the black dye used for that dress was worth a fortune. He still couldn't fathom why they treated Audrey so well. A tingle of suspicion was always on the back of his head. "Who told you I received letters? Calub?"

"I doubt anyone will miss fifteen mounted armed guards escorting two carriages," Audrey replied as she continued to massage Lansius's shoulder.

Lansius licked his lips and felt that he might be overreacting. Messengers from high-ranking nobles usually came with armed men for protection, which easily attracted unwanted attention. "I got two letters. One from Lord Bengrieve and another from Sir Stan."

"What did they say?" Audrey asked.

"Sir Stan, your adopted brother, is praising us for our surprising victory. He also sent sizeable gifts to commemorate it."

"I've noticed the fully loaded carriages. How about Lord Bengrieve's letter?"

"That's the tricky one."

"I doubt it's that bad," Audrey said as she kneaded his shoulder.

"Well, he . . . congratulated me for a brilliant victory."

"That's a good start."

"But he rejected my pleas to send one of his captains along with fresh troops to take over Korelia." Lansius exhaled deeply.

"That means we're not going back then," Audrey said, surprisingly calm.

"You don't look unhappy?" Lansius asked.

"Why should I? Better to reign on the farm than serve in a castle," she said eloquently.

Lansius tried hard not to grin at the wise words. Her education in Toruna was showing its fruit.

"Is that all he said?" Audrey asked.

"He thinks I'm foolish for believing that Midlandia would want to endeavor into another Lowlandia territory. I guess the last thing they want is to open an even wider front . . . He also calculated that it'll be hard to achieve peace, with all the neighbors at each other's throats, thus requiring great manpower just to keep the peace. And all that for a province with nothing but a sea of grassland."

"Go on," Audrey encouraged. She sensed that the more Lansius spoke, the more at ease he became.

"Umm . . . since we won the battle and were able to make an interesting deal with Lord Robert, he instructed me to . . . rule and survive."

Audrey's fingers froze. "Rule?"

Lansius met her gaze. "He offered me this land if I could survive."

She took a step back. "Lans, that means lordship. Korelia is a barony."

Lansius tried to downplay the issue. "The title may sound grand, but while the land area is huge, Korelia's worth a mere fraction of Sir Stan's Toruna. It's all bark and no bite."

"Did he really offer you that?" she asked again.

He looked up briefly, gathering his thoughts before revealing, "Attached to the letter is a vellum bearing the seal of the Lord of Midlandia. It's a duplicate of a recommendation letter for patent to the High Court."

Audrey gasped and covered her mouth.

Clutching his fur coat tighter, Lansius added, "I don't know what Bengrieve's scheme is, but that's what he's offering."

Barely recovered from her surprise, Audrey tapped Lansius's shoulder. "You realize it's still a grand offer?"

"A grand prize for a grand risk," Lansius quipped. "Lowlandia's feuds run deep. Everybody has a claim to another's land. Soon, they'll be knocking on our door with a siege engine."

Audrey seemed to struggle to find a response as Lansius continued. "That Bengrieve is dangling a prize in front of his pet and waiting to see whether I'll bite or not."

Dangling a morsel in front of a mongrel was a known proverb in Midlandia. It meant that it was likely a ruse, because the master would always eat it and leave only scraps for the pet. Still, Audrey sensed something was amiss. "Lord Bengrieve is taunting you."

Lansius caught her eyes. "Even if he isn't, my hands are too small for a prize like this. It's unthinkable to defend Korelia against a siege without reinforcement from Midlandia."

"I say we risk it," Audrey declared.

Lansius chuckled but went quiet after sensing her serious gaze.

"You're making ditches and fences, also inviting blacksmiths, carpenters, fletchers. Don't tell me you didn't come prepared," she pointed out.

A hint of a smile was on Lansius's lips. Noticing that, Audrey leaned closer and whispered, "I know your ambition too well, my lord."

Lansius blushed at her words and tried to refute them. "You know well that I just want a peaceful place to live," he said.

Audrey played along with his game. "You still thinking about returning to village life?"

"I have to say that I still fancy the idea," Lansius admitted. "No politics, no responsibility, no guilt." To live as a hunter in a distant village like Torrea was Lansius's go-to escapist imagination.

But Audrey didn't share his enthusiasm. "I only see hardships," she remarked grimly. "Hunting weekly, butchering game, stitching my own torn cloth. Stuck in rainy seasons and only visiting town a few times a year for supplies."

Lansius chuckled at her answer.

Undeterred, Audrey continued. "I'd rather live in a big city with a servant who does groceries. But then, I prefer to eat out when the weather's nice. Also, watch plays or go to the festival," she finished with a smile. "Trust me, I've been there. Secluded life isn't fun."

Lansius couldn't help but tease her. "And what about cooks? You often say it's a necessity."

"Indeed," Audrey replied. "I need someone who can indulge me with a variety of seasonal dishes for lunch. Glazed fire pit roast for supper. And don't forget a maid who'll help this lady bathe and dress."

The image of this stiff-faced cavalry captain being pampered like a princess sent Lansius into a fit of laughter. Normally, Audrey would hit him when he laughed at her expense, but this topic turned out to be an exception. Audrey looked proud of her jest, even delighted.

Despite his laughter, Lansius felt that Audrey's dream was justified. She had gone through so much in her life: been driven out of her family, lost her knight master, and been a victim of war twice, even almost sold into slavery.

"How about marrying a baron?" Lansius teased.

"I hope not one of the small barons who till the land and shear sheep," Audrey replied almost deadpan.

The image of himself dressed in gaudy clothing, wielding shears against a flock of sheep made Lansius laugh. "All title, no substance," he exclaimed as if venting out frustration.

Audrey happily added, "All glitter, but not gold."

Their shared laughter reflected a deeper understanding between them.

Afterward, the wind picked up again, causing the canvas above them to flap noisily. Feeling the chill in the air, Audrey signaled their entourage in a separate tent to ready the horses. She then turned to Lansius with her last concern: "Was the battle that hard on you?"

Lansius tried to shrug it off, but the memories were still fresh in his mind. "The battle was gruesome," he admitted. "But what shocked me the most was the aftermath."

This memory triggered a wave of guilt inside him. Around forty had fallen in battle, but almost a hundred had died after from blood loss, infection, and gangrene. Despite Calub's stockpile of alcohol, Lansius's knowledge of sanitation, and his order not to perform bloodletting, they still lost that many.

"I seriously think that you got sick because you exerted yourself too much," Audrey disagreed.

"Is that so?"

"You were doing so many things, taking care of the wounded, also the deal with Lord Robert."

"Well, there are so many things to do. Our men need treatment, supplies, and housing. And I certainly couldn't treat Lord Robert and his men badly, since I wanted them as allies."

"See? You're doing too much," Audrey replied warmly. "Next time, put more faith in your subordinates. After all, it's not your first time leading men into battle."

Lansius felt a weight on his mind. "You know, the first time I led men into battle was against slavers, and I didn't pity them. But the last time . . . I don't hold any grudges against the Lion and his men."

"Lans, we're not fighting without a cause," Audrey reminded him. "The end goal is to get our home back. That's as noble as it gets."

Lansius disagreed with her take but realized that modern values were not always applicable in this feudal world. He reminded himself that Audrey was born and raised in this society. Still, he tried to explain his stance. "Trampling on others who are not our opponents to advance our cause isn't exactly noble."

Audrey almost laughed. "Nobles fight, and men die all the time for lesser causes. A little blood on our hands is tame compared to them."

Lansius understood that Audrey was merely pointing out the reality, but he couldn't help feeling a churn in his stomach. "I'm not heartless. Witnessing men die haunts me."

"You're a softie, you know," she remarked.

"Sorry, but not sorry."

"Hey, I didn't mean it badly." Audrey turned to face him. "I mean, I actually like it that way."

Her words surprised him.

"What's the word . . . ? Ah, compassionate heart! Perhaps you're the rare kind of noble who could rule with one," Audrey remarked, teasing him gently.

"I take that as a compliment?"

"Rightly so, my lord," Audrey exclaimed, bearing a rare, cute smile.

Lansius noticed a squire, a pageboy, and a cup-bearer girl coming from a smaller tent in the distance, leading the horses.

"Can't we choose older candidates?" Lansius asked, feeling bad for employing underage children.

Audrey shook her head. "They're the lucky ones. Their parents fought hard to put them into your entourage. And that was before Lord Bengrieve said anything about making you a baron."

Lansius looked Audrey in the eyes. "Do me a favor, even if I'm a lord, call me by my name as usual."

"Not possible, my lord. At least not in front of people."

As her hair swayed in the wind, Audrey continued, "You know, the locals speak ill of the wind. They believe it carries diseases and miasma."

Lansius nodded. Even with his fur coat, he wasn't feeling all that well. "You're right. Let's head back."

Without waiting, the two walked toward their entourage.

In the first month of fall, 4424, Lansius declared himself as the new Lord of Korelia, claiming the support of Midlandian nobles. This news spread quickly, and Lord Robert of White Lake confirmed the transfer of ownership and pledged his support to Lansius.

Lord Robert's support was driven by his own predicament. As a fallen lord, he and his house faced the possibility of ruin or exile. Even if Robert had escaped to his castle, life would not have been the same. His own nobles would betray him and plan to oust him from power.

Lansius's decision not to imprison or exile Robert and his loyalists came as a surprise to Robert, and he knew it was his house's last chance to survive in Lowlandia politics. In their struggle, Robert and his loyalists grew to rely on Lansius's mutual support.

This bond was further strengthened when Lansius made generous terms, allowing Robert to rule nominally as the Lord of White Lake. This was in stark contrast to the brutal takeovers often seen in Lowlandia.

Lansius's aim was only to claim a portion of White Lake's income instead of ruling directly. To ensure submission, he integrated a portion of Robert's men-at-arms and stationed them in Korelia. He also incorporated neighboring estates owned by Robert's knights to gain their service.

However, Lansius was not the only one making moves. Behind the harvest and festivities, the seeds of conflict were being planted and set in motion in the shadows.

## CHAPTER 39

# UNSEEN HANDS

Korelia Castle and its town were perched atop a plateau, providing a breathtaking view of the vast steppe that stretched out in all directions. The castle towered high on the hill, while the town was nestled on one side. The people of Korelia relied on a small stream that flowed from a nearby river for their survival.

To the north of Korelia lay their only forest, a verdant expanse of towering trees that stretched as far as the eye could see. In stark contrast, the eastern side of the region was characterized by sheer cliffs and treacherous, rocky terrain that posed a challenge for even the most skilled climbers.

Despite the presence of a meandering stream, the area had little arable land for farming, and most of the townsfolk were shepherds who tended to their flocks of sheep and goats that grazed on the sea of grass. A few brave families also raised ducks, which were almost as big as ponies and aggressive, yet they yielded prized eggs and feathers.

Located halfway between the east and west parts of Lowlandia, Korelia had the potential to become a trade hub. However, the city's small population and the long arduous journey to the west discouraged most traders from doing business.

Despite being economically meager, Korelia was strategically significant as it served as the gateway between the east and west. Its possession meant military supremacy over the entirety of Lowlandia, and every ambitious lord sought to control it. While no House had ever united the entire province, the greed-fueled vision persisted.

The unforeseen losses suffered by Lord Robert, coupled with the unexpected emergence of Lansius as the new Lord of Korelia, shattered the precarious balance of power in the region. Almost instantly, the wheels of war turned once

more, and the people of Lowlandia braced themselves for the inevitable storm
that was to come.

*Korelia Castle*

Two weeks had passed since Lansius declared himself the new acting Lord of
Korelia. There was no ceremony or preparation. He simply sent letters to adjacent neighbors notifying them of the change. Because of this, the Small Council chamber was abuzz with clerical and administrative tasks. Inside, two men
worked tirelessly, facing each other across a long mahogany table.

Hugo glanced up from his work and asked Calub, who was poring over a
scroll, "What do you make of our lord's relationship with Audrey?"

Calub raised an eyebrow but didn't look up. "What's prompted this sudden
interest?" he asked.

"Well, I just think it might be good if they marry." Hugo chuckled as he
spoke.

"Midlandia wants Lansius to wed a nobleman's daughter to secure his position," Calub reminded him. "I believe Lord Robert's daughter is the prime
candidate."

"I'm aware, but with them already allied, there's little to gain." Hugo gave his
take and later added, "Meanwhile, the rumors are wild, I tell you."

"Really?" Calub asked and gave his full attention to Hugo.

Hugo leaned over and lowered his voice. "Well, for a young and success-
ful man without a lover. There are all kinds of rumors, even whispers about his
virility."

Calub exhaled deeply, sounding both amused and tired. "Give the man a
break. He should have a good reason."

"Well, the guys were just curious why he remains unmarried." Hugo defended
his men passionately, but he had exhausted the topic.

The two men returned to their work, busily tackling the daily tasks of
running the small town. They were responsible for feeding and clothing soldiers for the winter, managing supplies, overseeing construction projects,
and more.

Most of the clerical duties understandably fell into Calub's hand. As a member of the Merchant-Alchemist guild, Calub was highly educated and had taken
on most of the clerical duties, including the role of Lord Lansius's treasurer.
Meanwhile, Hugo's background was more of a warrior, a squire with an enviable
commanding experience.

Calub finally finished cross-checking Lansius's calculations. These were the
projected incomes for nascent House Lansius.

| Income | In gold |
| --- | --- |
| Lord Robert's captured baggage train | 1,400 |
| Capitulation, a share of accumulated Lord Robert's wealth | 2,100 |
| Ransom payments from knights/squire families | 800 |
| Confiscated, looted items from war | 600 |
| A share of White Lake's annual tax for next year | 300 |
| Korelia annual tax after harvest | 200 |
| Total in gold | 5,400 |
| Total in silver (1 gold is 20 silver) | 108,000 |
| Total in copper (1 silver is 12 copper) | 1,296,000 |

Calub mulled over the numbers. They looked impressive, but he knew the expenses would be equally staggering, especially considering the potential siege they anticipated next year.

As the man responsible for managing Korelia's finances and ensuring that everyone, from the men-at-arms to the servants, was paid, Calub was constantly busy. Still, he wasn't opposed to the idea of adding more men. He knew all too well that they still didn't have enough. In the face of impending war, they needed every defender they could get.

While Lord Lansius managed to retain most of his forces with lucrative contracts, side jobs, and year-round housing and meals, a portion of their forces had returned to Midlandia. Anci and Thomas were among a dozen cavalrymen and scores of men who had returned.

As far as Calub knew, Anci wasn't interested in the affairs of Lowlandia. He had only been there because Lord Arte wanted him to make a name for himself and for monetary gain.

Meanwhile, Thomas was motivated by more personal reasons. He wished to protect Lansius, and after seeing Lansius win the battle and command an army, he felt his presence was no longer needed. His loyalty ultimately lay with Sir Peter and House Arte.

Both returned to Lord Arte's side to act as escorts. The future Lord of Arvena needed to make a personal appearance in the capital to plead his case and garner support. If he managed to gather enough, then a campaign to retake Arvena would be in sight.

Meanwhile, Sir Justin had been busy setting up his prize, a new manor just east of Korelia.

It was close to midday when Calub groaned, dropping a scroll onto the table.

"Problem with the blacksmiths again?" Hugo asked.

"No, it's bigger. The food price keeps rising," Calub answered as he rested his back against the chair.

Hugo knitted his eyebrows. "But the harvest was just last month?"

Calub sighed. "Indeed, but the price won't come down."

"That's funny . . . Do we need to buy supplies from other towns?" Hugo suggested.

"I'm afraid we can't. The letters say it's the same everywhere," Calub replied.

"In all Lowlandia?" Hugo was alarmed. "This doesn't sound right . . . Anything we can do about this?"

"Not much, I'm afraid. The merchants noticed the disturbance and kept their stock tight," Calub said pessimistically.

Hugo's instincts told him that something was off. "Do you suspect foul play?"

"I do," Calub replied. "They want to limit our supply. They're probably planning for a siege next year."

Hugo was alarmed. "Has Lord Lansius been informed?"

Calub shook his head. "No, he's still recovering. I don't want to burden him with this."

Hugo made up his mind. "I'll talk to Audrey first. This is too urgent to ignore."

He left the council chamber in search of Audrey, knowing that rising food prices could lead to famine and spell disaster for Korelia. The town's people were not wealthy enough to have food surpluses, and many depended on trading their livestock for grains to survive the winter.

If grain prices were rising high, then nobody in Korelia could afford it. With their troops stationed in the town, the shortage would only worsen. Famine was a dreaded word in this world, and if it were to strike Korelia, no strategy they possessed could save them from utter destruction.

Lansius had started to feel better this week, and despite Audrey's wishes for him to rest longer, he was determined to check on the forest to the north. So, today they had gone for a ride, accompanied by ten riders and his entourage. At Lansius's insistence, nobody walked. Audrey rode with the blond cup-bearer girl, and Stirling, the new squire, shared a ride with the pageboy.

Although many believed he was merely bored with the castle, Lansius had been conducting an inspection. After an hour or two, they returned to the castle.

As Lansius's horses slowly climbed the small hill, they soon saw the sturdy oaken gate and the weathered stone curtain walls of Korelia Castle. The castle had endured many sieges, some victories, but many more losses.

As their group approached the castle, the guardsmen stationed at the gate readily opened the heavy wooden doors with a creak. The sound echoed through the courtyard as Lansius and his entourage rode in, the clatter of their horses' hooves filling the air.

In the distance, they could see Hugo and some of the staff waiting near the entrance of the imposing Great Hall.

They dismounted near the entrance, and the stable boy took care of the horses.

Lansius asked Hugo, "Did anything happen while we were away?"

Hugo replied, "No, my lord, it's been quiet around the castle."

Lansius nodded while still getting used to being called a lord.

"My lord," Hugo said again, "may I have a word or two with Lady Audrey?"

Audrey looked at Hugo questioningly.

Lansius chuckled and replied, "Sure, granted. Let's not be too formal between us."

"As you wish." Hugo bowed his head slightly.


After a midday meal and some rest, Audrey informed Lansius about the rising grain prices. He froze momentarily but quickly formulated a contingency plan in his head.

He drank another cup of boiled water and went straight to the Small Council chamber, where Calub and Hugo were waiting for him.

"My lord." The two rose from their seat.

"Help is coming." Lansius tried to liven the mood, but deep inside he was deeply troubled.

Audrey closed the door behind them as Lansius headed straight for the wooden cabinet, where he kept his scrolls and parchments. He rummaged through it for some time, but despite his efforts, he couldn't locate the specific item he sought.

"My lord, why don't you tell me what you need and let me search for it?" Calub said.

"It's all right, Calub. Maybe I missed it the first time," Lansius said with a smile. He continued searching until he finally found the parchment he had been looking for.

Calub watched him intently as Lansius began to make calculations in his head. "Not enough," he muttered after a few moments.

Calub let out a weak sigh while Hugo looked troubled.

"Is it about the grain?" Audrey asked.

Lansius nodded, then paused. "Give me a moment. I need to think," he said, walking to his seat and slumping down. Audrey and Calub followed suit.

*I should've known . . . Starving an opponent is a valid tactic, and price manipulations are as old as history. This also means we're up against a capable opponent. Nasty and morally questionable, but possibly a genius.*

The looming threat of famine could undo everything they had worked hard for in Korelia. If the people and troops rebelled due to food shortages, their defenses would be rendered useless.

Sitting across the large mahogany table, Hugo coughed once before speaking up. "My lord, I can arrange to get supplies from White Lake. I reckon we could make three return trips before winter sets in."

Lansius looked at Hugo and replied, "I believe Robert is in the same situation. After our last battle, he needs fresh supplies. Asking him for food right now will risk a revolt from his men."

"Can't we just purchase more food? I know it's expensive, but we got the money, right?" Audrey's bluntness loosened up the tension somewhat.

"Well, we could buy enough, but at this price, that would put a big hole in our treasury," Calub remarked.

Lansius disagreed. "We can't do that. If we suddenly buy a great sum of food, the price will rise higher. Then everybody, including our allies, will suffer."

Lansius's explanation caused Hugo to cross his arms and exhale deeply in frustration. "We're really in a mess then," he muttered.

Silence hung heavily in the room as Lansius stared blankly at the ceiling, lost in thought. Meanwhile, Calub furrowed his brow as he scanned his scrolls, hoping to find a solution.

It had only been two weeks since their proclamation, and the emerging forces in Korelia had already witnessed the cruelty of the neighboring Lowlandia lords. Their gift to Lansius for his daring declaration was a famine in the face of their first winter.

## CHAPTER 40

# FOG OF FAMINE

The chill of autumn crept through the small window of the Small Council chamber, causing shivers among those gathered inside. Within the nerve center of Korelia's bureaucratic operations, the new lord and his most trusted retinue strained their minds against the looming threat of famine.

Despite their efforts, they were still struggling to devise a plan.

"Say, Korelia's townsfolk are mostly herders, right?" Audrey brought up an interesting point. "Can't they survive by eating the livestock?"

"A butchered lamb can feed a family for two weeks. But if you trade that lamb, you can get enough grain to last more than two months," Calub explained from a practical standpoint.

Audrey nodded in agreement with Calub's explanation.

*Meat is many times more expensive than grain. To survive winter with just meat would be impossibly expensive.*

Lansius had a sudden idea. "What's the current price of food in Midlandia?" he asked.

Calub quickly searched through his scrolls. "It's normal," he replied. "In fact, the price of grain in Midlandia is currently at its lowest."

Turning to Hugo, Lansius's mind was already focused on the most efficient way to travel. "Can we travel directly to Midlandia?" he inquired.

"We can," Hugo answered with a renewed spirit. "We'll need cavalry escorts to deter outlaws, but that's easy to arrange."

"Hold on," Calub interjected. "We only have ten horse-drawn carts. They're narrow and can only hold three barrels. If we want to transport larger quantities, we'll have to use the merchants' wider carts."

"Hugo, can the wider carts travel alongside ours?" Lansius asked.

"Speed and terrain may be a problem, but the ground is firm this season. I'm sure we can find someone who knows the route," Hugo replied.

Lansius tapped the table softly, lost in thought. He realized that even with the fastest carts available, a second trip would be too risky. If winter arrived sooner than expected, they could get stranded. "That's all right. We probably can only manage one trip," he remarked.

Calub expressed his doubt. "Only one trip?"

Meanwhile, Hugo and Audrey exchanged surprised glances.

Calub pressed on. "Even if we managed to convince all the merchants to lend us their carts, we would only have around thirty at most."

"Still," Audrey chimed in, "thirty cartloads full of grain sounds like a lot to me."

"It may be so, but the grain isn't just for winter alone. We also need enough for next spring and summer. There's no trade going on in spring with the roads muddy from winter and the start of the rainy season. Come summer, they're probably already marching on us," Calub warned.

Audrey clicked her tongue and looked at Lansius with concern. She had been the one who drove Lansius to claim Korelia instead of returning to Midlandia.

"It's okay. War is inherently chaotic, but we can be flexible and adapt to changes."

The chamber fell silent.

Calub massaged his forehead, having been mulling over this problem since morning. Meanwhile, Lansius gazed at the ceiling to collect his thoughts.

*Thirty carts . . . With one return trip, I can probably feed the troops with rationing, but there won't be enough for the townsfolk to get through a famine.*

He could follow Hugo's suggestion of three return trips or settle with two, but he couldn't shake the feeling that it was still too risky. There was always the potential for an unforeseen variable.

*We have the money, but not the transport.*

Lansius took a deep breath as he found his position ironic. Medieval-era transport was crude, inefficient, and largely ineffective.

*If only there were other places to buy food . . . Hang on . . . this isn't a food shortage.*

In a fit of surprise, Lansius slapped the table, attracting everyone's attention. "Get that cup-bearer girl."

"You're that thirsty?" Audrey misunderstood and went to the door.

Lansius let it slide. "Ah, yeah, tell her to bring drinks too. We could use some refreshment."

Non-council members were forbidden to enter the chamber, so their entourage waited outside.

Calub read through Lansius's actions, but before he could voice his suspicion, a lovely girl entered the chamber. Cecile's hair wasn't the usual brown, but a pale blonde.

"You asked for me, my lord," Cecile said gracefully with a hint of fear.

It was understandable, as she had only known Lansius for two weeks, and rumors about the black-haired foreign lord who defeated the Lion were rampant among the servants.

"Relax, nobody will try to harm you," Audrey said in a friendly tone as she snatched the embroidery-covered flask from Cecile's hand and proceeded to pour drinks for them.

"I believe you can ride a horse?" Lansius asked Cecile as calmly as possible. He didn't want to look brutish in front of a new employee.

"Indeed, my lord. I'm able to ride," Cecile replied.

"Good. Go with Carla and Stirling, and please summon Sir Callahan for me," Lansius ordered gently.

Cecile was surprised. Nonetheless, she bowed gracefully, and left the room. Her father, Sir Callahan, was the first of Lord Robert's knights who had switched allegiance to Lansius.

Soon, there was a knock on the door.

"Come in," Lansius answered.

A swordswoman who had gained fame in the last battle entered the room with Stirling, the new squire.

"My lord, I've been told to escort the cup-bearer lady to her estate and summon Sir Callahan?"

"Indeed. Can I trust you two with this task?" Lansius asked.

"At once," Carla answered firmly.

"Stirling," Lansius called out before they left.

"My lord," the good-looking lad responded.

"Audrey mentioned that you're a skilled rider and familiar with my horse's temperament," Lansius said, mulling over his thoughts but not hesitating. "I want you to ride it. If you can handle it, I'll put you in the cavalry."

Stirling's eyes sparkled with excitement. "Yes, my lord," he replied, bowing slightly before closing the door behind him.

One of Lansius's constant thoughts was to strengthen his cavalry, but there was also another more personal reason.

Audrey brought Lansius his cup. "He's a good lad."

Lansius nodded and took a sip of pale ale.

"I heard his knight master died in the trench," Hugo said.

"A crossbow bolt to the jugular," Lansius answered. "Likely mine."

Audrey leaned in closer to Lansius, her voice low and serious. "His knight master was abusive. He hated him."

"If you want to, I could rotate Roger with him," Hugo suggested, fearing Lansius might feel guilty whenever he saw Stirling.

"No need. He's under my care, now," Lansius replied, taking a sip of ale and putting aside his guilt. He rested his back on the solid wood chair and tried to focus on the matter at hand.

*Now that things are in motion. I've got to plan for contingencies.*

Sensing a lull, Calub cleared his throat, gathering everyone's attention. "My lord, you've yet to explain your plan?"

"Well, we can't purchase grain in Lowlandia, so our only option is Midlandia," Lansius explained ever so briefly.

"Midlandia's prices are better, but it's a month-long journey. We also don't know how much the merchants would ask for their carts," Calub reminded them.

"Who says I'm going to pay for their carts?" Lansius refuted his assumption, causing confusion to run over the trio's faces.

Ignoring them, Lansius rose and approached the window for some cool breeze.

"Then how do you suppose . . ." Hugo's face turned serious. "My lord, do you intend to force them by arms?"

Lansius glanced at Hugo. "No, we don't need to. Just tell them that we're going to assemble a return journey to Midlandia. If they apply, then we'll provide escorts for a small fee."

"That's all? You sure they would take it?" Hugo wasn't convinced.

"Of course, merchants love cheap escorts. Also, there's a big opportunity for profit in Midlandia," Lansius explained passionately.

"I see . . . but why the fee?" Hugo asked curiously.

"Merchants are suspicious by nature." Lansius snorted, "If they hear that something is free, then they'll get worried about unseen risks."

Hugo nodded slowly, impressed by Lansius's explanation. He had never considered the merchants' distrust, but it made sense.

Still, Calub saw a flaw in the apparent plan. "My lord, we have no control over what the merchants will load into their carts," he pointed out.

"I realize that. They may load other goods, but I reckon mostly grain and foodstuff because profit dictates so."

"That solves one problem. Still, even if they all buy grain, a mere thirty cartloads won't be enough. And there's no guarantee they'll sell it cheaply when they return." Calub's words alarmed the room.

Hugo and Audrey stared at Lansius, who gestured for them to calm down.

"It's true that thirty carts won't be enough. After all, there are six thousand people in Korelia. It also true that it won't be enough to push the grain price back to normal."

Calub nodded and asked, "Then, my lord, why are you smiling?"

"Eh?" Lansius licked his lips, trying to hide it from the rest.

"You have a plan?" Hugo was surprised.

"Lans!" Audrey vehemently protested. Like hungry wolves, they pressed him for an answer.

"All right, I might have a solution, but it's a gamble and a risky one at that," Lansius finally conceded, revealing his plan. "First, we buy salt. Nothing but salt."

Everyone was taken aback. Before anyone could question him, Lansius motioned for silence and continued. "The issue with Korelia isn't grain; it's currency."

Calub instantly understood, having worked with the scrolls. "My lord, are you serious? You intend to pay people in salt?"

"Why salt?" Hugo inquired, looking puzzled, but was ignored.

Lansius let out a sharp exhale. "That's why I said it's a gamble."

Hugo cleared his throat. "I still don't understand, but how do you plan to pay for it? Even a cart is worth tens of gold coins."

Lansius licked his lips and murmured, "The Seneschal of Midlandia, our supreme benefactor, Lord Bengrieve."

Hugo groaned, while Audrey scoffed.

"My lord, please don't say you're taking a loan from him," Calub objected.

Lansius nodded resolutely. "It's better than facing a famine."

Their relationship with Lord Bengrieve had become strained after their recent victory. Furthermore, the seneschal was a formidable figure in his own right. They owed him a great deal, and he held all their dirty secrets. Even Lord Arte and Lansius's family were at his mercy.

Calub sighed, realizing they had no other choice. He helped Lansius write two letters. Once finished, he dripped purple wax onto each, and Lansius used his newly minted silver signet ring to seal them.

"Do you think this will work?" Lansius asked Calub afterward.

Calub patted Lansius on the shoulder and replied, "It had better, or else . . ." He shook his head, leaving the consequences unspoken.

# CHAPTER 41

# LION TAMER

The following morning, Lansius met with Sir Callahan at the castle. After a brief conversation, he shared the details of the plan and handed Sir Callahan letters to be opened in the presence of Seneschal Bengrieve of Midlandia.

Sir Callahan, Cecile's father, was chosen for his charisma and intelligence, qualities that enabled him to effectively connect with both nobles and merchants. His blond hair bore evidence of his northern aristocratic lineage. With this background and gifts from Lansius, Callahan was expected to help smooth relations between Korelia and Midlandia.

Lansius also entrusted Sir Callahan with five keys to chests filled with gold, silver, and jewelry from their recent victory. Although there were five chests, they were intentionally filled to less than half capacity to mitigate the risk of an attack on the convoy or betrayal by one of their own.

Callahan was considered trustworthy enough to handle the vast sum of money involved. In this regard, his daughter's employment at Korelia Castle served as an added layer of security, making Cecile akin to a hostage.

Without delay, preparations began, and news of a planned return trip to Midlandia with an armed escort spread throughout Korelia. Lansius gathered all the military carts he had and loaded them with leathers, furs, and other local commodities.

Since winter was approaching, he believed he could make a profit by selling these items to offset their expenses. As expected, all merchants who owned horse-drawn carts jumped at the opportunity. Affordable armed escorts and a direct route to Midlandia were too good to pass up.

By the end of the week, preparations were complete, and the last element of Lansius's plan arrived: Sir Justin and forty riders, half of whom were new recruits. Though satisfied with Sir Callahan, he wanted people from different backgrounds as an extra measure of protection to prevent collusion.

Now, with Sir Justin on the team, the convoy escort consisted of a diverse mix of Lowlandians, Arvenians, and Midlandians.

The following morning, just after dawn, Lansius bid farewell to the caravan and cavalry escort. Cecile's farewell to her father was particularly emotional. The last time they had parted, Callahan had returned with a large gash on his back.

With a gentle stare and a nod, the two silently said their goodbyes. Cecile held back her tears until the caravan and her father were out of sight. The fate of Korelia now rested squarely on the caravan and its cavalry escort.

Three weeks after the caravan's departure, the air in Korelia turned dry, and a chilly wind blew from the north. Animals such as bears and foxes had gone into hibernation, signaling the onset of winter.

Despite the usual slow season, Korelia bustled with activity this year. Digging work accelerated, and two wooden towers were under construction. An enlarged, crude picket fence encircled the west side of the town, its sharpened tips positioned to deter cavalry attacks.

The upcoming war weighed heavily on Lansius's mind. After surveying the region, he realized that nothing would stop an enemy from the west from reaching Korelia Castle. With no river, bridge, or natural bottleneck, the open steppe left Korelia vulnerable. Despite its size, Korelia was like a city-state with only the castle and town worth protecting.

As winter approached, Lansius faced challenges in improving his situation. The Lowlandian nobles predictably wouldn't build relations with him, as doing so would mean recognizing his claim over Korelia. Furthermore, he was a non-Lowlandian, non-noble, and not even Imperium-born, so his neighboring lords would treat him like a pariah, lest they attract hatred from their peers.

Lansius planned to train his troops, but Sir Justin, his new marshal, advised against it. Although Lansius introduced a new system and paid salaries, a lord could typically muster his troops for only forty days, and Lansius had already exceeded that limit.

Quietly abandoning the plan, he recognized that the concept of a standing army was still foreign in this era. After surveying their billets, he also realized that he might be asking too much from his men. They were primarily Midlandians, and this year they had marched, fought an uneven battle, and dug trenches to earn extra money. Now they spent their winter away from home to guard Korelia from daring surprise attacks. So, Lansius decided to tread carefully, lest his men grow resentful and desert.

Instead, he concentrated on bolstering defenses and producing crossbows. Interestingly, while no Lowlandian nobles sought him out, a steady stream of guests arrived, eager to meet the new Lord of Korelia.

Baronets, knights, and village elders with nothing to do in their lands after the harvest ended traveling to Korelia for hospitality, as was customary for a new lord. They had no immediate reason for the trip other than boredom and the chance to enjoy a free feast at the new lord's expense.

For Lansius, the guests were a source of constant annoyance. Because of them, he needed to dress up in bright, colorful, and uncomfortable tunics and fur coats to show his status.

He referred to them as his circus costume, but wearing them alone was not so bad. For him, the worst part was engaging the guests in pleasantries.

Lansius dreaded small talk. On a personal level, he found the exchanges mostly hollow and superficial. He also had a lingering suspicion that people ridiculed him behind his back because of his crude language and abysmal social skills.

Nevertheless, his sense of responsibility and the presence of Audrey made him tolerate it. She became his social and emotional crutch during social events, giving him the confidence he rarely possessed.

As was customary, the lord would dine together with his retinue, old and new, along with socializing with the guests.

That day, a pair of elderly knights had come to greet Lansius. Although they were too old to answer his call, Lansius wanted to show his benevolence and invited them to join him for supper in the great hall.

The airy hall was filled with a warm glow from the chandeliers, casting flickering shadows across the polished floor. The high ceiling soared above, supported by old but sturdy wooden beams.

Long wooden tables with benches ran down the center of the hall and were adorned with platters of roasted meats, loaves of bread, and bowls of steaming vegetables.

At the far end of the hall, a massive fireplace blazed, its crackling flames casting cheerful light and warmth throughout the room. The walls were decorated with tapestries of ancient battles, while at one end of the room stood a raised platform where Lansius and his closest companions sat.

A skald had just finished reciting an old poem about the tales of a heroic Lowlandian boy and a Midlandian princess.

The atmosphere was lively, filled with the sound of chatter and laughter, and the occasional clink of goblets being raised in toast.

"Well, as long as they didn't brag about themselves for too long and don't borrow money," answered Lansius.

Audrey chuckled. Both had had their share of wine.

"I doubt they're that insidious, my lord. They're merely wanting to see the powerful Lord of Korelia."

"The Black-Haired Lion Tamer of Korelia," Lansius corrected her.

Audrey smirked but tried to hide it, knowing that Lansius disliked that moniker. She then resumed her meal, gracefully using her fork to pick up a small piece of cheese from her plate, eating it with the poise of a lady.

"You seemed to enjoy this yourself, Lady Audrey?"

"Nonsense, I'd rather stand behind you in armor than wear this frilly gown."

Lansius couldn't resist himself. "Your clean plate clearly shows otherwise."

"My lord, food is food. I'm against letting a good meal go to waste."

This time, Lansius chuckled. "You know, I always think lowly of a lord that holds feasts in the face of a famine."

Audrey snorted. She remembered how Lansius was against throwing a daily feast, but then he realized it was just a means to feed his retinue.

"A feast is hardly a party," Audrey commented. "Just with a bit more food and entertainment. Besides, we have plenty of fresh meat available."

Lansius nodded his head in agreement.

Due to the large number of herders in Korelia, there was an abundance of meat and poultry. However, the townsfolk could not survive on meat alone. They needed grains to sustain them until the next harvest. Wheat and oats for the wealthy, barley and rye for the poor.

Lansius was acutely aware of this problem, but he had to push his concern aside for the time being, as he could do nothing but wait for the caravan to return.

He gazed upon the lively great hall and sighed.

Audrey noticed, so Lansius explained, "I feel bad letting Calub and Hugo labor hard while I'm enjoying a fancy supper."

She sipped her cup of watered wine and replied, "We need to keep you healthy, my lord."

"So I can plow the land and pluck chickens in spring?"

It came so out of the blue that Audrey burst into laughter and frantically covered her mouth. Her innocent laughter made the hall even more pleasant.

Unbeknownst to them, the restrained affection between Lansius and Audrey became a sought-after interest for everyone in their presence. The love between a lord and his squire was scandalous, but everyone, including the guests, was delighted.

They spoke highly of a man who chose to love his squire instead of some noble-born woman. After all, the Lowlandians were a hardy breed of people. They admired women who were strong and as capable as men.

This sentiment naturally grew because the region was often inhospitable and marred by frequent wars and conflicts.

As the feast ended, as was customary, the lord and Lady Audrey were the first to retire. Leaving the great hall and walking through the inner corridor, they were accompanied by Cecile and Stirling.

The two new members of his retinue were enjoying their work. Lansius had proven to be a just leader. Personally, they thought that the new lord was too soft, but his reputation as a war leader was undisputed.

They grew to respect Lansius despite his lack of superior physical or social qualities.

They took the stairs, and Lansius turned around to address them. "Thank you for the day. You may retire now."

"My lord." The two bowed their heads.

"Thank you and good night," Lansius warmly said.

The two left the premises. Stirling headed to the great hall where squires and other male servants slept for the night. Meanwhile, Cecile went to a room she shared with Carla and another servant.

Even without them, Lansius and Audrey couldn't spend their time together. The guard posted on the stairs kept a watchful eye.

Lansius could tell them to leave, but that would arouse even greater gossip.

That didn't stop intoxicated Lansius from trying. "Don't you want to come in?" he asked.

Audrey's answer was a strong gaze that made Lansius blink and shudder. "It went off again."

"Not sorry," Audrey said with a pout.

Lansius grinned, remembering what the magus they had befriended in Midlandia had said about Audrey's eyes. She said they were not normal and likely the result of an unknown magic Audrey's master had bestowed upon her without her knowledge.

"So, see you tomorrow?" Lansius asked.

Audrey nodded. "Good night, Lans," she said with a smile and left for the night.

While Lansius was openly showing affection, Audrey was more reserved about it. She had grown to care for Lansius, but she feared she would be a hindrance.

Despite her expensive gown and silver accessories, Audrey knew she had no land or estate to her name, and her social status was unclear. Not even a bastard, her adoption into a baronet family held little weight.

Audrey couldn't help but feel like a burden to Lansius, knowing that he would gain nothing from marrying her. As a rising star, it seemed inevitable that Lansius would eventually wed the daughter of another nobleman.

Pausing by a small window, Audrey took a moment to breathe in the cool evening breeze, a welcome respite from her swirling thoughts. Each day was a renewed struggle to maintain a careful distance from Lansius, yet each day, he managed to draw her in afresh, making her fall in love all over again. With these conflicting emotions swirling in her mind, she retreated to the sanctuary of her guest chamber for the night.

*  *  *

A week had passed, and a new day dawned in Korelia, marked by its bustling routine. Ever since the new lord had settled in, there had been no idle moment. Each day brought progress, whether in building up the inside or outside the city.

The defensive network advanced rapidly until today's busy work was interrupted by a single cry. "They're back. I've seen them. The caravan is back!"

Just after midday, the trade caravan from Midlandia was spotted in the distance. In droves, hundreds of men, women, and children rushed out to catch a glimpse of it.

The return of the caravan quickly became the highlight of the day. With rising grain prices, their return was filled with hope, especially for the most impoverished, who could barely afford even the cheapest grain for their bread.

As they watched, they noticed an additional ten horse-drawn carts. Now, there were forty carts of different sizes, accompanied by a hundred cavalry escorts. For the first time in weeks, the most impoverished had a sparkle in their eyes. Not even the hot midday sun could dampen their spirits.

As the first caravan made its way into the city, a wave of cheering erupted, filling the air with excitement and anticipation.

The jubilant crowd soon discovered that the ten additional carts were a gift from the Lord of Midlandia to commemorate Lansius's victory, and the news spread like wildfire. The cheers grew louder, echoing through the main road and into the surrounding streets. It was a moment of pure joy and celebration.

The merchants wasted no time, quickly unloading their goods at their respective shops and immediately opening for business. Hundreds of eager customers lined up to purchase the affordable grain, with the long queues lasting until sundown.

For a few days, the arrival of affordable grain led to a dip in local market prices. However, this brief respite was short-lived, as prices began to rise again on the fourth day.

Despite the arrival of the grain caravan, Korelia's situation only experienced a slight improvement before continuing to decline. The crisis had not been averted, and Calub's words of caution rang true.

## CHAPTER 42

# LITTLE TIMMY

Despite the grain caravan's success, the relief it brought to Korelia was short-lived. The price of grain dipped for a few days, before steadily rising again.

The next morning, Lansius visited a worksite, accompanied by Calub, Cecile, Carla, and Stirling, along with two guards who provided security.

Arriving while the sun was still in the east, he closely inspected the progress made on the site, ensuring the ditches were deep enough and equipped with a simple sewer system to prevent mud accumulation.

He also checked the nearly finished picket fence. Though rough and crude, it would serve as an effective deterrent. Now, not only the castle, but also the town, had additional protection measures.

While a wall or a wooden palisade would be better, Korelia didn't have the timber and resources to build one. Even building the picket fence likely put some strain on Korelia's only forest for decades to come.

In this regard, Lansius envied the Romans, whose region could supply them with endless timber for fortifications. Compared to them, Lowlandia was akin to the Eurasian steppe.

Satisfied with the inspection, Lansius approached the wooden tower, which was halfway completed. Calub had informed him that the platform could be used to address the men.

Lansius climbed up and gazed at the numerous workers toiling away on the defenses. He took a deep breath, but the tension refused to leave him. Nevertheless, he turned to Stirling and said, "Go ahead. Get their attention."

Stirling nodded, turned toward the workers, and bellowed in a loud, crisp voice, "Attention, all! You stand in the presence of the Lord of Korelia! Gather around and listen!" His energetic tone made his presence felt.

The workers took notice, dropped their tools, and gathered around. Lansius saw many familiar faces, mostly the troops that had stayed with him since the previous year.

"Please, do not be alarmed. I am here to speak with you briefly," Lansius said, projecting his voice so that everyone could hear him over the sounds of wind and other noises. "First, it's the third day, so we're here to pay for your work."

This announcement attracted short cheers from the crowd.

"It's usually the treasurer's job, but there's a slight change. Today, we're giving you a new option . . . You can choose to be paid in cash or salt."

At the mention of salt, there were murmurs among the crowd.

"The usual rate is three days of work for two silver coins. Now, I can offer you a cup of salt for the same—"

The crowd grew lively all of a sudden.

"Order! Order," Stirling shouted, trying to maintain control.

"Three days of work for a cup of salt. The rate stays until winter ends," Lansius paused. "Next week, the ground will probably be too hard to work on. However, the workshops will be ready."

The crowd listened intently.

"I'll pay the same rate for the workshop. Two silvers or a cup of salt—"

Just like a beehive being struck, the crowd was buzzing. Their faces were overjoyed. For many, their biggest fear of not having enough food for winter was now allayed.

"Order, say your piece after the lord is done." Stirling tried to rein in the crowd.

"The workshops will remain open throughout the winter, and if you choose to work there, while it won't be much or taste as good, we'll provide you with two free meals a day."

At this point, the crowds just couldn't believe what they heard, leaving Lansius to continue his speech. "We will also provide firewood for the night, and those who do not have access to firewood for their families can spend the night there."

This time, there was only a little cheering. Instead, all Lansius got were murmurs and a different kind of look from the crowd.

*Did I say something wrong?*

However, Lansius pressed on. "Lastly, the small amount of salt you'll get probably won't be enough for meat curing. So I've ordered the castle, just for this winter, to buy more fresh meat, and we'll pay in salt. A bucket of salt for a fat lamb, less for smaller ones."

Despite Lansius's expectations, the crowd reacted differently. Doubt was etched on their faces.

Calub took the stage after Lansius had said his piece.

*I'm really not a good speaker . . .* Lansius thought as he descended from the tower.

"Fellow Korelians," Calub began, addressing the crowd. "I have the lord's speech in writing. The town crier will share the details in the main plaza over the next few days. With that said, let's get down to business."

Afterward, Calub started the roll call, and each worker was given the option of taking coins or salt.

Now, only time would tell if Lansius's plan would work or fail.

Last summer, little Timmy lost his job, shelter, and meals when the family he worked for faced difficulties due to a livestock stillborn disease that had afflicted their herd.

Timmy joined forces with other similarly unlucky children and resorted to begging for alms or food in the streets of Korelia. Although his situation was dire, he wasn't the unluckiest. Little Tia held that title, having lost her flock to a wolf attack, which also left her with a limp.

The children formed a group to survive. Tia's knitting skills came in handy for making winter clothes from scraps of leather or unused rags. However, they struggled to find food.

It was a well-known fact that the poorest inhabitants of Korelia faced a bleak fate every winter. Korelia was a harsh place to live. Its winter mercilessly culled those unfortunate enough to lack food, fire, and shelter.

A shepherd family without enough livestock faced hunger or death. It was a deadly dilemma.

Butchering too many of their herd would make them poorer the following year, but butchering too few could lead to the loss of a family member from hunger.

Timmy had lost his last aunt and several friends the previous winter, and this year, the situation was even more dire as food prices rose so high, making it unaffordable for most.

After the harvest was over, there was very little work to be found, and many resorted to pickpocketing and even robbery.

Before the situation became critical, the new lord took over. They called him Black-Haired Lion Tamer, and his reputation preceded him, leading many to expect the worst.

Unexpectedly, the new lord initiated a series of works with the promise of pay. Most of the work involved digging trenches just outside the town. It hardly required any specific skills. Naturally, many of Korelia's poorest applied, including Timmy.

Sadly, little Timmy was deemed too small.

However, many of the older kids in his group were accepted. The promise of pay materialized every three days. They were ecstatic. For the first time, they could sleep with a full stomach.

The work and pay continued to enable them to sustain themselves. But they knew winter was coming. Fear lingered in their minds that there would be no work if they couldn't dig as the ground froze in winter.

As luck would have it, the situation improved when a much-talked-about caravan arrived, and grain prices dropped, much to everyone's delight. But the price drop was short-lived.

For the poorest in Korelia, even with all their savings combined, they could only secure a paltry amount of grain.

That close to winter, things were looking grim. Many joked that the lord's digging project would be a fitting burial site for them.

Then one day, the lord showed up and offered payment in salt. The poorest took the offer and ran to the market to trade their cup of salt for grain.

For them, it was nothing less than a miracle. The amount of grain they received from trading a cup of salt could feed a person through winter.

Suddenly, the situation changed rapidly for the better. Many were called back by their shepherd master. Now that everybody had salt, they gathered what they had and started a meat-curing process.

More and more shepherds sold their livestock for salt and gained enough to produce sausages, corned meat, and even meat jerky. Processed meat products fetched a high price at the market and boosted Korelia's meager economy for the upcoming year.

Timmy and Tia weren't the lucky ones. There was no work available for children and the crippled, but that didn't deter them. They heard about the workshop that provided free meals twice a day and a working fireplace every night.

It sounded too good to be true, and naturally, there was a big crowd of applicants. Unsurprisingly, the two weren't accepted, but they were permitted to spend the night.

Their first evening spent in the workshop would forever be etched in their memories. The warmth of the roaring fireplace, fueled by an abundant supply of firewood, provided a comforting reprieve from the biting cold outside.

To their delight, they were even given a woolen mat to sleep on, which felt like a luxurious treat. The skilled craftsmen employed by the lord kindly offered the children gruel in exchange for their help with cleaning.

During the day, they were assigned simple tasks, and in return, they received a slice of bread and a bowl of hearty stew, ensuring everyone had enough to sustain themselves.

As winter settled in, the first snowfall was quickly followed by a blizzard. Timmy and Tia watched and learned as craftsmen, carpenters, and apprentices crafted crossbow parts, strings, and bolt shafts.

The situation in the workshop was far from ideal, but now even the likes of Timmy and Tia could survive Korelia's winter and hope for a better future.

Hundreds, if not thousands, of Korelia's poorest residents shared the same sentiment. Whether they were daily laborers, shepherds, orphans, or destitute townsfolk, they were all equally grateful. Under the rule of the new foreign lord, they sensed they could not only survive but also thrive in Korelia.

Though they had not yet fully placed their trust in him, they were beginning to see him as their beacon of hope.

What had started as a move to prevent an uprising had inadvertently galvanized support at the grassroots level. Unbeknownst to Lansius, he had mobilized the entirety of Korelia to his cause.

# CHAPTER 43

# SALARIUM

Winter had arrived in Korelia, and the landscape had turned into a beautiful white blanket of snow. As was the norm, many of the original staff had gone on leave to spend time with their families. However, this custom was not for the benefit of the staff, but mostly due to the constraint of the castle's design.

Built mainly as a defensive structure, it had limited living space. When the outside castle grounds were buried in snow, the castle's inhabitants were forced to conduct all their activities in the great hall.

This winter, around twenty staff, a dozen retainers, and guardsmen shared the castle's limited living space.

Despite the lack of space, they carried on with their daily activities. Training, lunch, downtime, supper, and sleeping were done in the great hall. There, the younger staff members learned to read and write under the tutelage of their seniors, while some even practiced poetry, music, or singing.

The place was lively, but despite Lansius's effort to free some space, comfort and personal space were still a challenge.

As for Lansius, he spent most of his time in the Great Chamber, a private place reserved only for the lord's family. Without one, he surrounded himself with his closest circle around the large fireplace.

The chamber was a good place to relax, with a high ceiling that made it airy and more spacious. Its walls were fully plastered and painted white, while the ceiling boasted colorful decorative plants and floral patterns.

In there, Lansius ate, read books, and chatted with Audrey, Cecile, and Stirling about everything. However, two topics were off-limits: his origin as a farmer in Bellandia and his true origin.

For Lansius, the time was a well-deserved break away from guests and other responsibilities. Only at the start of winter could he enjoy a peaceful dinner.

Not everything was as enjoyable as he wished. Every day without fail, Audrey would drag him up for sword training and indoor archery.

Today, after sword and archery training, Lansius was talking with Stirling, who showed a keen interest in how Lansius had solved Korelia's rising grain prices.

Lansius, bundled up in three layers of thick clothing and a warm fur coat, winced as he shifted in his padded chair, the bruises from a brutal sword sparring session still fresh on his skin. "First, tell me everything you know about the situation."

Stirling, the only one standing in the room, straightened his back and gathered his thoughts.

The crackling from the fireplace filled the Great Chamber as they waited for an answer. Sitting next to Lansius, Audrey and Cecile also showed interest in the topic.

"My lord arranged for thirty carts to travel to Midlandia to purchase food."

"Go on," Lansius said.

"But while the merchants bought grains, my lord ordered all ten of your military carts to buy salt secretly."

"That's correct. Please continue."

"After that . . . my lord paid the workers in salt. Also bought sheep and meat with salt. And then everybody seemed to have enough food for winter." Stirling expressed his confusion.

Lansius smiled as Audrey and Cecile watched him intently. The two were also curious.

"Try to answer this question: is the problem in Korelia the rising price of grain, or the lack of grain?" Lansius prompted the group.

The lad and lass furrowed their brows, clearly thinking hard. Meanwhile, Audrey pursed her lips and looked away.

"You should give it a try," Lansius encouraged.

Audrey held onto her golden fur coat tightly before stating, "I'm only interested in solving problems with steel."

Lansius let out a chuckle. "You'll make a poor baroness if you think that way."

"I only need the money, not the title," Audrey responded without any hint of regret.

Lansius snorted and shook his head in amusement.

Meanwhile, Cecile and Stirling listened intently. As the lord's closest confidants, the two were privy to such information. While at first, the lord and Audrey tried to conceal it, they eventually grew tired and displayed it openly in front of the two.

Lansius, thinking he had given enough time for Stirling to think, eventually asked, "So, what's your answer?"

Stirling drew a deep breath before answering, "The problem in Korelia is the rising price of grain, not the lack of it."

"Exactly. As was usual after harvest, there was enough grain in Korelia. The only problem was the price."

Stirling nodded, while Cecile and Audrey kept looking with great interest.

"To lower the price, we could bring grain from outside, but we know it won't be enough. After all, thirty carts of grain cannot feed a whole town and troops through winter and spring," Lansius mused.

"That's what happened, right?" asked Audrey.

Lansius nodded. "Indeed, the merchants bought twenty carts of grain, and the Lord of Midlandia gave us another ten. But that only pushed the price down for . . . four days? As more people buy, the price will always rise."

"Then, my lord, why don't you force the merchants to lower the price?" Stirling asked.

Lansius leaned forward, emphasizing his point. "A town needs merchants. They're the ones risking their lives and money to bring goods to us. It's not the nobles, but the merchants who purchase linens, medicine, or even a simple iron nail from other places and bring them through winding routes to Korelia."

Lansius glanced at Cecile's face and saw that the girl was also listening intently.

"Coachmen and guardsmen need to eat and places to sleep, right?"

Cecile nodded quickly. "Of course, my lord."

"And those cost money, correct?"

"They do. Even horses need fodder, and it's not free," answered Cecile.

Lansius chuckled. "Smart lass. You make your father proud."

Cecile blushed and found herself staring at the stone floor. Audrey patted her on the back gently, saying, "Take the praise and wear it proudly."

Lansius focused on Stirling again. "Everything costs money. If you send people to buy things, you'll rack up considerable traveling expenses. And those expenses will be counted toward the goods they carry. And only then they'll take profit so they can embark on another journey."

"But, my lord what's this got to do with the price of grain?" asked Stirling.

"I wanted you to understand the merchants' situation. Most of the time, they don't govern the price. They're merely buyers and sellers. If the price rises, they're not the ones who are at fault."

Stirling nodded deeply. The lord just challenged what his cruel knight master had taught him about merchants.

Lansius looked at Cecile and continued. "The merchants aren't evil. They're greedy, but mostly only motivated by profit. They have no schemes other than avoiding losses and getting a good trade."

"Now that we have that cleared up, let's move on to the topic of salt," Lansius declared, sensing a growing interest. Deep into the winter, they had exhausted everything, so anything new was met with excitement.

"To me, salt is just another currency."

"Currency, my lord?"

"You have gold coins, big silver, and small silver, also copper and iron. Think of them as currency."

"I see." The young squire nodded his head. "But, why salt?"

Lansius reached into his purse and drew two silvers. "There are at least two good reasons. Name one and get a coin."

"Because salt is useful in meat curing, my lord," the blonde blurted out.

"That's correct, and here's your prize." With a smile, Lansius put a coin into Cecile's open palm.

"Gratitude, my lord."

"Now, is there any other reason?" Lansius asked the squire while showing a silver between his thumb and finger.

Stirling thought hard. "Because salt is expensive?"

Lansius smiled but balled his hand into a fist. "We all know that. In land-locked Lowlandia, salt is worth its weight in silver. Can you tell me the reason?"

"My lord, salt has many uses. For medicine, cooking, also alchemy," answered Stirling proudly.

Lansius motioned for Stirling to take the coin.

"Gratitude, my lord." The lad humbly accepted it.

The crackling from the fireplace again filled the chamber. This time, the flames had dwindled, and the embers were barely glowing. Cecile rose from her seat and hurriedly shoved two small logs of firewood into the fire.

"Salt is so expensive here. I've heard almost nobody in Korelia has even a plate of it in their homes," Audrey commented.

"Only the richest and the town butcher have that much," Cecile said as she returned to her seat.

Stirling stood uncomfortably. "But why is only my lord buying salt? Why don't the merchants buy grain too?"

"That's because almost everybody in Korelia is poor. Merchants don't stock items that people can't buy," Lansius explained.

Lansius watched the ember in the fireplace grow brighter and decided that he had provoked enough critical thinking in them. "Let's summarize," he began. "First, we don't have the resources or time to transport enough grain to Korelia to lower the price."

The trio understood that much. Nobody batted an eye.

"So, what I did was to bypass the high grain price using salt. Remember, the problem isn't a shortage of grain in Korelia." Lansius paused. "There's enough grain in Korelia, in the merchants' storages."

They showed slight surprise.

Lansius continued. "Our problem is the merchants. They can't sell their grain cheaply because they follow the market to maintain their margin."

"And salt fixed it?" Audrey asked.

"Yup. The value of ten carts of salt we brought from Midlandia could probably purchase enough grain to feed Korelia for more than two years."

The trio's eyes widened in disbelief at the amount of grain that could be purchased. They exchanged surprised glances before Audrey spoke up. "But then, why make it complicated? If the goal is just to buy grain, why can't you use silver and gold to buy grain?"

"That's the monster hiding in the shadows," Lansius remarked. "If you use silver to buy grain, the price will keep increasing in Korelia and neighboring cities. You can say the merchants will have so much silver that they don't want it as much as before."

Lansius could see that the concept was difficult to understand, but he pressed forward nonetheless. "However, if you use salt to buy grain, the price increase is small."

"But why?" Stirling asked.

Lansius chuckled. "But you have answered it already. Remember, salt has many uses: to cure meat, medicine, and all. Meanwhile, silver is only good for trade, making cutlery, or jewelry. Silver has little real usage for common people, unlike salt."

The trio began to grasp the concept.

Lansius knew he had his work cut out for him if they wished to learn more, but for now, he was satisfied that they were trying to understand the basic principles.

"That's why salt is just as acceptable as silver or copper. It's even better in our case because many Korelians can find real use for it."

*A currency that also has direct utility, imagine . . . No wonder the Romans loved it.*

Lansius recalled how the word salary itself was believed to be derived from salarium or salt. Because the Romans once paid their soldiers with salt.

"I still don't get it, but if it's fixed, it's fixed," Audrey commented lightly while reaching out for her cup on the small table. Cecile readily filled her cup with pale ale.

"Though I'm still curious, how did you know that the merchants would react well with salt instead of the usual coins?" Audrey asked after she had sipped her drink.

"It was a gamble," Lansius admitted. "But a currency that has real usage is powerful. It's resilient and stable. That's why the merchants played along. They took the risk because they can sell salt easily for profit outside of Korelia."

As he finished his explanation, Lansius leaned back in his chair.

Stirling rubbed his chin as he pondered. Suddenly, Lansius recalled something, "And you know what the funny thing is?"

The trio looked at each other but mostly shrugged.

"It's only working for Korelia." The lord laughed, leaving his friend and two attendants puzzled.

Korelia was a special case. It had an unusually large number of poor shepherd families who benefited greatly from Lansius's salt scheme. Salt was heavily used to preserve meat and make delicacies, such as sausages, ham, and long-lasting meat jerky.

Lansius hadn't thought about it, but it was the missing component in Korelia's nascent industry. With products to sell, many gained more than just enough to survive the winter.

Naturally, the same scheme wouldn't work for other places whose main populace was farmers. A farming community didn't need a large amount of salt. Thus, there was no incentive to take salt payment or use it as a bartering commodity.

Still, Lansius didn't disclose everything. He kept the fact that his scheme to pay in salt was causing him to lose money, with a little loss on every payment. His treasurer, Calub, had raised concerns, but Lansius viewed it as an investment.

He wanted to give something to the people of Korelia, something for them to hope for other than just another war in the future.

But Lansius knew that despite averting famine, the threat of war loomed large. Despite all his preparations, there was a high chance that he would eventually need to abandon Korelia to its fate.

## CHAPTER 44

# THE FIRST WINTER

*Maester Calub, the Alchemist, Treasurer of Korelia*

The harsh lady of winter had blanketed the Korelia landscape in fresh, pristine white snow. It was a cycle that had begun since time immemorial. At first glance, it appeared that nothing had changed in Korelia; the cold and bitter winds that battered the landscape were the same that their forefathers endured.

However, upon closer inspection, one could see that the Korelians this year had a different look in their eyes. Warmer, but more vigorous, as they no longer had to abandon their unlucky neighbors to die at the height of winter.

Although nothing appeared to have changed from the outside, a long-lost hope had been rekindled within. Everywhere in Korelia, whether at home or in winter shelters, people spoke highly of the new Lord of Korelia.

The old mentioned his name in their toasts, while the young were eager to pledge their support to his cause. Not even the cold winter weather could dampen their spirits.

Likewise, the scrawny troops from Midlandia shared the enthusiasm. Typically, contract soldiers like them were only called upon for wars and left to fend for themselves during winter and spring. However, the new lord was providing them with steady pay and winter quarters, complete with food and blankets.

Although the lord sheltered inside his castle, his name was on everyone's lips.

Calub, who had recently bought a house in town, faced daily questions about what the lord was like. Everybody who met him at the workshop was curious—the carpenter, fletcher, and local merchants all wanted to know.

The alchemist, who knew little about Lansius, only divulged small details, fearing he might reveal things he shouldn't have. Although he knew from Audrey that Lansius used to work as a clerk and a teacher, he had never worked as a merchant or noble. However, Lansius was suspiciously knowledgeable about trade, military, and leadership.

*No wonder Lord Bengrieve wanted him as his henchman.*

Lord Lansius remained a mysterious figure, even to his closest confidants. Audrey, who had known him the longest, still didn't know everything about him.

Calub's move to a house in the town was done hastily. Along with Hugo and the rest, he had planned to just stay in the great hall for the winter. While as the treasurer, he had a separate room, it was almost ancient and unsuitable for winter.

When Lansius heard about this, he urged Calub to buy a house in town, preferably close to the workshop, so he could easily reach the workshop if weather permitted.

Lansius was fully supportive of the move and even allowed Calub to bring along Margo, the pageboy, and Roger, who had recently recovered from his injury.

Calub was thrilled with the new arrangement. He was able to purchase a spacious two-story building with an attic at a discounted rate because the owner was keen to get into the new lord's good graces. But the most important feature was the cellar.

The house boasted a large stone-walled cellar that was perfect for his alchemy lab. With the winter downtime, he planned to replenish his dwindling supply of alchemy concoctions. Although he could conduct his experiments anywhere, he preferred not to do so in the castle, as it posed a risk of fire or hazardous gas leaks.

For Calub, following Lansius's leadership had been a highly rewarding experience.

*Better than crawling through the depths of the earth, seeking a rare find in dwarven catacombs.*

The memory was bittersweet for Calub and his comrades. They had lost a dear friend in the labyrinth. That was when Felis and another member decided to call it quits. They had made a name for themselves, but reality caught up with them. Entering the labyrinth was always a gamble with their lives.

Calub had buried many friends in that place, but the last one was special. She was a fifth-generation beastgirl—tough, headstrong, and playful like a child. They had met when they were little and grown to become adept explorers together.

Like many who arrived on the vast shore of Progentia, the old continent, they tried to better their lives and their family. One big haul of artifacts from the depth of dwarven catacombs would net them enough money for life.

However, the depths of that underground world were home to horrors that claimed the subterranean as their lairs.

Calub and his last team were among the few lucky ones who returned mostly intact. With enough money for retirement, Calub officially entered the Alchemist guild, while Felis started a tavern in Feodosia.

As a member of the prestigious guild, Calub mingled with the educated class in Midlandia and was quickly enamored with a number of freethinkers. With his capital, he sponsored several projects, the most ambitious of which was the school for the commoners and landless gentry.

For the educated Midlandians far from the center of the Imperium's seat of power, the world was changing. In Midlandia, there were more landless gentries than ever before, intellectuals, guild members, or entrepreneurs who stood on their own without farmland to support them.

People like Felis and Calub became part of this burgeoning new social class. Although the term "landless" was a mockery from the nobility, they wore it proudly as a token of their free-willed spirits unbound to the old idea of feudalism.

In preparation for winter, Hugo and his group of young officers also faced a new arrangement. Initially, they had planned to sleep at the great hall as was usual. It would be cramped, but such was life in a castle during winter. However, Lansius sent them to a mansion east of town.

The mansion was old, and only a portion of its fifteen rooms were in good condition, but this freed quite a bit of space for people who stayed behind in the castle.

Hugo and his men happily received this order. This arrangement gave them more freedom to socialize with the townsfolk before winter set in and heavy snow began.

The benefits went both ways. With Hugo gone, the castle staff could relax a bit. Audrey was the only high-ranking staff member left in the castle, and she tended to overlook minor issues and avoid any actions that might demoralize the staff.

All these arrangements were made because Lansius knew winter was harsh, and he took every precaution to ensure the castle ran smoothly and comfortably for him and his staff.

### *Lansius, the Acting Lord of Korelia*

"Ugh . . ." Lansius panted weakly after reading the letter from Midlandia. Despite sending ten of Lowlandia's finest horses, Bengrieve's reply was still razor sharp. That was why he had delayed opening the letter brought by Sir Justin and Callahan.

Audrey, on the other hand, was lively. She leaned from her chair to hear Lansius better. "Is there any mention of me?"

"No, you're safe," he reassured her.

"So, what does it say?"

"Well, he thanked me for the gift, but I'm still getting lectured." Lansius sighed. "He wrote that I shouldn't do rash things like purchasing ten cartloads of salt. And also, he advised me against playing a hero."

Their benefactor wasn't keen on risky gambling. Securing ten cartloads of salt without advance notice wasn't easy even for Bengrieve.

"That salts must've been really expensive," Audrey commented.

"Yeah, it cost a fortune. It could pay for an army for ten months. Thankfully, the salt plan worked."

"If it didn't, then Bengrieve would . . ." Audrey left the sentence unfinished, grinning mischievously.

"No, please don't say it. That's too much," Lansius pleaded, slouching in his seat.

"I'm still curious how Bengrieve decided to help you."

"Well, I assured him that I'm his pet. Inside those five chests was all the wealth left from our victory. Now, I'm nearly penniless. There was only enough for troops and the castle staff's expenses."

Audrey nodded. "So no more building projects next year."

Lansius shook his head.

She sipped her drink and changed the subject. "I'm still curious how five chests can purchase that much salt."

"I borrowed a little."

"Eh?" Audrey was surprised. "And what's the collateral?"

"Besides my neck and my family, also you . . ." admitted Lansius.

"I figured . . ." Audrey let out a sigh.

"I tried to pawn this castle, but he didn't see the value."

Audrey snorted at the notion. "At least he sees value in us. So, how much are we in debt?"

"Well, the plate armor we ordered, even just partial sets, was still quite a sum. But no worries, I'll work hard and shear lots of sheep next summer," Lansius joked, making Audrey chuckle.

Despite his words, Lansius sensed that Lord Bengrieve was supportive of his cause. As if the seneschal was gambling on Lansius's future victory for reasons Lansius had yet to decipher.

*Is he that rich to give me big loans so easily? Or is it simply cheaper to send money than men to help Korelia?*

As Lansius pondered Bengrieve's inexplicable support for his cause, despite refusing to send any form of reinforcement, the sun's intense rays baked his bedchamber walls. He had removed his fur coat and mittens, feeling the warmth.

The staff referred to his chamber, located on the upper floor of the castle, as the lord's chamber. It was furnished with tapestries hung on the wall. Made from thick wool like a carpet, the colorful tapestries served as decorations as well as insulation. The castle's stone brick was frigid during winter, and without the tapestries, the room would feel like cold storage.

"Well . . . at least you solved the famine. The people loved it. Everybody got enough grain for winter and salt to do stuff. I've heard it's the first time Korelia was this prepared for winter."

Audrey's words brought Lansius back from pondering. "Huh, really? Where did you hear such a thing?"

"Mm, is it from Cecile or probably Calub? Could be Sterling or Hugo, can't remember."

"Sterling?"

"Oh, that's the squire's real name. Turns out, his abusive knight master even changed his name out of spite," she explained.

"Poor lad . . ."

Audrey continued, "The point is, the Korelians are happy under your rule."

The way she proudly said that made Lansius grin from ear to ear. "That's funny. A long time ago, a certain squire told me that I'm dumb because I don't know how to prepare my straw bed or clean a bowl using firewood ash."

Audrey whistled nervously. "I don't know what you're talking about, my lord."

That made Lansius chuckle.

Audrey suddenly exclaimed, "Oh, I think it's almost ready," and went to the fireplace.

At Lansius's urge, she had prepared a pottage, a kind of stew cooked inside a metal cooking pot, inside his chamber.

The stew was made of wheat and beans, mixed with a bit of cheese and eggs. Although it was considered a poor man's food, Lansius had been eating it for three years and felt that winter wouldn't feel right without it.

As he enjoyed a bubble of peace and familiarity, Lansius asked himself just how long he could enjoy this peace before paying the price. He also wondered whether he could enjoy this again next year.

*Where will I be next winter?*

# CHAPTER 45

# ECHOES OF CERESIA

The lord's chamber boasted a fireplace spacious enough to fit a small caul-dron, which now was bubbling and steaming over a wood fire. The aroma of simmering pottage mingled with the sweet scent of burning wood and the cool, crisp winter air that wafted in through a small, narrow window.

Audrey carefully stirred the pottage with a wooden spoon while Lansius took in the delightful aroma.

"It smells delicious," he commented.

Audrey brought a bowl of the pottage and placed it on the small table by the fire, topping it with slightly charred bread. "Let me taste it first," she said as she sat across from Lansius and slowly blew on the porridge-like mixture.

Lansius cut the bread in half, revealing a soft and warm interior beneath a crispy crust. Audrey took a spoonful of the pottage and murmured something incoherent, but Lansius understood from her gesture that he should try it too. He scooped up a spoonful of the savory concoction.

*Gah, it's still hot!*

As the taste of the pottage hit him, memories flooded back, but then some-thing hit him squarely on the tongue. "Audrey, why is it so salty?"

"It's . . . err . . . it's a superior version?" She seemed nervous.

"A what?" Lansius suspected that Audrey had put too much salted meat Into the pottage.

*This isn't a mistake; this is gluttony.*

"Needs more peas," Audrey exclaimed, grabbing the bowl and spoon from Lansius. She scooped another mouthful as she ran to the fireplace. There, she added more water and stirred the pot vigorously.

"You know, Audrey, you can be quite puzzling," Lansius said.

"Why's that?" she asked.

"Just a while back, you wouldn't share a cup with me, yet now you don't mind sharing a spoon."

Audrey made a clicking sound with her tongue before replying. "What choice do I have? The castle's kitchen only has metal ladles, and all your spoons are silver. The pottage just doesn't taste the same without a wooden spoon, and I only have this one."

"Right . . . Sorry for complaining then," Lansius responded, realizing he should simply be grateful for their return to normalcy. The issues of his lordship had put a wedge in their relationship.

Their bond reminded him of a castle, its sturdy walls creating a distance between them. Despite their apparent closeness, an unseen barrier always lingered. Audrey had built this barrier intentionally, with the goal of protecting Lansius's future. No matter how hard he tried to scale the walls, he always fell back down.

"By the way, Lans, was there any news about your family?" she asked, leaving the pottage to simmer. It needed some time to cook.

Lansius's expression grew serious. "The letter didn't specify much, but I believe smuggling people out of Arvena isn't a simple task."

"I trust him," Audrey stated, taking a seat.

"Really?" Lansius was surprised by Audrey's confidence.

"Lord Bengrieve isn't the type to speak cheaply. If he says that he'll even employ the Hunter Guild to get your family out of Averna, then he'll do so."

Lansius paused for a moment, contemplating Audrey's certainty. "How can you be so sure? You've only met Bengrieve a few times."

"It's in the eyes," she explained bluntly. "When he said that, he meant business." Audrey's straightforwardness made Lansius feel somewhat guilty for doubting the man.

"I hope so . . . It's been years since I last saw my family . . ." Lansius stood up and approached the narrow window, peering out at the vast open plains below, now covered in a white sheet of ice. The reflective surface made for a beautiful display of sunlight.

The winter in Korelia was harsher than Arvena's, though less snowy. The snow barely reached ankle-depth, but the cold seeped in much deeper.

Suddenly, Audrey muttered something that sounded like an apology.

"Hmm? Did you say something?" Lansius questioned.

"I said I'm sorry," she replied with a frown and a bitter expression.

Lansius looked at her, surprised. "Sorry for what?"

"If I hadn't messed up back then, you could have returned to your family and escaped Arvena. Instead, I made you wait for nothing."

"That's not true. It was chaotic back then. Even if we had met, I still wouldn't have been able to escape west and reach my family," Lansius said, comforting her.

Despite his words, Audrey remained consumed by guilt. She was still haunted by the idea that she had willingly chosen to stand with Riverstead's defense rather than fleeing away with Lansius, only to end up in a hospice after the city's surrender.

It pained Lansius seeing Audrey shouldering a guilt that wasn't hers to bear. He held her hand, looked deep into her eyes, and spoke. "Audrey, it was me leaving you. You haven't wronged me in any way."

She averted her gaze, but her face softened. Lansius noticed how her head injury was now covered by thick, healthy hazelnut-brown hair. The big scars that made her wear a veil last year were now fully covered.

*This is such a mood wrecker for such a beautiful day.*

Thinking quickly, he called out, "Stefi! Stephania!"

Audrey was taken aback. "Lans!" she shouted and immediately charged at him, unleashing a flurry of punches. The first punch stung, but the rest were playful.

Lansius laughed at her reaction, shielding himself from her blows. "Okay, okay, I apologize."

"Humph! Don't ever call me that again," she threatened with a pout.

Lansius nodded, struggling to contain his laughter. Audrey turned away. He understood her reaction; after all, she had narrowly escaped being sold into slavery. The stigma attached to slavery was so strong that many changed their names once they regained their freedom.

Audrey's case was even more complicated because of the Sabina Rustica incident. Although the slavers were operating illegally, the fact that Arvenians waged an armed conflict inside Midlandia was a serious crime.

Moreover, with Lord Arte's involvement, the risk heightened, making it crucial to cut all traceable links. As a consequence, even though she wasn't involved in Sabina Rustica incident, Sir Stan's father felt compelled to adopt Audrey into his family.

That was the official reason, but Lansius and even Audrey herself were doubtful. However, one thing was certain: Audrey's origins as a citizen of western Centuria made her adoption an easy fix, with people naturally suspecting Arvenians and not Centurians.

Reflecting on all this stirred something within Lansius. "Come here, girl."

Contrary to his words, Lansius was the one who moved toward her.

"Eh, what are you—" she began to protest as Lansius enveloped her in a hug from behind.

"I can't help it. You look so cute today."

"Stop it, Lans," Audrey protested, her cheeks turning pink. "If you want to succeed, you need to marry a noblewoman. *Uwaa*, don't sniff my hair. It's dirty and sweaty!"

Ignoring her protests, Lansius buried his face in her hazelnut brown hair. Audrey made a quick attempt to free herself from his arms, but Lansius held her firmly. "But it's winter, you can't possibly be sweating that much . . . Oof, okay, maybe just a little," he teased.

Audrey gripped his arms and managed to break free, displaying her strength. "I'm practicing daily. That's why it's sweaty," she retorted while staring at Lansius with a hint of killing intent.

*No, it's just her usual gaze.*

"Your eyes, Audrey . . . they're a bit unnerving," Lansius remarked, his thoughts drifting back to an event that took place in Toruna the previous year. Spring had yet to fully arrive when a black carriage trundled up the mud-soaked country road to the manor's entrance.

That day, Sir Stan had welcomed a member of the Hunter Guild. The person was invited to confirm the mage's suspicions about Audrey's eyes. The guildsman, a man in his fifties, expressed surprise to see someone outside of the Hunter Guild with a skill akin to Carnivore Sight.

This ability could trigger a primal fear in beasts. It was useful to deter aggressive beasts from attacking, or to stun a rabbit from running away.

Audrey herself confirmed the guildsman's assessment, revealing she seldom faced problems with wild animals. Although the guest wouldn't elaborate further, Lansius suspected that the ability also worked against humans, as he had experienced during their regular sparring sessions. It was nearly impossible to fight Audrey while maintaining eye contact.

"Not sorry." Audrey glared.

"Ah, right, I'm sorry," Lansius apologized, though he felt the hug was worth it.

"I need to go," Audrey announced, grabbing her golden fur coat.

"Where to?" Lansius asked.

"To practice. I need to teach Carla and Sterling."

"Why don't you stay a bit longer? Like you used to . . ."

Audrey looked at him quizzically. "What do you mean?"

"Audrey, I feel like you've been avoiding me more. Are you hiding something?"

She clicked her tongue. "I keep no secrets."

"Then why?" asked Lansius.

Audrey hesitated for a moment before responding. "It's not you. It's me . . . If I stay by your side, no noble will offer you their daughter."

Lansius drew a deep breath. "I already told you, I don't want that."

"Lans, you're the smart one," she pleaded. "You should know that marrying someone like me is a dead end. Worse, I'm oath-bound to—"

"I know about your vendetta. I can help you with that," Lansius interrupted, trying to comfort her.

The sound of the cooking pot boiling filled the room. Audrey looked down, deep in thought. "I don't think I can accept that. I'm sure you'll find someone better. A proper lady . . ."

Lansius grabbed her hand, feeling the warmth of her palm and fingers. "Remember Ceresia?"

Audrey looked away. "What about it?"

"Just us and Horsie in a barn, and a roaring fireplace."

She smiled softly as she remembered those simpler times. "There were also two old men and a couple of boys in there."

Lansius chuckled, but his laughter faded quickly. A thought came to mind. "Audrey, what if I weren't a noble?"

Audrey furrowed her brow, caught off guard by his question. "What do you mean? Are you thinking of giving up?"

"No, no, I mean, just imagine for a moment, what if I were just a simple clerk from Riverstead?"

"If that were the case," her words trailed off as memories from the past resurfaced. Suddenly, her expression changed, as if she had figured out the answer to a long-standing riddle. Acting on impulse, she rose on her tiptoes and gently pulled Lansius's head toward her, pressing her lips against his in a tender, unexpected kiss.

Their lips locked together, and time stood still. Lansius was surprised at first but quickly melted into the kiss, his heart beating wildly. They parted too soon, and Lansius wished it had lasted longer.

Audrey took a step back, her cheeks turning a deep shade of red as she covered her mouth with her hand. Lansius couldn't help but stare at her, grinning happily.

*I always thought she had issues with me!*

Audrey dashed to grab her fur coat and left the room in a hurry. Lansius chased her and called out to her shamelessly, "Mwah!"

"Nuoo!" Audrey objected furiously, quickening her pace along the corridor. The guards and attendants looked at each other, probably thinking the two were out of their minds.

Later, Lansius heard that Carla and Sterling had received the sparring of their lives. Lansius felt bad for them, but he couldn't apologize since that would require explanations.

In the following days, Audrey avoided him as much as possible, which was difficult since they shared a castle. They only met at dinner, where she would sit near Lansius, where the best food was served. However, she intentionally kept her mouth full at all times and wasn't involved in the conversation.

The staff smelled something fishy and tried to pry information out of Lansius, but he wouldn't give them anything, fearing they might try to stage something.

After all, the Korelians had a vested interest in this matter. They would benefit greatly if Lansius married another Lowlandian noble's daughter.

This situation led Lansius to understand that, in the end, it was just Audrey and him against the world. But for once, he was at peace. For months, he had struggled to define their relationship, and only now he was sure that Audrey loved him back. For Lansius, that was all that truly mattered.

He had made a mistake in the past, but he wouldn't let it happen again. He would no longer negotiate with his happiness. Even if people who depended on him would hate him for it, he would gladly shoulder the blame.

# CHAPTER 46

# THE COMING OF SPRING

*Cecile, Cup-Bearer to the Lord of Korelia*

The burgeoning romance between Lord Lansius and Captain Audrey soon became the castle's chief topic of conversation. The tale of a noble falling for someone of humble birth never failed to captivate the people's hearts. As a cup-bearer, Cecile was privy to the unfolding saga. Initially skeptical, she eventually grew to admire the couple.

Cecile understood that the staff's fascination with the love story stemmed largely from Audrey's humble beginnings, a reflection of their own. Most of the staff hailed from esquire families, contrasting with Cecile, whose father was a knight.

Esquires, descending from squires or knights, held a distinct social position—not quite nobility, but more than mere commoners. This status of lower nobility was not hereditary and expired with the individual's passing.

Many of the younger staff members were absorbed in this love story that transcended social boundaries. The skald, a soldier bard named Sigmund, clandestinely fueled their fascination with epic songs of forbidden love on the battlefield.

To them, Audrey symbolized their hopes and dreams. However, the older staff members, fearing a tragic end, disapproved of such a union.

Cecile's initial impression of Audrey was far from favorable. The intensity of the Lady Captain's gaze had been disconcerting. Even Cecile's knight father had never displayed such ferocity during training sessions.

However, beneath her intimidating façade, Audrey proved to be warm and helpful. Cecile discovered that her powerful gaze came naturally, even when Audrey attempted to suppress it.

In time, Cecile and Audrey formed a bond. As the highest-ranking women, they became the defenders of the female staff, with Audrey assuming the role of matriarch and Cecile serving as her second. Any complaints of harassment were directed to them for resolution.

Thankfully, such incidents were infrequent in Lord Lansius's household, where discipline was strictly upheld. The Korelian troops, unlike those in other baronies, received regular payments and supplies, which created a small but efficient force.

The peaceful environment was also a testament to Lord Lansius, who refrained from womanizing and treated his female staff respectfully.

Likewise, Lady Audrey, despite her rank and intimate relationship with the castle's lord, integrated effortlessly with the staff. Although occasionally brusque, her behavior was likely influenced by her squire upbringing. Cecile would remind herself that Audrey was not raised to be a lady-in-waiting; she was a fighter at heart.

Once, Cecile inquired about Audrey's decision to become a squire. Audrey recounted how her knight master, Isolte, had made that choice for her.

As a child sold off by her family, Audrey served in a baronet's household. When a bear threatened their lands, the baronet hired Isolte, a renowned huntress, to deal with it. Unable to provide sufficient payment, the baronet offered Audrey to Isolte instead.

This practice was not unheard of. Baronets, essentially wealthier knights, often struggled financially, a fact Cecile knew well from her own family's experiences.

Despite her hardships, Cecile found herself envying Audrey. As captain, Audrey demonstrated exceptional swordsmanship and horsemanship, outshining many of her male counterparts.

While Cecile took pride in her own equestrian skills, Audrey was in a class of her own. A few more feats would earn Audrey knighthood. Furthermore, with the lord's affection, her future seemed secure.

However, life seldom unfolds as expected, as Cecile would later discover.

During the harsh winter months, the female staff slept together in a large, well-heated chamber, while the male staff, squires, and troops occupied the great hall. Given that Korelia was a small castle, only the lord's chamber and the guest room possessed decent fireplaces.

One night, while they were huddled together, Audrey casually revealed her vendetta to the curious servants, a story that even Cecile hadn't heard before.

Audrey confessed that her ultimate goal was to vanquish the beast that had slain her knight master and the rest of her group. The survivors of that disaster, mostly from the younger generation, had vowed to reunite when they came of age to hunt down the beast.

When a servant inquired about the beast's strength, Audrey admitted that it was more than formidable; it was a monstrosity.

She also confessed her doubt about their chances of success. Audrey felt she didn't hold a candle to her master, an extraordinary Mage Knight and a member of the Hunter Guild.

Ultimately, Audrey knew their chances of victory were slim, but she was resolute in her determination to try. Revenge or death, those were her objectives.

Cecile felt a mix of pity and envy for this female warrior. She understood that Audrey's status as a squire and her oath stood in the way of reciprocating Lord Lansius's advances. If Audrey were to marry him and bear his child, it would complicate the pursuit of her oath.

When Cecile asked if Lord Lansius knew, Audrey confirmed he did. As the older staff had forewarned, such relationships rarely concluded well. Their prophetic words rang true.

Winter finally gave way to spring, marked by the melting snow on the roof.


Cecile cleared her thoughts and knocked softly, twice. "Excuse me, my lord. It's Cecile, your cup-bearer."

"Come in," came the response from within.

As she pushed open the sturdy wooden door, Cecile saw the lord in his blue doublet, absorbed in his work at the desk.

"Just a moment," he said without lifting his gaze.

Cecile, understanding he was deep in thought, replied politely, "Yes, my lord." Unprompted, she replaced the water jug on the table, readied a clean cup, and filled it with water. She then waited patiently.

Cecile had adjusted quickly to her new role. Her upbringing as a lady-in-waiting had prepared her well. She knew how to appear engaged while waiting, to avoid prying, and to keep her opinions to herself unless asked.

Her tutor had also cautioned her against being overly sociable, to recognize her status, and to prioritize her master above all. However, Cecile had never anticipated becoming a cup-bearer, a position of considerable influence.

A cup-bearer was a trusted confidant who not only attended to the lord but also accompanied him throughout the day. The lord valued her insight and commentary. The role signified complete trust, as a lord would only drink from a cup served by the cup-bearer.

However, Cecile's appointment was unusual. Usually, a lord would choose a longstanding friend or someone he trusted unconditionally. It was uncommon to select someone he had never met. Initially, Cecile felt unsure about this arrangement.

She was aware that she obtained this position due to her father's shift in loyalty to Lord Lansius. Despite this, she refused to let it discourage her. She recognized the potential it offered her house and resolved to commit wholeheartedly.

It wasn't long before the lord finished his work. "Apologies for the wait. Please, take a seat," he invited, approaching the table and drinking from the cup.

He preferred water in the morning and a pale ale during lunch and supper, with his only stipulation being that the water must be boiled to ensure purity.

"Have you eaten?" he asked once Cecile was seated.

"Yes, my lord. Your servant had some porridge this morning."

"Was it good?"

She nodded politely. "It was, my lord. It was warm and hearty."

"Ah, that's good to hear. Umm . . . I still have some fresh bread that Sterling brought this morning. Feel free to help yourself to a slice or two."

"Thank you, my lord, but your servant must decline."

The lord offered a smile and settled into his seat.

Raised among nobility where social grace was paramount, Cecile could easily tell that the lord wasn't fond of small talk. Nevertheless, he made the effort, even for a subject like her. Having spent the entire winter in his company, Cecile recognized the lord's genuine friendliness.

Unlike many nobles who sought to exert power and control, the Lord of Korelia was approachable. He treated his subjects fairly, as if they were family. The castle's discipline was primarily maintained by Hugo, the marshal deputy and, to a lesser extent, by Audrey as the captain.

Cecile was uncertain about the arrangement's effectiveness, but the castle staff appeared content and in high spirits.

"Today, let's visit the workshops to check on working conditions. Let's go incognito," the lord announced from his seat.

"Understood, I will need to fetch my traveling cloak—"

"Yes, please do. No need to hurry. We have plenty of time," he responded cheerfully.

". . . but first, my lord." Cecile paused.

The lord noticed. "Speak up. What's on your mind?"

"Thank you, my lord. It's about my father, Sir Callahan. Your letter when he visited Midlandia last fall ensured that he received the best treatment possible."

The lord nodded. "Ah, think nothing of it. It's my duty to look after my retainers. How is he? Is he recovering well?"

"Indeed, my lord. I received a letter this morning. Father's injury has fully healed. Before, even the chill of the night caused him pain, but now he can bear the winter like everyone else."

"I'm glad to hear that," he replied with a smile. "You should visit him. After being confined to the castle all winter . . . Why not take a week or two off, starting tomorrow?"

Cecile was surprised by the unexpected offer.

"If the messenger managed to deliver the letter, the roads should be clear of snow by now . . . Oh, take a bag of salt, some fur, and freshly made meat products as gifts. I hope that's enough," the lord suggested casually as if these weren't valuable items.

Overwhelmed, Cecile fell to her knees. "M-my lord, you're too generous. How could we ever repay this?" She trembled. Deeply homesick, Cecile had never expected to see her home again after her appointment. Yet, she had been granted a visit last season and now another opportunity arose.

The lord was taken aback. "Please, Cecile, there's no need for this. Stand up."

"My lord, you arranged for a saint candidate in Midlandia to heal my father and paid for the treatment. My house and I are forever indebted to you. Please, at least let me pledge my loyalty."

"But I already accepted your oath as cup-bearer, remember? Cecile, please stand up," he urged her again, extending his hand, but Cecile remained kneeling.

She knew her family had never experienced such generosity. Despite the hair color and the knight status, her once-great house had fallen. Aside from her father's horse and the armor set, they were no better than the average townsfolk in Midlandia.

The treatment by a saint candidate for her father was already a luxury, and now a considerable gift was promised. One that would easily secure her family's livelihood for another year or two.

"I, Cecile, daughter of Sir Callahan, pledge my life in your service, my lord," she declared solemnly.

"That's too much, Cecile. It's unwise," Lansius warned her.

His disapproval surprised Cecile, who assumed her pledge had been refused.

Lansius sighed deeply. "Listen . . . we're likely heading into war soon."

"War, my lord?" Cecile asked, holding back tears.

"Yes, and probably against a larger force. I can't guarantee victory, so I don't want you to risk your life for me. Pledge it to someone you love dearly instead."

His fatherly words deeply touched her. Lansius didn't behave like a typical lord, eager to accept any loyalty pledge from his retainers. He genuinely cared for their well-being.

"My lord, forgive me, but even if you refuse, it's my wish to serve you."

The lord sighed again. "How old are you, Cecile?"

"I'm turning sixteen this year, my lord."

"You're too young to make such a weighty commitment. You have a long life ahead of you, and I don't want you to have any regrets later on."

"My lord, your words are too kind. I'm just a servant . . ."

Lansius extended his hand once more, and this time Cecile accepted. She stood up, her face flushed and eyes glistening with emotion.

"Cecile, you may rest for today. I'll have Sterling accompany me."

"There's no need, my lord. I will fetch my cloak immediately." She exited the chamber and sped to her room, her dull blonde hair trailing behind her as she ran.

In the lawless province of Lowlandia, where loyalty and mercy were rare virtues, Cecile discovered a lord who stood apart from the rest. Her heart swelled with pride after pledging herself to her lord's cause. From now on, their fates would be intertwined.

His fall would be her downfall. Cecile was determined to serve a noble who truly deserved her unwavering allegiance.

# CHAPTER 47

# CHILDREN FROM THE NORTH

The first light of dawn broke through the dark clouds, casting a soft, golden hue over the small castle. The rainfall from the previous night had ceased, leaving the air cool and fresh. Lansius stood by the window, gazing at the transformed landscape outside.

The ditches had turned into a water canal, and some sections had inadvertently created a crude-looking irrigation system. It would have been a great success if it had been intentional, but Lansius had no such plan.

Despite his insistence that it was a mere coincidence, the people of Korelia praised him, believing their lord was simply being humble.

*Good things do happen sometimes.*

As Lansius observed the canal-like structure, he wondered once more if the land could benefit from diverting the river stream slightly. A small man-made lake could prove advantageous, especially if it could support the fish delicacy he'd enjoyed in Torrea.

"Sterling," Lansius called, his gaze still fixed on the window.

"Yes, my lord," the young squire replied, bowing slightly.

"Were you present when I invited the old staff to discuss farming and fishery?"

"I believe so, my lord."

"Please, remind me of their responses," Lansius requested, prompting the squire to gather his thoughts before replying.

"About farming," the squire started, "they complained about poor soil quality. They said they tried many methods, including plowing, but most of Korelia's land remained barren."

"But Korelia does manage to grow barley and wheat?"

"Only in the areas with the best soil, my lord."

Lansius nodded in acknowledgment. "And the matter of fishery?"

"They informed us that the river was too shallow and with few fish. In the past, a lord attempted to dig a man-made lake, but it only resulted in a swamp and a breeding ground for undesirable insects."

Lansius sighed softly, weighing the risks.

*And they can't use ducks to combat insects, because this world's ducks are large, aggressive monsters. Even the young ones are half the size of an ostrich.*

It was known that only the bravest men bred ducks. Even at a few years old, ducks could trample farms and were strong enough to either jump or kick most fences. Their eggs and feathers were valuable, but sadly, their meat was difficult to cook.

The Lord of Korelia exhaled deeply. He had no experience in farming or fishery. Worse, he had no experience living in the steppe. He knew about yurts and cheese, but that was about it.

Last season, Lansius had tried consulting with Calub and Sir Callahan for assistance. They came up with several ideas but had to wait until the road cleared from mud and the rainy season.

Lansius looked at the parchment again that detailed his projected expenses for half a year. The biggest one was for the trench work, which he paid for in salt. Each worker received the equivalent of 5 copper per day for work that lasted effectively 90 days.

The combined cost of the trench work and the salt scheme was more than twice the upkeep of his army. However, he saw this as an investment and aid relief.

The second largest expense was the cost to maintain his military of 400 men-at-arms and crossbowmen. The standard rate for men-at-arms on a campaign was about 4 copper daily, including meals, while cavalrymen cost around 8 copper daily.

The previous year, Lansius and Sir Justin negotiated a standby rate that also included free lodgings and armament leases. This rate was half of the original campaign rate: 2 copper daily for each man-at-arms, including meals, and 4 copper daily for cavalrymen.

Considering that even master smiths, carpenters, and artisans only earned 4 copper daily, this was already a good living wage.

| Expenses (half a year, 190 days, standby rate) | In copper |
| --- | --- |
| 400 men-at-arms and crossbowmen. 2 copper daily | 152,000 |
| 70 cavalrymen. 4 copper daily | 53,200 |
| 15 squires, captains, lieutenant. avg. 5 copper daily | 14,200 |
| 200 crossbow trigger mechanism. 20 copper | 4,000 |
| 50 arbalest. 6 silver (72 copper each) | 3,600 |

| | |
|---|---|
| 40 half lance armor. 3 gold (720 copper each) | 28,800 |
| Workshop 20 maesters. 4 copper daily | 15,200 |
| Trench work, salt investment 1000 men. 5 copper | 450,000 |
| Total in copper (1 silver is 12 copper) | 721,050 |

With an estimated 1.3 million copper in cash, commodities like salt and horses, and other assets, and 720,000 in expenses, Lansius's current wealth amounted to around 600,000 copper, or slightly less than 2,500 gold coins.

While 2,500 gold might seem substantial, Lansius and his treasurer were far from comfortable. Their expenditures were hemorrhaging funds, threatening to deplete their reserves within two years. Moreover, they hadn't factored in their debts to Lord Bengrieve.

Feeling stumped, he turned away from the window, grabbed his fur coat, and headed to the door. "Let's ride a little."

"Should I ask for Lady Audrey, my lord?" asked Sterling.

Lansius almost chuckled. Audrey was still avoiding him because of what happened a few days ago. "No need. Just you and a few riders."

When the weather permitted, Lansius forced himself to ride as practice and to ensure his horses' stamina. Spring rides were especially important because the horses were restless after spending almost the entire winter in the stable. As their rider, Lansius felt responsible for taking them out as often as he could.

Lansius and his squire, Sterling, rode aimlessly through the countryside, allowing their horses to find their own paths. The landscape was a mosaic of vibrant colors, with the sun casting a warm glow over the spring grassland. Their journey eventually led them to a cluster of three yurts nestled among the grazing white sheep.

A shepherd with a round face and long brown hair emerged, a welcoming smile on his face. "Welcome, guest, welcome," he greeted them warmly, noticing their fine clothing and horses.

Lansius looked at Sterling, who rode beside him, saying, "Let's have a rest. Tell one to be on alert. The rest can dismount."

"Yes, my lord," Sterling replied.

Upon hearing that, the shepherd's reception grew even warmer. As they realized the guest was Lansius the Salt Giver, the shepherd's family sprang into action, bustling about in a flurry of excitement.

The child dashed off to fetch water from the small stream; two women hurried to gather firewood; and an even older man, leaning on his cane, grinned happily as he held open the flap that served as their home's door.

"Please, my lord, come in and rest. I'll prepare fresh drinks and sweets for you," urged the shepherd.

Lansius and Sterling dismounted. "Thank you. I just need a place to rest my legs. Don't let me bother you."

"Please, my lord, it's a great honor to have you here." The shepherd gestured politely, inviting the guest to his house.

The yurt was more spacious than it appeared. It was warm but airy and had an abundance of natural light coming in from above. The floor was covered by a combination of carpets, leather, and rugs.

Before entering, Lansius began to remove his boots to avoid tracking dirt inside, which immediately caused a commotion. The old man with a cane reached out to Lansius, attempting to stop the esteemed guest from taking off his footwear. The shepherd did the same, speaking rapidly in protest. Meanwhile, Sterling, alarmed by the sudden change in atmosphere, instinctively rested his hand on his hilt and yelled, "Don't touch the lord! Stay away!"

Seeing their reaction, Lansius laughed, defusing the confusion. Lansius was aware of the custom, as he had heard dozens of stories from the staff regarding the nomads of Korelia and its culture, so he asked, "I insist on leaving my boots and entering barefoot; will that be acceptable?"

There was a back-and-forth argument, but the host, while a bit embarrassed, was exceedingly pleased. "Please, my lord, our carpet isn't clean."

Lansius chuckled and entered barefoot. A table and cushion were provided for him, so he sat there and made himself comfortable. Sterling quickly followed and sat beside his lord.

"Thank you for your hospitality. We brought gifts in return for your refreshments." As Lansius said that, Sterling reached for his bag and opened it up for his lord to decide.

"My lord, please, you don't have to," the shepherd said bashfully.

"I insist," Lansius said as he selected several items from the bag. "A lacquered comb for the women; salt and spices, also for the women; dried medicinal herbs for your father; and honeyed mead for our gracious host."

Lansius's gifts stirred up a commotion as the host initially refused them out of respect. However, Lansius knew the custom and insisted on offering the gifts.

Sterling could only blink. He had heard about the custom but had never experienced it firsthand.

As everyone settled down, the host poured a milky-gold beverage with a strong buttery aroma. With Cecile the cup-bearer on leave, Sterling did his best to scrutinize the drink. The butter tea was too rich for him, and he shook his head, not knowing whether it was safe or not.

Lansius laughed it off and drank heartily. In truth, he knew his lactose intolerance would cause issues later, but he couldn't resist trying the unique beverage.

*Just a cup . . . Oof, a bit strong smelling, but buttery smooth. Wait, a hint of tea?*

Lansius realized the golden color must come from somewhere, so he inquired, "What did you use to make this?"

The host eagerly shared the ingredients. Lansius noticed dried leaves and asked for some along with boiled water, which the host happily provided.

Soon, the women and child returned and joined in the feast. They prepared the snacks over an open hearth at the center of the yurt.

Stirling, following instructions from Cecile, tried to engage in conversation on behalf of their lord. He asked about the winter, their herds, and recent news in this part of Korelia.

Though their dialect was difficult for Lansius to understand, he grasped that the winter had been milder, and spring had arrived early. The shepherd also personally thanked Lansius for his salt payments and mentioned that his brother and son were working in Korelia before winter, digging trenches and later in the workshops.

Lansius nodded happily.

The old man urged his son, the host, to bring another beverage. Lansius politely refused, but the host had brought a wineskin and poured two cups for them.

"Horse milk wine," the old man introduced. Stirling drank it, and his face said it all, much to the host's delight.

Lansius sampled the alcoholic drink and found it more enjoyable than anticipated. Next, the snacks were served on a large wooden platter. He chose a honey-glazed baked pastry and a tofu white crunchy morsel.

"This one is made from dried yogurt," the host explained, noticing Lansius's curiosity.

Lansius tasted both, finding the sweetness refreshing but not overpowering. He glanced at Stirling, who seemed thoroughly impressed by the treats.

Around that time, Lansius took the cup of boiled dried leaves and smelled it.

*Definitely smells like tea.*

He took a sip and was taken aback by the bitter taste.

*Smells like tea, colors like tea, but tastes like burnt charcoal.*

"It's good medicine for a long night with the ladies," the host informed, and everyone burst into laughter.

As they enjoyed their snacks, the host prepared steamed dumplings filled with minced meat. When they were ready, Lansius accepted one graciously. He let it cool briefly before taking a bite, finding the mutton flavor quite strong but managing to swallow it down, pleasing the host.

*A sauce would be perfect for this . . .*

Soon, a vegetable dish with dried meat on the side was served.

"Well, this has certainly turned into a big feast," Lansius remarked, bringing a smile to his host's face.

* * *

After the feast, as a parting gift, the host opened one of his wooden boxes and pulled out two remarkably lightweight shawls. "A modest gift for your men," he said, presenting the shawls to Lansius for him to bestow upon his men.

Intrigued by the quality of the shawls, Lansius furrowed his brow. "Why for my men?" he asked, examining the delicate, warm, yet strong fabric and its astonishing lightness. "Such a gift is fit for a lord."

The host shook his head modestly. "I wouldn't dare, my lord. These shawls are worn only by nomad families like us."

The subject was of great interest to Lansius, so he dared to ask, "Friend, I apologize if this may offend you. Could you tell me about your family history?"

The shepherd appeared uncertain but glanced at the old man, who nodded, granting permission. "Our great-grandfather came from the Caladan Sea in the north."

"The northern sea of grass." Lansius acknowledged the name.

The host nodded and continued. "He and many of his relatives were enslaved during a raid, and somehow, they were smuggled this far south to Lowlandia. They labored for the old lord in Korelia, who granted them their freedom on his deathbed."

Lansius nodded respectfully, taking in the story.

"Now, we're free, but not exactly welcomed to live in the town, so we live as our ancestors did, on the pastoral lands, grazing and dwelling in our yurts."

*Discrimination is rampant everywhere, even when they have the same skin color as Sterling. It's simply because they're different.*

"How many of you live like this?" Lansius asked.

"Now, there are at least a hundred families," the old man replied proudly. "Many more than when I was a child."

Lansius was pleased to hear this. He had always thought that Korelia felt like a colony, with its people trying hard to live like those in Midlandia, but the land and climate were entirely different.

Here, it was more suitable for a pastoral lifestyle, and seeing these shepherds thrive confirmed his view.

With the quality of the shawls lingering in his mind and sensing a potential trade opportunity to elevate all of Korelia, Lansius made his decision. "I would like to meet as many tribes as possible for a discussion. Perhaps a grand banquet on the west side of the castle. What do you think?"

The old man seemed surprised. "We will do as we are told. The land belongs to you. But what would you ask of us?"

"Be at peace. I won't ask for tax or tribute. I want to talk about friendship and trade among our people. I sincerely believe it would benefit everyone."

The old man smiled. "There's an old saying that unity is the ultimate strength. My family and I will do our best to send your invitations to the other tribes."

Lansius nodded and extended his hand. Without hesitation, the old man grasped it firmly to seal the deal. As the sun cast golden rays over the plains of Korelia, Lansius found an unexpected ally in his quest to defend his realm.

The newfound bond signaled a crumbling of old barriers and the dawn of a new era of trust. Spring had arrived, and summer, bringing with it the threat of wars and sieges, was fast approaching.

# AFTERWORD

Hello! I'm Hanne, the author. Thank you for reading *Horizon of War*. I hope the story of Lansius etching his presence in a new world has been as enjoyable for you to read as it was for me to write.

If you enjoyed this journey and wish to leave a mark, here's how you can illuminate my day:

- Leave a review! I'm used to reading all the comments and reviews my readers leave on Royal Road. You can bet I'll do the same for reviews on Amazon!
- Follow me on Amazon to get updates on upcoming books!
- Support me directly on Patreon! Visit Patreon.com/HanneLee to access early drafts if you want to read ahead before the definitive version is published.
- Join the lively chat with fellow readers in my Discord server! Discord.com/invite/ABdm3yfyg7

# ABOUT THE AUTHOR

Hanne is the author of the Horizon of War isekai series, originally released on Royal Road. An avid reader and writer, her "realistic" fantasy stories feature historical details with military-grade accuracy (i.e., gambesons, poleaxes, logistics, and all the intricacies of the feudal nobility).

# DISCOVER
# *STORIES UNBOUND*

PodiumAudio.com